LIMERICK CITY LIBRARY

Phone: 407510
Website:
www.limerickcity.ie/library
lib@limerick

The Granary,
Michael Street,
Limerick.

the Library.

D0275140

The Naked Name of Love

The Naked
Name of Love

Sanjida O'Connell

JOHN MURRAY

First published in Great Britain in 2009 by John Murray (Publishers)
An Hachette Livre UK company

1

All characters in this publication are fictitious and any resemblance to real persons,
living or dead, is purely coincidental.

A CIP catalogue record for this title is available from the British Library

Hardback ISBN 978-0-7195-2154-6
Trade paperback ISBN 978-0-7195-2164-5

Typeset in Monotype Baskerville by Servis Filmsetting Ltd, Stockport, Cheshire

Printed and bound by Clays Ltd, St Ives plc

John Murray policy is to use papers that are natural, renewable and recyclable products
and made from wood grown in sustainable forests. The logging and manufacturing
processes are expected to conform to the environmental regulations of the country of
origin.

John Murray (Publishers)
338 Euston Road
London NW1 3BH

www.johnmurray.co.uk

To my father, James O'Connell

Good God. When I consider the melancholy fate of so many of botany's votaries, I am tempted to ask whether men are in their right mind who so desperately risk life and everything else through the love of collecting plants.

CARL LINNAEUS

Prologue

I was wondering, she said, if you might expand a little on the bones you found in the Gobi.

She flushed slightly as he focused his attention on her but persevered.

Do you think that they were truly from a creature that existed thousands of years before? Could they not, do you think, have been a clever fake? After all, she said hesitantly, some might say that a flying lizard, a reptile with feathers and teeth, is a monstrosity that could not possibly have existed.

As he looked down at this woman, staring up at him with wide, hazel eyes, biting her lip and clasping her hands as she waited for his reply, he realized that this was the moment he had longed for all those years ago. He had been desperate to be revered, to be recognized in scientific circles, to have the upper echelons of society crave his company and his opinion. And now that this moment was here, he found that it was not quite what he had expected or wanted. How to answer this woman with her strange, almost preposterous question, which was not what she really wished to say to him but only a means to be near him? How to answer her when her words conjured up images of scraping through sand until his hands bled under a sun so vicious it had cracked his skin and killed his camels? And she thought that what he had unearthed in the middle of the Gobi where no living soul had previously ventured might have been a counterfeit?

What he truly wanted to do was to sip a glass of champagne with Lena by his side and raise a toast to his dear friends. He'd just finished his talk at the Royal Society on *The Fauna and Flora of Outer Mongolia* and had been about to join the others in the library where a small party was being held in his honour. But he had only managed to reach the connecting hallway between the two rooms when he had been besieged. There was a queue of people waiting to speak to him, including this woman. He smiled to himself. In the past that would have thrown him. Now he realized that for a certain sort of woman being the kind of man he was presented a challenge. Then, of course, there was the fact that he was well known in some circles. And, perhaps, he could finally admit to himself at the age of thirty-five, he was not unhandsome. Mongolia had taken its toll, of course, and he now had wrinkles round his eyes and lines etched more deeply across his forehead, but there were also laughter lines. Lena had taught him to laugh.

He caught sight of her. She was looking up at Patrick, her grey eyes glowing like the sea where the sun sends its surface silver. Her wild, dark blonde hair was pulled into a bun at the nape of her neck but stray curls had escaped. She was wearing a dress the same deep green shade as a hart's tongue fern, which Mrs Craven had picked for her. But, in spite of the fashionable attire, there was no mistaking the roundness of her face, the slant of her eyes, the high cheekbones. Framed by the library door, glazed sunlight pouring through the tall, thin windows on to the great glass goblets of flowers that stood around the room, she appeared as if she were surrounded by lilies.

How he had imagined them on that interminable journey through the barren, arid desert with its suffocating heat, these lilies he had risked his life for. And here they were, just as he had fantasized – five feet tall with golden stamens and perfect, marble-white blooms. Once he had thought only of the lilies in terms of the fame they would bring him. Now Lena turned to smell one of them and in that moment, half twisted away from him, bent towards the waxen petals, she looked just like her mother. His heart quailed within him. Was this to be his punishment – the great and unexpected joy of a child – and yet, for the rest of his life, seeing the woman he had once loved reflected in the features of her daughter?

PART I

A small flock of purple doves was clustered in an apricot tree, the first peach and cream blossoms beginning to unfurl along its crooked branches. Against the molten butter of the rising sun it was like a delicate Chinese painting. Joseph did not look behind him: he knew dogs with sharpened ribcages would be licking the stones; nor to his right, in case he saw the silent mill and the putrid river; nor down at the streets save he caught sight of an opium addict, half frozen and silently delirious. He wanted to leave this godforsaken town with this final and beautiful image intact, a sign that God was everywhere and that none, not even here, had been deserted.

Beyond the town, hanging over and caging them in, were battlements and turrets, the ruins of the last Great Wall of China. Past that barrier was freedom; the wide open steppes he longed for, the pure fresh air he had dreamt of. There were soldiers, border guards, by the wall, but they were sleeping. Joseph nervously angled his mule as far away from them as possible. As he passed by, his mule slipped on the rough cobbles, its hoof scraping loudly against the stone. Joseph held his breath and looked round. One of the soldiers opened his eyes. He sprang to his feet with a cry, waking his companion. The second soldier snapped his head back and stared unfocusedly about him and then staggered upright, twisting his rifle round towards them. The three of them came to a ragged halt. The first soldier was still shouting. The second advanced upon them, blocking their path and aiming the bayonet at the end of his rifle at Tsem. They were both Chinese, dressed in dark blue uniforms that were fraying and unravelling at the hems with tears at the elbows. Their rifles were dark with rust. It was impossible to tell how old they were, their faces were so smooth, their eyes hidden in shadow beneath their caps. They could be but boys, thought Joseph, boys with lethal weapons. Mendo and Tsem now slid from their mules and Joseph did likewise. The first soldier seemed to be gesturing towards something, barking orders at them in a harsh, guttural language. Mendo started tying up the mules to the broken remnants of the gate.

What's happening? whispered Joseph.

He wants to see what we're carrying.

Surely they can see we're not the type to transport opium.

Tsem said something and Mendo translated.

He says, how much we have to bribe them will depend on how valuable our luggage is.

Have you explained to them who we are? asked Joseph, raising his voice a little.

The first soldier now swung his rifle around and dug the butt into Joseph's shoulder, while shouting something at him. He felt his heartbeat rise and a cold sweat break out across his palms and chest. The soldier pointed and shouted again and Joseph stepped back, away from the mules and his companions. Mendo and Tsem finished tying up all the mules and started unloading their packs and lining them up in the gateway. Joseph wiped his clammy hands on his cassock. He tried to take deep breaths to still his racing heart. His shoulder throbbed. What frightened him was the unpredictability and arbitrary nature of their encounter. These men, no, boys, could do anything with impunity and, at this time of the morning, there was not a single person who would witness their actions.

Mendo and Tsem now started to undo the oiled canvas holdalls and peel back the hessian layers wrapped round Joseph's precious equipment. The soldiers, who had been standing threateningly close to the two men, their bayonets at the level of Mendo's and Tsem's stomachs, now bent closer, curiously examining the herbarium paper, Joseph's collection of tools for prising fossils from rock, his taxidermy kit with razor-sharp scalpel blades and waxy thread for sewing skins, discs of beeswax, pots of ink and leather-bound notebooks. One of the soldiers kicked a pile of specimen jars with the toe of his boot and Joseph had to restrain himself from pulling the man away. The first soldier reached forward and pocketed one of the jars and a blade. He strolled over to Tsem who was unpacking their food. He slipped a bundle of dried meat in his jacket pocket and tossed a packet of *tsamba* to his companion. Then he barked something at Mendo.

Mendo turned to Joseph. He wants to see our paperwork. Tsem snorted.

Mendo said, He says he wonders if they can even read.

Joseph pulled the bundle of papers from the inside pocket of his cassock and handed them to the soldier.

It was a horrible reminder of when he had first set foot in Pekin. He'd been weak from months at sea and still sick. The ground had felt unsteady beneath his feet. The harbour police had demanded to see his papers and had pored over them endlessly, while other officials had made him prise open his luggage, packed in wooden crates, and empty out his belongings. Wood shavings and hessian had littered the docks and a couple of dirty urchins had made off with some of his possessions. One of the customs officials had pocketed a fine bone-handled knife when he thought Joseph wasn't looking and then given him a nasty smile when he saw him watching.

The soldier now peeled off the first couple of sheets, which were in English, and held them up. The papers fluttered in the breeze and the man opened his hand and let them go. They drifted across the desert, reflecting the first rays of the early morning sun.

Joseph felt sick. He had worked for years building up contacts: men who would help him, men who would want him to work for them, men of means and men with the right connections. And once the expedition had been agreed, he had laboured for months to amass the right equipment, to plot his journey, to secure the necessary permits and permissions, to book his crossing and hire the two men who now stood helplessly in front of him while his precious possessions were scattered across a filthy cobbled street in the shadow of a decaying wall.

The soldier gave a grim smile and let another sheaf of paper blow free, this time the Chinese translation of the English papers he had already released. The sheet below, he crumpled and started to stuff in his mouth, watching their reaction as he slowly ate the document. The second soldier stood alongside him and released the safety catch on his gun. The weapon was so rusty, the catch snapped off suddenly, making them all jump.

Can you do nothing? said Joseph, through gritted teeth.

Mendo's back, which was towards him, was implacable. Tsem started to walk nonchalantly towards the wall. The second soldier swung his rifle round and trained it on him. Tsem held his hands in the air, walking backwards, and said something to the soldier. The man lowered the gun. Tsem leaned against the wall and started to roll a cigarette. The first soldier swallowed and then spat a wad of chewed-up paper against the stones. Tsem handed him a cigarette and lit it for him. He rolled another. There was almost complete silence apart from the men's breathing and the chink of the mules' bridles as they shook their heads and nuzzled against each other. Somewhere behind them, back in the town, a dog barked. Tsem handed the cigarette to the other soldier and then rolled one for himself. After a couple of puffs, he spoke to the soldier who appeared to be in command.

Joseph slowly took a few steps forwards so that he was standing alongside Mendo. The soldier's dead eyes never left him even as Tsem talked.

He's explaining who you are, said Mendo quietly, and that you're not a threat to them.

Once Tsem had finished talking the soldier dropped the cigarette and ground it beneath his boot. He barked a couple of orders at Tsem.

And now he wants to know how much you will pay them to let you pass.

I should not have to pay anything, said Joseph angrily.

It's the lesser of two evils, my friend, said Mendo simply.

Finally, Tsem told them the figure. It was extortionate.

And he wants one of the mules, said Mendo glumly.

Joseph counted out the money and handed it to Tsem who gave it to the soldier. He passed it to his second-in-command who made a great show of counting it twice. The first soldier took another cigarette from Tsem and then walked over to the mules. He walked in front of the animals a couple of times and then chose one. He pulled the mule out in front of the three of them. But instead of leading the beast away, he half turned and lunged, burying the bayonet in its chest. The mule brayed, an inhumanely loud sound, its lips curled back exposing its pink and black gums. The soldier pulled the bayonet out and then slashed the animal's throat open. Its eyes rolled back until only the whites showed and it fell to its knees, its head lolling at an unnatural angle. The soldier dropped his cigarette in the mule's blood where it sizzled. The two sauntered off, dividing the money unequally between them. The mule, now stretched out at Joseph's feet, struggled to breathe, its breath rasping in its broken windpipe. They stood and listened for what seemed like a long time before the mule stopped breathing. Joseph stepped past the prostrate animal and started to repack his equipment, hastily moving some of it away from the widening pool of blood. His hands, though, were trembling and he found it difficult to rewrap his specimen jars. They rattled and clinked and slipped between his fingers. Mendo leaned over him and put both his hands on Joseph's shoulders.

Joseph, he said, and Joseph felt himself being firmly but gently pulled to his feet.

Joseph, said Mendo again, leave it. Tsem and I will repack. Take a walk. We'll be with you shortly.

And he steered Joseph towards the wide open expanse of the desert.

On 4 March 1865 Father Joseph Jacob had left Pekin with ten mules heavily laden with all his equipment and a Mongolian whose name was Tsembel. His horseman was short and stocky with black hair and smooth skin, the colour of a peeled hazelnut, stretched taut over round, high cheekbones. His eyes were small and green and he wore black leather riding boots and a dirty, blue *del*, a calf-length, felt coat fastened at the throat with silver baubles. His hands were lined and there was dirt worked into the wrinkles and calluses. He knew no English, and Joseph knew only a little Mongolian. But in the short time that they had been travelling together Joseph had formed an impression of the horseman as a man whom he could trust: Tsem appeared light-hearted and uncomplicated yet honest.

It had taken the best part of two weeks to cross three mountains and the wide plain that led to the ancient capital of the Mongol emperors, Suanhwa. The city was surrounded by high walls and ornate gates, as was the custom, at each of the compass points. Joseph noted, using his own compass, that they were a few degrees out. To the south-west was the vast Yang Ho, the Yellow River, and encircling the city a smaller stream which flowed haphazardly through fields of rice planted in neat squares. Tsem had pointed out the west wall to him, but he had already noticed: sand blown up by the ever present wind had reached the top, and men were scaling its slope and jumping over the ramparts rather than walking round to one of the gates. This was where he was to meet his translator.

When they finally arrived at the mission and he was shown to his room, it was full of sand. A light dusting coated the furniture and there were heaps of sand, as if from an hourglass, in the corners. One of the brothers brought him a basin of hot water, a luxury he had already become unused to. He sank his hands into the water, resting them on the bottom of the basin, revelling in the warmth. He cupped his hands and splashed his face, feeling grit from the desert in a thin film across his skin.

He found the brothers taking tea in the narrow study, which ran alongside an internal courtyard. They were seated round a long dark table in near silence, small earthenware bowls cradled in their hands. M. Lefèvre rose as Joseph entered the room. He was a tall, thin man with narrow lips, sunken eyes and high cheekbones. A faint layer of stubble combined with the deep eye sockets lent his face an ashen cast.

Father, allow me to introduce you to your translator.

He held out one hand.

A man rose from where he had been seated cross-legged in the shadows and walked towards Joseph. He touched his palms together and half bowed. He was the same size and build as Joseph – medium height, lean and wiry. He was wearing a floor-length orange robe, and his exceedingly short hair was covered with a dark red velvet skull cap.

But he is, he is a . . . stuttered Joseph.

A *bonze*? said the translator, in perfect English, his mouth twisted in a slightly sardonic smile.

A Buddhist, said Joseph. My apologies, he said quickly, turning to the monk. It was not my intention to offend you. I was merely a little . . . surprised. Joseph had hoped his translator would be one of the brothers, a Lazarist, a man with whom he could converse about God and who would be company for him across the Mongol wastelands, a man who might share his enthusiasm for the natural world, who might aid him with his plant collections.

My name is Mendo, said the monk. I am a lama of the Yellow Hat Order of Buddhism. I believe I know enough English to be of some service to you.

I think you will find that he is more than suitable, said M. Lefèvre, drawing himself up to his full height and looking at Joseph imperiously. We simply cannot spare one of our brothers for what is essentially not a missionary's job. Moreover you will find his English, Mongolian, Chinese, Tibetan and Russian to be of a high standard. I trust, Father Jacob, that you require no religious tuition at your stage in life, hence it matters little what spiritual tendencies your translator possesses.

The monk's eyes were dark and inscrutable but he held out his hand and Joseph shook it. He realized that what M. Lefèvre was aching to say, but did not, was that Joseph was lucky to have anyone at all.

Joseph, in spite of his impatience, had agreed to spend an extra day at the Lazarist Mission to express his gratitude to M. Lefèvre. It was exceptionally cold at night; Suanhwa was 2,700 feet above Pekin, and the summers, he had been told, were short. He had to get up in the night to put more clothes on and add extra blankets to his bed. The incessant crowing of the rooks conspired to keep him awake. But the following day they rose early. Mendo and Tsembel repacked and replenished their provisions. Joseph, after prayers and breakfast with the brothers, left the mission by himself. The city appeared deserted in the thin light of morning. In any case, it was only half populated, the walls crumbling and decaying, dogs and emaciated cats trailing through the narrow alleys. The trading city of Kalgan, nestled under the Great Wall, was only a few miles north of Suanhwa, and he supposed that the fluid transaction of money had leached the life-blood from the older Mongol citadel. The few Chinese that he did see were noticeably different from those he'd come across in Tientsin and Pekin. Their skins were pale, their hair was lighter and they had more prominent noses; only their eyes gave away their race.

The banks of the Yang Ho were frozen. In the middle, where the current was strongest, blocks of ice flowed jaggedly downriver. Reeds along the edges were stiff with frost; a heron flew out of one clump as if rising from an iron crown. On the far side a long-legged plover stalked through the sedge, displaced from its natural element. He crossed a thin rope and wood bridge and spent the remainder of the morning poking through the fine yellow soil and digging beneath purple-red rocks that he suspected were porphyry. He unearthed several small yellow bones, scratched and gouged, as if by teeth, along their length. He thought they were the frail bones of marmots, and the leavings of jackals. Still, each time he heard the hollow tap of metal on bone, he felt a rush of excitement. It could be a skeleton from an animal that no longer existed, a creature that walked the earth unimaginable aeons of time ago, a beast whose life had been witnessed by God alone. The last skull he dug up did not look old – a small antelope with spiral horns. He let the sand drain from the eye sockets.

Ssu-pu-hsiang, in Chinese, said Mendo when he saw the skull. It's a deer. Its name means the four characters that do not match: it has the tail of an elephant, the nose of a horse, the ears of a rabbit and the feet of a pig.

Very early the next morning he prayed with the brothers and then took leave of them, the mules stepping over the raggedly cobbled streets with soft footfalls, slipping a little where ice had pooled in the cracks between stones, their breath drifting in crystalline clouds. The darkness had the grey quality of morning without moonlight before the sun has risen above the rim of the earth. They travelled west along the bank of the Yang Ho, the flow of the river muted beneath its layer of ice, the middle section black and glassy. Gradually the sun rose, the stony ground turned orange and the sky deepened to blue. Joseph was cold; the chill from the night still had not left him and he held himself stiffly on the mule until the sun began to thaw his bones. The saddle and the mule's gait felt even more uncomfortable than before, if that were possible. The days away from his mount had only served to tenderize and not heal his aching muscles.

By midday they had left the river behind and reached a vast crater surrounded by a ring of shale-grey hills. The land itself was flat and desert-like, covered with row upon row of pebbles, almost as if they had been raked by a cultivator of stones. Blades of grass were rare. In the distance the air seemed to shimmer: sheet ice grown across the sky. The hills surrounding the crater were probably volcanic, he thought, and the crater itself could have been formed by a flood, or might even have been the bed of some ancient sea. When they stopped to brew tea for lunch, Joseph poked through the diluvial sand and found a couple of shells, smooth, white and coiled. They were probably fossils. He thought of his father, who'd dreamt of being a sailor, and wondered what he might say – shells from a land without a sea. He imagined himself as a child holding out his tiny fist and opening it slowly to reveal them. He smiled and put them in his pocket. Tsem and Mendo were crouched by a small fire, watching him. It was a period of waiting, all three trying to assess the others, held back by barriers of language, religion, race, culture and simple lack of acquaintance. Mendo and Tsem could be equally distant from one another, he thought, separated by class – such as it might exist out here – and education.

Do you think we have sufficient food with us? asked Joseph.

Tsem held out a bowl of tea and one of *tsamba*, a kind of gruel made of barley flour. It was barely edible and he only managed by washing it down with the tea.

Mendo nodded. It is not so far to Ta-t'ung-Fu – and the border. He looked up quickly and then added, But I think we should not delay.

There might be fossils.

There are fossils everywhere. Believe me, Father Jacob, there are better places to find old bones.

You can call me Joseph, he muttered and looked at the two of them. Even Tsem's normally cheerful countenance was muted. He felt like a child who had been reprimanded. Tsem swiftly stamped out the fire and clattered their bowls and saucepan roughly as he cleaned and repacked them. There was something disquieting about this, Joseph thought. Here he was, in what had been the bottom of the sea in the country he had always dreamt of, with his expedition in place, his translator, his transport and his horseman, and yet he had done no work, had hardly started to explore, collect, preserve, dissect. His old impatience was welling up; he burned with excitement.

It will become easier once we cross the border, said Mendo quietly. Now we have little time, but there will be time. And he smiled as he repeated, There will be time.

Am I so easy to read? wondered Joseph.

As if in answer Mendo said, There is a man – and here he hesitated – many call him the White Warlord. He has an army and spies everywhere. The further away we are from people the more easily we can travel. Without feeling that we are being watched.

And are we being watched? asked Joseph as he stiffly climbed aboard his mule.

Mendo shrugged. We will be safer when we are over the border, he repeated.

Joseph was still thinking of himself. He believed that he had perfected the ability to be expressionless. A closed book, he had been called, and that had been one of the politer phrases. If growing more open was a virtue, showing one's flaws and weaknesses was not, he thought.

Further into the crater the land was threaded with streams as if by fine blue veins and in the centre was a swamp. The edges were lime green with moss. Lapwings and plovers rose in a cloud above it as they approached. Joseph took out his gun and fired twice. One of the lapwings came spiralling to the ground, wings outstretched. He urged his mule into a rickety trot and retrieved the bird from the outskirts of the swamp. The water was vaguely warm as if heated by an underwater spring. He laid the lapwing across his saddle. Mendo and Tsem were waiting for him.

Tsem looked distressed and Mendo's face was blank.

He said, In Mongolia we believe it is bad luck to kill birds. If it is essential, please refrain from shooting them in front of monasteries. We believe that the cycle of life is never-ending. When I die I might return as a bird. Or you may.

Birds have souls?

That is one way of expressing it.

Joseph stroked the soft feathers and felt the damp warmth of the bird's blood stain his fingers.

All animals are God's creatures. We have been given stewardship over living creatures. I am afraid, he sighed, it is a necessary death. It is part of my work. In the future it will help naturalists identify these birds and even learn a little about them. But wanton death, that I disapprove of.

In his heart, he knew that the joy he felt at firing the gun and hitting his target accurately was short-lived, displaced by sadness at killing the creature, and then that emotion was overwhelmed by his fascination: now he was able to see in detail each intricate pattern on its feathers, the fine scaled skin around its eyes. Did the lapwing have a soul?

At least we shall not go hungry, said Mendo, interrupting his reverie, but his smooth face creased with worry. We should make haste.

Joseph looked up at the sky. It was a peculiar colour of white, hard and brittle. A thin wind, sharp as a knife, picked up, gradually growing in strength. The sand started to shift ominously, skating across the ground, rustling round the mules' hooves. As the wind grew stronger, the sand whipped their faces, grating their skin, boring into their eyes and ears. Joseph's eyes began to water, clogging up his eyelashes with dust and tears. The sandstorm, fast as a river swirling around them, was so thick he could barely see his mule's head. He had to trust completely in the animal and hope that it, somehow, was aware of where the others were and was continuing to follow them. The mule stumbled disconsolately on, head lowered. The cold was incredible. His hands became numb, metal claws welded to the bridle, and he thought the skin on his face might split; his nose began to bleed a little. He hunched himself into his coat as much as was possible and resolved to make sure his scarf and gloves were in easy reach. It was one of the worst moments in the entire journey, including the sea crossing; he felt like cursing the very idea of travelling through such an inhospitable country. The thought that niggled depressingly at the back of his mind was that there might be many more situations like this. God will keep me strong, he hissed through gritted teeth.

The terrain changed: out of the storm loomed giant stacks of stone, rounded columns as if lava had oozed upwards and solidified. Joseph's normal interest in these odd formations was rather more muted than usual. It was only when they left the stone forest and the crater through a pass in the mountains that they were able to escape the worst of the sandstorm. They travelled for another two or three hours before they came to a village and an inn. Sand had blown into every crease in their clothes. Joseph left Mendo and Tsem haggling over the price of eggs and rice and where they might leave the mules and crouched in a small plot of land behind the inn where he prepared the lapwing's skin. He found that its stomach was full of tiny black beetles.

On the road to the border town of Ta-t'ung-Fu they were overtaken by a small band of men walking alongside a cart. Neither Tsem nor Mendo looked at the Chinese, though they stared viciously at the small party of travellers. They all carried guns and were chewing ferociously, their teeth ground down and rotted to blackened stumps. The man sitting on the back of the cart facing them watched them through narrowed eyes until he and his cargo finally disappeared from view.

Opium, said Mendo, when the men were gone. If you ever doubted your God, this is the place where doubt can grow.

Not only grow, but flourish like some anaemic weed sprouting from dung, taking root and becoming fat as it sucked the nourishment from its filthy origins. Or so Joseph thought as they entered the mire of dirty, tangled alleyways of Ta-t'ung-Fu. Every inn they called at reeked of opium, the air thick with its heavy stench, the inhabitants emaciated, comatose. A woman, whose face was powdered white and lips painted in a perfect ruby bow, attempted to fondle him; he recoiled as much from her touch as her sweetish smell, her thick floral perfume barely masking her unwashed body. The streets stank of human excrement and at every corner lingered the same faint odour – the milky sap of poppies which made him feel nauseous and gave him a headache. Beggars didn't even attempt to pluck at his clothes, they simply crouched in misery, holding out wasted and dirty hands. The men who strode through the town instead of lying limply in doorways all carried guns and thick curved swords.

Down by the river the air was a little cleaner. A group of women in jewel-like silks were working on the banks and there were tilled fields with the first green shoots sprouting in neat rows. But even this scene proved a false promise of beauty, as if he had witnessed a cloud of iridescent butterflies only to discover that they were feeding on human waste. As they approached the river he saw that it was dark brown and sluggish, swarms of flies hovered above it and he could smell the thin, almost high-pitched odour of sewage; its surface was slick with fetid bubbles that would not burst; breaking through the yellowish scum were the remains of animals and decaying tree branches. The fields were full of opium poppies; the women were filthy, their clothes torn. They were turning heavy stones by themselves – there was not a man to be seen.

What are they doing? asked Joseph.

Grinding bark.

Bark?

Yes, to make flour.

With a sudden guilty pang he thought of how he had abandoned his adopted father Patrick – and for what? To witness the kind of human degradation that was rife in English slums? Patrick, now alone and lonely and old in Bristol, would be measuring the days of his absence by the slow metronomic tick of the clock in the hall.

When Joseph was three years old his father had met a sailor who, for the price of a bottle of stout with a drop of gin on the side, told him a tale of a man who had conquered Asia, from the Yellow Sea to the Caspian. His name was Genghis Khan. At twenty he became a leader; by the time he was twenty-seven he was called the Universal King. His empire was the greatest known to man. He came from Outer Mongolia, a land where you could walk until you died and you'd never see the shore, where the sky was always blue and the steppes rolled on for ever. The sailor had spread his hands in astonishment.

His father had told this story to Joseph over and over again before he left him. And after he had found the abandoned child, the old priest had nourished his obsession with the land of Genghis Khan; it was Patrick who bought him a book full of dragons and bloodthirsty armies, Genghis wielding a silver sword that spat his enemies' heads to the far corners of the globe; Patrick who taught him to how to read it.

In a land beyond time, in a country far, far away, it began, *a baby was born with a blood clot as big as a knuckle clasped in his tiny fist.*

He could not have expected that land to spirit him away so soon and for so long.

On the outskirts of Ta-t'ung-Fu they found an inn that was not as bad as the others. They tied up the mules in the inner courtyard, and brewed tea and *tsamba* rather than risk the inn's food, such as it might be. For the first time Joseph was able to find out more about Tsem from his translator. Tsem, through Mendo, said that he lived on the steppes north of Pekin where Inner Mongolia began. He led a traditional nomadic existence – he had sheep, cows, horses, a beautiful wife and three children. But his wife was a capable woman and she and his oldest son could manage without him and, as he often came into contact with the Chinese trade routes, he had earned himself a reputation as a trustworthy hand when extra help was needed. Much of his income now came from working as a horseman, providing horses and caring for the cargoes of salt and stone, furs and spices that passed between Inner Mongolia and China. He talked long into the night, describing his family and became quite maudlin. The three of them were sleeping in one room on straw mattresses, their belongings at their feet and in their beds. When they finally lay down to rest, Joseph realized that the place was crawling with lice; all through the long night, he felt their small bodies creeping intimately across his skin.

Now in the ashen light of early morning the plains stretched ahead: an alien wasteland, sparse, volcanic, hostile, littered with a crop of stones. The ruined wall with its ragged battlements cast dark shadows that crept towards them with spindly claws. He itched all over from the lice and his spine ached dully from the constant jolting. But at least they were free. That morning they had crossed the Chinese border and escaped from the soldiers with their lives, although when he thought of the poor mule they had so callously slaughtered he shuddered. He still felt fear like a hard, crystalline rock inside his chest.

In this lawless land he wondered how many more encounters of this kind they might have. He realized that he had, up until this moment, only thought of the success or failure of his expedition in terms of the number and magnificence of the specimens he returned with, not whether he lived or died.

And yet, even as they rode away from the wall and the steppe stretched in front of him, wide open and limitless as he had always imagined, he felt his flesh creep as if he were being watched. He tried to dismiss the feeling. It was only Mendo and his curious haste to distance himself from the Chinese and his mutterings about the White Warlord that were making him anxious. As the sun rose and the shadows shrank his thoughts became less morbid. Larks began to sing – he noted both the common and shoe-toed variety – the birds rising and falling on the threads of their songs. They passed a herd of *huang-yang*, Mongolian gazelles, which raised their heads on graceful necks, tendons locked tautly, but did not take flight. They had a yellowish tinge to their coats, and blended in beautifully with the sandy soil. It was, though, he thought, as he watched the gazelles, a triumph that he was here at all.

Three years ago, on a late afternoon in early autumn, he'd been dead-heading chocolate cosmos and miniature sunflowers, their petals blood-orange red. Gnats and spider silk glowed in the dying sun and cigar-blue tendrils of smoke drifted through a clump of Panama grass. Out of the corner of his eye he saw John Turndike walking towards him. He was a stoutish man with a large girth, and a penchant for wearing green baize waistcoats with yellow silk cravats. He considered himself a gentleman gardener, which, in reality, consisted of rarely dirtying his hands, an occupation suited to his position as part owner and manager of the Bristol Royal Botanical Gardens. An ambitious man but lacking in the necessary drive, Joseph had known he would find it useful to hire a young, ardent scientist who, moreover, would not leave to start a family. In addition, one need not pay a priest a large salary. He'd started working for Turndike as a way of staying near Patrick while being close enough to the British Museum to maintain the links that he had forged with the scientists there. But, above all, he loved the work: the feel of the earth beneath his hands, the theoretical nature of planning the planting, the almost ecstatic pleasure he derived from knowing he was moulding God's better beauty.

Turndike looked like a man with something important to say who was reluctant to look as if he did.

How are the zinnias? he asked as he drew near.

They were Turndike's favourite flowers with their clusters of daisy-shaped stamens; the new ones he'd bought were green as envy and Mexican red.

They are faring well, said Joseph. They're about to flower.

And the plans for the Chinese garden?

It's progressing. I will show you, but we need more species. If we knew of someone who was planning an expedition, it would be of help.

Ah, said Turndike and nodded, turning away from him towards the fading embers of George's bonfire.

Joseph continued working, waiting. He moved round the bed and Turndike followed, his hands clasped behind his back, still out of breath.

I have news for you, he said, looking up at last and suppressing a smile. He drew a magnolia-coloured letter from his coat pocket, the red wax seal broken and crumbling.

Joseph's heart suddenly began to beat faster. Turndike slid his finger under the seal and started to unfold the thick, creamy paper. Joseph's obsession with Outer Mongolia, the land of Genghis Khan, his childhood vow that one day he would visit the Mongol king's country, everything he had strived for now seemed focused on that letter. It would be a small tribute, no, more accurately, a way to show that he, Joseph, was not worthless, a cast-off to be abandoned; that instead he was someone, someone capable of travelling to such an alien country and making his mark upon the scientific world.

When he was thirteen he'd heard that the plant hunter Joseph Dalton Hooker had brought the first specimen over from China, and, even at so young an age, he'd thought that if Hooker could bring such a precious plant to Britain, then one day he too might travel to Outer Mongolia and return with a strange and wondrous cargo.

For years now, he'd plotted and planned, had cultivated extensive links with the British Museum, hoping against hope that one day his constancy would pay dividends. He had learned to decipher what the scientists most desired and sowed small seeds in their minds: how maybe this specimen, that species, could be found in a land without an ocean – maybe even an undiscovered type that might bear their name within its new Latin nomenclature. And as for him, well, there would be many ways in which a young scientist who had run such an unusual expedition might make his name. From China's Forbidden City came rumours of floating beds of orchids; any one of those precious blooms could not be worth more if it had been cast in silver. And any one of those twisted flowers would be recompense for another man. But from the floating city had also come whispers of another flower: a pure, white lily so rare no foreigner had laid eyes upon it. A lily plucked from the vast wastes of Mongolia. To find such a flower, that would indeed be a singular treasure.

Turndike had been both easier and more difficult than the scientists. He was avaricious for new plants for his garden and could be flattered and beguiled, even by academics. But he had to believe that the idea to send Joseph to Outer Mongolia was his own. To this end, Joseph, not naturally a man of Machiavellian temperament, had worked with stealth and patience. And now, at last, he was to hear whether his machinations had been successful.

I have been working on your behalf with your contacts at the British Museum and I have proposed an expedition to Outer Mongolia to procure stones, specimens and what not for them and, naturally, plants. And finally, after much persuasion and considerable effort on my part, they have agreed partially to fund such a voyage.

And who would go? asked Joseph as his knife slid, soft as butter, through a flower stem. He held his breath.

Why you, of course, said Turndike, seeming visibly to swell with pride at his own endeavours.

Joseph took a deep breath and glanced at the triumphant Turndike. He wondered that Turndike could not sense the quiver running through Joseph's body, the slight tremble that translated itself to the flower he held between his fingers. He remembered that moment for a long time afterwards: his mind had emptied but the world around him took on a heightened clarity: a drop of plant sap on the blade of his knife, the darkened veins of the dead flower in his hand, a crab spider crouched like a jewel, its flesh suffused the identical hue of its floral surroundings, a broken blood vessel at the edge of John Turndike's left eye.

You will be participating in a noble voyage, one in a long and distinguished line of men of bravery and courage, said Turndike. The first record of plant hunting was documented in 1495 BC when the Egyptian queen Hatshepsut sent an envoy to Somalia to collect incense trees. And naturally plants are highly valued in our society today. A house in the Netherlands was exchanged for three tulip bulbs in 1635. I have no doubt that you will bring back many rare and wondrous specimens which will advance the fortunes of our humble garden.

Joseph smiled to himself. Turndike was repeating almost verbatim facts that Joseph had told him three months ago. It was only afterwards, after the elation and pride (yes, dear God, there had been pride), that he'd felt a cold creeping around his heart as he thought of Patrick and what his absence might mean to the elderly priest.

Joseph felt England's narrow meanness like a physical sensation. People pushed and jostled him, the houses were cramped together and leaned inwards as if making contact with those across the scant streets, the boats were crowded together in the harbour, packed so tightly there was scarce space for the eddies of oil, packing cases, orange peel and the corpses of rats and dogs; it seemed a long way to the open sea. Even the many hills within Bristol conspired against him so that he could never see a horizon, and the smell, rising in the warm summer air, enveloped him like a choking blanket: sewage, hops, rotten fruit and the acrid stench of burned coffee grounds. Now that he knew the expedition was going to take place, he could not wait to leave.

Patrick interrupted his thoughts. They had attended the sermon at St Mary's and he was asking Joseph if he wanted to take a little turn about the quay. As it was a Sunday, it should be safe enough, thought Joseph, and nodded his assent. There was a queer light: the sky was almost navy and the clouds were thick, heavy as bread soaked in buttermilk. A brassy light skittered across the surface of the water, back-lighting the boats against the darkening background. They walked out past the chandlers and the refitting of the SS *Great Britain*, where smaller boats were moored in smaller har-bours, and alongside the shanty slum of cardboard and crates that had been his home for a couple of years as a child after his father had abandoned him. Seagulls flew about his head, wingspans like pterosaurs, screaming for scraps.

As was his wont, Patrick stopped every few minutes to talk to people. He had a terrible memory for names and often called his ex-parishioners whom he'd known for twenty-odd years by the wrong ones, but he knew exactly the details of their intimate lives: how many children, who had lived and died, whose husband had run off with a whore from Cleve-don, whose mother had died of the plague, whose sister's aunt was coming to visit this autumn, which child was ready to receive confirmation and who was expecting to be bap-tized, who could not afford to pay a penny towards the upkeep of the church and whose son was shortly for the workhouse.

The constant stopping disguised the old priest's shortness of breath and his general frailty, but Joseph was not fooled.

After half an hour or so, he negotiated with a horse and trap to take them home.

He was just passing, Father. I thought I would stop him now in case we did not see another one, he said, steering Patrick towards the waiting driver.

They ascended jerkily up Park Street, one of the steepest hills in town, the trap bone-shaking over the cobbles, the horse leaning full into the harness, its flanks matted with sweat.

You know, said Patrick, his breath shaken out of him with every word, when you were a small boy, you were so . . .

Difficult?

Spirited, spirited is what I was going to say.

There was a long pause. The horse reached the lip of the hill and scrambled over the rim and round the corner. Joseph had told Patrick about his proposed expedition to Mongolia the night before. Patrick had merely closed his eyes for a long moment and said nothing but he had heard the priest praying long into the night. Joseph wondered whether this reminiscence about his childhood was a preamble to talking about the trip.

Over the years you became a little calmer, Patrick continued. The prayers helped and your years at Stonyhurst. Yes, you worked hard at smoothing over the anger and I cannot say I blamed you, that you felt a certain antagonism towards society as a child. I mean to say, no, I cannot say I blame you at all. And, of course, God listened and answered your prayers.

Joseph made a face. He'd found Patrick's goodness, his kindness, his peacefulness all hard to take as an eight-year-old rescued from the gutter. He'd been insufferable. And then there had been Patrick's godliness: his brand of Catholicism was entirely alien to the son of a would-be sailor. But because he quickly grew to love Patrick, he learned to love the culture and customs, the trappings of God, that surrounded the older priest, until they had become part of his fibre, part of his very soul.

It was why I chose you, Patrick liked to say to him as he was growing up, I could see God in you.

At first he'd thought Patrick was referring to some inner goodness that hadn't been crushed by his life on the streets. But later he took it to mean that Patrick knew, somehow, that Joseph had the makings of a priest within him; that Patrick had glimpsed the start of that fierce flame which would one day consume him.

The trap pulled up outside what Joseph always thought of as the new house. While he was at Stonyhurst, Patrick had retired and moved from the church at St Mary's to a small house in the village of Clifton Wood on the outskirts of Bristol. The new house was on the intersection between two thin streets; it was odd-shaped and angular, with dark corners and green velvet curtains that swallowed light and a clock in the hall with a swinging pendulum that seemed to measure the minutes in slower units. Now Joseph leaned forward and paid the driver, then jumped out and reached up to help Patrick.

Once inside, Patrick called for the maid.

Now, Joseph, what will you have? Will you take tea?

Joseph did not know what he wanted. A glass of iced lemonade, a quart of milk, black coffee with a dram of brandy. He was in a ferment of agitation. He wanted to begin to plan his expedition but was paralysed, unable to do so until Patrick had given him his blessing.

Yes, tea would do nicely.

He sat down opposite Patrick who pulled out his backgammon set. He looked at the long red and black lozenges as Patrick laid out the counters with quivering fingers. He'd aged perceptibly in the time that Joseph had been at Stonyhurst. A tall man with thin, withered legs, he was hunched with a spreading paunch. His hair was grey, streaked black, and was long and wispy, receding from his forehead in twin peaks. He had thick sideburns and his brown eyes were ringed rheumy cataract-blue. The skin across his large hands had become so pale and thin that his veins rose through it like twisted cord; there was an ashen pallor to his face. Joseph felt guilty that he was about to leave him for so long and his guilt manifested itself as a queer kind of anger.

He fidgeted in the high-backed chair. The maid brought tea and thin slices of Madeira cake. He ate slowly, tasting nothing, craving meat, chunks of lamb in thick gravy. He felt a violent need to overload his senses. He had a sudden image of torn peaches, the flesh wrenched from the stone, blush-red and striated, clear juice pooling against amber skin. Patrick poured milk into his tea with a shaking hand and added a spoonful of sugar. He stirred thoroughly.

Have you seen today's paper? He pointed at the folded-up square of thin newsprint. Another death in the Fox-Jones family. The youngest two died while you were away, and this is their second oldest son. It's a terrible blow to the poor mother.

He scattered the die across the board and looked up at Joseph again.

There's been a murder down by the docks. A sailors' brawl, so they say. He shook his head slowly. It's an awful thing what the drink will do to a man.

I'm surprised it was reported at all.

Patrick's hand hovered over the board. He touched the die tenderly and counted out the numbers across the coloured lozenges. Recounted. Reconfigured his moves. Joseph jumped up, hardly able to contain himself. He paced across the living room floor and peered out of the window, the glass slowly pooling in a thicker drift towards the sill.

Yes, yes, crime is on the increase. A fight between sailors is a commonplace incident these days.

Patrick read the paper from cover to cover and, for as long as Joseph could remember, he'd learned about the workings of the city second-hand from his father who summarized in sad tones the evil that had taken place in a voice that quavered with incomprehension while he yet retained a fierce optimism for the fate of human nature.

He suddenly looked up at Joseph as if he judged the time to be right to broach the subject.

Now, Joseph, my son, what I do not understand is why you are concerned about this trip in particular? It seems such an awfully long way to venture for a few plants. An extravagance. Not to mention the difficulties you will face and the considerable risk to your life.

But, Father, as I said . . . here, let me.

He walked over and took the pot from Patrick's trembling hands and poured them both more tea. He added milk and stirred sugar into Patrick's.

It isn't just plants, he said, forcing himself to sit down.

Thank you kindly, and I might take a little more cake, if I may.

I'm bringing back other specimens for the British Museum too – rocks, mammals, reptiles, liverworts for Dr Craven, no doubt.

It's very fine cake. Will you not take another slice?

No. All right, yes, I shall, thank you. I would have thought that you would be pleased such prodigious scientists are requesting that I do this work for them.

Only because they are too lazy or too unfit or too cowardly to do it themselves, answered Patrick heatedly. I sometimes think people believe Jesuits to be expendable; they seem to burn so brightly and for a shorter period of time than others. And, of course, they have no dependants and can be paid a pittance.

Father!

It is true. You know we can barely afford to live on what you earn and my pension. Still, it keeps us close to God and we have more than most. Naturally I am proud of you, Joseph, he added.

Joseph sipped his tea and leaned back. A leaden tiredness seemed to have overcome him. He suddenly foresaw the amount of work it would take to launch his expedition, all the while counting the months, the weeks, the very minutes until he could leave.

What I meant to say, said Patrick, is that Outer Mongolia is a completely unknown quantity. I do not know what it is that you hope to gain, but I think you should count the cost of going and ask yourself if it be too great.

I don't know what you're talking about, said Joseph shortly, drinking his tea.

Ah, Joseph, son, you always pushed away those who loved you the most. I shall retire to my room. Ask Marie to bring me a small glass of hot port in an hour if you would be so kind.

Despite the strangeness of the landscape and the incident at the border, Joseph continued to dwell on Patrick, with only the maid for company, until they stopped for tea and boiled rice at midday. Joseph carried his bowl of tea with him as he wandered around the steppe, anxious to stretch his tense muscles. He found a piece of purple rock, riven with green crystals, and a grey pebble marbled with cloud-coloured quartz, as smooth as if the sea had rolled it in its maw; he cupped it in his palm and felt God's spirit like a physical and palpable presence in the very constancy of the small, grey stone. He handed it to Mendo.

To me God is in everything, even this. He grinned with barely contained excitement.

That is very Buddhist, said Mendo. He turned to translate Joseph's words for Tsem. He added, I told him that you think God is everywhere, in everything. This stone. A blade of grass. Even a bird.

Tsem said something in his sharp, choppy tongue.

He says, Mendo translated, if God is everywhere, do you tread on Him?

Well, He is in the earth, in the air, He is a part of everything.

Tsem gestured animatedly towards their small fire.

He says, If He is in the air, I must swallow him. He is inside me. And he says, Is God in this iron pot? If He is, he must be scalded by the hot tea. Mendo laughed and continued to translate for Tsem. And he says, If God is in the pot, the pot must be alive.

Joseph crouched down by the fire opposite Tsem. If a fly were in the pot, the pot would not be alive.

No, said Mendo quickly, but the fly is only a tiny creature, it is flesh and blood. God has no substance. If God is everywhere and in everything, He must fill the whole space inside the pot.

He turned to translate what he had said to Tsem.

Joseph stood up and stuck his arms straight out. I fill my coat, yet my coat is not alive.

It was, he thought, an argument designed to win the argument rather than the truth, for the truth was that God was woven into the very fabric of his coat, melded with the metal of their cooking pot.

Tsem's face creased into a grin. He jumped up and slapped Joseph across the back as if to congratulate him on winning the dispute, and then picked up the pot from the fire. He opened the lid a little, peered in and lifted the lid away, jumping back in mock horror and astonishment as if God had escaped like a genie with the steam from the tea. He burst out laughing again and his laughter was so infectious Joseph laughed with him. Tsem threw away the dregs of tea and stamped out the fire.

Mendo handed the pebble back to Joseph with a small bow. You have – possibly it was an accident – taught us in the Buddhist way. You posed a riddle and gradually led us to the solution. Your solution.

Joseph could have replied that the master–pupil relationship, the question and the answer, was a traditional Western format that stretched back at least as far as Socrates. But the heart of the matter was that his excitement had momentarily overflowed and these two, the Mongolian horseman, and the Buddhist monk, were the sole human beings with whom he could share his thoughts. Whether they agreed with him or not. He put the pebble in his pocket.

Although he had expected it, he was still disappointed to see that there were no flowers. No doubt it was still too cold: the only sign of plant life he could make out were lichen, yellow and black, clinging to crevices in some of the stones, and the odd fern, curled and wizened as if coated in cracked leather. At this time of year in the Royal Botanical Gardens, snowdrops and aconites would be beginning to melt away, daffodils carpeting the ground beneath the apple orchard and the tulips would have grown tightly sealed buds. He remembered digging in the first shipment of tulips from Amsterdam; George, the head gardener, had told him that some of the more unusual hybrids with cream stripes, beaks like parrots – even serrated petals – cost a small fortune.

What they all want, he said, was a black or a blue flower because nature had no cause to make such a kind.

To Joseph, even the plainest variety was a miracle in itself; it was a gift worthy of prayer merely to hold the bulbs in his hand, their papery skin flaking away against the first signs of roots.

It's science, said George. The horticulturists in Holland breed the best with the best. They know what they're about: hardy ones bred with them that has the prettiest flowers. 'Course, sometimes they make monsters that keel over and die, their stems be ever so weak. Other times they surprise even themselves with the beauty of their creation.

God's creation, said Joseph, smiling up at him, as he planted a tulip which would flower the year he rode across Outer Mongolia: white with lime-green lines and muted pink veins.

The path they travelled was narrow and rocky, with sheer, slate-grey mountains rising on either side. It was the width of two mules; they walked in single file. The sun caught only the mountain tops, but its fractured rays cast a red stain across the lower slopes. Joseph scrambled up to see what the cause might be. He was hampered by his cassock which tripped him, snagged on stones and distracted him from the real business in hand. It would, of course, be sacrilegious to abandon it, as well as cold; the one advantage it had, as well as almost infinite capacity for carrying small items short distances, was that it was not dissimilar to the garments worn by the Mongolians themselves. Tucking the heavy folds of cloth into his belt, he climbed to the top of the hill and discovered the source of the reddish caste: thousands of tiny red succulent plants nestled between the stones, their buds pink and foetal. How well suited they were to this bleak and barren life, he thought. He dug up several. He shook the soil from their vestigial roots and wrapped them in hessian. That, of course, was the key to life itself – the struggle for survival and the survival of the fittest. This to Joseph was evolution at work, in these gritted, twisted roots, a theory that haunted his thoughts like a forgotten melody, an unsatisfied hunger, a promise to be kept, a summons to be answered.

In 1859 Joseph had been twenty-six years old and had just become a priest. At Stonyhurst there had been a flowering of knowledge within him that had left him breathless but, in the end, the Jesuit school was cold and damp and he had felt far from home. The year of his twenty-sixth birthday he'd returned to Bristol and taken up the post at the Royal Botanical Gardens. Patrick had already retired and left St Mary's to a younger man, a Jesuit; Joseph was sometimes asked to preach guest sermons. But what had really changed him was a book which was published that year. It was one of those works, although rambling, anecdotal and perhaps a little overlong, that cut to the core of what it means to be alive; it seemed to him that it explained the very essence of being. It united his beliefs and his thoughts in a way that nothing else had, and perhaps never would again.

On 22 November the book was officially published. Joseph was first in the queue to buy it. It was *The Origin of Species by Means of Natural Selection, or the Preservation of Favoured Races in the Struggle for Life* by Charles Darwin. It gave him some comfort as he read it to think that Darwin was himself also trained as a geologist and was a man of the cloth. Further, Darwin was settled at the spa in Ilkley at that very time, a town on the edge of the Yorkshire moors not so far from Stonyhurst itself and, as he read, he imagined Darwin looking out over the same windswept heather and gorse that he had spent many hours walking across, his stomach twisted into knots at the thought of his book's reception. Joseph had a small office at the Botanical Gardens from where he planned the garden's layout, ordered new bulbs and seeds, corresponded with travellers and anyone else who might be able to procure unknown and remarkable plants. It was here that he sat and read *Origin* looking out over the wet bones of the garden while George heaped rotting compost and manure on to the beds, and a robin hopped boldly in his wake.

It was a remarkable book, revolutionary almost, for it explained how species arose and diverged, changed through time, adapted to their surroundings, competed with other species, became like finely honed machines suited to their niche and their lifestyle; and yet, were one to dissect them, one would see that not all the parts worked perfectly, that there was redundancy, profligacy and waste, that old solutions solved new problems so that the very history of a species was recorded like a series of hieroglyphs within its biology. It was, as Herbert Spencer was later to say, survival of the fittest. On a practical level Darwin's words resonated with all that Joseph had thought and seen of the natural world. George and he spent hours in the summer extracting pollen and painting it on to the female part of plants when they wished to take the best traits of the males and cross them with the females. It was complicated by plant biology, the fact that some were not one sex but both and that one could create hybrids which existed but rarely in the animal kingdom. Nevertheless, the principle was the same, and he could see it in dogs, pigeons, cats, horses – wherever man had intervened and chosen who would mate with whom and how, ultimately, that species would evolve. The rest of the living world was merely an experiment running on a different timescale, with different needs and existing without teleology.

In the late afternoons he walked through Leigh Woods, allowing *Origin* to permeate into his very fibre. At this time of the year, the woods were bare, the trees crowded thickly together, their branches naked, rimed with moisture, their roots a porous mass of moss and the precious orange of stag's horn fungi. Holly berries, bright as beads of blood, the ruby gems of deadly nightshade gathered together in pewter clasps, and spindleberries, like cracked ball gowns the colour of old roses, all glinted through the semi-darkness. Woodpeckers, jays and magpies flitted through the tangled branches, wrens and dunnocks wormed their way into the densest undergrowth and, come nightfall, bats and foxes and barn owls would flicker between the trees and the patches of meadow trapped in the heart of the wood. The wood felt as if it were throbbing with electricity; he felt its muted vibrancy and saw that its very essence was composed of separate species evolving together and apart from every other living thing in this close-knit community. He felt, as he trod the secret paths and byways of the wood, that he was its spiritual keeper, a part of the very same process, yet knowing and understanding, carrying the key to life itself in the palm of his hand.

He came to the edge of the cliff and looked out from the darkness of the wood; below him the Severn, burnished as brushed steel, flowed through banks of mud, and the rock face opposite flared and flamed salmon and peach in the light of the setting sun.

He's caused quite a commotion with that there book, said George when he returned. Some say he's given us apes for grandfathers, and others say it is the death of God.

Well, I sincerely do not believe that my grandfather was an ape – nor yours. And it would take a lot more than a few words to silence God.

He was almost high, drunk on words and fine feelings, his cheeks burning. George contemplated him slowly.

You don't believe a word of it?

Oh, I do, I do. It is very much what I have always felt without knowing it, if you see what I mean. It is science, George, that is all. Scientific knowledge cannot diminish our love of God, only increase it. For why is there something rather than nothing? Why did this world spring into being? God begat everything. He created the means to our beginning. Once the earth was here, and God had primed and readied it, why, it was fertile ground for the creation of life which evolved for thousands of years until we see the world and all its animals and plants as they are now. How one creature became another, how whales drew breath in the depths of the ocean, and fish gained lungs and walked on land, that is a matter for science and yet one for which we can also praise God.

George stroked his chin and the stubble grated roughly beneath his callused fingers.

In the Bible it says the world was created in seven days. There was no mention of thousands of years before the sons of Adam, nor no mention of mussels turning into men.

The Bible is a story; we do not have to take all of it literally. It is the message – that God loves us and cares for us – that is important.

Well, I don't know about that. Seems wrong to me for a priest such as yourself to think such things. I shall be on my way home for me tea anyway. I'll be seeing you tomorrow.

Joseph laid a hand on the gardener's arm to delay him.

Think about your tulips, George. That is the heart of the matter, that is at the bottom of Mr Darwin's book. Listen to this, George, this is what it says. He opened the book and read:

As man can produce and certainly has produced a great result by his methodical and unconscious means of selection, what may not Nature effect? Man can act only on external and visible characters: Nature cares nothing for appearances, except in so far as they may be useful to any being. She can act on every internal organ, on every shade of constitutional difference, on the whole machinery of life.

There, George, what do you think of that? *The whole machinery of life.*

George grunted doubtfully. I think you and Mr Darwin between you are killing God. Don't be forgetting to lock up now, Father Jacob.

A few minutes later Joseph saw him cross the garden and leave through the great wooden gates, an old man stooped and weathered and worried through with the prejudices of his age. Joseph watched him go before he opened *Origin* again and reread the final chapter.

*

When Joseph first met them, he was still at Stonyhurst. They were taking tea out of an ornate pewter kettle and eating dainty cherry scones with raspberry jam and clotted cream. They had invited him to join them and he was so nervous the scones lodged in his throat. He did not realize then that these little cakes were a special treat in his honour. He was still over-awed by the exterior, the great scope of the building and its granite reputation. He choked on the scone and they slapped him on the back and made him drink scalding tea thick with cream and sluggish with sugar. For the first time he felt out of place in his dog collar and black vestments among these waistcoated men, dangling watch fobs and handkerchiefs, monocles and magnifying glasses, stirring their tea with the blunt ends of scalpels, who smiled with kind amusement. There were three of them: Dr Harold Holyoake, Dr David Craven and Dr Samuel McKendrick. His tutor, Father Theodore Pritchard, had secured him an interview at the British Museum with them. He asked that they provide secular guidance, of a type that he could not, and that, God willing, Joseph could be of some assistance to them in the future.

Dr Craven was a botanist who studied mosses and ferns, liverworts and lichens, but prided himself on his knowledge of Asiatic flowering plants; Dr McKendrick was a geologist with a particular interest in minerals and gems; and Dr Holyoake was an ornithologist and specialized in diving birds. Later he would tell Joseph how dippers literally swam underwater, how cormorants must hang their wings cruciform-fashion once they had surfaced as they were so primitive they had no natural oil glands, and that herons had the capacity to see through a sheet of water and make split-second calculations that took account of the differences in refraction between where the eye on land and the eye under-water believes the fish to be.

There was an uncomfortable pause and then Dr Craven said gently, Father Pritchard says that you are well versed in Darwin's works.

Joseph nodded. I have just finished reading his first great monograph.

Good God, man, interjected Dr Holyoake, surely you do not mean the barnacle book?

Joseph nodded again.

From cover to cover?

There are few who could say the same, said Dr McKendrick. There are a hundred pages on fossil barnacles and over a thousand devoted to the living specimens.

Dr Holyoake patted his stomach. The most memorable part for me was when he described males as astonishingly negative creatures for they have no mouth, no stomach, no thorax, no limbs, no abdomen. They consist in their entirety of the male reproductive organs in an envelope. He chuckled and added, Darwin once found twelve cemented to a single female.

And what of his latest, *The Origin of Species*, what do you think of that? asked Dr Holyoake. Must have created quite a furore in the Church.

They are not the only people to be upset by his theories, said Dr McKendrick. I would say a good sixty-five per cent of people here at the British Museum are set against it.

Is that true? said Joseph. Why would that be?

No science in it, said Dr Holyoake. Nice theory, but not a lot of facts.

But it is full of facts, said Joseph in astonishment, bursting at the seams with facts. He spent twenty years amassing evidence.

What Dr Holyoake means, said Dr Craven in his quiet voice, is that evolution, or natural selection, however you want to refer to it, is not written in a scientific way. It is a series of anecdotes intended to prove his point.

Quite, said Dr Holyoake, it is too speculative. Mr Darwin is a little premature with his theory.

Oh, said Joseph.

Perhaps you'll take another scone, said Dr Craven kindly.

Joseph took one absent-mindedly. He received the cream from Dr Craven but then put down the bowl.

I do believe, he said, that Darwin is using, let us call it, a hypothetically deductive method. By his method one needs theories at a very early stage. His theory then enables the scientist to decide which facts appear to be significant, and will also indicate which phenomena are worth investigating and what investigations and experiments and so on will be fruitful. Now this might sound like special pleading but, in fact, the plausibility of the theory is judged by the success of the experiments, whether the facts do, in truth, fit it, and by how well it advances our knowledge.

I agree Mr Darwin is somewhat short of hard, observational evidence. But, do you not see, he has created a framework within which geology, anatomy, embryology, ornithology, conchology – any branch of science you care to name – will fit. As a method of reasoning it works brilliantly and I feel sure, gentlemen, you would agree that his theory has advanced our knowledge considerably.

There was a queer silence around the table. The three men looked at each other and then back at Joseph.

Dr Craven put down his teacup and said, Father Jacob, we'd be delighted to help and instruct you in any way you and Father Pritchard see fit. I am sure that we can come to some arrangement that will be mutually beneficial to all of us. We are, as you can imagine, overwhelmed with facts, often without the benefit of a hypothetically deductive, or otherwise, framework, and any assistance you might be able to provide in preserving, conserving, annotation and administration would be most welcome. In return we will teach you anything you care to know and which is within our abilities.

By Jove, young fellow, said Dr Holyoake, I only agreed to this meeting because I knew Dr Craven would bring along his wife's excellent home baking. I had not expected a man of the cloth to be so well versed in science.

He is a Jesuit, said Dr McKendrick patiently and slightly petulantly as if he had said it before. Many Jesuits are scientists themselves, is that not correct, Father Jacob?

It is indeed, Dr McKendrick, said Joseph, who now grinned and slathered his scone thickly with cream.

And it was chiefly due to these three men that Joseph was now travelling across Outer Mongolia. Dr Holyoake, for all his pomposity, was a brilliant if maverick teacher. Dr McKendrick, as well as sharing everything he knew about rocks and stones, how the bones of the planet formed, how gems grow and where to find the best-preserved fossils, had taught him the benefits of patience, the value of precision, and the advantages of a certain level of pedantry. But it was Dr Craven to whom he was most drawn, a kind, softly spoken man, with a passionate enthusiasm for plants, and an almost selfless desire to further his knowledge through Joseph's ambition – as well as a touching degree of uxoriousness.

As Joseph returned down the hillside with his carefully wrapped specimens, he saw that Tsem had taken advantage of his open luggage to tear a thin strip from the paper he had brought to preserve his plant specimens and had rolled it into a thick cigarette with a twist of tobacco. He was squatting in the solitary shadow of a mule, smoking.

He is celebrating, explained Mendo. He says we will soon be able to buy horses.

Tsem pointed at the mules, screwed up his face at them and spat on the ground.

We are first and foremost horsemen. Riding a mule is, how would you say it? An insult.

They are damnably uncomfortable, that much is true, said Joseph, his spirits rising at the thought of horses, with a smooth gait and broad back.

The path in front of them eventually opened out into a plain as it was growing dark. There was a river to their right, but Joseph couldn't quite see its outline, only the black slash where its banks might begin. There was movement in the dusk: over the hills flocks of sheep and goats were pouring down into the valley in a marbled stream of cream and tan. He had that creeping sensation again, as if he were being watched. He looked up and saw a man on horseback on the

far side of the river. He had halted his horse and was looking at their small party. Joseph thought at first he was there
to herd the animals but, in fact, the flock had taken flight
because of him. There was something slightly odd about the
horseman and then Joseph realized that it was a woman.
She was wearing a fur-trimmed hat and a *del* that in the half
light was the colour of old blood. As she urged the horse into
a gallop her long black hair streamed out behind her. Tsem
whistled softly, under his breath; Joseph assumed that he
was admiring her fine horse. It was white and its coat glimmered in the gloom long after she had melded with the
darkness.

He was so caught up with watching the woman, Joseph
hadn't noticed the large, white, round tent in the valley
bottom. Tsem was now half cantering – in as far as the mule
could and would – towards it.

It is called a *ger*, Mendo explained.

Tsem shouted out something before he reached the opening. A couple of mangy dogs at the entrance began to bark
but as Tsem approached their tails wagged and the barks
became more a clamour for attention than a threat.

Mendo snorted. He is giving the traditional Mongolian
greeting – hold the dogs – but in this case, he doesn't need to.
He smiled at Joseph.

To Joseph's surprise, Tsem vaulted from the mule and
walked straight into the *ger* without knocking on the red
wooden door or announcing himself. He reappeared a
moment later.

Welcome, he called, beaming. This is my home, and he
stood aside for them to enter.

It was the first time Joseph had been inside a *ger*, and he was impressed by how clean and ordered it was.

Tsem's wife was small and pretty and plump, with dark brown, slanting eyes, neat as almonds, and high, round cheeks, flushed plum with pleasure. She bowed to Mendo and Joseph and said her name was Khulan.

My son is still out with the goats, said Tsem, beaming and hugging his wife, but these two cheeky little monkeys are my daughters.

A toddler and another child of about five stared fiercely at the three of them but ran to hide behind their father as soon as Joseph smiled at them. He scooped them up and threw them in the air and they screamed with delight. Tsem's wife offered them a tray piled high with slices of dried apple, some deep-fried dough biscuits and hard pieces of curd. *Bordzig* and *aaruul*, Mendo explained, as Joseph bit into the cheese, which had a high, pungent odour.

You must eat what they offer you, whispered Mendo. It would be bad manners not to, but you should not take more. These sweetmeats are for visitors and not to eat in large quantities.

Khulan now handed round bowls of tea. It was white with globules of fat floating in it; almost completely masking the flavour of the tea was the rancid tang of sour milk. Tsem drank his with obvious relish and handed his bowl back, which was promptly refilled. Joseph sipped his very slowly hoping he would get used to the taste for he was hungry. He looked around him. Part of the material at the apex of the tent had been pulled back to reveal a triangle of deep blue sky, but most of the steam and smoke from the fire filled the *ger*. All the cooking utensils and ingredients were neatly stacked to the right of the door as one entered the tent. To the left were coils of ropes, saddles and some tools, clearly Tsem's area. Small wooden beds masked by thin cotton curtains were pushed against the side of the *ger* and at the back was an altar to the Buddha with offerings of food, a blue silk scarf and what looked like a rosary. Below the altar was the low table they were seated or squatting round and between it and the door was a bubbling pot of stew.

Delighted to have an excuse, Tsem opened a bottle of white liquid and poured a little into a bowl. He dipped his third finger into it, flicked the drop of milky liquid in the air, towards the hearth, and over his shoulder, moving his hand across his body as if he were genuflecting. He poured more of the liquid into the bowl and handed it to Mendo who repeated his actions. Joseph was at first entranced by the gesture but Mendo said, when he handed the bowl back to be replenished and given to Joseph, that they were blessing the earth, fire and sky.

We use the third finger because it is the cleanest and also because the Chinese love to poison people. It is their preferred method of dispatching those who are out of favour with them. A Mongol prince had a ring fashioned that would change colour when it came into contact with poison. He wore it on this finger of his hand, and he said to the Chinese officials that he was praising his country and blessing the elements by making this gesture. In truth he was testing his *airag* for cyanide.

Joseph took a cautious sip. It was a creamy concoction and tasted of a perfect, or an imperfect, blend of milk gone high and alcohol. Mendo's explanation served to remind him how

53

far from home he was, surrounded by people with alien customs and religion and who, as a priest, he should perhaps be attempting to convert. In reality, though his heart burned with his faith in God, he could not bring himself to take away from them something he had no understanding of and replace it with a religion they had no real conception of. There were few, he knew, who believed with his fervour, but the small and swiftly quenched thought returned again and again that the simple truth was that God was here in this room, God believed in them and it mattered not one iota if these people did not believe in Him. Christ, the Son of God, had died for them too.

Mendo quickly took the bowl away from Joseph and gave it back to Tsem who filled it to the brim. The heat and lack of food was making Joseph feel quite light-headed. Eventually, Khulan served them all from the pot of stew. It was a thin stock with large lumps of lamb in it, the off-cuts and leftovers, and there was not a vegetable to be seen. Nevertheless, he ate the mutton soup with gusto and thanked Tsem in his grammar-stricken Mongolian. Mendo watched him quietly, half smiling in the semi-darkness.

Suddenly Khulan started to speak. She talked quietly and rapidly and Joseph struggled to understand. Tsem grinned.

Of course, why didn't I think of that?

He turned to Joseph and Mendo helped translate what he had to say.

He said, My wife says that there was a trader here earlier, a woman from the north who was selling furs.

The woman on the white horse? interrupted Joseph, and Mendo nodded.

Khulan says that this woman's tribe lives where one of the most beautiful flowers in Mongolia grows. It's only found in the mountains and, in the middle of the summer, the slopes turn white as snow. It's very tall, as tall as a man, the colour of the first frost, and the smell is one that can never be forgotten. We should help you find it.

Joseph smiled to himself. It sounded like the white lily he had heard rumours of. It would indeed be a prize worthy of his expedition.

Tsem now took out an instrument and held it flat and lightly in the palms of his hands and smoothed it with his callused thumbs. It was like a fiddle made of wood but it was small and square, with a long thin neck that curved into a horse's head with flared nostrils and a flowing mane. There were two strings made of horse's hair and Tsem played it with a bow.

Morin khuur, he said, grinning at Joseph and indicating the fiddle.

Joseph leaned back against one of the beds and listened. The *morin khuur* danced between the Mongol's hands, and the sounds that it produced were mellifluous, yet rhythmical: they were the sounds of the herds that roamed the steppes, camels, goats, sheep, yaks and horses. Joseph could hear their pounding hooves, the sweep of the flock as it passed by, the rolling gait of camels, the charge of heavy-shouldered yaks. He heard them gallop across steppes and over mountains, cross rivers and skirt great lakes. He felt the pulse of it beating through his blood long after Tsem had stopped playing and they had rolled their bedding mats up to the fire and lain down for the night.

That night he dreamt of Alfred Russel Wallace, the man who had prodded Darwin to complete his twenty-year research into natural selection by coming up with an extraordinarily similar explanation of the origin of species. He dreamt of Wallace's voyage to the Spice Islands where he caught a butterfly with a wingspan of seven inches, green and velvet black, its body gold, its breast crimson, and he had written:

It is true I had seen similar insects in cabinets at home, but it is quite another to capture such a one one's self, to feel it struggling between one's fingers, and to gaze upon its fresh and living beauty, a bright gem shining out amid the silent gloom of a dark and tangled forest.

Wallace had eaten bats and Maleo bird's eggs and thought birds of paradise ethereal creatures who never came down to earth, for they had been born without legs. Joseph dreamt that one day he too would write for the Royal Society, and would correspond with Darwin, and other men might dream of his journeys and his treasures.

He thought: *Of all lands of the whole world thou hast chosen thee one pit: and of all the flowers thereof one lily.*

And in his dreams he saw fields of lilies, white as frost, their scent as clear as snow, and men knew his name because of that single, inimitable flower.

Tsem snored loudly all night and Joseph slept badly. In the morning he woke early, stiff from the hard floor. The inside of the *ger* was now bracingly cold, as the fire had gone out in the night. He pushed open the door and slipped outside. Mist lay in long swathes across the stony grass which glimmered with a fine dusting of frost. The river curved from east to west, round an outcrop of rock touched with gold from the rising sun, the water black and flecked with gilt and strawberry light. Away in the distance, almost like a dream of mountains, were snow-topped peaks level with the clouds. The air was sharp and he felt as high as if he'd been drinking liqueur. He became aware of the vast expanse of space and sky around him, the clear blue heaven that was Mongolia; a sensation that was not to leave him until he left the country. And yet he still felt as if he were being watched though he could see no one and there was nothing here, save for the rocks, that could have hidden a man.

He tried to shrug off the feeling as he went to kneel by the river and pray. His words mingled with the sound of the water, as if, he thought, nature itself was offering up thanks to its creator. When he opened his eyes, he was startled to find Mendo sitting a few yards from him, swathed in his orange robes, and huddled in his *del*, still wearing his velvet skull cap. He was meditating. He knew his superiors would have been angry: allowing a heathen to conduct his meaningless and blasphemous rites alongside his holy prayers, but what Joseph felt, like a blow to his heart, was an overwhelming sense of connection with this man who sat beside him, his head bowed, his breath humming in time with the river's eternal sound, his beads moving through his fingers. Joseph wanted to reach out and touch him, connect with him in some physical way, though he only sat and waited until Mendo had finished. When he had, he turned to Joseph and smiled, deeply and broadly, as if he had known all along that that was what Joseph would do.

*

For four days they travelled north-west, staying in *gers* at night, where the welcome was always hospitable and the people still had a slight Chinese character to their features. At each one Mendo presented the family with a small gift of barley flour and poured out a bowlful of sorghum brandy before they left. But at each one, the families looked at Mendo and his lama's attire and talked fearfully about the White Warlord.

The second time it happened Joseph asked Mendo directly who the Warlord was.

Mendo replied, He is a Tibetan who wields great power across Western Mongolia. They say he was once a lama.

It is a rather abrupt change of occupation.

He made a journey, a pilgrimage, and was away for so long that the monastery thought he had died. They even found his replacement. They believed the spirit of the lama had been reincarnated in a child. When he returned, the monks refused to depose the child. There was a feud and the original lama left with men, money and a change of heart.

Could that cast doubt on reincarnation? asked Joseph wickedly.

Mendo ignored him but his look clearly said that Joseph wasn't taking the situation seriously. He added grimly, He now seeks to wreak vengeance against all monks and lamas.

Joseph felt suitably chastized.

On the fifth day they arrived in Hsi-Pao t-ou. The town, like all the others they had passed through, had narrow streets and delicately curved roofs in the traditional Chinese pagoda shape. They stopped at an inn for their midday meal. The rice and salted egg with fine shreds of some kind of meat and broth of boiled noodles were a welcome change after the last few days of mutton. They sat outside on wooden benches to keep an eye on the mules and their bags. Mendo talked to Tsem for a long time and Joseph leaned against his luggage and closed his eyes, turning his face to the sky to feel the sun's faint warmth.

Eventually Mendo said, Tsem needs money. He will buy horses for us. We will go to the lamasery and he will join us later. This is a very Chinese town as you can see. After this, we will be in Mongolian territory even though the Chinese claim to rule us everywhere. It is the last large town we will see for many months, so we need to buy many things. I think we can also rest here for a few days. You need have no anxiety, there will be plenty to occupy you.

He turned back to Tsem briefly and then told Joseph how much money they needed. To Joseph it seemed on the one hand a paltry sum for food for several months and to buy horses but, on the other, it was a great deal of the money he had available for the trip. He started to count out a large pile of *togrugs* when Tsem's face changed. He snatched the money from Joseph and stuck it in his *del* and said something tersely to Mendo, who immediately got up.

Remember, said Mendo, you are not a priest, and he swiftly disappeared into the darkness of the inn.

Joseph turned to see what it was that Tsem had been looking at but the horseman kicked his boot and mimed drinking his tea. Tsem started to take out his tobacco to roll a cigarette. But Joseph had already seen. Coming up the street behind him was a ragged band of men, the weak winter sun glinting on their swords. He bent over his tea, his neck naked, feeling vulnerable and exposed. The sound of their boots on the cobbles grew louder, then stopped. Joseph glanced to one side.

The motley army had halted next to them. There were about twenty of them. They had an approximation of a uniform – navy trousers and *dels* with heavy boots and sashes that had once been white tied round their waists and heads. But they were filthy, their clothes dirty and greasy, their weapons old and lethal. There was nothing, he thought, men like this – hungry and impoverished – would not do. He wondered if they were the White Warlord's soldiers and hoped that they had not seen Mendo slip into the inn.

Their leader started speaking to Tsem. They were clearly talking about Joseph; they both gestured towards him. A white man on the edge of Outer Mongolia; it was surely a rare occurrence. He cursed his fair skin and European eyes. He stood up. Within seconds he was surrounded by swords levelled at his stomach and every soldier was staring at him with clear malevolence. He swallowed and held up his hands. He could feel cold sweat trickling down his back and his legs started to tremble uncontrollably. He looked at Tsem and very slowly mimed drinking. He inclined his head to take in the men clustered around them. Tsem slapped his thigh and stood up. He said something to the leader who nodded curtly and shouted an order at his men. They stepped back and lowered their swords.

Tsem went into the inn and Joseph remained where he was. The men stood in disorderly ranks watching him, taking in every detail of his clothes and appearance. He had no doubt that they would have killed him if he hadn't been travelling with a Mongolian horseman. Their leader stood barely a few feet away from Joseph and picked his tobacco-stained teeth as he gazed coldly at him. Opposite, a door in one of the houses opened a crack and shut swiftly. On the ground a male rock dove stalked a female, up and down the path beneath the tables, his chest puffed out as she walked in staccato fashion, trying to get away from him. It seemed an interminable length of time before Tsem finally reappeared with two bottles of clear liquor and the landlord followed with a tray of shot glasses.

As the men fell upon the alcohol, he and Tsem picked up their bags and loaded them back on to the mules. They undid their tethers and walked up the street leading the animals without looking back. Behind them the men's voices rose, drowning out the clink of glasses. Joseph shivered. He half expected a knife to punch between his shoulder blades as they walked slowly and carefully away. When they had turned off the main road and down one of the narrow streets, Tsem looked behind him and then grinned at Joseph and clapped him on the back. Joseph, his legs still trembling, smiled weakly.

Tsem led him to the edge of the town and pointed to the horizon. Way across the steppe was a lamasery, a long, white building set into the cliff. He tied the pack mules to Joseph's mount and then slapped them on the rump. He turned his own mule back towards Hsi-Pao t-ou and set off at a brisk trot. After about an hour Joseph drew near the lamasery, which backed into a steep-sided hill of granite stained with feldspar, glowing red in the afternoon light. Behind it was ridge after ridge of jagged mountain peaks and clinging to the lower slopes surrounding the lamasery were stunted mountain elms, birch and dogberry. A river snaked across the steppes in front of the temple and widened into a small lake. Between it and the temple itself about a hundred monks, clad in brilliant red or orange, were chanting and dancing. Flashes of colour, as if the monks, like birds, were taking wing; the white of the lamasery, the folds of red stone and the deepening blue sky were reflected in the still surface of the lake.

A single copper bell rang out as he rode up the steep and stony path to the lamasery. The space all around was breathtaking. The monks at the door looked at him uncertainly but they helped him tie up his mules and carry his luggage. Up close the temple itself was worn, the paint and plaster peeling, the corridors inside faintly dank, the flagstones cracked. The room they gave him was at the back of the lamasery and was small and cell-like, but the monk who accompanied him lit an oil lamp and built a small fire with fine kindling wood, which quickly banished the smell of damp. Joseph sat in front of it and waited.

A couple of hours after darkness had fallen, Mendo walked in.

Joseph stood up quickly.

Are you all right?

Yes, I am fine, said Mendo gravely. He suddenly smiled, his teeth gleaming white in the light from the dying fire.

That was quick thinking, he said. I imagine the soldiers will still be at the inn now. It gave me time to get here.

They were the Warlord's men?

Mendo nodded and then said heavily, It's like coming home, being back here with my fellow monks. But I wonder whether it is safe. Perhaps I have done wrong by bringing you here. In the past it was always the most secure place to be. But now . . .

The monks did not seem that concerned, said Joseph. Would they have been outside chanting if they felt uneasy?

Perhaps you are right, said Mendo with a sigh. I may be worrying unnecessarily. There were not that many of them and there are plenty of us. They may not be brave enough to attack us, or they may be waiting for others to join them. But come, let us think of other things. Shall we eat?

He led him to a dining room next to the kitchens. The monks were already waiting, seated cross-legged at the long, low table. Young novices brought them bowls of yak butter tea and a watery mutton stew, stepping in and out of the dark like shadows given coloured substance.

When Joseph woke in the morning, the hillside and steppe were covered with a light blanket of snow. He dressed quickly and walked towards the lake. The edges were frozen solid, the ice appliquéd with fine flowers and sharp-sided crystals of frost. A flock of white-headed ducks took off as he approached. Among the frozen reeds he found a nest, quickly abandoned by ruddy shelducks as he approached, which contained two large, reddish eggs. He put one in his pocket to blow it later and felt it warm against his thigh. Around the lake were footprints from hares, a sprinkling of fleet-footed toe marks left by foxes. A sliver of moon hung in the water in the centre of the lake, and the early morning sun cast long rays of light like shards of ice-gold glass across the steppe. He crouched by the lakeside to pray, grinding frozen grass beneath his heels.

All of a sudden he knew with certainty that he was being watched. He looked up, half expecting to see – what or who he was not sure – but his heart started to beat sharply. Yet it was not what he was expecting. A wolf was staring at him from the opposite side of the lake. Its deep tawny eyes seemed suspended in space – the light was still low – and the wolf was pure white, its outline blurred and spent by the snow. It held his gaze for a long time and then loped away into the scrubland.

Joseph spent the next couple of days hunting through schist for fossils and finding few, save those of leaves and once a shell, preserved perfectly in the stone as if pressed between the pages of a book, and setting snares to trap small birds – rock partridges, a rose-collared dove, a sparrow with a blue beak and a crimson iris – at a suitable distance from the lamasery.

On the third night at the lamasery Joseph discovered a small, windowless room in the temple. He held up a candle and peered intently at the walls which were covered with pictures painted directly on to the stone. They were grotesque visions of torture, of the depravity of humanity, worse than anything by Hieronymus Bosch. Men were being tortured, molten metal poured down their throats, roasted alive, hung from hooks inserted into their anus.

You have discovered hell, said Mendo quietly, making him jump. He had not heard him come in.

These are the eighteen hells which sinners will travel through, eight hot, eight cold; this is the neighbouring hell and this, the ephemeral hell.

Joseph looked at the neighbouring hell Mendo had pointed to.

You see this is the hell of ultimate torment and surrounding it are these five realms – this one looks like a cool ditch but is, in fact, full of blazing embers. And this appears to be a river, but when sinners run to it, hot and thirsty and in pain, they discover it is nothing but a swamp of putrescent corpses – men, horses, dogs, decomposing with a stench worse than anything they have ever smelled, where worms with iron beaks devour their stinking and rotting flesh. When they emerge they will see a pleasant green field, but it is full of razors, and this is the forest of swords, which will hack them to pieces. Their bodies become whole once more so they are chopped up over and over again.

And this one?

This is our own special domain in hell, said Mendo. It is the hill of iron trees. It is designed for monks or nuns who succumb to lust. See, they are at the bottom of the hill and they hear their lovers call them. They run eagerly to the top to join them. The leaves of the trees bend down and pierce their flesh. At the summit ravens and vultures gouge out their eyes. As they try to escape, the iron leaves slice into their chests once more. When they reach the bottom, men of iron chew their heads like sweets until their brains trickle out of the corner of their mouths.

Joseph looked at the stricken faces of the monks, their bodies weeping blood, the red eyes and gaping beaks of the ravens and the dense forest of sharpened metal.

It is frightful. There are more torments for the damned than the Catholics have created, said Joseph.

And over here . . .

Stop, I do not wish to hear more.

Come then, I have something to show you, said Mendo.

He followed the monk through the long dark corridors, ducking and weaving under low, arched doorways, in and out of the light of his lamp. Outside there was a touch of frost in the air and the cloudless sky was thick with stars. They walked towards the lake. A drum was rolling out a monotonous beat as a procession of monks carrying lighted candles made their way down to the lake. As each man reached the water, he poured a little oil in a cabbage leaf and lit it before setting the flaming boat free. The lake, slick and black, was filled with these small boats, their cargo of flames bleeding gold and red, flickering across the surface. Some were caught by the current at the far side, and spun and tossed downriver until their tiny incandescence was extinguished. Mendo, crouched by the water's edge, his eyes and face lit by fire, was staring intently out across the lake, his velvet cap twisting and twisting in his hands. It was almost as if he were naked without his cap; Joseph realized why he seldom took it off. All around his head were Cyrillic letters carved into his skull, the skin smooth and hairless. Joseph bent his head and uttered a short prayer, but he could not be sure for whom he was praying as the drum beat through his body, quickening his heart, and the flames glittered across the obsidian smoothness of the lake. He poured some brandy from his hip flask into the bottle's cap and offered it to Mendo. The monk took it without looking at him and downed it quickly. As he gave it back he looked up at Joseph, his eyes dark and unreadable, his face expressionless as a ritual mask, and Joseph felt himself slipping in this alien culture, slipping like sand between God's fingers.

*

In the morning, the lake was full of fish, their bellies floating pearly side up. The oil was from the candle nut tree and poisonous. Joseph was appalled at the waste of life only momentarily. He rolled up his trousers and waded into the freezing waters to hook out some of the fish. They were of no kind he knew and he hoped to preserve their skins to take back home.

You have the appearance of a heron, said Mendo. Although a little more ungainly, he added as Joseph staggered back to the bank.

Good morning to you too, said Joseph.

The monk watched him as he gutted the fish and removed most of the flesh, sadly tainted by the poison oil. Your head, he said, not looking up, as if he could read the answer in the entrails.

Ah, said Mendo. It is a few letters only, from the Tibetan alphabet, carefully drawn by the monks who raised me. They wrote on my skull with sharpened quills and small knives.

Were they as cruel to everyone?

I think others were treated more severely. The Tibetans never killed, they merely helped death along. Some of the junior monks, children, you understand, were tied up and left outside with no food. Naked. They rarely survived the night. This was a punishment; the monks had not personally taken their lives. Some of the young boys were kept as special friends. I am sure you understand my meaning. My scars are few in comparison.

And yet you still became a lama.

Yes, said Mendo, I had no choice. My parents encouraged me. At least one boy in a family must spend some time with the monks. My brother would inherit my father's livestock. For me it was a way of receiving an education, however harsh. From the beginning I knew that the suffering I underwent would ultimately help me find the way of the Buddha. I knew that I would take that way, that I could do no other; as the bird must sing, and the wolf must hunt, I had to be what I would become.

But your parents? When they realized what was happening to you? How badly you were being treated?

They didn't know, said Mendo quietly. At first I didn't tell them. I didn't wish to worry them. They had enough problems of their own. I had a little sister . . . He stopped speaking for a moment and then, collecting himself, continued in his normal, calm voice. She was so full of life, so happy, so lively . . . but she became ill and died. And whatever it was that had ailed her, my parents caught from her. We were poor and could not afford medicine. They both passed away.

And your brother?

Dead too, said Mendo shortly.

I'm so sorry, said Joseph. We have this loss in common. My mother and father are both dead and I have never had brothers and sisters.

It is not so bad, said Mendo, trying to smile. I have my family around me; the monks at the lamasery are my brothers, my family.

Mendo briefly put his hand on Joseph's arm and Joseph, looking down at his strong, slender brown hand, felt the deep core of sadness at the heart of this man who seemed so outwardly calm and impassive.

But tell me, said Mendo, resuming his former line of discussion, you also felt a calling, as I did?

Yes. Even as a child I felt the presence of God at an early age, yet not, I think, as God. I met a man, you see, who changed my life. I owe everything, maybe even my belief, to him. He became my mother, my father, my family.

He wiped his hand on a rag now stained with oil and blood. The fish skins were spread out to dry and he'd rubbed salt and preservative between their scales.

I have had to keep my prayers to a minimum throughout this trip. I might now take advantage of our time here to pray more fully, he said by way of explanation to Mendo as he stood to take leave of him.

Yes, your God took second place to the fish this morning, said Mendo, smiling up at him. I think you will find this place very conducive to prayer, he added. I will go and buy a tent today and see Tsem. If he has bought horses, I will sell the mules. They will fetch too little, he grumbled.

Joseph went to the long hall where the monks frequently prayed and meditated. There was a stone Buddha at one end with remnants of gold leaf burnishing his round cheeks and crossed legs. A few monks were already seated in the lotus position in the middle of the hall and round the edges candles and sandalwood and rose incense sticks were burning. The early morning sunlight slanted through the high, narrow windows, and lay across the floor in pale bands of white gold. The room was pervaded with a silence of a deep and immense quality that seemed to flow from the vast expanse of hill and steppe that fell away from the monastery walls. The stillness calmed his mind, filling him with an inner silence. He wanted to pray but could not, yet felt that without his will, every fibre in his body was speaking to God. A monk brought round small bowls of green tea; the warmth from his fingertips coursed through his body; the smell from the tea, of wood warmed in the sun, crushed green shoots, aftertaste of gunpowder, the musky rose incense, stone and snow combined to make him feel a little high, as if his body were expanding, stretching into every corner of the room.

That afternoon Tsem and Mendo returned triumphantly with the horses. They looked comical astride their mounts, for the horses were so small, the men's stirrups had to be hooked up high so that they were almost in jockey position, and their size, though neither Tsem nor Mendo were large men, quite dwarfed the horses. Joseph resolved not to say anything. Although the horses looked pretty enough – there was a grey, two bays, a dun with eel-like stripes on its legs that betrayed his relation to Mongolia's race of wild horses, a black one with white stripes across its flanks, and a couple of chestnuts – they were thin, their ribs stuck out and their coats were rough. But Tsem cantered up the hill towards the lamasery waving his hat and hollering with joy and his tiny horse never missed its footing once.

The following morning they left the lamasery early while the stars were still blurred by frost and the moon was a jagged splinter in the lake. They seemed to be heading straight up past the monastery and, despite the chill, Joseph was soon hot and he could feel the steam rising from the chestnut's coat. His horse was marginally more comfortable than the mule, but he realized he would have to get used to its narrow girth and uneven gait. The others looked as if they had been born on horseback. They rode as if part of the horse and yet distanced from it: they put their weight on one buttock and rode like that for some time before swapping sides and held the reins slightly loosely with one hand. With the other they swished a long lead rein over the horses' flanks to keep up their pace. Eventually they reached a wide flat plateau and with a mighty yell Tsem galloped straight off into the distance. Without prompting, Joseph's horse broke into a gallop too, as did Mendo's and the packhorses. They raced across the steppe, the sun low in the early morning sky, and a herd of wild horses, manes trailing to their fetlocks, took flight and cantered away to the west.

As it grew warmer, Tsem rode almost as if drunk on the cold, rarefied air and he sang in a pure, high-pitched voice.

Joseph couldn't make out the words.

What is he singing about? he asked Mendo.

He is singing about Mongolia – about its rivers and its plains, about its mountains and the blue sky that gives its name to Tengger, the sky god. He sings that this country is so beautiful, no other can surpass it. Tell me, Joseph, how does this compare to England?

Joseph looked around him. The vast wide steppe stretched for miles on either side of them; in the distance were mountain ranges of dark crystalline granite, fading into the blue of the sky like an overexposed photograph. To the east red-gold sandstone rocks bubbled out of the plain. There was a herd of gazelles grazing north-west of their party and overhead circled buzzards with wingspans greater than the length of a man. The first new green shoots of grass were pushing through the dead blond stems, softening the harsh outline of the rocky ground. He remembered the wild horses, racing from the sun, the white wolf by the lake, the rock doves on the apricot tree. There was an incomparable feeling of space and light.

Mendo smiled, as if he needed no other answer.

It will become even more beautiful in spring, you shall see. But tell me, what is your home like?

I grew up in Bristol, said Joseph. I think you would find England hard to imagine; there are people everywhere, the land is so small. We are an island surrounded by sea, a sea vaster than the biggest lake. My town has a river that runs through it and leads to the sea. Giant boats with masts as high as the lamasery, sails and a network of ropes spread across their bows, glide directly into the heart of the city and moor in front of St Mary's Church, even in front of houses and shops. My father used to work in a coffee warehouse. When I was young, I lived with him and helped him bring the beans in from the ships, and grind them to powder. They would then be carried, by ship or train, to other parts of the country.

How could he, he wondered, describe the smell of the beans, the mustiness of the hessian sacks, the odour of coffee roasting, the particles of ground coffee floating in motes of light in the warehouse? The view of the boats coming and going, coffee, oil, hemp, cotton, rum and sugar piling up on the quayside, the sailors with their swagger, their gin-soaked breath, their tales of faraway lands and improbable peoples, their unexpected finds – a shell, a giant spider, a hand of bananas, concealed among the cargo – these were the things that were part of the fabric of his childhood, part of what had made him a man.

Mendo's normally smooth brow was creased. Here he was trying to describe the smell of a raw coffee bean and Mendo had no idea what a ship was like, or even an Irish church on the shores of an English river. All the words Joseph could think of using referred to other words and another world, frames of reference that had little in common with the desolate wilderness before him or the richness of Mendo's inner but alien spiritual life. If he'd been a man of means he could have brought photographs of Bristol, the docks, the boats, horses and carts, tinkers and sailors, the Avon Gorge, and even a camera to document his experiences, to show Mendo one day what his own face looked like, to explain to Patrick the meaning of infinite space, to remember, when he was old, what true wildness existed beyond the hearts and minds of men. He held his palms sky-up in a gesture indicating the burden of words and his horse tossed its head abruptly at the sudden loosening of the reins. Mendo smiled in mute sympathy.

Later a north-west wind sprang up that made Joseph long for the damp mildness of Bristol. It came from Siberia, it had fed on glaciers, grown sharp on razor blades of ice, and torn its lonely way across the frozen wasteland, picking up speed and acerbity on its million-mile route. Joseph felt as if he had toothache in his whole body. The wind chiselled into his bones and scoured the skin from his face until he was raw. The muscles across his back seized up with the cold, and his hands screamed in pain. Even the horses seemed to weep as they trudged forward into the teeth of the wind. Pain, he thought, was never worse than when one felt it. As a child he had often wept or been numb with cold, his whole body racked with hunger, and yet when he thought of his experiences, it was intellectually; gruelling nonetheless, but a memory of the mind rather than the soul. Face down, barely inches from his horse's mane, he noticed his small hooves were delicately threading their way through a carpet of the first alpine crocuses, the faint purple and white flowers bent almost flat to the stony ground on their frail, waxy stems. He made a mental note to dig up the corms when the flowers had died, and the leaves had somewhat replenished the nourishment spent on winter's only bloom.

For the next five days they kept a course by or near the river, following its twisted route into the mountains. The ground itself was a dark chocolate but in the mornings the sun turned the stone blood-orange gold. In the distance, like a far-off torch, were the Wu-la-shan Mountains, their ridges and peaks glittering with snow, fusing with the clouds. Some mornings the edges of the river were glazed with ice inherently flawed so that it cracked along the weakest seams as the day drew warmth. He saw spoonbills and demoiselle cranes, their plumage soft grey, dancing together, shaking their tail feathers like ladies' bustles.

One day he woke before the others and found snow glazing the ground, blindingly brilliant in the strong sunlight. As he stood rubbing his hands together and breathing on them to warm them he had the feeling he was being watched again. The hairs on the nape of his neck prickled. He spun on his heel. A few yards away was a pure white horse, its breath freezing in clouds around its flared nostrils. Its rider was a woman, wearing a long, dark blood-red coat and a fur-trimmed hat. Her straight black hair fell almost to her waist. In the slanted light of the sun he was half blinded and could not see her face but he felt a spark of recognition. And then he remembered the rider they had seen before reaching Tsem's *ger*. He took a step towards her, his hand outstretched, but she pulled back on the reins and the horse whinnied and half reared, then horse and rider turned and galloped away. He watched until she was a distant spot on the horizon and then he stamped his cold feet into life. Who was she? Why was she watching him? Could it be a coincidence that they had seen her twice now? He felt deeply uneasy. He wondered if perhaps she was a spy; as Mendo said, the Warlord had many and a woman and a trader at that would be a good disguise.

During this period the only other person they met was a *tarbagan* hunter, with a bow slung over his shoulder and arrows in his boots. He slouched on his horse and whistled as he rode. Mendo explained that the *tarbagan* – marmots – just beginning to come out of hibernation, were suicidally curi-ous. A hunter had only to dangle a white flag on a stick near their hole for the creatures to come out and investigate. Tsem traded barley flour and a twist of coffee for three marmots and a pouch of yak's milk. Once Joseph snared a partridge and roasted it on a juniper fire. Tiny and scrawny though the bird was, it was a welcome relief from mutton stew and *tsamba*.

They forded the river at a low point and bore west up into the mountains. The vegetation, such as it was, grew sparser. The river bed with its occasional tree and bowers of juniper began to look like an oasis. The horses picked their way along a path so fragile that the merest hint of a misplaced hoof sent slabs of slate sliding down the hillside. By late afternoon of the first day in the mountains they reached a ridge of stone and half fell from their horses, weak with fatigue. They were in an exquisitely shaped bowl of rock, the mountains curving round them on three sides, and in the heart of the bowl was a brilliant green lake, its edges white with mineral deposits. Joseph walked down to it. The water was translucent for a few yards and then sank to depths unimaginable. He splashed his hands and face in its icy chill; it tasted of cold stone. He wondered what kind of life forms could possibly live there – fish marbled moss green, salamander the colour of algae with a flash of flame along their flanks or only simple animalcules. The rock surrounding the lake was mainly granite and quartz, but he turned over a large lump of andalusite to find it riven with pale pink crystals in the shape of a cross. The crystal had often been chiselled out in times past and sold to pilgrims as Stones of the Cross. Perhaps it was a sign, he thought, that his God had not deserted him in this godforsaken land. He took the rock with him.

Look, said Mendo, when he returned. He beckoned to him and led him along the stone ridge and up the mountainside.

Soon the winter will be gone, he said.

He pointed to a clump of iris. The flowers were tiny and shone a deep and perfect purple in the dark shadow cast by the opposite mountain.

We call them little daughter-in-law because they are Mongolia's most joyous flower. Our own daughters leave when they marry so the son's new wife is a gift to the family; she

76

brightens the *ger* and our lives, as these flowers brighten the steppes.

Joseph carefully plucked a couple of the blossoms and leaves to press later. He gave them to Mendo to carry back to the horses. He climbed further up the mountain, his heart glad that the bulk of his work would soon begin. They were high already, and he soon reached the snowline and passed beyond it to the peak which was shrouded in a light mist. From the top half of the mountain his vision was crystal-clear; the valley below was obscured by cloud. In front of him stretched the Wu-la-shan chain, ridge after ridge of glittering granite, lakes trapped like gems between bright bands of ice and snow. The plains beyond swept away to the west, a precious green, inlaid with rivers of molten platinum and *gers* as white as polished pearls. A flock of wild swans flew past; the leader called twice, its cry reverberating and echoing round the mountain slopes. Behind him was a bank of mist, swirling about his feet and eddying above his head; the piercing light of the setting sun splayed his shadow across the cloud, the refracted light fragmenting into a double halo, two perfect rainbow circles, one the inverse order of colours of the other.

Joseph held his breath at the beauty of the phenomenon and tears sprang to his eyes. It seemed as if he were in another world, one created aeons earlier but that had remained fresh and whole, untainted by the presence of man, and that he but glimpsed because God loved him so. Now, even more than at any time in his existence, he felt God in the ground beneath his feet, the air surrounding him, felt His spirit coursing through his veins, flying north in the bones of swans. He stretched out his arms, and his shadow extended across the cloud, his rainbow halos quivering, and though he believed that Christ was with him here, he offered Mongolia to God, in that land where none yet knew His name.

For a couple of hours every day as they rode Mendo taught him Mongolian. He was a thorough and patient teacher. Tsem, on the other hand, was quite different. He rode alongside for part of the lesson, giggling at Joseph's pronunciation and tried to teach him swear words. Sometimes he sang and Joseph attempted to sing along with him, out of tune and in badly pronounced Mongolian, and at these times Tsem laughed and seemed to be laughing for sheer joy because Joseph was joining in. And Joseph could not help but laugh with him.

One day he said it was his turn to teach Joseph something. Mendo looked concerned but Tsem clapped Mendo on the back and said he had nothing to worry about. He took out a sheep skin from his pack and stuffed it full of dried grass. He took a charred stick from the fire and made a black dot in the centre of the skin before drawing concentric rings around it. Then he gathered together a pile of small boulders and propped the sheep's skin bundle on the top. Next he took out a pair of knives and wet the blades before sharpening them on a stone. He held them in the palm of his hand, as if weighing each one individually. He passed one to Joseph and started to speak using a lot of hand gestures.

Joseph couldn't really make out what he was saying but got the gist of it: Tsem was going to teach him how to throw a knife. The horseman demonstrated the position – a wide-apart stance, knees soft but slightly bent, one shoulder angled and he gripped the handle between his fingers. He bent his arm back and threw his body forward, at the last moment releasing the knife. It hissed through the air and landed with a satisfying thud on one of the outer rings on the sheep's skin, the blade buried almost to the hilt.

Now you, said Tsem, turning and grinning at him.

Joseph tried to copy Tsem's stance. Tsem nodded and moved him slightly, manhandling him as if he were a horse, a cigarette dangling from one lip. Mendo stood and watched from a distance, his face implacable, his arms clasped behind his back.

Joseph took a breath and let it out as he released the knife. It shot way past the target and over to one side. Tsem let out a whoop and a laugh and clapped him on the back, then ran off to retrieve the knife.

Keep going, it takes time. It's even harder than learning Mongolian, he said, winking at Joseph, as he handed the knife back.

On his fifth attempt, Joseph hit the edge of the sheep skin and Tsem shook him by the hand. Joseph grinned and shouted, waving his knife in the air in a rare display of high spirits. He turned to Mendo, slightly breathless.

I think you should not be excused from all the fun, Joseph said, handing his knife to the monk.

Mendo half bowed and took the knife from him. He rolled up his sleeves and with one fluid movement half turned and threw the knife as if it were an extension of his body. It pierced the skin right in the middle on the dot of charcoal.

Tsem whistled.

Mendo suddenly grinned broadly. Years of martial arts training, he said. The Tibetans were good for something.

You, my friend, will be good too. A little more practice is all that is required.

It was the opposable thumb, he suddenly thought, that allowed men to throw knives and wield swords; the opposable thumb that had separated them from the rest of the animal kingdom.

The year before *Origin* was published, 1858, had been momentous. The anatomist Hermann Schaffhausen discovered a skull in a cave near Düsseldorf in Germany. Its forehead sloped back, its brow was solid bone and overhung the large, cavernous sockets of its eyes. Its whole demeanour was brutal. It was named Neanderthal, the head of a race of beings as like and as unlike modern man. Huxley examined a cast of the cranium at the Royal College of Surgeons and pronounced:

> Brought face to face with these blurred copies of himself, the least thoughtful of men is conscious of a certain shock, due perhaps, not so much to disgust at the aspect of what looks like an insulting caricature, as to the awakening of a sudden and profound mistrust of time-honoured theories and strongly rooted prejudices regarding his own position in nature and his relations to the underworld of life.

That men might be shocked, in this Huxley was correct, but few shared his privileged position. Huxley, one of a handful of men, had first-hand knowledge of Darwin's claim that human beings were descended from apes. The subject, taboo in the best Victorian circles, was not even examined in depth in *Origin*; at the last, Darwin gave way to his innate cowardice and saved his ideas on man's descent for another book. But within *Origin* his theories on ancestry lurked like barracuda, all teeth and sleek muscle, between sentences and in the reefs of paragraphs. In private, Darwin had little sympathy for those who were appalled and shocked that man might indeed be descended from an ape. To him descending from an ape was neither here nor there; he had set his sights on an origin much more distant. He wrote: All the organic beings which have ever lived on this earth have descended from some one primordial form, into which life was first breathed.

Darwin had 300 million years to play with or so he thought, and apes, by his calculations, and thus, by inference, man were closely intertwined relatives when one compared them to the primordial prototype. Seeing the 'blurred copy of himself' at the College of Surgeons had only served to heighten Joseph's determination that one day he too would bring back an object, the skull of the missing link, a rare orchid, a new species from a foreign land, and men as able as Hooker and Huxley would talk about his find in grave and sonorous tones. And now he thought that the rare white lily, the colour of frost, with its incomparable smell, could be his legacy.

What had made more of an impact upon him was the baby gorilla he'd seen three years earlier. From time to time the East India Company Trade imported young chimpanzees and orangutans who arrived at the docks, sickly and feeble, with bulging eyes, wild cries and a grip as tight as any bereft child's. Joseph read about their arrival in the papers but it was not until 1855 that he saw an ape first-hand. He was back from Cambridge for the holidays and was, as he was frequently inclined to, wandering up and down the docks, the arterial life-blood of the city, a stinking reminder of his own origins. Just past St Mary's was a sugar warehouse; men were stacking the dark, sticky cones of sugar ready to ship them to Gloucester. The air was thick with syrup and sulphur, harsh with the stench of flayed animals and preservatives from the tanneries. The river was bloated on sewage, blood, fat from the soap factory; the body of a pig drifted past, its corpse swollen, its snout misshapen where fish had eaten away its nostrils.

He crossed the river opposite the coffee warehouse, skirting horse manure and human excrement, ducking back along the docks to the sea. Two boats were unloading and he stopped to watch the sailors at work, worn to sinew by months at sea. One boat was full of timber from Norway, the trunks redolent of pine where the bark had been cut and resin oozed like amber from the wounds. The other was a more precious cargo from Africa – a pile of elephant's tusks, barrels of rum and palm oil, tiny wooden boxes like miniature trunks glittering with a mica of gold dust. And then he saw it, the small, dark shape cradled in the first mate's arms, its limbs, longer than humanly possible, wrapped round the man's chest. Its fur was so black it glowed a deep blue where it caught the light. Joseph pushed his way closer and was there, slipping on putrescent fruit, yesterday's leftover rock salt crunching beneath his shoes, when the creature turned its head and stared at him. The skin on its hairless face was black too, black as wood from a peat bog; its brow was furrowed and ridged and its eyes were round and dark.

He reached out to it, but the creature huddled closer to the sailor who said, I'll thank you not to touch her, sir, she's worth her weight in gold.

It was a baby gorilla, the first to arrive alive on British soil; two men from Wombwell Travelling Menagerie were already waiting by the quay, a wooden and iron-barred cage at the ready. The ape didn't want to leave the sailor. She showed her teeth in what looked like a smile and shrieked, clutching at her original captor with tiny, black hands with square finger-nails. Joseph could see the whites of her eyes. By now a small crowd had gathered, pushing and pulling around the cage and the men from Wombwell.

Make way, now, make way, said one of the men, his cream waistcoat torn and soiled. You shall all have your turn, we'll be back to put on a show in two weeks' time, ladies and gentlemen, two weeks' time, and then you shall see the gorilla.

Come, sirs, give us some air, the other complained as the two manhandled the screaming ape in the cage on to the back of the cart and wrapped her in sackcloth.

Joseph had a final glimpse of the animal, her fists curled round the bars, her snub nose pressed against the metal, her large, dark eyes peering at the mass of people pushing against the cage. In those features he saw misery and fear as clearly as if he were looking into the face of a small child. What he felt was less a profound mistrust of time-honoured theories but more a deep-seated, almost instinctive sense of belonging. Looking into those eyes was to gain a knowledge that could never be unknown: the knowledge that in the dark jungles of Africa lived a race of creatures from whence we have all come.

*

And here we are, he thought, a species that walked across continents, from the burning African savannahs to the glaciers of northern Europe; a species that was supremely adaptable – even to this climate, one that he still continued to find harsh. Although the sun was now pleasantly warm during the day and he could see that his hands were beginning to brown, it was bitterly cold at night, and high in the mountains there was almost always a thin wind that drew the breath from his lungs. Sometimes his nose bled in that rarefied air.

From the time when their small party had been in the lamasery, Mendo seemed to have become increasingly inscrutable and withdrawn. It had been an extraordinary place, Joseph reflected. He thought of the deep religious feeling he had experienced in the prayer room and the other, the out of consciousness – possession, one could almost call it – in the dark by the flaming lake where the monks beat time with his heart. And it had been there that Mendo had opened up to him, allowing him to see his other side, the part of him that had been damaged. Like a shellfish, he seemed to have snapped his protective covering tightly shut. He concluded that he would merely watch and wait for Mendo, clam-like, to crack open his shell and perhaps dance, as clams dance, castanet-style, through warmer waters. He believed, in any case, that one should always hold something of oneself back from one's fellow man, and that the only constant on this earth was God, for the love of all else would eventually turn to dust and disintegrate before one's very eyes.

The descent to the plains on the other side of the mountains was nearly vertical. Joseph clung to his horse's mane and prayed silently. By the time they reached the valley, he was bathed in a cold sweat and there was something wild about the horse's eyes; it too was wet and he could feel its limbs shaking. But there was no let-up. Mendo set off at a terrific gallop, dragging half of the packhorses behind him. Joseph called out but Mendo merely stood up in his saddle and spurred the horses on. Tsem came cantering back and whipped his horse across his rump until he laid his ears back and bolted from fright. Tsem cheered him and then swiftly overtook him, racing neck and neck with Mendo, their horses trailing behind in a multicoloured stream. Joseph gritted his teeth and clung to his horse with dogged determination. At least his companions had not entrusted him with the burden of leading any of the other horses but he was worried that his precious luggage, his stones and skins and specimen jars, might tumble from their horses during this needless and headlong flight. What was even more irksome was that he could not tell where Mendo was heading; moreover, it was the middle of the afternoon and there was no need to worry about reaching a suitable spot to camp before dark. His mount swerved violently to avoid a marmot hole and Joseph almost careered straight on. He grasped the chestnut's neck and attempted to retrieve his stirrups. No amount of encouragement was needed now, the horse was determined not be left behind and was wheezing with the effort of keeping up. Joseph had for some time suspected that he had not been given the best horse, but still, there was no need to overwork the animal in this way.

His path through the valley twisted round an outcrop of rocks and about the base of a mountain and then he saw the *ger* they were aiming for. Tsem and Mendo were already tying up their horses outside and talking to someone on horseback. As he approached he saw it was the woman on the white horse he had seen a few days ago. Tsem and Mendo disappeared inside the *ger* but she remained outside, almost as if she were waiting for him. She was looking directly at him. In the clear afternoon light the sun burnished her long, black hair, which hung straight and thick as a horse's mane, and he could see that her large, almond-shaped eyes were green. She was the most beautiful woman he had ever seen. He couldn't look away from her, yet he was gripped with the sensation that something was wrong. What had brought her here? Was she following them? But before he could speak, she turned the horse suddenly and it pivoted on its hind legs and galloped away.

When he reached the tent, he took longer than usual to secure his horse, and attempted to rub him down. He was concerned for the animal, but he also recognized in himself the stubborn desire to make a point. Mendo came back out and stood scanning the valley before realizing that Joseph was standing right beside him with the horses.

Ah, Joseph, you must come inside and meet my friend.

He held his arms out to him and ushered him inside, beaming so broadly that all Joseph's ire melted. Mendo was holding his hat in his hand, and it was this one gesture that indicated what an old and trusted friend this person must be. Joseph was on the point of asking about the woman on the white horse but was prevented by the arrival of a small black shape that hurled itself at Mendo. It was a boy who clung to his knees. The monk lifted him easily and showed him to

Joseph. The child kept hiding his head and squirming closer to Mendo. He had a shock of raven-black hair and dark impish eyes. His name was Boldt.

It means hard, strong, like steel, said Mendo. And this is Munke. Her name is forever flower.

The woman approached and bowed her head to Joseph, smiling gently. She gestured to him to sit in one of the seats of honour at the head of the hearth.

All the homes Joseph had visited had been clean and orderly, but Munke's *ger* was even tidier than most. The tapestries that hung on the walls and over the two small beds were exquisitely embroidered. She herself was also very beautiful. Her hair was the colour of obsidian, and hung straight down her back. Her face was flat with large, slightly slanting eyes and a small nose; she'd woven coral beads into her hair in a line down the central parting, and she wore a man's blue felt *del* with red and black leather boots; the toes curled upwards. She served them yak butter soup and then she and Tsem went out to kill a sheep in their honour. Joseph watched, intrigued, from the doorway. The pair of them rolled the sheep on its back and in one motion slit it open from throat to belly. Tsem put his hand into the opening and grasped the sheep's heart. He squeezed until it stopped. It seemed a remarkably short time between the death of the sheep and the assembly of its constituent parts around the *ger* and in the giant stew pot. Munke added bundles of dried herbs and small, wild onions which pleased Joseph, although after days of *tsamba* and only the odd boiled marmot and the scraps of roast partridge, he was warming to the idea of mutton stew.

While they waited for the meat to cook, Munke and Mendo talked. Mendo didn't translate and they were speaking too quickly and too quietly for Joseph to be able to understand. Tsem smoked and sipped a bowl of *airag* contentedly. Joseph lay down on one of the thick rugs below the statue of the Buddha and drifted off. When he awoke, Munke was ladling out the stew, and he felt ravenous. To his surprise, although Munke served him first, she gave him a large piece from the stew that was mostly fat and gristle while proceeding to give the meatier parts to the others.

Mendo, who missed nothing, said with a smile, It is traditional to give the best part of the sheep, the fat tail, to the guest. If you would care to share your tail with us, I am sure we could give you a piece of meat in return.

Joseph gratefully parted with the fat but even as he ate and enjoyed the stew, he wondered how much longer he could eat mutton with equanimity. Both Tsem and Mendo had three helpings before lying flat on their backs, their hands resting on their swollen stomachs. The boy had become over-excited at their arrival and although he was tired he was still refusing to go to bed. His mother wrestled with him quietly in the corner, trying to take his clothes off while he resisted.

Come, said Mendo, holding his arms out to him. I will tell you a bedtime story, and I will translate it into English for Joseph. When I have finished, you will both be tired and want to sleep.

He held the boy in his lap in front of the fire and began to recount the legend of Erkhii Menger, the archer. Mendo began.

Once upon a time, long, long ago, there appeared seven suns in the sky. The heat from all these suns was terrible; they burned up the earth and dried up all the rivers and streams. The poor people who lived at this time had nothing to eat, and nothing to drink. Now in this time, there lived a young man called Erkhii Menger who was famed throughout Mongolia for his skill with a bow and arrow. It was said that he could hit anything in the whole world.

One day, the people decided to ask Erkhii Menger for help. They visited his *ger* and they begged and pleaded with Erkhii Menger. They said, The heat from all these suns is too hot, please shoot down the suns or we will all surely die.

And Erkhii Menger replied, Not only will I shoot down all seven suns, but I will use only seven arrows. If I fail, then you can cut off my thumbs so that I can no longer use my bow. I will become an animal that never drinks pure water, and eats last year's grass and lives in dark holes under the ground.

Erkhii Menger was proud of his strength and skill and the people were pleased that he was going to shoot the suns out of the sky for them, yet they were puzzled by his bravado and his confidence.

The next day the archer climbed to the top of a mountain and he aimed his bow and arrow at one of the seven suns. He let off his arrows, one after another, until he had released seven arrows. Each one pierced one of the suns and it died, but the seventh arrow hit a swallow. The arrow shot through the swallow's tail and sliced it into a fork. The arrow flew off course and it did not hit the seventh sun.

The sun saw that all the other suns had died. It was afraid and it quickly disappeared behind one of the mountains in the west. But Erkhii Menger was angry with the swallow. He was determined to try to catch the swallow and teach it a lesson. His loyal piebald horse said to him, I will gallop after that swallow and I will catch it. If I do not catch it by the time the seventh sun begins to set you can cut off my forelegs and leave me in the desert.

So Erkhii Menger mounted his trusty piebald horse and he chased after the swallow. They galloped and they galloped but they never caught the swallow, for the bird ducked and dived and whistled round their ears. The seventh sun began to set and the sky turned blood red and still the horse and the archer had not caught the swallow. So Erkhii Menger cut off the horse's forelegs and left him in the desert. The horse turned into a jerboa, which hops about because its front legs are shorter than its hind legs. Erkhii Menger kept his boastful promise and ceased to be a man. He became a marmot who never drinks pure water, and eats last year's grass and lives in holes under the ground. On each one of his paws there are only four fingers because he cut off his thumbs.

Even today there is a part of the marmot that remains partly the meat of a man and, out of respect for the man who saved our world from the seven scorching suns, we do not eat it. The seventh sun is still frightened of Erkhii Menger and so it hides its face behind the mountains. That is why we have day and night. As for the swallow, it still has a forked tail and it swoops around us when we ride as if to say: You will never catch me.

I could catch a swallow. I could, said Boldt, looking up at the monk.

Tomorrow you can show me how you can gallop so fast you can catch a swallow.

The child was almost asleep in his arms and Mendo laid him gently on his bed. Munke turned to Joseph and said something; then she took a large bundle from a chest under the bed and handed it to him.

Mendo hesitated and then he said, She wants you to have this old *del*. It is warm and it has been mended so there are no holes in it. I told her how cold you always were and this is her gift to you.

He paused again and then said, You cannot buy *dels*, they are made by women for men and passed down within the family.

Joseph felt awkward. Mendo's face was impassive and partly in the shadows. He was not telling him everything. Joseph hesitated, wanting to accept the gift, realizing how useful it would be. He did not want to offend Munke, but he knew how precious a *del* was and how poor many of the nomads were. He continued to hesitate until Munke seized him roughly by the shoulders and pulled him upright. She pushed his arms into the coat and bound it round the waist.

Joseph looked at Mendo. The *del* fitted perfectly over his cassock and was even almost the same length; the double layer of material would, at the very least, keep him warm. But he knew, and he knew Mendo had known, that it would fit, for both men were the same size. Tsem staggered to his feet, laughing delightedly, not a little inebriated on *airag*. He slapped Joseph across the back, kissed Munke and hugged Mendo before stumbling over a stool and collapsing. The tension was broken and Joseph was able to turn to Munke and thank her profusely in his new Mongolian; her eyes sparkled brightly and she smiled up at him. He kissed her hand, and she laughed again.

That night he felt as if someone were watching him. He opened his eyes and half sat up. The woman in the long, red coat was standing at his feet. She took off her hat and her long, dark hair cascaded over her shoulders. Her coat was unfastened and beneath it she was naked. Firelight glowed and flickered across the flat plane of her stomach, the just visible curve of her breasts, along one smooth thigh. He realized that there was a fire next to him: he could feel its heat on his bare skin. He was lying on a sheep skin, the pelt warm beneath him. The woman slipped off the coat. She knelt and then, in one sinuous movement, she stretched out and pressed herself against him. He felt his flesh burning where her skin touched his. She looked down at him and he was transfixed by her wide, green eyes. He could hardly breathe. He tried to turn away but he felt his body respond to hers and he dug both hands into the rug in an attempt to control himself.

And then suddenly, confusingly, he was outside, kneeling on the ground, the grass damp against his legs. His hands were tied behind his back and he'd been gagged. His wrists were raw from the rope; he felt his saliva creeping at the edge of his mouth. There was the smell of raw earth. It was still night: there were thousands of stars in the sky. But in a line on the horizon was the first cold, gelid white of dawn. The woman, now fully dressed, stepped to one side. Her expression was blank. In front of him were three men. One of them had long hair and a scar like a knife slash across his face, the middle one had a broken nose and the third was wearing a hat; one of his eyes was the colour of a raw egg. They leered, their mouths full of blackened teeth, and he could read his sin on their faces. They advanced upon him, raising their swords, the metal catching the first rays of the sun's light.

He woke with a start, his heart pounding, his cock uncomfortably hard, his chest slick with sweat. Next to him Tsem was snoring loudly. He could see one star through the hole in the roof of the *ger* against a pale lilac sky. It was nearly morning.

Tsem and Mendo rose early. Joseph lay a little longer, half asleep, exhausted by his dream. When he finally dragged himself out of bed Munke explained her plans for them: bridles and saddles had to be mended, some of the poles and the trellis for the *ger* needed to be repaired, a bed and a couple of stools had been broken. When she'd finished giving out her orders she placed the handle of a large wickerwork basket round her neck and went out to gather dried dung for the fire. She *was* like a flower, Joseph thought, both frail and strong. He wondered how she managed through the long winter nights on her own.

He shrugged on his new blue felt *del* and walked towards the horses. They'd been hobbled together and some of them were resting their chins on the other's withers but his chestnut hung apart with his head down and didn't even look at him as he approached. He untied him and led him back to the tent as if to make a point to the others: the horse wheezed and choked and his eyes were clogged with pus, his hair matted across his chest and flanks. His ragged breathing only emphasized the animal's thin ribs. Mendo and Tsem watched in silence. Tsem tied the horse to a stand by the *ger* and, holding his nose out with one hand, he took out a small silver knife and sliced open one of the horse's nostrils. The horse quivered and Joseph winced. Tsem held the animal's nose tightly, his head lowered towards the ground, and let the bright blood spill on the stones. Taking a rag and a pail of water, he wiped the horse's eyes.

Is that horse sick? asked Boldt.

Tsem nodded, whistling through his teeth.

Will he be dead soon?

He might.

The child went and sat next to Mendo and played with the wood shavings at his feet.

Tsem will go and find herbs and maybe the horse will be well again, said Mendo, stroking his head.

The child was nearly as indifferent as the adults, Joseph thought. The horse, to them, was no more than a means of transport and there was no point in wasting sympathy on what was merely a machine. Mostly their horses ran free but one would be caught and kept hobbled near the *ger* for a week at a time before being swapped for another. That way all the horses managed to fend for themselves and survive the harsh Mongolian winter without needing extra food. But in spring they were almost wild, Tsem had told him, laughing and miming being bucked about by a recalcitrant horse.

Joseph left them to it and went to find a quiet spot to pray. There were indeed many herbs in the grass, with small flowers of pale pink and purple; as he walked over them they released the scent of mint and marjoram and lavender, both a floral and a meaty smell. It made him feel hungry although he'd already drunk tea with mutton scraps that morning. By the edge of the river, a spring welled from the cliff face above it and trickled down to join the main body of water. Next to it was what looked like a shrine, a gathering of stones and dry sticks, crowned with a sheep's skull. Blue silk scarves and horses' hair had been tied to the twigs and these fluttered in the gentle breeze. Joseph drank from the stream which was pure and cold, and seated himself to pray.

Anima Christi, sanctifica me. Corpus Christi, salva me. Sanguis Christi, inebria me. Soul of Christ, sanctify me. Body of Christ, save me. Blood of Christ, fill me with life.

Ah, you should honour the *ovoo* by walking around it three times clockwise, not by crouching below it and muttering to Jesus, said Mendo, holding out his hand and helping Joseph to his feet.

He proceeded to demonstrate and added a small coin to the shrine.

I asked that our horse be made well again, said Mendo gravely and Joseph reflected that he too had asked for the same but in a somewhat different manner.

The two men walked back over the grass and herbs to the chestnut. His head hung almost to the ground, his coat was matted and his eyes were dull and glazed. He looked abjectly miserable. Joseph stroked his ears, which twitched listlessly against his hands. Tsem had smeared a green paste across his chest and the slit in his nostril that smelled of mint and camphor but the horse was now making a rattling sound deep in his lungs as he breathed.

Joseph spent the day picking different kinds of herbs and observing a family of ground squirrels that had emerged from their long winter underground. They were beautiful, inquisitive creatures, almost tame, with cream and chocolate-brown fur, and thick tails like the squirrels back home. As he walked back towards the *ger*, Boldt galloped out to meet him. The child was so tiny, his feet didn't reach past the end of the saddle flaps yet he controlled his horse far more adroitly than Joseph could ever have done. He said nothing, but sauntered back with him, gazing at the priest curiously from time to time, for he had surely never encountered a man who picked flowers and stared at squirrels. He led him round the back of the *ger*. The horse was now lying on his side, his flanks rising with difficulty under his laboured breathing.

Tsem had been whittling wood to mend one of Munke's stools and he came and stood with them. He shook his head.

The horse will die tonight, he said.

There is no hope? asked Joseph.

None, he replied, and, wiping his knife on his *del*, he returned to his spot at the front of the *ger*.

Joseph loaded his shotgun, placed the barrel against the horse's skull, and pulled the trigger. The sound echoed throughout the length and breadth of the long and narrow valley. After an unseemly short time, Tsem skinned the horse and cut up his flesh. Munke's two dogs rolled on their bellies and slavered in anticipation. Joseph, who was pressing his herbs by the light from the hearth beneath the grisly remains of the butchered sheep, felt his stomach churn at the thought of eating horsemeat. While Tsem was still butchering the horse, Joseph took the opportunity to ask

Munke in his halting Mongolian about the woman he had seen.

Oh, her – she's a trader. She lives up in the mountains. She brought furs to show me, said Munke.

Joseph felt his cheeks burn as he suddenly recalled his dream. And then he remembered how the woman had tricked him. He might have thought it an omen if he believed in such things. He swallowed and said, You don't think she could be a spy for the White Warlord?

Munke looked at him searchingly. Then she shook her head. You never know. You never know who to trust these days.

She looked so sad suddenly, he decided not to ask her any more about the woman. Instead, he enquired about the white lily.

She said she had not seen it but she had heard of it. It was said to be very tall, as high as a man, and beautiful. She said, Men say the smell will stay with you for ever.

Joseph murmured:

> *Have you seen but a bright lily grow*
> *Before rude hands have touched it?*

Mendo, who walked in at that moment, frowned.
Rude hands?

It's part of a poem. It means that the lily is so pure it will be tainted if touched. I hope to find it, he said to Munke, and bring it back to my own country so that my people will also smell it and be haunted by its scent for ever.

They spent two days with Munke. She sang to them in the evenings, her voice like a fine, clear mountain stream, and while she sang she salted the horsemeat. Joseph wondered whether any of his precious specimens or his many jars and phials would be abandoned in preference to the meat, given that they were now one pack-animal short. Perhaps because of the enforced rest he felt inordinately tired. One night he dreamt he was walking through the mountains, following glimpses of a pheasant whose feathers were royal blue. The bird led him deeper and deeper into the heart of the mountains until he came to a narrow cleft within the hillside whose slopes glimmered white as the first frost from the pale reflection of a thousand lilies. He walked among them; they stood tall as a man and their stamens dusted his shoulders with a thick, rich pollen. The very air felt heavy, humid with their intoxicating and heady scent.

The lines from a poem came to him unbidden:

> *A lily of a day*
> *Is fairer far in May,*
> *Although it fall and die that night –*
> *It was the plant and flower of light.*

When he woke he had been sweating and his skin was cold and greasy from the mutton he'd been eating; he lay on his back and tried to recapture that elusive scent but it was lost in the dead smoke from the dying fire.

On the day they were to leave, Mendo and Tsem packed and repacked the bags. They squabbled with each other, listened to Munke's advice and rejected it; Tsem threw his hat on the floor and scratched his head, picked it up, grinned and they started all over again.

I told him we should have purchased a camel, said Mendo grumpily.

Tsem made a face. They're nasty and they spit and sometimes they die of loneliness for their own kind, he said. More trouble than they're worth.

But at least they are large, said Mendo, sighing. He double-checked Tsem's knots to Tsem's obvious annoyance before he finally nodded and pronounced that they were at last ready to go. He held out the reins of the dun horse with the eel stripes on his fetlocks to Joseph.

Munke came towards Joseph and held him under his arms, touching her forehead against his chest. It was a gesture he had never seen or experienced before but he presumed that it had some significance. Tsem gave her a vast bear hug and grinned from ear to ear before picking up Boldt, who had been hiding behind his mother, and throwing him in the air. But Mendo and Munke held each other gently for a long time. Then Mendo took the child from Tsem and kissed him on both cheeks before giving him back to Munke.

Munke held herself very straight and still as she watched them go; they too were quiet and set off slowly, Joseph trying to adjust himself in his saddle, the only sound the leather creaking and the faint notes from a solitary lark.

It was the beginning of May and the long winter seemed finally to be over. It was almost impossible for Tsem to remain sad for long, and he soon began to whistle and sing. Joseph noticed with delight the profusion of small flowers on the steppe and he felt God's presence like a living, breathing energy dancing through the bones of the earth, humming in every blade of grass, boiling with an effervescent delight in the breath of the horses, the flight of a bird, a ground squirrel's chirp.

Their path through the valley took them closer to the tiny stream Joseph had prayed alongside. On the slopes of scree above it rock roses clung, their pale yellow flowers beginning to unfurl. The first swallows of summer wove deftly above their heads and Joseph saw terns and plovers alight in the grass after the horses had passed.

They stopped for tea at midday and Joseph was able to snare two stone chats and dig up a couple of the rock roses. A lizard, its back a mosaic of lichen and slate, with chips of blue as clear as porcelain, basked on a stone near by.

It's a suncatcher, remarked Mendo.

Joseph, caught in the act of creeping towards the lizard, looked up at the monk. It was the first thing he had said all day. Joseph wondered how he could bear to look him in the eye after they had met Munke and the child. Mendo, on the contrary, seemed quite at ease, only a little reserved.

The lizard disappeared into a crevice in the rock. It was a wonder that such a creature had, in the marrow of its bones, the imprint of a thousand thousand years of evolution from the original prototype through to the legacy of the sauropods. In its blood it held a million years of shape-changing from the infinite variation of the lizards of today to the promise of a reptile of the future.

That is a long meditation on a lizard that is no longer there, said Mendo.

I was thinking, said Joseph, of the imperfection of living things.

He sat up and said, This lizard was once a dinosaur and now it is a suncatcher. But it only had what is contained within its own self – it cannot pluck fleeter legs and sharper eyes from thin air. Because nature must change what is already present to suit a different purpose, animals like this lizard cannot be perfect.

No wonder you have been so quiet all morning, said Mendo, smiling at him.

I've been quiet? said Joseph.

But I see you have been writing essays in your head, said Mendo.

It's going to rain, Tsem interrupted, starting to put out the fire.

Either that or . . .

Or what? asked Joseph, starting to feel irritated.

You are here in body but your spirit is elsewhere. Back in the *ger* with Munke and her son perhaps.

It is not *me* who is lingering in that *ger* in his mind, said Joseph.

Mendo, sitting cross-legged on the ground, gestured to him, as if presenting him with a gift in the heart of his cupped hand.

Please explain.

Joseph started to pace back and forth in front of the monk.

When I was talking of the imperfection of beings, perhaps what I really meant was us. Men of faith. You, as I did, took a vow of chastity.

I did, Mendo inclined his head.

I know how hard it is, to resist temptation, the torment of the situation . . .

He stopped and reflected that, really, he did not. He had never been surrounded by women in his life. He had, of course, that visceral sexual urge, the desire for cool hands touching, no, burning against his naked skin, but never for one woman specifically, one woman who would lie in wait at night and haunt his dreams.

Brother, I know, believe me, I know, said Mendo, smiling up at him. Is there something you would like to share with me?

Me? said Joseph, wheeling to face him in astonishment.

The monk's face was blankly open.

I was thinking of you.

You have been listening to too many stories. Yes, I agree, there is corruption, there is profligacy, said Mendo, and yes, many lamas do keep women. But how does the expression go, you should not tar us all together.

Joseph did not move.

So how do you explain Boldt?

Mendo got to his feet and faced Joseph. He was so close that Joseph could see the sun pooling in his eyes, like the shallows in a dark river; the edges were green-gold. He felt as he had done when the white wolf had stared into his soul.

There was a long pause and then Mendo said, Munke is my brother's wife. As you know, the White Warlord pledged to kill any Mongolian priests he finds. He and his men thought that my brother was sheltering me. They killed my brother. Ever since that day I promised to look after my brother's wife as well as I am able. Boldt is my brother's child.

A wave of confusion and embarrassment washed over Joseph and his anger dissipated almost as quickly as it had come. He looked down at his *del*.

Then I am wearing . . .

Yes.

I am sorry, Mendo, truly, I am sorry, he whispered.

It's no matter, said Mendo, gripping his upper arms. You are wearing my brother's clothes. Now you are as a brother to me.

Gentlemen, said Tsem, coming up and slapping them both on the back so that for a brief moment they were caught in an off-kilter triangle, it really is going to rain. Can we leave the theology to another day?

Joseph looked up into the clear blue bowl of the sky unmarred by a single cloud, but Tsem was right. In the late afternoon the sky turned an eerie green glowing ominously along the horizon and the wind was wet. The stream became broader, steeper, a torrent of foaming water above which they could no longer hear even the sound of the horses' hooves. They were travelling through a narrow, rocky gorge, juniper bushes and crooked elm clinging to the slopes. The horses slipped on the dampening stone. There was something almost evil about the wind, the way it whined round jagged boulders, and tore down the funnel of the valley. One of the packhorses half reared and neighed and the others whinnied in consternation. The sky had grown black above the green. From far off came the rumble of thunder. The deluge, when it came, would not be deterred by their meagre tent, Joseph thought glumly. It was at times like this that he missed home comforts: the small fire in his office, fresh bread thickly spread with marmalade, a tumbler of porter by the fire, salted ham and the decadence of sweet hot chocolate. And, of course, Patrick. Patrick to talk to in the evenings. Patrick who might have made him feel better about what he had said to Mendo.

Above the roar of the river was another sound, louder, heavier, more sinister. Joseph wiped the sweat from his face and urged the dun on. They struggled over the lip of the gorge, unable to hear a thing. In front of them was a black lake and pounding into it from a great height was a waterfall, a single opaque white sheet. In one corner of the lake, a black stork speared a silver fish. It caught sight of them and rose languorously, its neck a sinusoidal coil, and flew away to the west. Both the horse and he struggled to catch their breath as he stared, mesmerized, by the giant waterfall. Round the rocky basin surrounding it were carvings of the Buddha and a demon astride a lion, filled in with blue and red pigment. Rattling and swinging against the black rock was what appeared to be a huge necklace until Joseph realized it was a rope strung with human bones, a skull in the centre like some ghastly jewel. And above them, at the edge of the waterfall, was the rider on her white horse. Joseph held his breath. For one long moment, the woman with the black hair and the blood-red coat stared directly down at him. In spite of the cold, he felt himself grow hot, recalling how, in his dream, she had lain across his naked body. Lightning cracked across the inhuman green of the horizon and almost immediately there was a clap of thunder that vibrated the very stones they were standing on. The horse and rider disappeared into the darkness. Joseph started to shiver.

Tsem beckoned them on and he and Mendo struggled to follow him with the overburdened horses. At that moment it began to rain, the water slightly warm, almost immediately becoming bitingly cold. They scrambled up a narrow and tortuous path to a flat and level plain where the black water flowed mind-numbingly fast and slick as molten glass over the lip of the rock to the lake below. On either side of the river were thick slabs of rock, taller than a man, poking at an angle out of the dank soil. At the root of these irregular teeth the soil had washed away and in some cases Joseph was sure he could see the grim white of bone. Through the sheets of rain loomed a stone man, a statue twice as tall as himself, staring with blank sightless eyes over the vast plains and twisted spine of the mountains they had left behind. He could barely see Mendo and Tsem ahead of him and spurred the dun horse on round the stone man and over the ground that now ran with water and mud, as the earth was so hard and the water so heavy that the one could not absorb the other.

How long they journeyed he could not tell; he sank into a kind of lethargic misery, shrunk inside his new *del*, the felt becoming increasingly sodden and heavy. The horses' heads hung low and they battled into the torrential rain, currents of water eddying round their hooves. Joseph hoped the tarps covering his bags would not let in any leaks that might destroy his precious specimens. Eventually, as the night drew in, Tsem let out a shout and pointed to the east. Above the river and with its back against a sheer cliff wall, a lamasery glimmered through the darkness, a milky shade of green, like the wings of a cabbage white.

They forded the river which had grown so high the water reached the horses' withers. Joseph gathered his *del* about him and crouched on his horse's back, feeling his painful struggle through the currents. He swept the rain out of his eyes with one hand, the other clutching the horse's mane as he tried to balance and check that the bags were not going to get wet. One of the horses slipped in mid-stream, the luggage slid to one side, the weight threatening to overbalance it. Mendo was behind the horse, and Tsem in front. Neither could reach it. Tsem, who was holding its leading rein, urged his horse on even more vigorously until it scrambled out of the river. He jumped off and pulled the lead rein taut and to one side, gradually winding it in, dragging the horse towards him. The animal struggled to regain its footing and finally stood upright out of the water, choking and snorting. It skittered across the shallows and clambered over the bank of the river. Joseph hit his horse on the rump with the reins and they progressed through the torrent and out the other side without further incident.

Behind the lamasery were some stone buildings where the monks' own horses were sheltering from the rain. They untied the baggage and hobbled the horses together. In England, after such a deluge, the horses would have been rubbed down and given a good feed, but there was no such treatment here. Joseph shouldered one of the packs and followed the other two, weighed down by his wet *del*. The lamasery, when they reached it, was locked. They stood shivering and shaking in the rain, shouting and banging on the door for a long time before they finally heard a giant internal bolt being drawn back. The door opened a crack and a monk looked suspiciously out, holding up a lantern so that its light blinded them temporarily.

Oh, it's you, he said in relief, when he finally recognized Mendo.

The monk stepped back to let them in; he was clutching his purple robe with his other hand to keep it out of the water.

Have you had trouble? asked Mendo, as they stepped past the monk.

He nodded. We've survived a couple of attacks. Fortunately no one was killed. We were able to barricade ourselves in. There weren't many of them and they lost interest when they ran out of food. But, he said gloomily, I expect they will be back. And next time there will be more of them.

The lamasery had flooded and the man led them up a tiny, winding stone staircase to the upper levels to where the monks had all retreated. The main prayer hall looked like a gymnasium on a wet afternoon: the monks were sitting or lying with their prayer mats in rows, some chanting, some sleeping; the rain beat against the wooden shutters, a cauldron of tea steamed in the huge hearth and the air was damp and thick with incense. The three of them huddled together in one corner and were given green tea and small bowls of mutton stock. Tsem and Mendo fell asleep and Joseph, watching them, envied their hardiness against the vicissitudes of life: hungry, wet, cold and surrounded by coughing, snoring and humming monks, they still slept well. He turned on to his back and stared at the stone ceiling imagining the lily towering over him, the pure petals flushed as if dipped in wine that had coursed through its veins, the stamens canary yellow, the centre a pool of molten butter.

White as the sun, fair as the lily, he whispered to himself.

There would be a stand of them in the Botanical Gardens growing round the magnolia tree that Hooker had brought back from China. He'd send Hooker bulbs, he thought, a compliment from one illustrious plant hunter to another.

Unable to bear it any longer, Joseph got up, his body stiff with a rigor mortis of cold. Taking one of the lanterns, he crept downstairs. During the night the lamasery had filled knee-deep with water. He waded through the flooded, labyrinthine corridors, the oil-black water lapping at the stone walls, creating strange currents and echoes of sound that bounced like the light of his lantern, disappearing and reappearing through dark doorways, narrow spaces and twisting culs-de-sac. As he had suspected, there were fish swimming blindly through this medieval maze, lost in the stone, their scales the gleam of sunken treasure, old gold, the verdigris of aqueous copper. With the lantern clenched between his teeth, he caught several fish, almost too easily; they gaped, confused in the darkness of air, and his lantern bled oil, spiralling in rainbows across the troubled surface. He carried them in the pouch of his *del* to the stone steps where he killed and gutted them, throwing their intestines out of one of the windows in the stairwell to the howling winds and rain and whatever creatures might make use of such a thing.

It was still raining in the morning, but he showed the monks his catch and, with delighted whoops, they ran through the flooded parts, splashing and killing. Egrets and storks clustered round the monastery's doorways, their beaks poised like daggers as they stalked this unexpected bounty, and the cook, exiled from his waterlogged kitchen, grilled fish fillets over the fire in the prayer room all morning.

Mendo wiped fish grease from round his mouth and laughed at Joseph.

All this so you would not have to eat your horse.

I am sure I have not escaped my fate.

Mendo cleaned his hands on his robe.

Help me unpack, he said. We will give some of the horse-meat to the monks as payment.

You do that. I shall check the rest in case my specimens are damaged.

He unwrapped the tarp and lifted out some of the herbarium paper.

Mendo, where do you come from?

Why, here. The country is mine. I travel, he offered by way of explanation.

Joseph said nothing. Some of his packets of seeds looked a little damp. He spread them out in the corner of the hall to dry.

Sometimes, Mendo continued, I stay in one place longer than others. I mainly live at a monastery a few days' ride from here. We will go there next and you will see my home, as much as I can consider anywhere a home. I grew up south of here and the Tibetan lamasery where I was taught is near Saratsi. Once I had left, I never returned. As you can imagine, it is not a place I like to visit.

Joseph opened one of the shutters and looked out. The river had burst its banks; the area directly beneath the lamasery looked like a field preserved in glass. It was still raining and the sky was the colour of curdled milk. Most of the monks had left to attend to other business and, as the fire was dying, the room was growing increasingly cold and damp, the green smell of mould and stone combined with the high odour of fish. He sighed.

We shall stay here tonight, Mendo said.

We have had sufficient rest already. At Munke's.

The horses need it. The next few days will be difficult and it is likely to rain. You may appreciate it later.

He was right of course. Their *dels* were still sodden. Joseph wondered how old Mendo was. Older than him? The same age? It was impossible to tell, his skin was so smooth; he was either laughing or his face was impassive, unreadable.

Joseph left the monk sorting through the meat and descended to the bowels of the lamasery. He waded through the oily water, now glinting with scales. He found himself a nook at the back near the kitchens that was sheltered from the rain and prepared the stone chat skins and some of the smaller fish he'd caught. The rain fell softly but continuously; he felt as if he were in a narrow corridor, the solid stone of the lamasery behind him, the dark cliff face towering in front of him. The wind whistled through this cramped passageway and, throughout the afternoon, the monks rang prayer bells and cymbals that echoed dully.

That night they ate bowls of stew swimming with fat and full of tough lumps of meat. Joseph swallowed it with difficulty. Again he could not sleep and in the middle of the night he rose and stepped over the bodies of the sleeping monks. When he came to the stone staircase, he thought he heard the faint tremor of water as if someone were slowly wading through it. He listened for a while but decided it must simply be the stir of the water as it slid, trapped like some kind of mythical and amorphous creature, between the walls. His footsteps were absorbed by the cold stone and his light cast hallucinogenic shadows so that sometimes he believed the corridor would stretch for ever; at other times it appeared to have ended and he walked in limbo.

In some of the rooms he looked into were statues of Buddhas and demons; in one there were *arhats* – men who had attained enlightenment but who return to earth and help mortal souls reach nirvana. There were offerings of rice and flakes of silver leaf at their feet and, as he approached, a rat knocked one of the bowls to the floor and disappeared into the darkness. Joseph hurriedly left. As he did so he had the distinct impression of someone drawing breath. He turned to go back to the prayer room. Behind him was a slight sound. It was the rat, probably, or one of its companions. He walked a little way on. The sound followed him. He stopped. It stopped. He peered through the dark, holding out the beacon of his feeble lantern. He could see nothing save stone. He walked a little further on and the sound behind him became distinct: faint footsteps, so soft they were barely there. This time when he stopped, the footsteps continued a moment longer and in the silence he could hear drops of water.

Who's there? he called out and his voice bounced and echoed, transmuted into a new and terrible form.

He walked on, more swiftly now, not quite sure whether he was heading in the right direction, or if he had branched down a side corridor away from the main prayer hall. This time the footsteps closed in on him and he could hear the faint sound of cloth brushing against the wall. He spun round holding his lantern high and something darted into a pool of darkness to his right. He followed quickly – he was now in one of the monk's cells – and the thing swung towards him causing him to call out involuntarily. It was a man, a man so white he had the semblance of a creature who had lived beneath stone his entire life; his hair was long and matted. He was covered with a trailing gown of black that spat water from its folds as he spun towards Joseph, his eyes glimmering dangerously. He was eating something, furiously chewing, and in front of the priest's face he ripped pieces of paper apart with hooked, clawed hands, the nails long and ragged, pouring the contents of the packets into his mouth.

Joseph suddenly realized what they were.

My seeds! he cried, and lurched forwards.

With what seemed superhuman strength, the man lashed out and struck his arm, the lantern fell from Joseph's grasp and the light went out. The man began to laugh, a high-pitched, savage sound, and Joseph staggered back, falling through the doorway into the darkness of the corridor. His arm throbbed, nearly deadened by the blow. The shrill laughter grew sharper, came towards him. He had a horrible image of those curved hands and vicious nails grasping him round his throat. He staggered to his feet and ran down the corridor, holding his hand out to guide his way. Suddenly, instead of touching the stone walls, he felt nothing, and he almost fell into the open doorway. He pulled himself up, breathing heavily, and tried to listen for the deranged creature behind him. The darkness was oppressive, a blackness so dense his vision spiralled into purple and bloated red. He walked slowly on, continuing to trail his hand against the walls. He stubbed his fingers and his right foot against stone. He stopped and spread out his hands before him. The stone stretched in front of him, sheer, impenetrable. It was a dead-end.

Faintly, now growing louder, came the manic laughter, echoing through the corridors towards him. He did not know whether to howl from fear in the hope that someone would come to rescue him and risk his pursuer finding him easily, whether to crouch in the corner and wait for the morning light and pray the creature overlooked him, or try another branch of the corridor. He turned back the way he had come and walked on cautiously, his hands outstretched in front of him. He took the first opening he came to. The passage seemed to twist and turn and double back on itself. Round a bend he saw a wavering pool of light and hastened towards it. The light spilled into the corridor and illuminated it; he stopped to shield his eyes. Two monks ran towards him carrying lanterns. One of them was Mendo. He took Joseph's arm and led him back to the prayer hall. He sat and faced him in front of the dying embers of the fire.

There is an intruder here, hissed Joseph. He stole my seeds and then he ate them. Look, they've gone. He flung out one arm, gesturing to where their bags were.

Mendo didn't even attempt to look at the absence of the seeds. He merely said quietly, He is not an intruder. That was the head lama.

The head lama?

Yes. He was once a brilliant and wise man. Now he is mad, said Mendo matter-of-factly.

He ate my seeds, repeated Joseph.

Mendo said nothing for a few moments but continued to stare at Joseph.

Eventually he said, It is possible that he could not explain to himself why a white man should come from the other ends of the earth to collect seeds from our beloved country. Maybe he read a pattern into them, a less than honourable intention on your part. It may have the appearance of thieving.

Joseph stared at him. Do you believe I am a thief?

Brother, it matters little what I think. We were speaking of the lama.

You could have told me.

Mendo shrugged, his palms uppermost. Joseph, I did not know you would spend your nights wandering through the corridors of the lamasery in the darkness.

He smiled and put his hand on Joseph's shoulder. Come, get some rest while you can. Soon there will be flowers as far as the eye can see and you will be able to steal more seeds than you can carry.

It was Mendo's talk of flowers that suddenly brought to mind his friend Jeremy and another time, almost another life, when he had not fitted in with the prevailing religious views, as Jeremy had taken pains to point out.

Look at that! Isn't it a miracle? Joseph had said.

He'd been crouching next to a wood anemone. In this dark and damp place where the winter had seemed interminable, this tiny, fragile flower with its frail veins like old blood seemed a triumph of God's will. He may have said something to that effect.

Dear Lord, you are such a pagan, Jeremy had breathed.

Looking back on it, there had been real consternation in Jeremy's voice. Jeremy was his best friend. They'd met at Cambridge and had transferred to the seminary at

Stonyhurst together. At Cambridge they were natural allies: neither of them had money, neither had class; all they did have was a burning desire to learn, in Joseph's case because he had a passion for it, in Jeremy's as a means to an end. In the free-structured and marginally free-thinking environment of Cambridge, Jeremy was a fish out of water. They called him Jeremiah and mocked his priestly ambitions. In Yorkshire they called him Jeremiah too, but with quite another intention.

As much as he had been out of place in Cambridge, Jeremy fitted in at Stonyhurst. It was a place of rules, a regimented sanctuary, a cold-hearted training ground for an army that would conquer the hearts and minds of men. He was fond of quoting the Third Jesuit General Francesco Borgia: We came in like lambs and we rule like wolves. We shall be expelled like dogs and return like eagles.

He liked to say that they were *Everything to God and all things to all men*. Moreover, Stonyhurst was in Lancashire, and Jeremy, from just over the border in Yorkshire, was used to the cold, the damp and the bleak austerity of the moors. The second-oldest child from a farming family, his father had always encouraged him in a gruff sort of way. He'd not inherit the farm, but he'd inherit the right to oversee a man's soul. Next to Jeremy, who was well over six feet, a strapping, broad-shouldered, freckle-faced, ginger-haired lad, Joseph was a dark slip of a thing and when they visited Jeremy's family – which they did as often as they could – Joseph was pushed in front of the fire and given a vast plate heaped with meat and potatoes, mushy peas and apple pie as if he were some kind of an invalid.

It was that moment in the woods when Jeremy pinpointed exactly what it was about Joseph that caused the fathers at Stonyhurst so much concern. There was nothing wrong with Joseph – he was intelligent, obedient, diligent – but that there was something awry they all knew to be true. It was all very well to see the Lord in a grain of sand, but not literally, not to such excess, not with such ecstatic fervour. The likes of Jeremy and his stolid, dependable views were in favour here; he was what was wanted – just about bright enough and imaginative enough to be a Jesuit. You could tell he would do what he was told; he would be a foot soldier of the Lord whenever and wherever they sent him. Joseph was quite another kettle of fish.

Go set the world ablaze! Loyola had commanded. To Joseph it was ablaze already, burning with God's grandeur.

You don't have to interpret the Bible in quite so many ways, Jeremy had complained to him. There's one way, and that's what's taught here. It's simple, Joseph, why complicate it?

Jeremy had written to him shortly after *The Origin of Species* was published. At the end of his letter he'd alluded to the book and added that he didn't want Joseph getting carried away with Darwin's fine ideas.

The fathers wouldn't like it. It would be heretical, do you not see?

They do not understand what is best for them, Joseph had written back.

In the chill damp darkness of the prayer hall, Joseph smiled, as he thought of his friend. Things couldn't have worked out better for him: Jeremy was teaching in a small school in Wales. He had settled in with remarkable ease: the Welsh were probably as mistrustful of outsiders as Yorkshiremen and perhaps recognized a kindred spirit, and then the area he was living in was almost as ruggedly forbidding as the landscape he was used to. Jeremy would never be a wolf or an eagle, but in the kingdom of God, or a remote Welsh valley, a lamb or a dog was just as good.

Joseph was woken at four by the monks rising and the darkness of his fitful sleep was woven with sandalwood and chants. Tsem shook him into full consciousness at six and with Mendo's help they repacked the bags and loaded them on to the horses. There was a light misty rain and to the east the sky was the colour of honey. Joseph felt as if his body were full of lead. His limbs would not function properly, his hands had turned into fleshy stumps and Tsem had to help him on to the dun. He was dog tired and almost in a state of shock.

They journeyed upstream for many miles until they found a place shallow enough to cross and left the river, travelling always to the west. The land was mainly level with rolling hills, towering rocks the colour of beeswax and tight thickets of tamarisk covered with violet flowers. The horses crushed wild mint and artemesia beneath their hooves releasing the bitter-sweet scent of absinthe. They saw herds of wild ass and *argali*, the sheep eating steadily despite the rain. At midday they stopped briefly at a spring and ate salted strips of fish, but otherwise kept riding.

As the afternoon drew to a close, the rain eased and they retreated to a tamarisk grove. Mendo struggled with the tent, attempting to erect it between the trees, while Tsem cursed softly as he tried again and again to light damp dung and wet bits of wood. Joseph was gathering a few herbs for the night's stew when a man approached him out of the gloom. Although the others were not far away, he realized that it looked as if he were on his own. The man was not fully of Mongol origin for he had a beard. It was thin and straggly and curled into wisps at the end. He had high, pronounced cheekbones and a sharp nose. When he opened his mouth to speak, Joseph saw that his front teeth were rotten and black.

Sain bainuu.

Sain bainaa. Are you by yourself?

Joseph shook his head. There are others.

There was something wrong. The man was staring at him in a cold, blank way, not with the normal welcoming friendliness Joseph had become accustomed to.

I would like a bowl of tea.

Joseph nodded. Of course.

His Mongolian did not extend to telling the man they were struggling with their fire and tea might be a long time coming. He gestured to the man and walked towards the thicket. He felt the first prickles of cold sweat stand out on his spine as the man stepped behind him. He looked around nervously and when they reached the trees he again stopped and glanced to either side before continuing to follow Joseph.

This man says he would like tea, said Joseph.

Tsem spat on the ground and looked up at him. Help me light this then. He nodded at the fire.

Where have you come from? the man asked, remaining exactly as he was.

Pekin. We have travelled many miles.

What do you have with you?

Our tent, some food. Tsem stood up and looked the man full in the face. Why do you ask? Is there something you need?

The man looked around wildly and took a step backwards. A second man pushed his way through the tamarisks and took up position behind Tsem. He was smaller and slighter than the man with a beard but he had the same kind of features – high cheekbones, a sharp nose and the same dead look in his eyes. He nodded to his companion and both of them swiftly drew long, curved swords and began to talk fast.

Mendo, who was standing next to Tsem, responded gravely, almost slowly, and, although Joseph didn't understand it all, the gist of it was that they were carrying nothing valuable, only things of value to him, Joseph, and that if the men wanted food, they were welcome to share a meal tonight, but that the three of them needed such food as they had to complete their long journey.

The first robber darted his sword towards Mendo and spoke quickly, harshly. The second robber was holding his sword above Tsem. The two had obviously concluded that the white man could easily be overpowered later. Mendo nodded to the men and turned to untie one of the bundles.

Joseph suddenly saw how easily his whole expedition, the months of travel and of work, could unravel; he might lose what remained of his specimens because they would not have enough food to last back to Pekin – they might not even have enough food to survive. Moreover, the men were highly unlikely to leave them their horses. He pulled out his pistol from the folds of his *del* and levelled it at the nearest robber.

Stop, he said quite calmly in Mongolian.

The bearded man swung round. Joseph aimed at his chest. With an ugly expression, the man swept his sword towards Joseph as if to strike the pistol from his grasp. Joseph lowered the gun and stepped back. As he did so, he tripped over a tree root and fell to the ground. The man laughed and came towards him, his sword flashing through the semi-darkness. He kicked the gun out of the way and held the point of the sword to Joseph's throat.

Joseph felt the metal against his bare skin and wondered who else's blood had run along its cold and cruel length. His heart swelled and he felt as if it would block his throat and he should choke. Dear God, he thought, forgive these men. But he felt his mind close in terror as he looked up at his captor, so close he could smell his rank odour. The tiniest sensation seemed to overwhelm him: the feel of mud beneath his fingers, the cold seeping into his forearm from where he lay sprawled on the ground, his elbow throbbing where he had grazed it as he fell, the tree root beneath him, digging into the flesh of his thigh.

But before the robber could push the blade home, Mendo whirled round, throwing the bag he'd untied from one of the horses at the man behind him who staggered back under its weight. Mendo leapt into the air and as he landed alongside Joseph he kicked the underside of the bearded man's arm. The man jerked back and the sword flew into the air. Joseph rolled out of the way, hardly knowing which way to turn to avoid the falling blade. When he glanced up, Mendo had caught the sword. Mendo swung back around and thrust it at the smaller thief who was darting towards him, sword outstretched. Joseph dived for his pistol at the same time as the first robber. He was dimly aware of the sharp ring of metal on metal as the man's fist closed around his as he gripped the gun. The two of them wrestled with each other, the robber now lying on top of him, pinning him to the ground. He could feel the man's sharp wheezing breath against his neck and gagged at the stench of his decaying teeth.

Then a great weight seemed to lift from him. He jumped to his feet. Tsem had pulled the man off him. The horses were wheeling and whinnying in fright as Mendo and the other thief continued to fight. Joseph slipped the safety catch from the gun and held it out level in front of him, his arms shaking. He could barely see in the gloom to aim properly. He felt rather than saw the man turn and flee, shouting to his companion. The smaller thief continued to swing his sword at Mendo for a few moments more before he too stepped back and sprinted after the first robber.

Joseph tucked the gun into the belt of his *del* and ran to Mendo.

You're hurt, he exclaimed, turning the monk towards him.

It's a graze. It's nothing, he said, shrugging.

Mendo's breath came heavy and jagged. The robber's sword had caught him across the cheek. It was a short, sharp cut, but he didn't appear to be bleeding too badly.

You might need stitches, Joseph murmured, tilting the monk's face towards the sliver of moon.

I don't think we can risk a fire in case they come back, said Tsem. Here, let me have a look. I think you'll be all right, he added after a moment. We'll get you some herbs and make a poultice tomorrow.

Your martial arts lessons with the Tibetans? asked Joseph.

Mendo was still pale with fright but he allowed himself a small smile. I'm a little out of practice though.

You saved my life, said Joseph. I thought they would take our horses and still slit my throat.

You're my brother, said Mendo simply, smiling at him.

Thank you, said Joseph, stepping forward and hugging him.

Listen, said Tsem, we were very lucky. But they're likely to come back. Someone should keep watch.

He looked pointedly at Joseph. He didn't need to add: with the gun.

Joseph nodded although he was so tired he could hardly keep his eyes open. The horses had trampled the beginnings of Tsem's damp fire and as there was no more of the cured fish and as no one was inclined to eat raw herbs, they prepared for sleep, wet, cold and hungry.

Try not to drop it this time, Tsem called out as he wrapped himself up in his bedding.

Joseph pulled his *del* around him, took the gun and went to sit in front of the horses. It was still very cold and even with the thick coat he was freezing. The boundless blue horizons of Mongolia translated at night into a perfect dome alive with a thousand constellations. Joseph counted as many as he could see. The wind rustled through the trees, the horses stirred sleepily and an eagle owl called incessantly, but there was no other sound that might have indicated the return of the robbers. He must have slept, for he woke with a start and grabbed his gun when Tsem touched his shoulder. Tsem laughed at him and handed him a bowl of tea. He thanked him and rubbed his eyes; he'd even slept through Tsem managing to light a small fire from tiny twigs gathered in the heart of the thicket.

Who were those men? Joseph asked, cradling the bowl in his numb hands. Were they just robbers? How did they know we were here?

Mendo, the cut standing out livid on his cheekbone, his face ashen and drawn, said, I don't know, Joseph. They could easily have been poor, desperate, hungry men.

Or?

Or they could be linked to the White Warlord. The fact that they didn't come back makes me suspect that they returned to someone to report on us. He has spies and emissaries everywhere. When the robbers we saw reach the Warlord's men, he may send more soldiers.

He might, but are we worth it? Our horses are few and not the best, we don't have enormous amounts of food or money and we are not carrying anything that he might consider precious. Why would he waste more men when he knows that we can defend what little we have?

My friend, you will never become a warlord with that attitude, said Mendo, half smiling. Do not forget he has made it his mission to eradicate all holy men, he added more gravely.

Can you two stop debating and get ready to leave? We should make haste – just in case, said Tsem, stamping out the fire.

There had been no time for prayers that morning, but Joseph attempted to pray as he rode although his very bones ached. Dear Lord, our God, thank you for keeping us safe through the night, protecting us from harm, delivering us from evil.

They travelled for several days. The rolling *nors* continued and then the whole land became flatter, the vegetation sparser. It was either hot and sunny or it rained and there seemed no rhyme nor reason to the vagaries of the weather. Sometimes they stopped at *gers* and ate mutton or marmot stew with the nomads or else they camped by themselves and finished off the horsemeat and made a gruel from the *tsamba*. Tsem bartered sorghum brandy for tobacco and continued to steal small scraps of Joseph's paper to make his roll-ups.

It was, Joseph reflected, all part of the life of a plant hunter, long periods of tedium punctuated by brief bursts of danger and flurries of excitement as new plants and animals were discovered. As they rode he thought of Darwin's friend, Joseph Dalton Hooker, who had inspired the craze for rhododendrons back home. Hooker had witnessed far more hardships than he had. He'd travelled to Sikkim in the north-eastern Himalayas in 1847. The terrain was rough, there were no roads and he and his porters had had to hack their way through thorny bushes and nettles. He was bitten by hundreds of gnats every day. Frequently they would ascend 5,000 feet only to drop back down a crevasse and have to ford a torrential river. Hooker suffered from altitude sickness and was habitually half snow-blind, crazy with fatigue and dizziness. It was often bitterly cold. At night he had to build small walls of stone or peat in front of his tent, which he constructed from blankets, to protect himself from the bitter, glacial winds. Yaks poked their noses through the makeshift tent and woke him with a snort of moist air, and once he discovered a huge rock had been dislodged during the night and had landed by his tent, just missing him. The final insult was when Sikkim men half beat his friend, Alastair Campbell, to death and the two of them were imprisoned for almost a month before Hooker could get word to the British consulate. But even while they were being marched to Tumloong where they were confined, Hooker secretly gathered rhododendron seeds along the way.

Hooker had discovered his first rhododendron in Sikkim – *Rhododendron argenteum*: its thick deep green leaves were silver on the underside, it grew to a height of forty feet, and its flowers were ivory white.

He wrote: I know nothing of the kind that exceeds in beauty the flowering branch of *R. argenteum*, with its wide spreading foliage and mass of glorious flowers.

Later he found *Rhododendron dalhousiae*, which smelled of lemons, growing as an epiphyte on *Magnolia campbelli*, a specimen more magnificent than any he had seen in cultivation in Britain, with its spare twisted branches and huge rose-purple, cup-shaped flowers.

Once when Joseph had been enthusiastically talking about Hooker and his travels to Dr Craven, the botanist had smiled and said, You have heard the story of Hooker as a child, have you not?

Joseph replied that he had not. Dr Craven said that Hooker had grown up in Glasgow and was one day seen grubbing about in a dirty wall in a dirty suburb of the city. He was about five years old at the time and when he was asked what he was doing, he said he had located a specimen of *Bryum argenteum*, a type of moss.

Hooker had once written:

> The isolation of my position, the uncertainly to the success of a journey that absorbed all my thoughts, the prevalence of fevers in the valleys I was traversing, and the many difficulties that beset my path, all crowded on the imagination when fevered by exertion and depressed by gloomy weather, and my spirits involuntarily sank as I counted the many miles and months intervening between me and my home.

Joseph had known it was going to be hard. He also believed he had the mental and physical strength to cope with anything. Although he was not counting the months until he returned home, for he felt as if his journey had barely begun, he did miss Bristol, Jeremy, Patrick, and, of his colleagues at the British Museum, Dr Craven in particular.

He thought of that first meeting at the museum.

Dr Craven had escorted him out and on the way had said, You see, Joseph, we are all bit prickly about Darwin here. It is a most unorthodox scientific method, and yet, as you say, quite brilliant. We are all a little envious of *The Origin of Species* and his success. But most of us, well, we are floundering, Joseph. I think you'll understand why more than many. We were – how can I put it? – almost intermediaries between God and science. It sounds rather conceited to say it so boldly, but we explained God's works to the public. Now what role do we have if Darwin has explained it all so clearly and no one can quite see how God fits in? You, I am sure, he'd added kindly and patted Joseph on the shoulder, will help set us straight.

Yes, he missed Dr Craven, with his reams of pressed plants, his skilful paintings depicting the minute details of moss, and his plump, pretty wife, her hair the colour of wild honey in thick ringlets, her olive skin and her large hazel eyes. She nearly always wore green and seemed quite to fade into the verdant velveteen wallpaper in their parlour. Mrs Craven, who baked biscuits that melted in buttery crumbs in his mouth and pressed small bottles of damson or rhubarb and raspberry jam upon him, frequently gave him tiny hampers for his return journey to Bristol containing quails' eggs, wedges of Stilton and thick, oaten cakes, pear and ginger torte and home-made lemonade. Dr Craven handed them to him with a slight air of abashment, as if he thought Joseph might be embarrassed, and a barely disguised pride.

As they crested the brow of the hill, Mendo turned to him and said, Joseph, I want to welcome you to the Valley of the Larks.

He was grinning broadly as if he personally had created a gift fit for a priest and was presenting it with the utmost satisfaction.

They were on the lip of a wide plain and the sight that greeted Joseph was so unexpected he reined his horse to a standstill and stared about him like a starving man feasting his eyes on a banquet. For two days they had been climbing steadily, grimly, alert for the slightest sign that might give away the presence of robbers. They had barely stopped even to eat and the land itself had been stony and barren. Yet in front of them was a tumult of colour and noise. At least a hundred men in their best *dels*, with sashes of fine jewel-like silk, were holding long poles with a wickerwork ball balanced on the tip. Inside these cages were one or more larks; other men were wandering between them, stopping to listen, their heads tilted to one side, hands behind their backs. The larks' songs drifted towards them as richly layered and intricately woven as a Persian rug. Trains of camels were tethered around the gathering of men and birds, cerulean-blue silk scarves tied about their throats. The grass itself was thick and lush, carpeted with flowers in blocks of dense colour: white, cream, carnation, daffodil, amaryllis red.

This is where the Chinese buy their best larks, said Mendo.

They have travelled so far!

The Chinese prize larks very highly, Mendo said dryly. And what is far for a Mongolian? We are horsemen, nomads. Distance is irrelevant. They will travel back to Chinese territory to sell these larks for an even higher price than they are paying for them today.

How do they catch them?

They gather the fledglings from nests on the steppes and rear them until they begin to sing. Only the males sing and so they keep them. Not all the birds sing equally well. Sometimes the young ones are kept with a master singer so that they will develop a better voice.

They must be costly.

The best are more expensive than a horse. We Mongolians find it strange, to pay so much for a bird in a cage when every day we are surrounded by their songs.

Joseph jumped off his horse and wandered between the men and larks who allowed their listeners a respectful silence to hear the larks sing before extolling the songbirds' virtues. He felt as if he were in the midst of a vast symphony and as he walked he wove a path through individual instruments and fragments of melodies. A couple of the men nodded and grinned at him in the hope he might stop and listen to their birds, but Joseph asked them in his halting Mongolian about the rare white lily. Neither of them had seen it, but one said that he had heard it grew in the hills and forests to the north of the Valley of the Larks.

Mendo caught up with him shortly and pointed out Batar Halek Sume, the Temple of the Larks, at the far end of the steppe where a rolling sea of hills began. Joseph could barely see it, for the distance from the lark sellers to the temple was covered with *gers*, horses and people.

In a week's time it will be the Maidari Festival, said Mendo. We will stay at the temple until the festival ends.

What is it for?

Maidari was – how would you describe it? – a prophet, a Messiah; he brought Buddhism to the people. The festival is in his honour; he requests that we reflect upon our sins and he will indicate whether we shall have a prosperous year.

But Joseph was barely listening. He was peering intently at the tapestry beneath his feet of wild thyme, mint, edelweiss, lilac vetch, white daisies with feathery dill-like leaves. He sank his hands into the flowers, his head throbbing with the melody of the larks, the heady aroma of herbs. This, then, was the entangled bank Darwin had written of, the incarnation of his vision of plants, birds, insects – these elaborately constructed forms – so different from one another yet utterly dependent upon each other. From such a simple beginning endless forms most beautiful and most wonderful have been and are being evolved.

This was evolution spread out before him, the magic word that haunted his thoughts like a tune, an unsatisfied hunger, a promise, a summons.

Dear God, he thought, it was for this I came.

For seven days Joseph made short forays from the temple, past the gathering crowds of people, to the steppes and hills beyond. He dug up spring bulbs, replaced his lost seeds, pressed flowers and feverishly sketched, described, annotated. The days were long and hot, the abundance of flora breathtaking. The steppes were covered with orchids that smelled of vanilla, their heavy heads as large as walnuts. He watched small bees shoulder their way into the flower, docking like tug boats. While the bees sipped from the orchids' nectaries, sacs of pollen were attached to their furry backs. When they visited the next flower, they were removed by the flower's stigmata. The beautiful and bizarre petals of the orchid were thus a way of enticing bees to be their pollen bearers; transporting pollen from one flower to another would ensure that the next generation of flowers would be stronger and fitter than if the flower had fertilized itself.

In 1862 Darwin had published a book on orchids: *On the Various Contrivances by which British and Foreign Orchids are fertilised by Insects*, which proved to be a hit among a certain sort of genteel lady, taking evolution into the parlour, as it were. One of the more eccentric forms he'd described was the *Catasetum* which was originally thought to be three different species. Darwin discovered that it was, in fact, three types of flowers: a male, a female and a hermaphrodite. Even more strangely, it was sensitive to insects and fired arrows with sticky pollen heads at them as they brushed past. Joseph, mindful of the fashionable nature of orchids, dug up a few to take home.

The hills leading up to the dense forests beyond were clothed in flowering juniper bushes, broom, peonies, delphiniums and red and yellow lilies. All of these were varieties he had not encountered and many were species that had no name or antecedent in his own tongue.

He picked wild garlic, onions, mushrooms and herbs and for the first time ate food that he considered vaguely palatable. In the evenings he and Mendo drank tea with the Mongolians surrounding the temple who sang and played the *morin khuur* and told tales of Genghis Khan: a child descended twenty-one generations after the union of a wolf and a doe; a child born with a blood clot the size of a knuckle clenched in his tiny fist; a child who became a warrior king. Tsem had his own agenda which included drinking copious amounts of alcohol.

The temple itself was very different from the ones they had stayed in before. It had a Chinese flavour, ornate pagoda-style roofs scrolling skywards at the corners, with rows of terracotta monkeys, dragons, fish and horses marching across the gables; the roof slates were brilliant green and shaped like scales. The first building was several storeys high with gold prayer wheels on each terrace and mandarin-orange, white and blue prayer flags. Through the elaborate gates there was a huge courtyard flanked by three more smaller but equally decorative buildings: chrysanthemums in gold filigree inlaid in ox-blood red onyx were set into the walls, and pillars of fire-breathing dragons supported the entrance to each section of the lamasery. In the centre of the courtyard was a giant statue of Maidari sitting cross-legged on a lotus flower smiling serenely; tatters of his gilt coating still remained.

The Chinese destroyed the original monastery. They paid for it to be rebuilt as a, how would you say it, a way of *healing* their conscience, Mendo told him.

The day of the festival was the first time Joseph had seen the Yolros lama, who, as Mendo explained to him, was a living god. He was wearing an orange sarong-like garment, and over the top a sleeveless tunic embroidered with gold thread. When Mendo presented Joseph to him, he stood up and looked straight at him. He was inordinately tall for a Mongolian and lean. That he was old, Joseph had no doubt, but there was a youthful vitality about him despite the fine lines that webbed his narrow face. His shorn hair was silver and in the light from the early morning sun, which streamed through one of the high side windows, he appeared to have a halo. The lama's eyes were not large, but the dark iris nearly filled them so that when he met Joseph's, the priest had the impression of looking into the depths of a creature both enduringly ancient and wholly feral who yet possessed a wisdom unfettered by words. For one moment Joseph was transfixed, but within an instant the Yolros lama's penetrating eyes had clouded and his consciousness was transposed to some other place or time. Mendo placed the last of the salted horsemeat at his feet. For a short while he and Joseph remained seated cross-legged near the door as scores of people knelt one by one in front of the lama and presented him with a gift: a silk scarf, a sheep's stomach full of butter, some grain, a pouch of *airag*, a little milk, and the lama leaned across and with his long, thin fingers dropped holy water on each person's forehead. Joseph shuddered involuntarily.

In the afternoon the crowd gathered in the courtyard and the heavy doors to the lama's quarters were swung shut and barred as if he were an animal of inordinate strength who must be contained.

Because he is the living incarnation of the deity, explained Mendo, he cannot participate in a festival to worship the gods. He paused and then said, The Yolros lama has asked that we see him before we leave. I will arrange it.

And we have sufficient . . . Joseph began.

Food will not be a problem, said Mendo. It's the white season, a time of plenty.

Without explaining himself further he rose and turned towards the crowds.

For the next two days Joseph collected specimens as long as there was sufficient daylight, the noise of the festivities a constant in the background.

PART II

*S*hortly after they left the Temple of the Larks, they passed a small stream whose banks shimmered with irises that cast a blue gleam across the bronzed surface of the water; the horses waded chest-high through tall, spindly, daisy-like flowers. Further up the slope, the ground levelled out and the stream broadened. In the dark recesses towards the edge of the forest were royal-blue delphiniums and rhododendrons, starred with vivid magenta flowers. Cream and white water lilies floated on the surface of the stream. They were not the only ones to have found this beautiful idyll. A small collection of *gers* was spread across the meadow, grazing between them were a few horses and, further upstream, a herd of yaks, all of whom had little ones. Compared to the Temple of the Larks and the festival, it was beautifully peaceful.

The three of them erected their tent and unloaded the baggage. By the time they were halfway through doing this, a small group of children and a couple of men had come to watch. Tsem said they were all invited back to one of the men's *gers*. Joseph had been dimly aware that there was something different about them but it was not until he was inside that it struck him. These *gers* were larger and more angular than the others they'd seen, the inner walls stitched with tapestries in bold, bright colours, the patterns and figures evenly spaced out, woven in a loose stitch. He had the impression of being in a large, airy and cool space. They were given yak's milk and big squares of *aaruul*, a hard, sour cheese.

The milk was welcomingly refreshing and Joseph stayed a short while out of politeness, but left as soon as he could. He felt as if the woods and the wilderness were calling him, and he was acutely aware that they would be beginning their journey back home soon.

For the next couple of hours he busied himself sketching, picking specimens to press and digging up roots. He was determined to create a herbarium of plants, which he could bring back alive to Bristol. It was the stillness that first alerted him, the absence of bird sound. He looked up and saw a woman leaning against a tree trunk watching him. He realized that to a Mongolian there was an absurdity to his posture: he was crouched on the ground, a bunch of flowers next to him, a pile of papers with rough sketches of parts of plants held down by a stone, grubbing in the ground with a thin metal trowel. The woman was staring at him with the frank and open gaze he had become used to. Like the other Mongolians he had seen in this clearing, she was very fair-skinned, with a long, flat face, high cheekbones and large, slanting eyes. Her hair was tied loosely, so that it framed her face before being pulled back into a thick black plait. Her eyes were a deep, yet light green, the colour of moss in a wood. She was wearing a red felt waistcoat over a white and red dress with deep blue trousers underneath. He had an almost visceral reaction to her: unease so strong it bordered on fear and another emotion that he suddenly recognized was desire. She was quite the most beautiful woman he had ever seen.

Sain bainuu?

Sain ta sain bainuu? she replied.

Sain bainaa, he answered, in the time-honoured ritual he had learned.

They stared at each other for a moment and then Joseph stood up.

It's you, he said.

Yes, it's me, she said, inclining her head towards him. I have been watching you. She smiled at him, revealing a mouth full of perfectly white, straight teeth.

Joseph was not a tall man, but she was a tall woman, barely an inch shorter than him. He noticed she wore a star carved from coral at her throat.

The fur trader? he asked suspiciously.

Yes, she said. My name is Namuunaa.

Were you spying on us?

No, she said simply.

I don't suppose you would tell me if you were, he said, wiping the earth from his hands. He held out his hand to shake hers. My name is Joseph.

I know, she said.

Without taking his hand she bowed her head towards him and walked away, leaving the edge of the wood and heading back towards the tents. He stood and watched her leave. But after she had gone several yards she turned back to him and called, Come, I have something to show you.

He hastily scrambled after her. She led him to the edge of the river and walked slowly along the edge of the bank, her head bent. Joseph waited and watched her. She had a very thin, strong neck; he could see the tendons at the base of her throat as she looked from side to side.

Ah! She gave a sudden cry, and bent down. Look.

He walked over to where she was pointing. By the bank was a plant growing half in, half out of the water. Its leaves were thick and soft, slightly serrated and it had tiny, yellow stars for flowers. She rubbed a leaf between her fingers and held it out for him. It smelled like pineapple, camomile, an after-taste of mint.

It makes very good tea for when you are sick, she said and smiled up at him as if she had just offered him something very precious.

Bayarlaa, he said.

It was indeed a good find. He could imagine it flourishing in a Victorian knot garden, or perhaps round the edge of an ornamental pond. She moved out of the way for him and he crouched down and dug it out carefully with his thin trowel. When he looked up to show her the whole plant, roots and all, she had gone.

It had been a good spot, the place where she had showed him the herb, half in, half out of the water, partly wood and partly meadow. He suddenly entertained a dim hope that she might be able to help him find the rare white lily. He packed the plants he had collected in earth and hessian and laid out the flowers on herbarium paper ready to be put in his flower press.

I am looking for Namuunaa, he said to the old woman in the first *ger* they had been invited to.

Namuunaa, she repeated, rolling the word like a stone in her toothless mouth. She pointed up the hill.

Where? asked Joseph, smiling.

There were three *gers* behind this one. She made a more expansive movement as if gesturing beyond them.

It was dusk and the sky was streaked with pink clouds, the same shade as the rhododendrons. Small bats flew across the glen and the grass exuded a wonderful smell as it released the last of the day's warmth; he could still catch the lingering scent of the strange herb on his lips and hands. He passed the last *ger* and at the end of the meadow he followed a narrow strip of land set steeply between the trees and the river. After about half a mile, the path eased off and became level, opening up once more into another, smaller meadow. There was one *ger* on its own against the trees. Two horses, a roan and the fine white horse he'd already seen, were hobbled together outside and a dog tethered to a post at the door. Joseph approached slowly, talking to the dog in low tones. Unlike other Mongolian dogs, it didn't yap or bark or leap up and attempt to choke itself on its leash before settling back into a kind of miserable despondency. It made no sound, but regarded him with its head on one side, its black lips curled into a vicious leer. He was on the point of putting his hand out to it when he realized that it was not a dog. The animal was a medium-sized wolf cub. As he was half crouched down, the wolf straining towards him, every muscle locked in its body, the door opened and a small child peered out at him. A moment later Namuunaa herself came to the door and welcomed him in.

There were feathers from some kind of bird of prey, maybe an eagle, round the door, that brushed against him as he entered the tent.

Sit down, please. We were about to eat. Will you have something?

Thank you, I will, he said, immediately accepting the hospitality as he had grown accustomed to, before realizing that, in fact, he was hungry. He'd had nothing but the milk and cheese since the morning.

The little girl leaned against her mother while she ladled out a milky stew with scraps of yak butter floating in it. She too was startlingly beautiful. She was about five years old with skin even lighter than her mother's, grey-blue eyes and blonde curly hair.

She's called Lena, said Namuunaa, ruffling the child's hair.

And your husband? asked Joseph, taking the bowl of stew from her.

Dead, said Namuunaa shortly, but then half smiled at Joseph's reaction.

He wondered whether it was appropriate for him to be here with this young, unmarried woman. She was, of course, quite safe with him, but the others were not to know he was a priest, and even if he were to explain that he was the equivalent of a lama, this would be of little value either, given the reputation of some of the travelling lamas.

He looked around her tent. It was very simple, plainer than the other ones he'd been in. All the furniture was hewn out of white pine and sanded smooth. There was a giant stove in the centre and the usual pile of saddles and bridles by the door. A string of beads and a bunch of feathers were the only offerings dedicated to the Buddha. Against the wall were two beds with white covers and white wooden trunks next to them. Like the other *gers*, the walls were embroidered with thick red, orange, blue and gold thread – flowers and birds and trees, forming an intricate pattern that began on the east dome of the tent, spread to the middle and stopped.

Namuunaa, seeing him looking at the pictures, tried to explain to him about them. Eventually he understood her to say, as she mimed parts and he knew a few of the words, that when a man marries a woman, she is given a new tent, and she embroiders designs on to it. The tent becomes her life's work. But this, she said, pointing to the last motif, a flower, was when he died.

Lena whispered something in her mother's ear.

Namuunaa smiled and said, She says your skin is even whiter than ours.

As she said this she ran her hand over her cheek to emphasize her words and he could not help noticing how smooth, almost translucent her skin was. She did not have a single wrinkle, only faint laughter lines around her eyes.

I come from a land, far, far away, he said, a phrase Mendo had taught him and which normally sufficed, but Lena immediately said, Where?

You must sail on a big ship to reach our country, he said in English, and taking his notebook out, he drew the girl a picture of the sailing vessels that usually moored in the harbour. He felt, as he drew it, a wave of nostalgia for the smell of the city, the seagulls that cried over the boats, the wind as it sang through the rigging, the sound of the waves as they slapped against the hulls.

Lena looked at him wide-eyed. She thought he was odd, the picture meant nothing to her. He quickly tore out the sheet of notepaper and folded it into a boat as she watched, bent over him.

Come with me, he said and held out his hand.

She put her hands behind her back, but she followed him to the stream and watched in fascination as he put the boat on the water, gave it a push, and let it sail away. Her face, which till then had been scrunched up in angry puzzlement, opened like a flower unfurling and she shouted in delight as she ran alongside the stream parallel to the boat which glowed a ghostly white in the semi-darkness.

Eventually her mother called her back and she came reluctantly, trudging uphill, the threat of tears not too far away. Namuunaa held the door open for them and she marched inside scowling silently. The wolf at the door watched them steadily.

She wants you to make her another one, for the morning, said Namuunaa.

Joseph smiled, and tore out another sheet of paper. This time he folded it very slowly into a boat, and Lena helped him smooth down the creases, but she still sat up in astonishment when the boat materialized, the paper miraculously transposing itself into another object despite her diligence. Like an English child of the same age she took the boat and flew it round the room, pretending to sail it in the stew and across the bed covers.

Joseph thanked Namuunaa and handed back his empty bowl before taking his leave. He'd got about halfway home before he realized that he hadn't asked her about the lily. Back at their tent, Mendo and Tsem had left some food for him and the nomads had given them milk, *airag*, a stuffed sheep's heart and a plate full of *aaruul*. Joseph took his penknife and cut them all thin slices from the heart. He lit several candles and spent the remainder of the evening painting a portrait of the white lily as it appeared in his mind's eye. Tsem took himself off for liquid refreshment at one of the tents, but Mendo remained cross-legged by the fire, his beads trickling through his fingers.

Will you tell them that I am a priest? Joseph asked him suddenly.

A priest? They will think you are like a lama or a monk if I try to explain.

Is that so bad?

It depends on your reasons for wanting them to know you are a priest.

You will just have to explain who God is and then they'll understand.

Ah! Are you determined to keep me here for months?

With your skills it should be – well, let us say a month.

How can you trust the interpretation of an unbeliever? Who knows what I might say on your God's behalf?

My God will understand. Especially if your intentions are honest.

Now you are becoming a Buddhist. The Buddha taught that if a man has the right intention, only good things can come from a good heart.

And I know, said Joseph, smiling at him as he held up his painting to dry, that your heart is, as we say, in the right place.

Take care that yours is not dislodged, said Mendo quietly.

You believe that you are wise, said Joseph, shaken by what Mendo might be implying, but you are also terribly – he struggled for the right word – ambiguous.

Good, said Mendo, getting up to go to bed. I have been practising all my life. That is the role of the lama, is it not?

In the late afternoon Joseph washed the dirt from his hands and the sweat from his face and went up to see Namuunaa. It was cool in her *ger*, though her face was suffused a delicate pink from exertion and wisps of hair stuck to the perspiration on her forehead. She was churning milk to make curds. When she saw Joseph she pushed out a low stool with her foot for him to sit on and gave him a bowl of milk before continuing. Joseph waited until she took a rest and then showed her his paintings.

Very beautiful, she said, struggling to catch her breath.

She held them out to him but he indicated that she should keep them.

Have you seen anything like this?

She took a long drink of milk before replying and then she nodded.

Yes.

They're called *lilies*, he said in English. Do you know where I will find them?

She started to speak and Joseph picked up the words 'difficult' and 'in the woods'. But then she pointed to the flower and, repeating it slowly twice, said, I will take you.

Thank you, said Joseph, grinning. When?

The day after tomorrow.

She put the pictures on either side of the altar and returned to churning the milk. Joseph offered to help, but she shook her head almost angrily. For fear he had overstepped some kind of boundary, he took his leave. As he walked across the grass, there was a loud sound, a kind of scratching cough. He walked a little way round the *ger* to see what it was, watched closely by the wolf all the while. On a low perch was a huge bird with a hooked beak and great curved talons. Its eyes were golden yellow, and as he stood there it spread its wings and hissed at him. Its feathers were russet brown and tawny flecked with white patches. The bird was magnificent, a foot and a half tall. It was a golden eagle. Joseph felt the hairs on the back of his neck rise. He backed away slowly and left the small clearing in the wood, the wolf following silently in his footsteps as far as its leash would allow.

What kind of woman was she? Joseph wondered.

Two days later they were sitting round a smoky fire which Tsem was trying to coax into life so they could have some tea when Namuunaa rode up to them through the pale morning mists. The three men looked at her in silence. She was on the white horse, her hair swept into a plait coiled tightly at the nape of her neck. She was clad in a deep blue *del* with trousers underneath and her boots were black and straight cut with a red dragon embroidered on the outside. The eagle was with her too, perched on a wooden arm-rest built into the saddle; it sat calmly, for its black leather hood covered its eyes. The bird was almost as tall as she was. Behind her was Lena, astride the little roan, the stirrups wound up to the edge of the saddle.

This is Lena, she said to Tsem and Mendo, my daughter, and this is *Shuvuu* and this is *Chon*.

Mendo and Tsem started to laugh.

A wolf called Wolf and a bird called Bird. Tsem grinned.

And all the more surprising since the Mongols named nothing, thought Joseph.

I would ask you to have some tea, said Tsem, but it will take a while.

I think we should go.

What, and deprive a man of his tea?

He can have tea later, said Namuunaa, smiling at Joseph.

He saddled his horse. He had only half-heartedly gathered some of the things he would need today; he had not thought that she would come.

As he finished packing he said in a low voice to Mendo, Should someone come with us?

Me? I am too busy explaining God to these people, he said, and Tsem is learning how to light a fire. He added more seriously, She has enough protection.

Joseph thought he meant the eagle and the wolf, which joined them from where she had been lurking in the shadows. And who knows what else Mendo meant, thought Joseph, sighing. Still, he was only concerned about obeying societal mores in so far as they would otherwise prevent him from attaining his own goals and if Mendo thought the situation seemed respectable, then he was happy. More than happy. He grinned ecstatically at his companions and they held up their hands in a silent farewell.

There was so much he wanted to ask her – about the animals and plants in this region, about herself, and her people – but he struggled to formulate these things, his Mongolian still not quite good enough. And then, too, he wasn't quite sure whether to trust her. Besides, for the moment they were in single file: Namuunaa, followed by Lena and then him as they passed her *ger* and continued to climb up the mountain. Like the other Mongolian women he'd seen, she rode as well as a man, almost becoming a part of her horse. Lena darted about, now overtaking her mother, now trotting alongside, falling back, stopping to stare at him, all arms and legs flapping but with a quick confidence that made it seem unlikely she would fall off.

There had been heavy dew during the night and every leaf and blade of grass was coated with a fine silver film. For the first hour of their journey, mist lay like wraiths in the clearings and above the stream but, as the sun rose, the colours became bright, hard and sharp. The forest gradually grew denser; alongside the narrow pathway by the stream there were small cream and purple azaleas, the trees were festooned with moss and lichen and the stream was choked with ferns and what looked like marsh marigolds. Joseph made mental notes to himself about places to return to.

By mid-morning they'd passed the treeline and come out above a rolling vista of mountains, the sky a limitless blue. Namuunaa held the eagle on her fist, the jesses between her finger and thumb, and carefully removed the hood. The eagle shook his head and stared about him as if getting his bearings. Namuunaa held out her arm and released the bird. He soared effortlessly, the great wings easily propelling him heavenwards; like a prayer, thought Joseph, there was something so magnificently simple about him. The eagle hovered above them and they watched silently, as if trapped in the golden lens of his eyes, then he tucked in his wings and plummeted to earth.

Namuunaa turned to look at the wolf cub and almost without another movement on her part the animal was running flat out across the grass over to the eagle and his kill. The eagle allowed the wolf to take his prey, though had he so wished, he could easily have snapped her backbone in two. The wolf deposited the hare at Namuunaa's feet and the eagle slowly, almost languorously, flew back to her fist. He made small panting and hissing noises as she skinned and gutted it; she gave the parts she did not want to the animals.

Lena was already gathering twigs and dried dung for the fire. Joseph rode back to the wood and found some larger logs. Namuunaa lit the fire, and heated flat stones in the embers on which she roasted the meat and boiled plain black tea. As his contribution, Joseph had brought some *aaruul*. It felt, as he ate, as if they were sitting on top of the world. The animals stared at the hare; they had already consumed their meat raw and bloody and it was not enough.

They have to be a little hungry, or they will not hunt, said Namuunaa watching the eagle pretending not to watch them. This eagle killed her mother, she added, pointing to the wolf. We mainly hunt for meat and fur – foxes, wolves, gazelles – in the winter.

Does no one else hunt like this?

They used to. But it is hard to find and raise an eagle chick. Not everyone has the luck or the patience.

He reached over and gripped her wrist.

Why, he said, were you following me?

She looked into the distance and then back at him. He felt himself being drawn into the depths of her deep green eyes. He let go her wrist suddenly as if her skin had burned him.

My mother is a shaman, she said. The spirits told her that I would meet a man from a land far, far away. A man of God. When I heard about you from the nomads and then I saw you with your pale, pale skin, I knew you were the one.

She stood up abruptly. Come, let us find the flowers.

She wiped her hands on the grass and stamped out the fire. Deftly she slipped the hood over the eagle's head and, grasping him by the talons, placed him back on his wooden perch and fastened his jesses securely.

Joseph wasn't sure what to make of what she had said but he was starting to believe that he had been wrong to be suspicious of her.

The three of them rode in a line again, Lena in the middle, talking to herself and making up stories. The wolf ran in front of them all, casting about at the maze of strange scents. They rode over a long ridge, like the spine of some curved sea creature, with a breathtaking view on either side of them – hills, mountains and woods as far as the eye could see – and, in the very distance, at the end of vision where land and sky melded, a shimmering mirage of bone white and deep ochre, the Bad Lands: the edge of the Gobi Desert. They descended the east side of the ridge into trees again – tall pines that were spaced far apart so that muted green light filtered between the branches as if through a stained-glass window. Joseph, staring up at the vaulted sky, felt as if he were in a cathedral. Namuunaa picked a path that wove through the trees and now, as Joseph glimpsed pure white light flashing through the trunks on the far side, he began to smell what could only be the lilies – a tide of scent: white musk and vanilla, a hint of jasmine, gardenias at nightfall, the purity of snow after the first frost, an after-odour of salt-rich sea water.

Lena cantered on ahead and Joseph followed, bursting through the trees. In front of them was a narrow, steep-sided gully and it was the light from this place that they had seen glowing through the trees, for every square inch of soil was covered with lilies. It was like a new snowfall, heavy and thick and blindingly bright. They were perfect: each one was no less than five feet tall with several blossoms on every elegant stem. The outer edge of the petals was the colour of rich cream, the inner, crisp, clean white. The stamens were wine black with golden pollen and the base of the petals was suffused with a glow like the pink flush of hawthorn blossom. The smell was overpowering. The wolf sneezed and remained at the edge of the wood.

He thought of Keats:

> *For there the lily, and the musk-rose, sighing,*
> *Are emblems true of hapless lovers dying.*

And he thought of how his name would be assured in all the best salons and in the Royal Society when this flower, his crowning glory, would blossom on English soil.

Joseph turned to Namuunaa in astonishment, but she said, It is our secret, and held her finger up to her lips in case he had not understood.

Who is she? Joseph asked later. She is so different. Where has she come from?

She is not so different. Mendo laughed. You have not looked at anyone else. They are all pale-skinned and some of them have blonde hair. She and Lena are not unique.

And yet, and yet . . . was she married to a chief? The head of the tribe?

She *is* the head of the tribe, said Mendo. She is descended from a long line of shamans. Her mother lives here too; she still exercises her powers and heals people. Namuunaa has inherited her skill with animals and herbs.

Yet she has a Buddhist altar in her *ger*.

Welcome to Mongolia, said Mendo impatiently. Everyone believes in both.

How do you know all this? asked Joseph suspiciously. About Namuunaa and her mother?

I do not spend all day looking at flowers, said Mendo with a smile.

It's unique.

Oh, yes, it is special, but then there are many peoples here. Further north, on the border with Siberia, are the Tsaatan who hunt with reindeer. They ride them, Mendo said with admiration.

I meant the lily, said Joseph, holding out one perfect specimen. Now that I have my heart's desire, do you think I will lose my soul?

No, but you are in danger of losing your head.

What nonsense, said Joseph, still staring at the lily.

Joseph painted and then pressed the lily. He spent the next couple of days gathering plants for his herbarium as well as collecting seeds and bulbs. He pondered what to do about the lily. It was far too large to become part of the herbarium. Normally a plant like this would be transported back as a bulb. The best time to dig them up was when flowering had ceased and the nutrients gathered by the leaves had been pumped back into the bulb. It would take another month at least before the bulbs would be ready to dig up and it would be better to leave them for two once they'd ceased to flower. Mendo wasn't willing to stay any longer. He warned Joseph that he'd seen nothing of winter in Mongolia – only the warm tail end as spring approached. Moreover, sailing back to Bristol in winter was not a charming prospect either. Joseph decided that he would just have to take the bulbs as they were and hope they survived the journey. George might be able to coax them into life at the other end.

Three days after he had first seen the lily, he set off for the hidden valley taking with him enough cold food for the day. He left early, in the grey light of dawn, for he planned to dig up as many bulbs as he could.

He had almost reached the lilies – he could smell their perfume wafting towards him on a wind already redolent of the pines he was travelling through – when he changed his mind. The lilies would go nowhere and it mattered little when he dug them up; the best time to see birds was early in the morning. He decided to look in the forest for new species for a couple of hours, then return to the lilies and journey back the way he had come. He was less likely to get lost by adopting this approach, he thought.

He imagined, as he rode, presenting Namuunaa with a huge bunch of the cut stems. He thought of them gracing the best parlours in hand-blown vases, adorning the entrances to the finest restaurants in Britain; opera singers would receive sprays of them, gardeners would vie to procure their masters these much sought-after bulbs and Victorian ladies would take tea alongside beds full of the flowers. He would grow them in the glasshouse at the Botanic Gardens and he'd have a pot or two outside Patrick's house. The lily should be named after himself – *Lilium jacobensis* – or may be Namuunaa – *Lilium namuunensis*. He hummed her name to himself: Namuunaa, like a psalm. That God should have made a creature so beautiful and so practical . . . He wondered what her name meant. It would, he felt, be fitting, whatever it was.

Joseph did not understand women. His world had always been one composed exclusively of men: the warehouse, the church, Cambridge and Stonyhurst all masculine domains. Patrick O'Farrell's housekeeper at the church was a waxy-faced and embittered reed of a woman who disapproved of Patrick's generosity, which included his adoption of a street urchin, and ultimately she might have had a point, for Patrick bankrupted the church sending Joseph to Cambridge; and Jeremy's two stout, large-breasted sisters, who bundled him about the kitchen with floury hands, amused and frightened him in equal measure. In spite of his inexperience, or perhaps because of it, there was a part of him that longed for some feminine figure to be beside him, like a note of music that would lend a tone to his whole existence, not to feminize him, for he realized that some of his exploits – his painting and his interest in botany – could be regarded as feminine, but more as a Mary Magdalene figure: support without sex, guidance without rigidity, discipline without authority, all of which would allow the essential part of himself that revered and worshipped God to grow and flourish beneath this benevolent touch.

The trees had grown sparse, and in front of him stretched an alien meadow; the hillside was covered by clumps of giant rhubarb with shiny, thick pink prisms for stalks and large, glaucous leaves. The flowers stood out from the centre of these clusters, white bracts five feet tall. In between were twisted trees, apricot and apple, the fruit ripening like small and precious stones. On one side was a steep-sided gully, a crack hewn in the rocky slope at the bottom of which was a tiny stream that barely wet the red limestone. He saw a number of small birds and through the trees came a call that sounded remarkably like a cuckoo.

Joseph saw a flash of blue through the trees. He reined in the horse and peered through the branches. Barely feet away from him was a male pheasant but the bird was unlike any Joseph had seen before: its feathers were a brilliant azure. It had a cape of feathers that curled gently upwards at the tips and its shoulders were metallic purple. He held his breath. It was high-stepping through the glade in front of him, oblivious to his presence. In that diffuse grey dawn, the bird drew all the light into itself. The pistol was not really the ideal way to dispatch the bird but he was so close, it was worth a chance. He knew he should really get off his horse but he was afraid the bird would fly away. He eased off the safety catch. The horse flicked his ears in slight alarm. Joseph aimed at the bird's breast and was about to press the trigger when, before he could fire, there was a hissing and a snarling and a snow leopard leapt from its lair in a cascade of rocks barely two yards away and made a dash for the trees. Joseph swung the gun round to take aim at the leopard, but his horse was faster: he put his ears back and bolted in terror straight down the mountainside.

The gun flew from his hands and as it hit the ground exploded towards him. Joseph was flung backwards off the horse but his left leg remained stuck in the stirrup. The blast had momentarily deafened him and his head felt dense with a thick fog, his ears ringing. He tried to pull his leg from the stirrup as he was being dragged after the horse, scraping and bumping across the ground. As his ears stopped ringing, he managed to twist upright slightly. He felt blood wet and slick against his skin and pain suddenly flooded his body. He let out a scream that shocked him in its intensity and inhumanity. He realized that his leg had broken when he had been jerked from the horse. It was only a matter of time before the horse dragged him straight into a rock or a tree and smashed him unconscious. He tried to lean forwards to grasp the trailing lead rope. The pain in his leg was excruciating and the skin along the back of his good leg, his hands and his elbows was raw. Thank God he had worn his *del*. Even so, he felt as if the small stones and tree roots he was being dragged across were cracking every one of his ribs. By twisting himself round and doubling up, he was almost able to reach the reins when his horse veered round a large clump of rhubarb and he was dragged straight through it, the prickly leaves wiping against his face like sandpaper. He grabbed hold of the thick, sinewy stems and held on, seizing the entire cluster between his arms. He felt as if he were being stretched apart on a rack and screamed in agony as his broken leg twisted. His foot came loose from the stirrup and he was released. He rolled painfully out of the rhubarb. There was a thick trail of blood smeared over the grass above him.

After he had got his breath back, he looked at his thigh. His leg was at a stomach-churning angle and the flesh a raw, bloody, meaty mess where the bullet had grazed the surface and burned his skin. With difficulty he took off his *del* and tore strips from his undershirt. He wrapped them loosely round his bleeding hands, and one around his thigh. He managed to cover himself as best as he could with his *del* before he drifted out of consciousness.

When he awoke it was late afternoon. He felt like a creature without substance, as if he were made of air. He could drift between the boughs of the apricot, float into the blue range of mountains opposite. He watched tiny flies lit gold with sunlight swarm in clouds as if particles of air had been made corporeal.

Two hours later his head felt full of space, though his flesh and blood exterior was all too real. He had a raging thirst and was growing cold. He had lost some blood and he was beginning to shiver uncontrollably. He remembered the leopard. He could not defend himself – the gun was somewhere on the hillside. He tried to think rationally but the pain that ate away at his leg and seemed to dart into the small of his back caused him to clench his teeth and shake. Water was out of the question; even if he could drag himself to the stream, he would not be able to climb down the steep rocky sides. He knew that he was unlikely to see the night through if he lay at the end of a trail of blood directly outside a leopard's lair. He half sat up, grinding his teeth as his vision swung into blackness and his stomach lurched. He dragged himself slowly towards one of the fruit trees. By pushing his good foot against the base of the tree and holding the trunk with both hands, he was able to inch himself into a standing position. He used his penknife to half saw through two of the straightest branches until the green wood had split enough to allow him to break them away. He broke or hacked off all the side branches. He tried eating one of the apples but it was so new and bitter he spat it out. It made his teeth feel as if they were coated in fur. Joseph tore a few more strips from his shirt and strapped the straighter of the branches to his shattered leg. Using the other branch as a crutch, he tried to hobble back up the hill. He blacked out for a few moments and had to cling to the tree for support. The sudden movement caused fresh blood to well from the wound on his leg and blossom across his makeshift bandage. There was no sign of his runaway horse.

Agonizingly slowly, he made his way back up the hill. He focused on the next tree, willed himself to make it, just two more yards, a few more steps. Once at the tree, he rested and wiped the sweat from his face before choosing another goal, another target a little further up the slope. It was well past nightfall by the time he found his horse. Shaking with pain, he rested against the animal, which started and would have bolted if he had not managed to grab the reins. He could not put any weight on his leg, so he leaned over the back of the horse – thanking God that it was so small – gripped its mane and swung his good leg over his back. Sitting upright caused a fresh outburst of pain. It seemed to have taken root and flowered in the base of his brain –

red and magenta with vivid streaks of blue that blinded him. The horse darted forward as if wishing to be rid of his rider. Joseph clung on desperately, his hands buried in the animal's mane. He could only hope and pray that this horse, which he could not control, for his legs were useless, would take him back.

When he woke he thought he must be lying on the forest floor – it was so comfortable and there was a sweet smell of pine. But then he moved slightly and the pain came flooding back. He winced and Mendo's face appeared above his own, looking down at him anxiously.

He could hear the crackle of a fire burning. He was bathed in cold sweat and his vision swung in and out of focus.

Have I lost my soul yet? he managed to ask. His lips felt as if they would crack if he spoke too much.

Mendo smiled weakly. You are in Namuunaa's house. She and her mother will take care of you.

Her house?

Yes, the villagers have houses made of wood for the winter. We found you in the woods and you were nearer the house than the *gers*.

My trusty steed did not succeed in carrying me home?

No, but your horse was covered in blood. We thought a leopard had caught him.

Joseph smiled. Nearly did, nearly did.

Mendo fetched a damp rag and wiped his forehead. He helped him into a sitting position and gave him a bowl of yak butter tea. Joseph gagged.

You must eat something.

I am too tired.

You have been feverish for days. We thought you might not make it. You are still sick, and weak, but you will live.

That's reassuring, said Joseph, taking a sip of the tea.

I presume you were attempting to shoot a bird.

I was.

Maybe you will listen to me in the future. Lie down now. Try to rest.

I did not manage to gather the lilies, Mendo. I do not have the lilies.

We have waited long enough, Joseph.

The voice seemed to be coming to him in a dream.

We must leave.

You are leaving me? he whispered.

You are too weak to travel. Your leg needs to heal. We shall come back for you, Joseph, Tsem and I, we will return in the spring.

You are leaving me.

Tell me what you want me to do with the plants.

In his dream he thought about what needed to be done. He thought: The seeds are all in individual packets of paper; they have to be kept dry in a tarps envelope with silica salts to draw the moisture from the air. Keep the plants damp. Take them all to an acquaintance in Pekin – Delaware, an Englishman – tell him he needs to make a herbarium – a big glass box for the plants – and then ship everything back to the Botanical Gardens in Bristol. All the rest, my paintings, notebooks, my equipment, I can keep with me. Delaware must tell Patrick, must tell Patrick.

He sat up suddenly. You are leaving me, abandoning me here in this wilderness.

But there was no one there. Embers from a small fire were glowing in the hearth and by his bed was a bowl of water and some cold tea. A chink of light came in from under the door and the windows, which were firmly covered with layers of felt. There was no other light. It was very still and very silent. It could be mid-winter for all he knew. Had they left him up here in this mountain hut to die? His leg was throbbing so badly it set his teeth on edge. He did not even want to look at it. He lay down again.

When he sailed into Bristol it was fine and sunny. He stood at the prow of the boat with the wind in his hair, blowing away the fresh, iodine scent of the sea, bringing him the smell of the city: roasting coffee, rotting fruit, manure, sewage, the faint tang of the estuary, oiled ropes and brewer's yeast. They sailed through the Avon Gorge, the cliffs glazed blood orange and gold in the evening light, the sun glowing along the fine arc of Royal York Terrace. They swung round the corner and up past the docks, the chandlers, the shipyard, the warehouses, past Harvey's Bristol Cream, into the heart of the city where the seabirds screamed a raucous welcome. There was St Mary's to his left. He waited impatiently for the pedestrian bridge to lift so that they could sail through and moor and he was first in line, running down the gangplank even as it was being lowered. He dodged crates of rum and sugar from Barbados, and sacks of cotton from Africa, past knots of sailors and horses and carts, down a narrow alleyway and into the coffee yard where the beans were piled high in shiny stacks like beads waiting for an abacus.

Father! he called. Father, I am returned. And look what I have with me – from the land of Genghis Khan – a lily, Father, a perfect, white lily.

The warehouse was deserted. The machines still. The fires dead. Not a soul to be seen. And when he put his hand in his rucksack, he felt, not bulbs as smooth and fertile as eggs, but dust, only dust that crumbled between his fingers.

You are, at heart, a pagan, whispered Jeremy in his ear. Do you not realize that evolution and God are not compatible? Listen to what the Reverend Sedgwick says in his sermon: If the book be true, the labours of sober induction are in vain; religion is a lie, human law is a mass of folly, and a base injustice; morality is moonshine; our labours for the black people of Africa were works of madmen; and man and woman are only better beasts.

Better beasts? Is that what you want, Joseph, is that what you believe?

Charles Darwin, who was seated on his other side, leaned forward and said sadly, My dear Joseph, it pains me to say this, but I cannot persuade myself that a beneficent and omnipotent God would have designedly created the *Ichneumonidae* with the express intention of their feeding within the live bodies of caterpillars or that a cat should play with mice.

You see? asked Jeremy. You see? Even he is struggling with God's existence. No good will come of it, Joseph, no good, lad.

No. Joseph shook his head. It is not like that. It was not what he meant; do you not see? Mr Darwin is speaking in favour of evolution and for God.

He turned towards the Reverend Sedgwick to elicit his support but he had become Benjamin Disraeli, who leaned back and hooked his thumbs in his waistcoat.

He gave a supercilious smile and said, Really, Joseph, you must read the Revelations; it is all explained. Aha! I see this was a section you neglected at the seminary. You see, what is most interesting is the way in which man has been developed. You know, all is development. The principle is perpetually going on, have you noticed, Joseph? First there was nothing, then there was something; then, I forget the next, I think we were shells, then fishes; then we come, let me see, did we come next? Ah, are you trying to tell me something? Never mind that; we came at last. And the next change will be something very superior to us, something with wings. Ah! That's it; we were fishes, and I believe we shall be crows. What do you think of that, Joseph? Wherein lies your God? Will we sprout wings – ape to angel, is that how it goes?

Once, the longest time ago, the Buddha was giving each of the twelve years in the Mongolian calendar the attributes of an animal. He had got to the eleventh year and he was struggling to think which animal should be the final one. Now the mouse and the camel had not been mentioned and they both wanted to have a year named after them. The two animals came to the Buddha and they each argued why they should be chosen.

In his dream-like state, Joseph heard the story wash over him as Namuunaa told it to Lena.

The Buddha listened carefully to them. They were both correct in their way and he did not want to offend one by choosing the other.

So he said, You two must decide between you who is to be chosen for the twelfth year.

The camel and the mouse looked at each other and they decided that they would have a contest.

I know, said the mouse, whomsoever sees the sun first will have the year named after him.

It is agreed, said the camel.

The two animals waited anxiously for the dawn, straining to see the first rays of light, their eyes half closed with tiredness. The camel had chosen to face east and the tiny mouse, perched on the camel's back, faced west. As the sun rose, one ray of light bounced off a snow-capped west-facing mountain.

The mouse shouted out, I see the sun.

The mouse had won but the camel was so outraged, for the camel knew that the sun rises in the east, that he chased the mouse. The mouse, fearing for his life, hid in a pile of ashes. The camel rolled and stamped all over the ashes attempting to kill the little mouse. Even to this day, whenever a camel sees some ashes, he will roll and snort and stamp all over them.

The mouse had won the contest so the Buddha named the twelfth year after him. But he felt sorry for the camel, so he told the camel that he would be represented in the whole of the Mongolian calendar, for he would possess one feature belonging to all twelve animals. The Buddha has kept his word because the camel has:

the ears of the Mouse
the stomach of the Cow
the paws of the Tiger
the nose of the Hare
the body of the Dragon
the eyes of the Snake
the mane of the Horse
the wool of the Sheep
the hump of the Ape
the head-crest of the Rooster
the crooked back leg of the Dog
and the tail of the Pig.

And to this day, the camel is very happy. What animal are you, Joseph, what kind of creature are you?

An old woman leaned towards Joseph. Her eyes were deep blue-grey and her skin was like pressed rose petals, fine and fragile with faint creases. She was holding the hollowed skull of a young child in the palm of her hand, and anointing his lips and forehead and temple with the dark and bitter brew contained therein. She muttered to herself slowly, softly, and dipped only the middle finger of her right hand in the potion.

This is my mother, Joseph, Uugantsetseg, said Namuunaa, coming out of the shadows. Do you not recall seeing her? You had a fever; she has been calling the fever like a dark spirit from your body. When it leaves, you will be well.

He could taste it now, an essence of plant sap, a green astringency settling on his tongue, tightening his skin.

The cabin was full of people, their faces half carved by fire-light, and the old woman, Uugantsetseg, was there too, but this time her dark eyes were glazed, and she was wearing a black dress sewn with many scraps of mirror and a headdress of eagle feathers. She was beating a small drum and twisting and spinning in front of him and his heart clenched in his throat. The tiny mirrors flashed firelight, filled with the watchers' eyes, the wound in his leg ached and throbbed in time with her drum beat. She was chanting but in an ancient tongue that seemed to him to speak of primeval events from a time when there were no words; harsh as the sound of chemical fusion, molten metals, liquid rock: the raw begin-nings of life. Uugan spun faster and faster, a tiny, thin woman, drawn tall and stretched beyond her limits by greater forces.

She collapsed against the watching people and spoke for several minutes. Her eyes were bulging grotesquely and there was foam at the corners of her mouth. Namuunaa was somewhere; he could hear her quiet, calm voice, like the still depths of water below a river of flames. He was unable to make out what she was saying – she was too far away and he could not focus his mind – but she appeared to be translating her mother's utterances, for sometimes the watching people spoke out in consternation or sighed in unison.

Behind his eyelids were starbursts of blood and cymbals clashing. He felt her breath on his neck and she said, though he knew not in what language, The devil has left you, Joseph, the *gurtum* has gone.

*

The next morning – and he was sure it was the next morning for there were shards of mirrored glass and many empty *airag* containers on the wooden floor – he felt wonderfully refreshed as if he had slept deeply for hours. There was a loud snoring coming from the bed next to him. Uugan was lying flat on her back in a blue felt dress, her mouth wide open, making an awful racket. She was a wizened walnut of a woman with clear skin the colour and translucency of an opal, a button of a nose and cheeks like wild plums, bright and sour. His leg was still sore and he could not rest his weight on it for long, but he was able to get out of bed and hobble around the cabin. At first he was quiet about his movements but he soon perceived it would make no difference to her what he did.

As well as the two beds there was a cot and at the other end of the cabin was a stone hearth with cooking implements and wooden stools around it. Though spartan and entirely hewn of wood, there was an opulent feel to Namuunaa's home: a thick woven rug, almost Persian in appearance, and large silk cushions were spread across the floor. Embroidered tapestries hung against two of the walls; the third was almost entirely covered by his flower paintings, glued on with resin. He pulled back the heavy felt coverings from the window and let the breeze sweep away the stale air. He peered in one of the small fragments of mirror. The sight shocked him and reminded him of an intrepid female explorer who had said that it only took a couple of days for men to wilt like unattended pot plants in the wilderness. He'd had several days – maybe even weeks – to wilt. He had lost much of the colour he had gained by living outdoors, his cheeks were sunken, his eyes were shadowed and webbed by deep lines, and his face was covered with the beginnings of a ragged beard. He smelled of wood smoke, mutton grease and the sour tang of sweat.

Outside, the hills sloped gently away and he could see that the glorious spread of mountain flowers were past their best and that many were beginning to set seed. In the forests below the odd tree was a darker green tinged with gold – larches or birches on the verge of losing their summer colour. A wave of bitterness welled up for one moment at the time he had lost and he felt that familiar cold pressure grip his heart when he thought of Patrick, alone at home, wondering what had become of his adopted son.

But he thanked God he was safe and well. In one corner of the cabin was his luggage. He unpacked his razor, a towel and a change of clothes and limped outside. As he opened the door the wolf, which had been lying there, stood up. Joseph stepped back involuntarily. She had grown bigger and leaner and had lost some of her puppyish look. She stretched out her nose and licked his hand. Getting down the single step from the front door was a difficult operation that served to remind him he should go easy.

Half a mile down the slope were another couple of log huts, and in between was a stream. He found the largest, deepest pool and immersed himself in the bitingly cold water. He unwrapped the bandage and examined his leg. The wound had healed without infection although the scar tissue was a livid pink. His leg appeared remarkably straight but he still could not put any weight on it. Every bone in his ribcage seemed to be sticking out and his muscles had wasted away. In disgust, he pulled his trousers back on, and sat down by the river to shave.

He'd almost finished when Lena rode over. She slid down from her horse and looked with interest at the skin emerging beneath his razor. She pointed to the pot strapped behind her saddle. It was full of yak butter tea, still warm; there were some curds. He was starving. He quickly finished shaving and then hobbled back to the house with Lena, using the palomino to support his weight. Uugan was still snoring loudly. Lena giggled when she saw her. The child sat opposite Joseph watching him eat.

Where is your mother?

With the yaks. It's milking time.

She will come here?

Lena nodded. Later.

He was exhausted when he'd finished and felt almost faint. He ruffled the child's hair and she made a face at him. He lay back down and must have drifted off because when he came to he had the impression of a lot of people in the cabin again. He sat up quickly, intending to tell them they need not try to exorcize the spirits from him again – but the old lady was still flat out, snoring.

Lena, Namuunaa, two dark-haired girls who looked like twins, and a young couple, presumably the girls' parents, were by the fire. They looked over as Joseph sat up.

Can you rise? asked Namuunaa, coming towards him.

Yes, he has washed already, said Lena. I was watching him.

She put her hand over her mouth and giggled. Namuunaa helped him over to the fire. The two villagers nodded at him and smiled shyly. Tsend, said Namuunaa, indicating the young woman, and Boshigt. Boshigt was whittling a piece of wood. He stood up and placed it next to Joseph. He realized it was going to be a crutch and smiled.

Bayarlaa, bayarlaa.

It's a pleasure.

Boshigt grinned back, and measured the crutch against Joseph's armpit. There was a second one on the floor which he marked up too.

Namuunaa helped him prop himself up on cushions, fetched them slices of dried apple and poured tea made from herbs, minty and fragrant. It seemed, as she hovered on the edge of his vision, stirring the tea over the fire, cradling the small bowls in her hands before passing them on, arranging the apples, that he knew each of her movements by heart. He felt, almost before it happened, her hold up the bowl and breathe its scent deeply before taking the first sip. The house seemed infused with her spirit. He saw the ghost of her past, drifting across the room, hanging up his paintings, bringing in firewood, chopping up herbs for his poultice. It was as if her presence had been burned into his unconscious while he was sick. He could feel the weight of her cool hand against his forehead.

Namuunaa and Tsend were talking about the yaks. One of the herd was ill and Namuunaa was trying to work out what might be wrong with it. Boshigt quietly continued to whittle the crutches and Lena and the twins played with a couple of dolls in the corner. Uugan was still snoring.

You could take her up to the high pasture past the three streams and let her graze there for a day.

The shavings of wood peeled away in small spirals and thick curls the colour of beeswax. It was cherry wood: the chips of bark glowed metallic red in the firelight and the smell was sweet, almost syrupy. Joseph prayed under his breath, thanking God for his recovery, asking forgiveness for his silence.

Over the next few days Joseph began to realize how much Namuunaa had taken on when she agreed to nurse him back to health. She was still living in the *ger* with Lena. The yaks had to be rounded up and milked twice a day, and butter, cheese, curds and vodka made from the milk. She spun wool from their thick winter coats, as well as gathering herbs and firewood and checking her small flock of sheep. When he'd been ill she'd ridden up to the log cabin twice a day to wash him, give him tea and dress his wound. Now that he was healing, there was no need. She came up once in the evening and brought him a meal as well as cheese and tea for him to have during the day. She fetched water from the stream and brought him more wood. At night he remembered her touch against his thigh, firm yet gentle. He was impatient, annoyed that his leg still pained him, that he was not strong enough to fetch water, that the crutches hurt his arms, that he still needed to sleep during the day. He felt starved of human company; he waited restlessly for her to appear, and was frustrated that there was little he might do to fill his time. He read his Bible and prayed, but his mind was apt to wander. He did sit-ups and chin-ups and press-ups to regain his strength. He learned lists of words and whole sentences in Mongolian that she had left for him the night before. She and her mother, being the elders in the village, were the only people who could read and write, he discovered. He watched the last of the summer pass before him with something akin to desperation.

One evening Namuunaa brought his horse back; Mendo had left him the dun with the wild black stripes. She'd lengthened the left stirrup with string so that he could ride.

Try to control him with your legs, she said, pushing his thigh against the saddle. It will be good for your muscles.

Now he was able to fetch water and firewood, using the horse as support, or piling the wood high in the saddle and limping back, leaning on his withers. He gathered seeds from the meadow flowers that were fast ending their short lives. Around the house stood large sunflowers with russet and flame-yellow petals, which started to wither as the centre of the flowers prickled with the growth of milky seeds, and behind the cabin bitter gourds and small squash swelled, pregnant with burgeoning flesh. For some reason, Namuunaa had strung hundreds of the white lily flowers together and long strings of them hung under the eaves to dry. Some days he could smell them, a powder version of the richness of their fresh scent.

Towards the end of September, he rode out one morning. Thistledown and spider silk drifted through the pale, chill morning air and he reined his horse to a stop as a flock of geese flew across the bleached sky, the first migrants returning home. It felt like a personal bereavement.

A few days later he was hauling water from the stream, gritting his teeth at the pain in his leg and his general ineptness, when the dun whinnied. Over the brow of the hill came a stamping cavalcade of yaks, their bells ringing, manes adorned by bright bows. Three of them were roped together, laden with large, white bundles, secured by rope. On top of this precarious load were lashed a number of red poles and a huge wheel. Joseph realized with a start that it was the internal spines and circular top section of a *ger*. Behind the yaks were Lena and Namuunaa on her white horse and the roan. She held up one arm, and he could imagine her wide smile and the way her eyes glowed in the autumn light like the warm edge of the sea.

He put down the water and rode over to greet them.

You are moving back up here? he asked, unable to hide the delight in his voice.

Lena made a face. It's too early, she said crossly. No one else is coming.

It is a little early but soon the others will be here too.

Namuunaa dismounted and tied the three yaks to the log cabin. The rest of the herd fanned out to graze. Joseph attempted to help her untie the bags from the horses, but his crutches kept falling out from under his arms and he struggled to pick them up.

Namuunaa laughed. Go back to fetching the water; we shall be all right.

I can't leave you to do this by yourself.

You don't have to, said Lena, still grouchy.

She was right: within a few minutes, Boshigt, another young man from the village, Batbaatar, and two elderly brothers, Delger and Amgalan, rode up with the rest of Namuunaa's possessions and her sheep, shepherded by Wolf.

In a very short space of time everything was unloaded, unpacked and in its rightful place. Joseph built up the fire and boiled a large pot of water for tea, perceiving that this was going to be his only useful contribution.

Delger passed him a small bottle beautifully carved from coral so that he might take a pinch of snuff to stop him, Delger said, from becoming too much like a wife.

The only thing missing, thought Joseph as he looked around, was Bird, the eagle.

Shall I fetch him? asked Joseph.

She knew instantly what he meant and hesitated for only a fraction of a second. She handed him her gloves.

Amgalan whistled and slapped his thigh. Delger grinned and looked at him with raised eyebrows over the pipe he was slowly filling.

He's a one-woman bird, he said.

I will be back in the space of one kettle, said Joseph, glad at last to be able to use his newly learned idiom.

Two, said Batbaatar.

Three, added Boshigt and laid down a tiny silver coin to start off the bet.

Joseph left his crutches outside the door and took Namuunaa's horse. He had not ridden as far as her *ger* since his accident and the horse was nervy under its ungainly new rider. Moreover, he could not put his left foot in the stirrup, for the leather strap was not long enough. He let his leg hang loose and controlled the horse with his leg muscles as he'd been practising. Eventually the horse settled down and they proceeded at a choppy trot down the mountain.

The grass where the tent had been was etiolated and flattened; the bird was perched at the edge of this white circle, blind to the world. He turned his head in Joseph's direction as he rode towards it. Namuunaa must have left the hood over him so that he would not become frightened while they were taking down the *ger*. Without getting off the horse, he leaned over and undid the eagle's jesses. Holding them between his fingers, he put his fist against the great, curved talons. Bird tilted his head on one side, opened his beak and hissed at him. He stroked the bird's chest feathers and then applied a little force, enough to push the eagle slightly off balance. He raised his wings, still hissing at him, but then stepped forward on to his gloved hand, squeezing with his talons. Joseph lifted the bird on to the back of the horse and rested his arm on the support built into Namuunaa's saddle. He was glad of it, for the eagle was heavy. He wrapped the jesses more securely round his wrist and urged the horse on. The eagle remained with his wings slightly open as if unbalanced by this mode of transport and uncertain of Joseph but he talked quietly to the bird and shortly he settled down.

The eagle's winter perch was next to the food store – a small version of the log cabin with racks and wooden hooks for dried meat and curds. Bird's section was like a porch, the roof extended over his perch, and it was enclosed on three sides, allowing the eagle to look out down the mountain. Joseph slid down from the horse and attempted to swing the eagle on to the perch. Bird, perhaps realizing that this was his last bid for freedom, stretched out his wings. Joseph leaned against the wall and spoke to the creature, stroking his back until he was still. He held his fist near the perch so the huge, curved talons touched it, and the bird walked on to it voluntarily. He tied him by his jesses and then slowly, smoothing his feathers all the while, undid the hood and eased it off. The eagle shook himself and glared at him with one golden, baleful eye as if accusing him of deception. He winked each eye closed, one at a time, the lids scaly and reptilian. It was a creature from an ancient time; he wondered whether Darwin had ever been stared down by an eagle and, if he had, what thoughts he might then have had about the struggle for existence and the ultimate survival of the ultimate killing machine.

Two kettles! said Batbaatar, when he limped in. I win!

Joseph was uncertain what Batbaatar had actually won, but the four men were clearly in good spirits, having drunk all the tea and moved on to their usual concoction of alcoholic milk.

Sain bainaa, he said, nodding to Namuunaa, before easing himself on to a stool near the fire.

Delger seized him by the chin and twisted his face this way and that.

He still has both his eyes, he said before releasing him.

Amgalan said, Namuunaa was just about to tell us the story of why the wasp lost its tongue.

It's a tale about Khan-Garid, the ancestor of all eagles, explained Delger.

He's so big, when he flies his wings hide the sun and the moon, said Lena, coming to sit next to him. She folded her doll on her lap and looked expectantly over at her mother.

Who will look after the stew if I am to tell the story? asked Namuunaa.

The two elderly brothers both pointed at Joseph and giggled like schoolboys. Namuunaa gave him a long-handled spoon and a bunch of herbs to throw in the pot. She sat down on a big cushion next to Lena, and began.

A long time ago when the world was very young, Khan-Garid was hungry. He called the swallow and the wasp to him and he said to them, From now on, I only want to eat the tastiest meat there is. I want you to fly around and taste all the animals and tell me which one has the sweetest blood. He commanded the wasp and the swallow to report back to him the next night.

Off flew the wasp and the swallow. But it was a sunny day and the swallow darted and swooped, flew high, flew low, and he forgot all about Khan-Garid and his request. But the wasp, he flew everywhere and he bit every animal he could find, like this.

Namuunaa demonstrated the painful sting of the wasp on her daughter who curled up and giggled.

When the sun set and it became dark, the swallow remembered Khan-Garid's terrible command and he became anxious.

Wasp, he said, have you managed to find out which animal tastes the best of all?

Indeed I have, replied the wasp, and of all the animals in the world, the human being tastes the best.

Now the swallow was even more concerned because he did not like to think of Khan-Garid eating people. So he said to the wasp, How do you know that people taste the best of all?

Why, said the wasp, because I tasted their blood with my tongue.

Is that so? said the swallow. You must have a very long tongue.

Oh, I have, said the wasp, look, and he stuck out his tongue.

As fast as a flash of lightning, the swallow darted in and pecked out the wasp's tongue. Before the wasp could react, the great Khan-Garid summoned the two animals before him.

Well, wasp, he said, have you found the sweetest meat on earth for me?

The wasp could not speak for he had no tongue. He could only fly round Khan-Garid making a whining buzz. Khan-Garid was annoyed and he sent the wasp away because he could not understand what the wasp was trying to say. He turned to the swallow and he said. Now, swallow, have you discovered the sweetest meat on earth?

I have indeed, said the swallow, it is the snake.

And Khan-Garid thanked the swallow and said that from this day onwards he would only eat snakes.

And do eagles still eat snakes? asked Lena sleepily.

Some of them do, said Namuunaa, and wasps still cannot talk and give us nasty stings. Time for bed, little one.

I don't want to go to bed.

Namuunaa picked her up and carried her over to the cot at the far end of the cabin and Joseph remembered that he was supposed to be stirring the stew.

I will help you.

She looked at him. It was a long, slow appraisal, then she smiled and he felt his face light up with hers. She gave him a pail and a small stool which he carried, one under each arm.

She asked him to wait outside the log cabin and, mounting her horse in one fluid movement, she rode away. He sat on the stool with his crutches stretched out before him and waited. The valley was shrouded in a thick blanket of blue-white mist. It hung in thin curtains diffusing the sun's glare into a soft, golden glaze. Namuunaa rode back with Bird at the hooves of her yak herd, and tied the females to a rail a few yards away from the food store. She waved for him to come over.

Milking the yaks was not quite as easy as it looked. The black and white female he tried first had large teats and she was able to withhold milk from his clumsy fingers. Even though she was tied up, she still moved about, which meant he had to shift the stool in order to reach her udders and her coat was so long he couldn't see what he was doing when he leaned his head against her hot flanks. His hands were aching by the time he'd managed to extract half a pail from the animal; Namuunaa had already milked all the others. She stood over him and watched for a minute and then she crouched down next to him and put her hands over his, showing him how to squeeze exactly right, how the rhythm should run. Her hands were hard and strong, the skin the colour of coffee and cream. There was a sudden loss of warmth when she let go. She stayed by his side, checking his performance until the pail was full. She took the milk from him as soon as he'd finished and poured it into an urn with all the rest. He would have protested that he could do it, but she was right not to let him; struggling with the crutches as well would only have resulted in spilled milk.

She really was a strange and wondrous creature, he thought, so strong and beautiful, vibrant, full of energy and delight. One moment she was aloof, the next she was singing and dancing with Lena; sometimes she was mysterious, and at others she was practical; one minute serious, the next frivolous. At times she was acutely aware of him, almost hypersensitive to his presence, and at other times she was oblivious. She had taken no notice of him in the last few days since she and Lena had come back to the cabin, in the sense that she did what she had to do and his wishes were of no account, or at least, she did not seek to consult him. In many ways he found it curious; he had, after all, been travelling with men whose purpose was to fulfil his needs and desires, yet it was oddly liberating and meant that there was little awkwardness in their sudden proximity. Of course, he reasoned, there was no need for her to change – it was her house, her child she had to care for, her animals she needed to tend and he was, at best, a burden. He felt as if she were a great, sleek cat that played and hunted, basked in front of the fire and prowled in the night and yet he thought a cat would be more predictable to a man who studied science than this woman. She might be the subject of a life-long experiment and still one might not fathom her, nor find the rules that could predict the vagaries of her internal climate.

Sometimes at night he woke sweating, his body reliving her touch when he was ill. He had, he felt, put a lot of faith in Mendo, hoping that Mendo had explained who he was and what his values were. It would be awkward to begin now, especially as she gave no clear signs that he was anything other than a creature to be healed, certainly not a man. He wondered, as he limped after her, if he had ever felt like a man, if he even knew how the vast majority of men felt.

He thought of Darwin's comment on the genders, how in most cases there must be a struggle between males for possession of females.

He had written:

> The most vigorous individuals, or those which have most successfully struggled with their conditions of life, will generally leave most progeny. But success will often depend on having special weapons or means of defence, or on the charms of the males.

He smiled to himself as he tried to think what a man's charms might be.

The next time the yaks needed milking he did not ask her, but took the heavy wooden stick from her to churn the milk into cheese. She let him and it felt, not quite a gift, but at least an acknowledgement. It was time-consuming, hard physical work – good for his arm muscles, which were gradually building back up, although he was still painfully thin.

About an hour later Lena came over. She put her hands on her hips and stuck out her portly belly.

Where's my mamma?

She's cutting grass. He couldn't remember the Mongolian word for hay.

Cutting grass? Cutting grass? She screwed up her face. That's a stupid thing to do.

For the animals. For winter.

Oh. Making hay, silly.

Making hay, he repeated after her like a child and she giggled at his accent.

Look at this cheese – do you think it's ready?

He lifted her up to peer in the urn. She stuck her finger out to taste a little bit, and then wiggled to be put down.

I don't know, do I? I'm only five.

What is five plus one? he asked, continuing with the churning. The milk had separated into curds and grown very sticky; he was sweating heavily.

That's a silly question.

No, it's not. Come with me and I'll show you something.

She waited until the last possible minute and then ran after him. He pulled off one of the heads of the sunflowers and scattered the seeds on the front step. He sat down next to her and counted out five seeds, and then added one more.

Four, five, six.

Six. Do another one.

Three plus two. Count out three seeds first.

And so he found a way of repaying Namuunaa to some extent. In the mornings after they had milked the yaks, he would make tea with the hot, fresh milk and wake Lena. For the rest of the morning he gave her lessons. As well as occupying his time, it made him feel useful. There was another unexpected benefit. Up until then Lena had treated him with a mixture of contempt and guarded affection. She quite clearly missed her father, or a father figure, but had been used to being with her mother by herself and was jealous of anything less than her undivided attention. She didn't always want to learn, but the mixture of play and education made her calmer and better able to accept him as a person who was not a threat. When Namuunaa wasn't around she hugged him and held his hand, although as soon as her mother reappeared, she would neither touch him nor listen to him.

Around midday he took an hour out to pray and in the afternoons explored the area, finding seeds and digging up bulbs. He thought about Darwin and his ingenious experiments into which his whole household were co-opted, boiling pigeons, breeding hens, collecting orchids. Even when he was ill he lay in his bed and watched the way climbers grew, recording the growth of tendrils from sweet peas, cucumbers, passion fruit vines, logging their green scrolls and curlicues. Just before Joseph left for Mongolia, Darwin had published *On the Sexual Relations of the Three Forms of Lythrum salicaria*. He'd bred wild purple loosestrife in his gardens and greenhouses. He'd noted what no one else had, namely that the female stigma was tall, medium or short and that there were two types of male pollen-producing stamen. If the female stigma was tall, the male stamens on the same plant were either medium or short. Darwin came up with eighteen possible sexual combinations. He brushed pollen from every size of stamen on to every size of stigma. Laboriously he counted out the seeds that resulted from his artificial crosses, and attempted to grow them to test their fertility. He found that only six types of marriage were viable and that crossing tall stamens with short stigmata from the same plant resulted in sterile offspring. Another one of nature's ways of ensuring cross-pollination.

He wrote of the loosestrife:

Nature has ordained a most complex marriage-arrangement, namely a triple union between three hermaphrodites, – each hermaphrodite being in its female organ quite distinct from the other two hermaphrodites and partially distinct in its male organs, and each furnished with two sets of males.

Joseph tried to be back in time for milking. Once he'd helped Namuunaa he sometimes sketched or mixed up pigments so that Lena could paint too. He was in a way content, though contentment sat oddly with him. He was also perturbed that his God was so quiet. It was not that He had deserted him, but the deep certitude that God was there, with him at every waking, living, breathing moment, had diminished. When he tried to visualize his exercises from the Bible, questions about what to teach Lena next, and how to make her lessons fun, intruded; or else a deep stillness descended, an image of the mountain ranges fading like old photographs into the horizon and the wide arc of blue sky that encompassed all filled his mind. His prayer had become unfocused, lacking in clarity, though his mind was in every other respect as sharp as usual.

The yaks' breath hung in a cloud around him. The first frost of winter had rimmed the grass with a dull steel edge.

I should like to visit the lily valley today. I need to collect the bulbs.

He limped over to the urn with the pail of milk. He was able to walk without crutches now, though he normally used one, for his leg was still weak.

Will you come?

He turned back to look at her. This morning she was wearing black trousers and a blue and white dress embroidered with coral beads and tiny mirrors and her hair was pulled back into a long sleek plait.

Yes, I will go with you.

He went back into the house and swept the ashes from the hearth, built up a fire and put a pot of milk and tea on to boil. Namuunaa was still outside with the yaks. Lena was curled up in bed like a small hibernating animal. He carried her still half asleep in his arms over to the fire, where he dressed her as she yawned and stretched. When Namuunaa came back in, they crouched by the fire waiting for the tea to boil and she combed the thick tangles out of Lena's hair. At times like this he suddenly seemed to see himself as if from another perspective, looking down from above, and it was with amusement, and then a cold chill that he realized how much they looked like a small family. It was almost with a shiver that he passed Lena a bowl of water so that she could wash.

The others will be here soon. Maybe in the next few days.

Good, good, he managed to say, though he was reluctant to lose this time with Namuunaa. It seemed to him that they were isolated, thrown together in the wilderness and that all they had was each other. It was a fanciful exaggeration, he knew, but the appearances of it would be spoiled if the rest of the tribe moved back up the mountains. They had learned to live with each other, after a fashion, but he felt as if they were intimate strangers. They were on the brink of something – he did not know quite what – perhaps a truer friendship, but that fragile bond might not even form if they were disturbed. He was placing so much on to her fine shoulders, treating her as if she were a key that would unlock the door to a greater understanding of the experience of

Mongolia, a deeper knowledge of what women were, and a keener perception of God's other face. And he still did not know who or what this woman was other than that she lay in the palm of his hand like a bright gem, ultimately precious, unfeasibly durable, shape-shifting contrary to all laws of physics even as he watched.

The tea was boiling. She ladled out bowls and added a lump of the hard cheese to each one.

Why do you want the bulbs? She looked him directly in the eye and there was a challenge in her voice.

To grow them in England. We don't have any flowers like them – nothing quite so beautiful.

And it is their beauty that interests you?

Yes, and their rarity.

They are special.

I know.

I mean, they can affect you in a certain way.

Like a herb?

Like a herb.

How? What do they do?

She drank some tea, not looking at him, and then said, You will not take many.

He was not sure if it was a question or a statement.

No, he said.

He had been looking for plants and returned late. The first stars were coming out, an early promise of the great swathe that would carpet the night sky. Even from a distance he could tell that something was different. He thought at first it was simply one of the village gatherings but as he drew closer he could not hear any voices, only the slow beat of a drum. He limped as fast as he could towards the house.

All the village were there, seated in a semicircle around the fire. Boshigt took his arm and pulled him down on the edge of the circle. One of the women threw a handful of juniper berries and pine needles on to the fire which hissed and cracked. The scent filled the room. In the centre of the room was a woman. She was wearing a midnight-blue dress covered with mirrors and tiny bells and a headdress of eagle feathers turned back to front so that the beak curved from the back of her head, and the feathers covered her face. She was slowly beating a drum which she held in one hand with a wooden stave. At first he thought it was Uugan, but she was too tall and slender and then he realized with a start that it must be Namuunaa. Boshigt passed him some vodka and he took a long, slow sip.

Now she began to beat the drum a little faster and as she did, she spun in a circle. The tempo of the drum increased and she whirled with ever increasing speed and gradually she began to sing. It did not appear as if she were singing in words; it was a high-pitched hum that came from the depths of her being. It was not her voice though the sound emanated from her. The villagers watched mesmerized. As she slowed down, the villagers leaned forward and placed sweetmeats and small bowls of *airag* on a makeshift altar that had been erected by the fire; as she spun faster, they drew back. He looked at her face, but he could see nothing beneath the broad, gold-brown and black feathers. Her eyes, when he did catch a glimpse of them, were black and blank; implacable as an animal's. He felt as if he were slipping, falling, being sucked into the smell of mountain flowers and vodka, his heart quivering in time with the drum, his ears ringing with the flashing bells. She had been an anchor to him in this strange and alien place where he had been left without his men, without links to his own society and the ties that had bound him to his home. Now he was cast adrift with nothing solid beneath him. He staggered to his feet, his mind light with alcohol, and pushed his way through the incense, the thickening sound and out into the cold night air.

Namuunaa said fifty bulbs would be quite sufficient. Joseph wanted to take more – there were plenty in this valley; his trowel hit at least one every time he sank it into the earth – but there was something that appealed to him about taking only a few samples of such a rarity. They counted them together and once their hands touched accidentally, fleetingly.

Lena pointed her podgy finger at the bulbs and counted too.

. . . ten, eleven, thirteen, fifteen, thirty, twenty-one.

Three and three, Lena?

Lena was about to work out the addition using the bulbs, but Namuunaa wrapped them up. She counted her fingers instead.

Don't touch your eyes, Namuunaa said. We should wash our hands as soon as possible.

Joseph's fingers were stained a light nicotine from handling the bulbs. His hands smelled of an acidic musk.

The last leaves clung to the larches, a rich golden orange. Near by was a strange tree covered with a soft down as smooth as the velvet on a reindeer's antlers and scarlet flowers shaped like foxgloves that welled directly from the bark. Joseph broke off a branch to paint. They found the last mushrooms of the year and brought them home.

That evening Joseph roasted squash and fried the mushrooms with wild garlic in yak butter and grated hard cheese over the top. Namuunaa ate it slowly, delicately, smiling occasionally at the unusual taste, but Lena spat out the squash and they gave her cheese and milk instead.

Later Joseph painted the delicate strawberry-coloured flowers and Namuunaa sat by the fire and sewed after the child had gone to bed.

Your husband, said Joseph, how did he pass away?

There was a long pause and then Namuunaa said, He had an eagle, like Bird only bigger and fiercer. They were hunting one day and the bird attacked a bear. Sometimes trained eagles can kill bears but Temujin thought the bird would die. He went to rescue it and the bear killed him and the eagle.

Were you with him?

No. We discovered him later.

She sighed, and then said, I was very young. Maybe nineteen, Lena was only a year old.

Joseph was struggling to paint the exact texture of the bark.

What kind of a man was he?

Temujin? He was . . . She smiled into the flames. Brave, bold, fearless. He was a born hunter. He drank too much, he was always singing. I loved him from when I was a very little girl.

As she said this Joseph felt an emotion which he could not describe in himself, but he thought that what he generally felt was gladness, for as a priest he would never be weighed and found wanting in the scales that men and women use to assess one another.

I taught him how to hunt with eagles when I was fifteen. In a way, it was my fault. I showed him how it could be done and he had no natural fear.

You must not blame yourself, said Joseph.

He washed his brush and returned to the flowers, adding veins and shadows to their fragile form.

I caught my first eagle when I was seven, you know. You can steal them out of the nest when they are fledglings. It's hard to do because there are few eyries and they're difficult to find. Eagles never lay eggs in places it's easy to reach. I raised the baby eagle from when he was a few days old. I fed him night and day and I never left his side. When he was old enough, I taught him how to fly and how to hunt.

The other way you can trap an eagle is to find out where the nest is and watch the birds until they are strong enough to fly and then you catch them. It takes a lot of skill too – to catch them before they go for good, but they must be strong enough to fly. That's what I did with Bird last year. I left Lena with her grandmother and lived for two months in the mountains watching the eagles, waiting for the right moment. Then I spent another three months working every day with Bird, teaching him to tolerate me and then to hunt for me.

Which way is better?

How I caught Bird is better because he is strong – he already knows how to fly and hunt by himself. But he will never become tame. He will always remain wild at heart. My first eagle was different; maybe not as fierce or as fast, but he loved me as much as a wild creature is able to love. He would have torn out the eyes of anyone who attacked me. If Temu-jin had had a bird like my first one, he would be alive today.

She was silent and he could think of nothing he could say that might offer her comfort, if comfort was what she needed. The conventional words that one would use in such a situation were from a religion and a culture unknown to her, and though he liked to think God's words were universal, his were tainted by their English origins.

After a while she said, with the resilience of youth, It was a long time ago, Joseph.

The smell filled the small wooden house, rich, dense, redolent of summer flowers, his office at the Botanical Gardens, Patrick's heavy dining room table, polished every Monday morning. It made him long for home.

What are you doing?

Namuunaa had come in, the smell of pine trees and fresh air clinging to her hair.

I'm preserving the bulbs for their journey back to England.

She walked over to him. He was sitting crouched by the fire with an earthenware bowl of golden wax, painstakingly painting it on to each bulb. A tin pan of water was sitting on the embers; he was using it to keep the wax soft.

I keep them outside. They last well in the cold.

I'm sure that's true but they shall not survive the journey by sea without some kind of protection.

Why not?

Here. He gave her the earthenware pot to hold.

He filled a bowl with water and broke off a piece of rock salt and rubbed it between his fingers and thumb until it crumbled into pink crystals. He stirred the bowl of water with his hand until they dissolved. She watched him intently. He licked his finger and then passed the bowl to her.

She copied his action, looking up at him as she did so.

That's what the sea is like, he said. Salty. If the water touches the bulbs, they'll rot.

I see, she said. She dipped her finger into the water and tasted the droplets again. We can cook with this water tonight.

She passed him the salt water bowl and he put it by her cooking utensils and then took the wax from her.

I could help you.

I would appreciate it greatly, he said, smiling at her.

She did not smile back, but she fetched more brushes from his canvas holdall. He put the earthenware bowl in the tin pan and watched as the congealing wax melted. She was fast, dextrous. He watched her out of the corner of his eye as she painted thick stripes of wax on to the bulbs, the wax hardening beneath her fingers, turning a pale mustard with fine white cracks. Her fingers were long and fine. The dying embers cast a faint red glow across her cheekbones, were caught in her silver and turquoise ring.

Once they've dried, we must paint them again. They need another coat, he said.

You're going to a great deal of effort for these bulbs, she said, not looking at him.

Indeed, he said, they're precious to me.

Precious because of what they are or what they will mean to you?

He watched her loosening hair fall forward over her shoulder as she bent over the molten wax.

They are precious in and of themselves. They are a gift from God, he replied softly, but at one and the same time he was thinking of science journals, of the Royal Society, of Wallace and Hooker and even of Darwin, of accolades and scientific plaudits, of women in cream summer dresses whose lace edges cast nets across the lawns in the Botanical Gardens, of men who would remark upon his courage and journalists who would describe the romance of a lily discovered at the edge of the world.

He held up one of the bulbs to the light of the fire. Its edges glowed like honey. To think, he said, that inside this is matter that will be transformed into one of the finest flowers known to man.

Perhaps it is the finest, she said, smiling at him.

The finest flower, he said, inclining his head towards hers in a mock bow, the very finest, and he let the bulb roll across the floor. She stopped its path with her naked foot.

When the other families moved back up the mountain, the two elderly brothers, Delger and Amgalan, Namuunaa's mother, Uugan, Boshigt and Tsend with the black-haired twins, Batbaatar and Enke, their three sons and Enke's grandparents, Ermek and Jargal, there was very little privacy. Each cabin was a mile apart, but in the evenings they often congregated at someone's house. Joseph had grown up more or less on his own and followed a solitary path, surrounded by colleagues yet essentially separated from them, and to have an interested and concerned community around him was something he both welcomed and resented. He found it hard, when they were all in a group, to understand them.

Namuunaa had to act almost like a translator for him; he knew the cadence and rhythm of her speech.

At first they were full of tales of evil: of the vengeance the White Warlord had unleashed against the monks and lamas. They were stories of unimaginable depravity and it distressed Namuunaa to translate them for him. She quickly stopped but he could tell from the emotions sweeping across her face what the others were saying. He hoped that Mendo was safe and he felt selfish and cosseted, shut up here in the mountains hidden from harm.

Quickly though, because he was the newest and most intriguing person they had met for some time, they turned their attention to him. He found the villagers frequently exhausting, though usually entertaining, and the effect was to make him value his privacy more than ever. If it was too cold for Lena to play outside, he walked or rode away from them all so that he had time to think and to pray without being observed.

Namuunaa sewed while a group of them were at her house, laughing, talking, drinking and smoking, and it reminded him of nothing so much as a dinner party at home where the women frequently continued with their needle-work while the men drank brandy and smoked cigars. When they had all left, he felt drained.

At least, he said, you're never lonely.

It's easy to be lonely surrounded by people, she replied without looking at him.

He was instantly sorry for the triteness of his remark, especially as he had been commenting with slight irony on his own situation. A little later she looked over at him and he could tell she had forgiven him.

Tell me about England, she said.

He thought instead of Mongolia, with its infinite sky, its fairytale palaces, temples hewn out of the cliff face, endless mountain ranges and vast, sky-reflecting lakes.

England, he said, is narrow.

He remembered how he had struggled to describe his city where the land enveloped a fragment of the sea, the boats, the gulls, sailors and whores, coffee and Harvey's Bristol Cream, sacks of sugar and bananas, to Mendo. Instead he found himself telling her about his father, fresh out of Cork – God's own town and the devil's own people – as he was fond of saying.

He had talked endlessly about Outer Mongolia to Joseph. He had also spoken to him at length about ships. He was obsessed with sailing. His father described the *Great Western*, built in the docks at Bristol the year he was born, a steamer specially designed for transatlantic journeys.

She was built of wood, weighed a sweet 1,340 tons, 440 engine horsepower, his father said. Joseph didn't remember her sailing but he must have seen her; maybe his mother had been well enough to take him; perhaps he had held both his parents' hands, caught as a loop in a chain between them, when the *Great Western* sailed on 8 April 1838, arriving in New York fifteen days and ten hours later, a record for the time.

Joseph barely remembered his mother. She and his father had come from Cork. She'd been consumptive and died when Joseph was four. As an adult, Joseph concluded that his father had never recovered from her death. A small son was no consolation to a grieving man. When Joseph was six years old, he'd come home from playing out to find that his father had left. Sailed away on a boat. Just like that. Left a pile of debts and unpaid rent on their lodgings.

He'll come back for you, they'd assured him at the coffee warehouse. They'd given him a small boxroom, practically a cupboard, to sleep in, and the odd penny for sweeping up, but there was little a boy of his size could do. His father never returned. Probably drowned, he has, they said. And one day the cupboard was locked, his pathetic pile of belongings outside. For two years Joseph lived rough, even rougher than before. He built himself a shelter down by the mouth of the docks, collected stones and fossils, searched in dustbins for food, talked his way into the odd job, collected horse dung and fallen coal to keep warm, and grew one lily in a small pot that proved to be his salvation.

He remembered asking Patrick once when he was about fifteen: Why me? Why help me, Patrick? There must have been dozens of other orphans you could have saved.

Patrick had thought for a moment and then said, Because there was something special about you, Joseph. I had a feeling about you. I knew it to be true the moment I looked into your eyes, even though you looked away, proud and angry, trying to hide your fear.

Patrick had described to him how he had been walking along the harbour, away from the town and towards the mouth of the river. It was growing dark and the seagulls were flying in, their white bellies lit by harbour-side oil lamps like souls rescued from the sea. He'd been about to turn back when he saw a flash of colour, a white glow, as bright as polished bone. He'd walked towards it and seen a hovel on the quayside, barely three feet tall, constructed of bits of packing cases and covered with hessian sacks. At the opening of this dilapidated pile of junk was a flower, a small white lily in full bloom, the leaves thick and luxuriant. Who, in all this filth, in these pitiful conditions, without light and warmth and food, would take the time to grow a flower? he wondered.

And then you poked your head round a piece of sacking and glared at me with those great eyes of yours, said Patrick, and I knew there was some spark in you I had to save before it could, as it surely would, be extinguished.

The priest had adopted him and for the next ten years, though it had not been simple or easy, he had lived at St Mary's Church. Patrick had been like a father to him and all that he had left of his real father, he felt, was this one story, endlessly repeated, of a warrior king riding across an ever-lasting land without a sea. He grew up longing to gallop with a vast, multi-coloured army across the steppes, battle cries bloody in his throat. And he told Namuunaa how, to his own surprise, but perhaps not Patrick's, he had become a priest in an order even more rigorous and demanding than Patrick's own. How he took on a religion that believed even before a written law came into being, the Law of God was written in the hearts of men. How he was to be everything for God, but all things to all men. How Jeremy used to say, We came in like lambs and we rule like wolves. We shall be expelled like dogs and return like eagles.

What Namuunaa understood of his long and rambling tale in grammar-stricken Mongolian he did not know, but she listened attentively as she sewed and she looked up at him and smiled widely when he said he would return like an eagle.

Even as he spoke he was overcome with a wave of nostalgia – for the damp moss and wild moorland of Stonyhurst and Jeremy's giant and gentle frame, for Patrick waiting anxiously in their small terrace cottage in Clifton Wood – and he was also plagued with his usual doubts as he said the words that would inspire a simpler man. How could the word of God be written in the mind of man when evil existed as if evil had existed for the sole purpose of being wielded by man? Was it possible that he could be eagle-like and was it even right to aspire to that kind of fierce, ruthless lawlessness? Could anyone be everything to all men and still retain the love of God? A greater man than he, he thought with a sigh.

I don't see you as an eagle, she said, but she was smiling and he knew she was teasing. I can't imagine you as a descendant of the great Khan-Garid. Maybe a sparrow?

God loves even sparrows.

Ah well, perhaps you're a sea eagle. Tsem told me you kept talking about your desire to eat fish.

I think perhaps it is you who are like an eagle, said Joseph quietly.

At first he found it disconcerting, but he smiled at them and carried on, and thought that it must just be their way. The two old brothers, Delger and Amgalan, sat opposite him in the weak afternoon sun, smoking quietly and watching as if he were paid entertainment. He continued to saw and sand the pieces of pine he had found, the ground around him speckled with a confetti of sawdust.

I told you, it's a trap for animals, said Delger.

No, it's too small.

It looks like a house.

Such a tiny house. Perhaps it's a toy.

Ah, it's for Lena.

Yet not a good house. See, parts of the walls are missing.

Aye, these foreigners are useless.

It's a herbarium, he said, to put them out of their misery.

They raised their eyebrows at the English word.

It's for plants, he tried to explain. Look, I'll put soil in here, and grow plants inside. I'll carry it back to Pekin and there I'll put glass in here to fill in the gaps in the walls.

Glass?

He struggled to describe it.

It's clear, and hard, but it can break. It lets light into the plants but keeps out water.

They shook their heads in unison and continued to pull on their pipes. Out of the cloud of blue smoke, Amgalan said, You will return to Pekin.

I will return to England with my plants and bulbs.

Are you certain that you'll go? asked his brother.

Yes. It's my home.

This is your home.

This is my home for now. But, and he stopped sanding as he attempted to explain. This is my living – finding plants and bringing them to England. I must return.

Namuunaa may not enjoy living in England, said Delger.

He looked up at the brothers swiftly; neither of them was smiling.

I cannot take her, he said quickly. I am a priest.

We know, said Amgalan. Mendo explained that you're like a lama.

But, asked Delger, are you not tempted by beauty?

Of course, of course, but I cannot, I must not, I cannot even think . . .

The two elderly brothers started to chuckle. We mean the beauty around you, the beauty of Mongolia, surely it tempts you to stay.

He smiled back, half in relief.

It is beautiful, he said, yet sometimes one misses that which is ugly and England is beautiful in its own way. And I miss my family and friends.

They nodded at him and then muttered to each other.

We'll leave you now, said Delger, with your house for plants, but we have one piece of advice for you.

Yes? said Joseph, looking up at them.

With your handsome face, you must be careful not to break too many hearts.

They chuckled and wheezed at each other as they walked back towards their cabin. Joseph was left with his herbarium half assembled, his hands raw from sanding and a constriction in his chest as if he could no longer breathe; as if he breathed, he would be unable to take another breath.

He woke one morning at the end of October with a terrible pain in his leg. The bone had healed enough for him to walk on it without the crutches, but he still limped slightly. It began as a dull ache in his femur and spread right up to his hip. It was still early; he could hear Lena's soft breathing. He levered his leg out of bed, wincing as he attempted to put his weight on it. He opened the door a crack and looked out. It had snowed during the night. Soft drifts had built up against the walls; the tops were crusted with a thin filigree of frost. Where the mountain fell away from the house, the snow dissolved into the grey-white of the sky so that it was impossible to see where one ended and the other began.

Lena, wake up! He shook her gently and carried her sleepily to the door. She opened her eyes in the cold draught. It was incredibly still and silent outside.

She gave a shout of joy and wriggled out of his arms. She put both hands flat in the snow across the doorstep and giggled at the cold.

Don't disturb your mother, whispered Joseph. Come on, get dressed.

He dressed Lena and then put on his own clothes. The two of them slid outside like thieves. The yaks and the horses had crowded round near the food store, perhaps for shelter, or because they could smell the hay stored inside. They huddled closely together in a cloud of damp breath. Joseph had brought a square of tarps that he'd saved for waterproofing his seeds. He put it on the ground and helped Lena climb on to his lap.

Hold tight, he said as he lifted up the edges of the tarp and tucked in his feet. They careered down the slope, the makeshift sledge increasing in velocity, Lena screaming and screaming until they reached a natural plateau in the mountain and he dug in his heels and held her, laughing and crying at the same time.

Can we do that again? she asked, as soon as she could draw breath.

Yes, but it's a long way back up the hill.

She kept pace with him for a few yards, and then started to snivel as she became bogged down in the snow. Joseph lifted her on to his shoulders.

Faster, faster. The child kicked her heels into his ribcage.

Do you want to carry me? Will we go faster then?

Lena giggled and pulled his hair as if she were holding on to reins. When they finally reached the top, Namuunaa was standing on the step looking out. She waved to them. She was still wearing her nightshirt but with a *del* over the top.

Joseph lifted Lena down and she ran over to her mother.

We went so fast, faster than a big leopard.

Faster than an eagle?

Faster than the fastest thing.

Would you like a turn? asked Joseph, holding out the tarp.

He showed her what to do, how to sit, and they stood back as she slipped over the snow, gaining speed and disappearing over the brow of the hill with a long-drawn-out cry.

Come on, let's go to your mother.

I want another turn.

You can have another turn, but let's help your mother up the hill.

They reached Namuunaa halfway down the slope. She was laughing and covered from head to foot with snow, her cheeks flushed, her hair falling out of her plait. He gave her his hand to help her up and for one long moment they stood hand in hand, staring at each other. He abruptly let go. Lena inserted herself between them and they walked back up the hill with her holding their hands, demanding that they swing her.

When they reached the top Namuunaa said, Go and wash and have your breakfast.

Lena started pouting.

You can play in the snow after breakfast, said Joseph. You can use my sledge, he added, holding out the tarp. He said the word in English, for he had no idea whether there was one in Mongolian.

All right then. But I'm going to eat my breakfast very, very, very quickly.

You are good with her, said Namuunaa when Lena had gone inside. She brushed the hair away from her face and looked up at him. Joseph banged the snow off the tarp and hung it over the rail where the horses were usually tied up. He went in and started to make the fire. He couldn't look at her; he couldn't even speak to Lena. It had hit him like a blow to the heart; he had known intellectually yet never felt emotionally that as long as he lived, he never could and never would have children. No matter how many years he was alive, he would be alone in some essential way, for he was not part of a family and he could not have his own. It was a pain that flooded through him, more intense and physically real than the ache in his leg.

The eagle quivered from head to talon, his wing tips vibrating slightly and he turned his head from side to side though he could see nothing. The brilliance of the snow made Namuunaa's eyes glow a deep green as if she had been submerged in salt water. There was a constrained intensity about her movements that matched the eagle's. Every time she looked at him, it made his heart constrict. She was quite the most beautiful thing he'd seen. And at the same time, he hated himself for the overwhelming desire that he felt.

There had been a fresh snowfall in the night and the prints of animals were ice blue in the early morning light. The sky had an edge to it, sharp as diamond, and Namuunaa had woken with only one thought.

Go to your grandmother, she said, waking Lena roughly, Joseph and I are going hunting.

He rolled the words, *Joseph ba bi,* Joseph and I, in his mind while he packed a small bag of food. It was the mutton season again but now he was less indisposed towards it. Even Wolf seemed to have realized what kind of a day it was, for she was waiting on the doorstep and ran in small circles around them, wagging her tail and sniffing the powdered snow.

The trees were coated with a thick layer of ice: rounded stalactites hung down from each branch and, as the day wore on, fell like glassware melded by a glass-blower with an alternate state of mind. They left the trees and climbed higher into the mountains where the air was thin and the country was laid before them in black and white and shades of silvered blue. She was grinning hugely and he was reminded, in spite of the child and her responsibilities, how young she was.

She unsheathed Bird. The eagle blinked solemnly in the brilliant light; as she pulled back her arm to release him, the raptor spread his wings, dwarfing the horse. They watched until he became a black pinprick, almost invisible against the glare of the sun, and hung motionless in the sky. After about twenty minutes when Joseph's vision had started to flare into black and vermilion shapes, the eagle came hurtling down towards the earth, skimming the ridge of the mountain, curving round a vast outcrop of rock, and dived into the snow.

Namuunaa was already galloping towards the kill and Wolf bounded after her, overtaking and streaking across the snow, lithe and fast.

There was a stand-off between the eagle and the wolf when they arrived, the carcass of a white fox lying across the divide, their killer instincts temporarily suppressed. Namuunaa picked up the fox and whistled for Wolf. The wolf pressed against her leg and licked her hand. She skinned the fox, and threw small pieces of the entrails to the two animals. The rest of the meat she wrapped up; she hung the bloody skin with its pure white and unsullied fur over the back of the horse.

Will you eat it?

No. She shook her head. I'll keep it for them. She nodded at the animals.

Bird caught another fox and two hares that day. The eagle was exhausted. Namuunaa let him eat a large piece of the fox and announced that they should go. It was getting much colder and the dark shadows were deepening. A fine and fragile layer of ice was swiftly forming across the snow. Wolf stuck close to the heels of her horse as they rode back. Joseph felt high on the fine, rarefied air, the exhilaration of the hunt. Even though it was still light, the first stars gleamed in the west and the moon was a pale fingerprint in the sky.

Who taught you how to hunt? asked Joseph.

My father. My mother taught me how to use herbs, but it was my father who encouraged me to hunt. He had no sons. I was the nearest thing to a boy.

As they rode back through the twilight, Namuunaa told him a story about their tribe.

It was about a hundred years ago, maybe more. The head of the tribe, Tomo, had a dream, she said.

He dreamt of an eagle that lived in a valley to the north. It had the head of a snake, golden eyes and big, fierce talons. In the dream the eagle laid an egg that hatched into a baby eagle. When Tomo woke, he remembered the dream and he travelled north to the valley he had dreamt of. When he arrived he found the eagle's eyrie with one baby in it just like his dream. He brought the eagle back and he thought that it would make a good present for Dundoi, who was his younger brother. Dundoi was very poor and Tomo thought the eagle would make him rich. And indeed, this is what came to pass. Dundoi took great care of the eagle and he trained it well. It grew up to be a fast and fearless hunter and caught bears, *argalis*, wolves and foxes. He sold the fur and became wealthy and his status in the village increased.

A few years later Tomo was walking past Dundoi's *ger* when he heard the eagle crying. He went to his brother and he said, Dundoi, the eagle is crying, it wants to breed and rear eagle babies of its own. Will you let it go?

Dundoi agreed that it was the right thing to do because the eagle had brought him so much prosperity and status. The two brothers tied a small gold ring with a scrap of blue silk to the eagle's talon. They killed a black horse in its honour and then they released the eagle.

Now around the same time, Tomo had made an agreement with a man called Tsedenbal to marry Tomo's son and Tsedenbal's daughter. All the preparations for the wedding were under way, but Tsedenbal requested that Tomo come and see the bride's dowry. Tomo did not think this was necessary because he was happy with whatever the bride would bring, but Tsedenbal was very insistent. Tomo went as requested and saw that Tsedenbal had prepared everything – he had bought a new saddle and all the cooking utensils and bedding for his daughter and Tomo's son's new home. But next to all these things was a perch for an eagle, and when he saw that, Tomo understood why Tsedenbal had asked him to come.

Tsedenbal, he said, I no longer have the eagle. My brother and I let it fly away because it wanted to rear its own eagle chicks.

At first Tsedenbal did not believe him. He said that Tomo was lying and that he did not want to give the eagle to him. Then he became angry. He said no daughter of his was going to marry Tomo's worthless son.

Tomo went outside to talk to his brother. They realized that there was nothing they could do because they could not get the eagle back. At that moment, Dundoi spotted a black dot in the sky. It flew lower and lower and perched in a tree near by. All the people from Tsedenbal's tribe came out to look at it but the eagle remained where it was. Tomo became excited. He thought the eagle might be his and Dundoi's bird. He took a small piece of meat and held it out and the eagle flew down and alighted on his hand.

Tomo and Dundoi went to Tsedenbal and showed him the eagle. Tsedenbal didn't believe it was their eagle, but Tomo told him about the gold ring they had tied to their bird and he pointed out to Tsedenbal that the ring was still around the eagle's leg.

Tsedenbal immediately said that a new *ger* should be erected and they would all have a big feast in honour of Tomo and the wedding would take place after all.

In that case, said Tomo, you should kill a white mare and allow the eagle to eat the first piece.

Tsedenbal did as Tomo requested and everyone stood outside the *ger* while the eagle was allowed in to feast on the white mare. But the eagle ate only one piece of meat and then it flew up through the hole in the top of the *ger* and away.

Tomo could not understand it: the eagle had been treated so well, given the best *ger* and the best meat and left undisturbed to eat. He thought that this could only mean bad luck. He said to Dundoi, I do not think my new daughter-in-law will live long. And Tomo was right. The wedding took place as Tsedenbal had promised but the girl died six months later.

She smiled across at him – an almost bitter-sweet expression – when she'd finished her story. They rode in silence and Joseph struggled with the words he wanted to say. His understanding was improving all the time but he still found it an effort to express himself sometimes; indeed, he often felt his terms of expression were unfamiliar to himself, as if he were wearing someone else's clothes.

He said, You usually hunt alone. Is it difficult when I'm with you?

No, she said, without hesitation. She paused and then added, No, because you are solitary in yourself. You are like a wild creature that lives in itself and for itself but likes the company of others. You are like Wolf. She loves me as well as she is able, but beneath her skin she is wild and there is a fierce freedom inside her. She's separate from her own kind, she'll always be aloof. It is in her nature just as it is in yours.

I am never alone, said Joseph. God is with me.

Ah, but I don't really understand what you mean by God.

He is in here. He tapped his head. He is in the flakes of snow, the first frost, the horses' breath, the blades of grass that will appear when the snow melts, in the rocks and stones and in the air around us.

She looked straight ahead and then she said, I understand. I feel the same but I would say it was the spirit of the Buddha, who is in the beginning and the end of the world, in all things and all people.

Joseph felt a sudden warm glow, glad to be understood by a person he so valued, but then equally quickly he felt his heart constrict. He remembered, as he had been reminded so frequently of late, Jeremy's words as he breathed, You are a pagan. How could he, a man of God, have an understanding and a belief system akin to those who were and always had been godless? How could they presume to understand each other? Could it be that the bedrock of his own existence was nothing but a will-o'-the-wisp, a chimera masquerading as the Holy Spirit? But doubt, he tried to reassure himself, was a natural part of a living faith, and as surely as he knew anything, he knew it was the mind of God that breathed life into the world and not an amorphous, nefarious consciousness.

Namuunaa flicked her horse's reins, urged it into a canter, the eagle swaying with the horse's movements on her arm. Every star was out now, a million more than one could ever hope to see in England. Joseph waited, tracing the constellations across the night sky, the smell of frost sharp as a nose bleed. He felt a hot breath against his leg and looked down. Wolf was waiting with him. He spurred the horse on and galloped after Namuunaa through the snow-lit darkness, the wolf at his side. He caught up with her just before the house and as she reined in her horse, she said quietly, Thank you for coming with me.

How was it possible to miss a person with whom you've spent almost every waking moment for the past weeks and months? He had ridden out that lunchtime to find a place to pray. He'd come across a frozen waterfall, the pool beneath it glassy and blue with trapped bubbles, the waterfall itself a single sheet with a fine column of water running like a vein through the centre. The stream was surrounded on one side by trees laden with snow; occasionally the weight of the snow was too much and the branch shed its burden with a soft sigh. He imagined the crucifixion then, in every detail, taking place in front of him. Christ, his skin white and waxy and cold to the touch, the first drops of blood melting the snow, his blue eyes blood-shot, the muscles silently tearing in his back; the tears that would not fall.

He'd wanted to tell Namuunaa about the waterfall but neither she nor Lena was there. He should have relished the peace and the quiet but all he felt as he sat by the dead fire was alone. He ached to touch her, to reassure himself, to smell the faint scent that rose from her dark and milky skin like musk and spice. The house was silent with the sounds of her past laughter and her songs of rivers and mountainsides, dead to her quick movements, the way she brushed her hair in front of the fire in one long jet-black stream burnished like melting metal, the deftness of her fingers as she sewed, her concentration as she sliced meat, the roughness with which she chopped firewood and hauled it into a pile by the hearth.

This, he suddenly thought, is what love is. An all-consuming desire to be with another person, to touch them, to hold them, to be held, and healed and made complete. And yet, for a man like himself, this passion that burned and flared and raged within him was wrong. Was this some trial of God's own devising: a torment to test his faith?

He thought back to the few days that he and Mendo and Tsem had spent at the Valley of the Larks. How on the very last evening before they were due to leave the lama's assistant had summoned Mendo and Joseph to his quarters. After the chanting in the temples, the monks' discordant music and the crowds' shrieking and screaming, the silence in the Yolros lama's temple had been immense. The room had been thick with incense: it smelled like clean snow and was lit with thousands of tiny candles. The lama had seemed to hover half formed in this muted light, his eyes locked into some distant epoch.

Mendo and Joseph had sat in front of him at a respectful distance. The lama had continued to chant softly and run his beads through his fingers as if he were not aware of their presence at all. The chants that could be prayers and the gentle click of the beads that could be a rosary had lulled Joseph into an odd sense of contentment. After some time – how long it was he could not tell – the lama, still chanting, had reached forward to grasp an oblong wooden box at his feet. It was inlaid with bronze and silver lotus flowers curling and floating over its surface.

He drew out a deep blue silk scarf and laid it on the ground between them. Then he took out a number of small objects and held them in his cupped hands. He whispered over them and touched the cradle of his hands to his forehead and then scattered them widely across the scarf as if he were casting bread upon water.

They were human bones – small vertebrae and finger joints. Joseph looked at them with horror. The lama's head snapped up and this time when he looked at Joseph all trace of his other-worldliness had gone and his eyes seemed to assess him with a keen and cool appraisal.

You, he said, and his voice was low yet powerful like the intake of breath a wolf might make before it snarled, will journey far beyond the boundaries of your imagination. You will meet and seize your heart's desire. It will be the death of your soul.

You mean that I will die?

After you have killed your own soul, you will be released.

Released unto what? To do what?

To another destiny.

You mean I will be reincarnated? said Joseph, taking care to keep the scepticism from his voice.

In a manner of speaking.

The Yolros lama was still staring at him, and Joseph felt as if his very marrow were being extracted.

Have you no advice for him? asked Mendo quietly.

He has everything he needs within him, replied the lama and his eyes glazed over like a lizard's.

Outside the temple, Joseph had taken a deep breath of the cold, crisp night air. Of course he had not believed a word of it at the time. And even if, by some chance, by some freak of nature, it were true, well, his heart's desire was to return to England with as many plant and animal specimens as possible; to make some kind of scientific mark on his return, to see the fruits of his labour growing in English gardens, transforming their Victorian tidiness into a tiny corner of Mongolian wilderness. He wanted above all to find the rare white lily that had captured his imagination. If he were to attain these things, why, he could not die before he reached England, and after that, naturally everyone must die – and as a lama in a Buddhist-Shamanistic country, of course, the lama had to mention reincarnation. But although he tried to dismiss it, deep in his heart he felt a gnawing uneasiness: it was the incense, the bizarre festival, the lama himself and his previous encounter with the madman in his stone labyrinth: an unquiet mind can discover many reasons to rationalize its discomfort.

But now, now as his desire for Namuunaa grew stronger and more uncontrollable, Joseph wondered if this then was what the Yolros lama had meant. His heart's desire. The death of his soul. He knelt in the snow throbbing with that very desire. He pressed his forehead through the fine crust of ice, brittle as sugar, and felt the cold grip him in its vice. His whole body ached and he groaned out loud as the snow balled between his palms, melted and ran across his wrists. He must, he knew, somehow cauterize this sensation. Yet even as he thought this, her image came unbidden into his mind; his desire for her was so strong he could not bear her absence even when she was in his presence, until she turned to look at him and included him within her own bright refrain, adding substance to him as a melody harnesses a collection of chords.

*

Lena was playing with a doll and Joseph, who was watching, wondered idly what her father had looked like. The child was, he thought, a perfect mixture of the two of them: she was going to be tall and broad-shouldered like her father, he assumed, and her hair was wild, blonde and curly unlike her mother's. Her eyes were the colour of Uugan's and their shape and slant, her lips and the line of her jaw were like Namuunaa's. It must be an incredible thing to create and bring into life an entirely new being that was a mixture of yourself and the person whom you loved most in the world. He did not know what to do with the pain that grew and spread within him like some kind of tumour; he wondered what a child of his would be like, knowing that all the possible children he might ever have, could ever have had, would remain unborn but in his mind and imagination. He felt like cursing God for making him suffer in this way. He wanted to take the child in his arms and hold her tight to ease his pain, but he knew Lena of old and from previous rebuffs had come to see that she gave affection only when she felt like it and was not a willing receiver. He let her play.

In a few days' time it'll be Christmas, he said to Namuunaa who was sewing.

What's that?

It's the day when Jesus was born. God sent his only son to spread peace and love among mankind.

He explained that it was a day for prayer, worship and reflection, but that there were other rituals, such as giving presents and having a Christmas tree.

Well, let's have Christmas. She was smiling at him.

He hesitated. It was all very well for him to pray to Jesus but was it not a sacrilege for a Buddhist to encourage him, even participate in the celebration? He had no desire to try to convert her, but neither did he want to see his own beliefs lightly taken.

Come on, she said, laughing at his solemnity, it'll be fun.

As he looked into her laughing face he suddenly thought of Patrick encouraging him in a different way, the sentiment the same.

I don't want to go, he'd said, scowling. He was ten at the time.

Come, son, it is possible that you may find it interesting, Patrick had answered patiently.

It was a few days before Christmas and Lord and Lady Bart Spencer had requested Patrick's presence urgently. They feared the elder Bart Spencer would not last the night. They had sent a trap and Joseph had climbed up with the coachman and sat suspended above the horses' sleek rumps, bobbing like apples below him. It was midday, the sky bright winter blue. They headed north out of Bristol, down narrow country lanes, the hedges stark trellises garlanded with autumnal remnants of deadly nightshade, ice glimmering in the crevices of the fields.

The house itself was enormous, larger than anything he'd ever seen before. Patrick was immediately escorted into its depths.

Be good, my son, he called behind him to Joseph.

The coachman showed him to the servants' quarters. Some great party had occurred, or was perhaps still ongoing. The kitchen table was laden with half-eaten food and dirty crockery. The servants sipped the dregs of flat, pink champagne; the lees of red wine silted the glasses. The cook gave him a meringue. He'd never eaten anything so exquisite. He slipped outside, still eating, breathing out to see his breath hang frozen. Round the back of the house he saw something that seemed to him like a dream, a mirage, an oasis in the frost. He hurried towards it and let himself in.

It was an orangery, a curved conservatory filled with orange and lemon trees in large wheeled pots. It was warm inside and from the outside it had gleamed in soft golden colours, like a petal preserved in a block of ice. The fruit were tiny, perfectly formed, the leaves as polished as if they'd been waxed, the scent sharp and fresh.

It was with considerable difficulty that they found him when Patrick was ready to leave.

Will he die? asked Joseph, ignoring the fuss being made, as he climbed into the trap.

Not tonight. He had merely imbibed a little too vigorously.

Look. Joseph pulled out the twig he had carefully severed from one of the orange trees.

Patrick, as he now realized, had had the grace and tact to say nothing of stealing. He only said, Well, we shall plant it on our return.

The twig grew roots and sprouted newly minted leaves but after a few weeks they cracked and shrivelled; and when there was nothing left save for a desiccated stick, Patrick made him throw it out. He had imagined the tree with its divinely smelling star-shaped flowers and its host of tiny oranges glowing like a beacon on his bedroom windowsill.

Patrick must have realized that the orange would not survive heavy cosseting, and had not pointed out the social differences between themselves and the Bart Spencers which meant they did not have the kind of money to dedicate to an orangery. He'd simply said, Some things cannot flourish in spite of our best intentions and our most indulgent ministrations.

Joseph tried to put the thought of Patrick to the back of his mind.

If you wish it, we shall celebrate Christmas, he said, smiling at Namuunaa. What harm could it do? he thought and, having made up his mind, he became childishly excited too.

On Christmas Eve he and Lena went out to choose a tree. They found the perfect fir, about five feet high, and Joseph chopped it down and they dragged it home together, struggling through the snow, Lena frequently falling and being swept along by the dense branches.

He cut stars out of his herbarium paper and they painted them yellow and sewed a loop of thread on to them and hung them from the tree. He drew an angel for the top and Lena coloured it in. They brought back ivy from the wood and wound it into wreaths to hang from the door and around the hearth and the ceiling. In the absence of a crib, he made a bed of hay for Lena's doll and above it he hung a picture he'd painted of the star of Bethlehem with Mary, Joseph, the three shepherds and the wise men looking down at the baby. Lena and he tied the frail orange globes of Chinese lanterns to the tree too and Namuunaa brought in a few of the strings of dried lily flowers and wove them into the ivy. She filled small dishes full of oil with thick wicks and placed them on each windowsill and above the hearth as he'd asked. Later on that evening he returned to the waterfall, which was still partially frozen, and conducted his own silent midnight mass. When he'd finished he turned to see Namuunaa and Lena watching him a few yards away. He walked back, Lena between him and Namuunaa.

In the morning he kissed them both and said, Happy Christmas.

Can we open our presents now?

He smiled over her head at Namuunaa. Yes, you can have your present. He went to retrieve their gifts and was surprised to find that a fourth one had been added during the night.

Lena tore hers open first. Namuunaa had given her a bracelet and a necklace made out of seeds and small polished stones threaded together. Joseph had spent ages agonizing over what to give her: his initial idea had been to make her a book for learning her sums in, but he thought that was a dreary present for a little girl. Eventually he'd explained the situation to Uugan who'd made him a doll for her in return for a small twist of coffee and a little brandy. Namuunaa opened his present to her next. She unwrapped it very carefully and held it in the palm of her hand before putting it on. It was a Celtic cross his father had given him when he was five, threaded on to a thin black ribbon. She came over and kissed him on the cheek. He felt the imprint of her lips burning against his skin.

The fourth parcel was from Namuunaa. She handed it to him eagerly. It was much the biggest of all the presents. Inside was a pair of loose-fitting trousers and a jacket made out of heavy blue felt, lined with yak hair.

He went behind the screen round his bed and changed into the outfit. The jacket fitted perfectly and the trousers were only slightly loose round the waist. Namuunaa felt the waistband critically.

I'll need to take this in slightly here, she said.

When she straightened up, he enfolded her in his arms for one brief moment. It was as much as he could trust himself to do.

They were Temujin's, she said. But I altered them for you and lined them so they'll be warmer.

Thank you, he said, looking down at himself. It felt odd to be wearing the suit after so many years of being draped in his heavy winter cassock. Physically he felt less encumbered but also more self-conscious, as if with the wearing of this suit he had become visible: it announced him as a man and not a priest. He wondered if it were wrong to abandon his cassock and if this was a sign of the loosening of his mind and his morals.

They ate a large roast pheasant for Christmas dinner followed by a drop of brandy and a rather unsuccessful attempt at a Christmas cake made from barley flour, brandy, sugar, water and dried apples and plums, baked flat like unleavened bread. Lena had three helpings: she didn't know how it was meant to taste.

It was, he thought, the perfect Christmas. That night after Lena had gone to bed, they sat by the fire. Although he loved the little girl, these were the times he cherished, the few occasions the two of them were on their own by the fire, the child breathing softly behind them, the vast stillness of Mongolia around them, the wolf at the door, and the fierce, wild creature on his perch outside.

You know in six days' time it'll be New Year.

Is that true? Our New Year won't take place for another couple of months. She was silent for a few moments and then said, Either way, you'll soon be gone.

Yes. I'm not sure when Mendo and Tsem will arrive, but they said they would come as soon as they could.

Did it ever occur to you that I might like to see England? She was staring at him hard.

He met her gaze full-on and said quietly, Yes, it did.

But you'll still leave here. Alone.

Yes.

Why? she raged suddenly. You came here from a land far, far away. You could have travelled anywhere, yet you came here. You accept our hospitality, you take our plants, you collect our seeds, you shoot our birds. And then you leave. What good is that to us?

He felt the colour drain away from his face despite the heat from the fire. He didn't quite know how to begin, what to say.

Namuunaa, if it had not been for you I would have died. You saved me.

And yet you will leave here without me. That is how you repay me. Do you not think that I would like to travel too? You talk of the sea. I have never even heard the word. You speak of ships and I do not know what you mean. You think that because I am poor and all I have are yaks and sheep, I do not want to see the world too?

Namuunaa, you should not like England. It's too narrow for you – there are houses and people everywhere. It's dirty and smells of shit, there are beggars, thieves, sick people. Here there's space, light.

Sometimes a person can become tired of space and silence, she whispered. A minute later she said, You lived all your life in England until you came to our country. You thrived there as you have here.

He sighed. Even if it were not for the differences in our language and our culture . . .

You've learned our language, and you're beginning to understand our culture. You could be my translator, my guide, as Mendo was for you. Do you not think that I could learn? What's the matter with you? Is it because I am a woman? Is it because you think I could not survive the voyage? That I am not able to travel? Well, let me tell you—

Namuunaa, you don't need to tell me anything. I know how strong you are, how resilient. The truth of it is, he sighed again, the truth is that I cannot take you because of who I am. I am a priest. How could I, a man who has sworn never to have a woman, return to England with an unmarried girl?

She got up and without another word left the house, banging the door behind her. Lena sat up and rubbed her eyes. She looked around.

Where's my mamma? I want my mamma.

Joseph came and sat next to her. Let me tell you a story.

All right, she yawned and lay down.

Once upon a time there was a big, tall ship that sailed out to sea . . .

Where's Mamma gone?

I don't know, Lena. Perhaps she's gone to visit Uugan.

Will she come back soon?

Yes, very soon.

It sailed far, far away across the water . . . The child fell asleep in his arms. He carefully eased her back into bed and sat by the dying fire waiting for Namuunaa. He must have fallen asleep because he was suddenly jolted wide awake wondering where he was and what he was doing, the dead ashes in front of him.

Namuunaa?

He heard her rather than saw her slip past him and behind the screen that surrounded her bed. She did not answer.

He woke late the next morning and she had already left the house. He gave Lena her breakfast and had just begun to teach her about Africa when Namuunaa returned. Joseph, who felt as tired and friable as if he'd drunk too much the night before, expected her to be angry still, or at least sad. To his surprise, she burst in singing, kissed Lena and rumpled his hair. He looked at her in astonishment. She cleaned and swept the house, still singing, occasionally sweeping Lena from her lessons and dancing with her round the hearth. If this was a mask, Joseph could see no flaw in it and he had, in the end, to believe she was genuinely happy. He wished that there were some kind of periodic table, better still, a conversion chart by which he could map her emotional weights and secure the full measure of her.

That evening Namuunaa sent Lena to play with the twins at Boshigt and Tsend's house and she boiled a big pot of water. She half filled their wash tub with cold water and added the hot. Kneeling in front of the tub, she brushed her hair and then lowered her head over the basin, allowing her hair to coil into the water in a thick, black spiral. Joseph watched, mesmerized. The weight of her hair dragged it to the bottom of the water before it fanned out, floating like a raft of kelp. Her neck formed a perfect arc.

Joseph, help me, will you?

She remained crouched down with her head bowed and handed him a small bowl. He knelt beside her and scooped up water with the bowl. He poured it over her, channelling it from the small indentation at the back of her neck, across the fine, wispy hairs at the base of her small skull, her hair slick against her head as if she were a seal or a mythical sea creature. He took a bar of soap and lathered it in his hands then worked the lather into her hair, using his fingers to massage it in and then gradually adding handfuls of her thick hair to the mass of suds piled on top of her head. He slid his hands through her hair to get rid of most of the soap and poured water over her head to rinse away what remained. She had undone the top buttons of her dress and folded it down past her shoulders so that she would not get it wet. The tendons in her neck arched and the small fine muscles around her shoulder blades tensed as he pushed gently against her. He cupped his hands around her ears, small, delicate and coffee brown, studded with coral and obsidian, so that the soap would not run into them. When he'd finished, he took her hair in a bunch as if it were a mare's tail and twisted it to wring the water from it before letting it fall across her shoulder. Namuunaa sat up. Fine rivulets of water ran along her collar bone and over the faint ridged lines of bones across her chest before trickling beneath the front of her dress. He had an overwhelming urge to trace the pattern of one tiny drop with his finger and stem its flow. He closed his eyes. He felt his entire body trembling.

Thank you, she said, turning to face him.

She picked up a piece of cloth to dry her hair with.

He could not look at her. He carried the wash basin outside and tipped the soapy water into the snow. When he came back, she'd buttoned her dress back up again and was brushing out the tangles in her wet hair.

Are you cold now? Shall I build up the fire?

A little.

She sat closer to the hearth while he piled on more pine logs. They spluttered in the heat as the resin popped and bubbled.

Have you always wanted to become a priest?

Always, he said, almost under his breath.

Why? She tossed her cape of hair over her shoulders.

He thought her slight smile supercilious and in that instant he almost hated her. How had he gone so wrong, allowing himself to become allied to a woman who neither shared nor understood his religion, who would not support him in his quest to become ever closer to God, and who sought to undermine the very foundations of his beliefs? He felt as if he were standing on soft sand that trickled between his feet and sank beneath his soles.

Because God loves me, He loves me, he practically shouted and in his heart he added the rest of the sentence against his will and better judgement . . . when no one else would or did.

The smile faded from her face. He looked down at his hands and steadied himself.

He said, I am a man of science, a rational and logical person. I see no discrepancy between belief in God on the one hand and in the discovery and workings of science. What I think is that God is there in spirit within every living creature, within every inanimate thing. That we are here – that there is something rather than nothing – is because of God.

He realized how angry he sounded; his desire for her coagulating into something gelid and cruel.

I would say that there is something because there cannot be nothing, answered Namuunaa. The Buddha teaches us that one thing causes another: a spark causes a fire, a yak mating, the birth of a baby yak, a bird singing in the forest makes us feel joy. The world is – because it cannot be and not have a cause.

He saw it now: how Namuunaa spoke to him as if she were handing him a bunch of flowers and he crumpled them into a ball, tossed it around and threw it at her, and yet she accepted the differences he created, the leaps he made in conversation, caught the ball, passed it back. He suddenly remembered what Mendo had said to him after he had received the Yolros lama's terrible prophecy and he repeated it in a whisper back to Namuunaa.

Knowledge is not important, love is.

He was still talking to her about Africa, drawing pictures of elephants and oranges, dark men with spears, explaining the difference between a cheetah and a snow leopard, describing how sugar grows in stalks. Lena was bored, her attention span was limited and sometimes it was a struggle for both of them; she was only young, and he was teaching her in a language not his own, a language that as yet had no words for Devonian and Cambrian, for ichthyosaurs and pterodactyls, a language whose words he had not mastered so that describing the workings of a volcano or a cyclone was more like a game of charades than a lesson.

It must have been an accident, a slip of the tongue, for she sighed and said, I'm tired of this. Papa, pass me my doll.

He picked up the doll almost mechanically, but held it in his lap. She held out her hand for it, but when there was no response, she prised his fingers away from the toy and hugged it to her chest. He felt Namuunaa's strong, hard fingers grasp his own.

Joseph, look outside. It's a long time yet till the spring.

That's what I'm afraid of, he said. He stood up, pulling her closer and put his arm about her waist. She was so slender his arm fitted around her easily. She looked into his eyes and her lips parted slightly. He let her go almost forcefully and left the house abruptly.

It was one of those rare days in Outer Mongolia where the sky was grey and overcast and a bitter snow was falling. He walked numbly up the mountain heading towards the ridge where they sometimes went hunting together. Namuunaa had amassed a number of furs and the exercise and fresh meat meant Wolf was in peak condition. She would sell the skins in spring, she said. Of course, he had realized how he was filling a niche, becoming an intricate cog that had been missing in the mechanics of this small family. Every day he found it a small torture to be with Lena who demanded attention and affection, whose features were Namuunaa's yet not Namuunaa's, who was a person formed by a union between Namuunaa and the man she had loved since childhood; a person, though young, with her own strong beliefs and desires, affectations and inclinations, and this young child served to remind him of how he had become drawn into a situation he should not be in, and who every day pained him afresh as he remembered that he would never have a child or a family he could call his own.

If the days were bad, the nights were worse. He thought that as an adolescent and in his early twenties he'd managed to work it all out of his system but that was the sin of complacency. He was feverish, his mind filled with the tantalizing glimpses he had seen of Namuunaa: part of her bare back, the frail arc of her neck, her shoulders, the quail's egg hollow of her clavicle, the strong fingers, her long cream-brown throat, thin ankles and firm hard feet; the curved indentation between her hips and ribs where his arm fit so perfectly, the touch of her hand in his hair, her faint smell of musk and cinnamon and the long-remembered and often revisited dreamtime in his illness when she undid the buttons of his shirt, one by one, and washed his naked body.

Dear God, he whispered, why have you sent her to torment me? Why are you testing me?

Was it not written that the best way to remain innocent was to avoid temptation? All his life he'd lived virtuously, he'd hardly spoken to a woman let alone touched one. Yet here he was locked in a mountain cabin, trapped by the snow, far from all his peers, with the most beautiful woman he had seen in his life. He could have wept from frustration as his body ached with desire.

Jesus, let the spring come soon, let it be fast, he prayed as he walked. Let the snow melt and the flowers bloom, let me ride far from here.

He had made mistakes, he could see that, but he would rectify them now. He would pray longer, harder. By dusk he could see his way through. The solution, as he saw it, was to remain polite but grow more distant; in short, behave how a person of his profession ought to have conducted himself right from the beginning.

When he entered the house, he was flushed from walking, his skin stung from the biting cold and the slanting watery flakes of snow, but he was glowing with his own resolution. Namuunaa was standing waiting for him with her hands on her hips. She barred the way to the house and looked squarely at him.

The break will come when you leave here with Mendo. Don't try to make it happen any earlier, Joseph.

He felt like a child who'd made a brand-new kite out of tissue paper and frail twigs, string and sealing wax, and on its maiden flight the paper had ripped, the frame had snapped and the sun had melted the wax. His face crumpled.

She looked at him hard for one long moment, and then she stood back to let him in. He half stumbled, half fell and she caught him in her arms. He held her so tightly he feared he might crush her ribcage. He wound his hand through her black hair and pulled her head back so that her throat arched and he kissed her hard. He felt himself melt into her, her lips yielding to his, and he let her hair go. It flowed across his hands as he grasped her shoulder blades, gripping on to the bone as if he might tear her apart with his love. And even as he held her, even as he gave in to his desire, he knew that one day, in some way, he was going to have to pay.

*

The next day she said, It's New Year's Eve today, isn't it? Your New Year.

Yes, he said, surprised that she had remembered.

What do you do to wish the New Year in?

Well, pray.

You pray all the time.

People make New Year resolutions – ideas about how they want to live their life the next year. But I make resolutions about being a better person every day. Making them on New Year's Eve doesn't mean they're more likely to come true.

What else?

Stay up until midnight and sing a song. Drink a toast to the New Year.

Shall we do that?

I don't really feel like it. It's not your New Year anyway.

Still, we can sing a song and have a drink. We could make tea from the lilies – I do it for special occasions.

That's what they're for?

Yes. The bulbs are more potent, but you're taking them away with you.

I'm not going to eat them.

You might change your mind after you've drunk my tea.

If you wish, he said. Lily tea with you at midnight. It sounds like a perfect way to see in the New Year.

After they had kissed yesterday, it had been only with a tremendous feat of willpower that he had broken away from her. Now he felt his whole being drawn towards her as if he were scattered metal filings and she was a powerful magnet. He couldn't take his eyes off her as she moved around the cabin.

On the stroke of midnight he chinked his bowl against hers and sang 'For Auld Lang Syne', right through to the end.

Slàinte, he said, as my father used to say, and he sipped the tea.

In those few moments the whole of the summer came flooding back to him: the brilliance of the flowers, the torrent of light through the trees, waves of scent drenching him in an exotic tide, his dream of a singer receiving a bouquet, back-lit by the stage lights, a single lily in a fluted vase on Charles Darwin's windowsill, a pot of five-foot-high magnificent stems by Patrick's door. Other memories came rushing back too: meadows full of delphiniums and daisies, Tsem grinning at him from the top of his horse, Mendo, his eyes dark and trou-bled, a handful of human bones cast from the hand of a man whose mind belonged to another era, burning boats floating across a jet-black lake, his heart pounding to an atavistic beat.

What was so incredible was how real and perfect his mem-ories had become, like gems being forged in a white-hot furnace. He sniffed the tea. It was pale green with fine fila-ments of petals floating in it. Some stamens fanned open on the surface like the blossoming of Japanese water lilies. The scent was the very same as that of the fresh flowers: white musk and vanilla, a note of jasmine, gardenias at dusk, pure frost at first light and salt-laden sea water. He looked up at Namuunaa.

She was smiling back at him enigmatically, drinking her tea in small cat-like sips, her heavy hair hanging forward obscur-ing part of her face. He drank a little more and felt his body loosening in some strange way. The colours of the tapestries, even of his own paintings, had grown richer, more intense.

You asked me what my name meant once, she said. Namuunaa means calm.

Her name seemed to glow in the darkness, hang for a moment in front of him, a perfect plum, a velvet peony red around the edges.

Joseph? she said, and his name had colour too, a deep blue serge with the sheen of oxidized steel.

As he sipped the tea, the smell took on a shape, a forest of columns, some thin, others wide, all smooth as glass and spearmint-clear. They pressed against his arms, his hands; he felt he could reach out and feel his way between their vitreous forms. But when he stretched out his arms, it was Namuunaa he felt, Namuunaa in his embrace.

Her skin was so smooth it was almost like trailing his fingers through scented oil. Images flooded into his mind unbidden, leaking colours, surreally bright as if painted on stained glass flooded with sunlight.

> a child on a swing in a field full of poppies
> a green-gold fish sliding sinuously through waterweeds
> clouds in turmoil seen between blades of grass
> the first drops of rain on parched earth
> a single lily unfurling at high speed. A waltz of petals.

When she kissed him it was as if he'd swallowed a molten sword; he was pierced to the core. He held her breasts, cupped in the palms of his hands, a sensation more intense than any he had yet experienced, for he felt the erotic charge that flooded through her surge through him. Every time he touched her he perceived this dual sensation, burning his fingertips, searing his skin where it ignited in correspondence with hers.

She whispered his name softly in his ear, over and over, creating him anew. As he entered her he felt her intake of breath, the slight pain and his own overwhelming need to move with her, her warmth gripping him, the sensation building between them so that they were utterly in tune, together as one, a single being with a dual desire.

They were shaking, pressed against one another so hard he could not tell where he ended and she began. There was a feeling of space in his head, a pure white light. Expanding.

In the morning he woke with cold air against his face, his body deliciously warm, Namuunaa cradled in his arms; her hair spread across his chest felt like a blanket of thick silk.

He ran his hand down over her ribs to her waist, the dip where the perfect curve of her hips began. Down her back, the ridges of muscle either side of her spine, lithe as a cat, the camber of her coccyx.

There you are! I've been looking for you. Lena was peering round the screen.

Why are you in Mamma's bed?

Joseph held his finger to his lips. Hush, Lena, go dress. I'll help you in a minute.

But why are you in—

Lena, go and dress as Joseph asked you, said Namuunaa, lifting her heavy mane of hair and looking sleepily at her daughter.

Joseph eased himself out of the bed and wrapping himself in his *del*, he took his boots, his clothes and a machete and headed for the river. More snow had fallen during the night and the path he had cleared between the house and the river had a new covering a foot deep. When he reached the river he broke the skin of ice that had formed across the central pool and stepped into the water. He submerged himself entirely and forced himself to look up at the jagged blue ice above him, the torn scrap of sky, the black water closing over him. The cold was excruciating. For those few moments it was as if his hatred had metamorphosed into a blindingly physical pain.

He felt a rising tide of disgust sweep like a sickness over him. He struggled to comprehend last night's overwhelming craving that had threatened to subsume his very person. It had now turned to a source of shame and guilt. He no longer felt as if he could inhabit his own skin. He wanted to wash every vestige of her from himself, scrub his skin so hard he could no longer feel the gentle touch of her fingertips, the trace of her caress, the mark of her teeth against his shoulder, the crescent-shape indentations of her nails.

He surfaced gasping and, convulsing violently, rubbed himself dry with his *del* and put on his clothes. He seized the machete and began to carve out chunks of ice from further downstream where it had grown thick and dense. He'd stack the ice like firewood by the side of the door and melt it when they needed more rainwater.

Do you think that is sufficient? he heard Namuunaa say from behind him.

He looked down at the heap of glacial-blue glass bricks he'd amassed. He finished cutting out the block he was working on and felt rather than saw her leave. He stacked the blocks next to the doorstep and fed Bird and Wolf on pieces of raw, nearly frozen meat, then scattered hay around the food store for the yaks. Taking the dun horse he rode to the forest to gather firewood. Every machete stroke biting into the wood was a blow he wished he could deal to himself. Every time the kindling splintered beneath the blade he thought of his own bones breaking. Eventually he stopped. He was sweating profusely, his breath and the horse's hanging still in the still air. He looked around at the frozen world, the dark forest capped with snow, the hillside sloping away from him, the mountains in the distance merging blue and mauve into one another, their peaks crystalline, the sky a hazy cloudiness like water in absinthe.

The only one of God's men to tread this particular piece of earth, he was the first to have sinned – and a sin so flagrant; he could almost imagine his virginal footsteps through the snow now boiling black as if beneath the corrupting influence of acid. But there was no outward sign of contamination and if God reproached him, it was by silence, a silence so immense he struggled to fill the space created in his mind by the enormity of his deed and the totality of His absence. He could have wept, but his tears would not fall.

He returned home with the wood and silently Namuunaa handed him a plate of hot stew and silently Lena watched him, her large eyes fastened upon his face though he would not look up.

He passed his days as if dumb. He could not speak, he could barely eat, his prayers were stillborn in his dry mouth, replaced by a stifled scream of bitter agony and at odd intervals he burned with images, sensations unbidden: Namuunaa's hand against his chest, branding him; the jut of her hip bone; the flicker of firelight through her falling hair.

He felt as if everything he touched were as thin as an eggshell. She filled his nights and slid into his waking hours like a succubus and he had to try to distinguish the living woman from the phantom; in reality she was neither wanton nor provocative and yet he felt the alchemical reaction that brewed in his mind, a toxic potion of desire and hatred, might poison them both.

Standing in the outhouse one morning searching for a joint of meat, he saw the lilies laid out in rows and threaded like fairy lights on coiled strings. He picked one up and crushed it in his hand. As he inhaled its faint, cold scent he realized that it was the lilies that had brought him to such a delirious state; the intoxicating brew that Namuunaa had concocted for him had undone his morals. He ground the petals into a powder and let it trickle to the ground. It was Namuunaa who was to blame: from a lily to Lilith, she had become a temptress, a seducer of men, the worst kind of whore.

He stood between the frozen carcasses, remnants of the petals clinging to his fingers, utterly wretched and burning with anger. To go and live with one of the other villagers was tantamount to expressing his shame, and in winter when their summer work had already been done he had nothing to offer them by way of help; an unwanted and uninvited guest, he would deplete their precious stores they had set aside with no thought of another mouth to feed. He was trapped with Namuunaa in a hell of his own making and as he stood there he remembered the Hill of Iron Trees, the leaves as sharp as razor blades, bending in an icy wind to slice the flesh of monks who'd strayed and, at the summit, the circling vultures waiting to peck out the transgressors' eyes.

I have been thinking, said Namuunaa when he returned with the meat she had requested, that Lena and I will go and stay with my mother for a while. You can stay here, of course.

There was defiance in her voice, but also fear. She was not sure how he would react. He wanted to say to her that he was glad she had realized the error of her ways and that it was best she remove herself from all temptation. He merely nodded, his jaw set.

Are we going to Grandma's? asked Lena.

Yes, my little one, answered Namuunaa, looking at Joseph.

Will I come here and you'll tell me all about Africa?

Namuunaa said nothing. She wasn't going to make it entirely easy for him.

He sighed and looked at his hands.

In England no one goes to school or has lessons at this time of year.

I want you to tell me about the noriges.

She still couldn't pronounce orange and there was no Mongolian word for the fruit.

Later, said Namuunaa soothingly, later. Finish your stew, Lena.

After they left he removed all the remaining lily flowers and threw them on to the fire. The petals shrivelled and glowed briefly before turning to ash. Outside there was a howling gale. He could hear it singing at the lintels and whistling round the eaves, keening through crevices in the wood. There was the occasional dull whine, which he thought part of the wind's effects until he heard scratching at the door. He opened it fractionally and Wolf slunk in, her coat matted with sleet, her tail between her legs. He was glad of the company. He rubbed the worst of the snow from her fur and she curled up next to the fire with him as he watched the slow drift and dance of the flames burning the string that had once held the lilies like a fuse along a firecracker.

The wind did not abate but began to build up into a terrible snowstorm. He must have fallen asleep by the fire, for he dreamt that he was lying on his stomach and Namuunaa had poured oil over his back and was crouched over him, massaging him with long, hard strokes. He felt his muscles relax beneath her touch and rolled over, his arms outstretched to embrace her, but she had become a giant black bird with a viciously curved beak, which she swung knife-like at his eyes. He woke with a start, his heart pounding, Wolf watching him cautiously from the hearth. He added more wood to the fire and made himself tea. His anger at her was like a palpable thing, a dark excrescence at the heart of him. He fed it and nurtured it through the long, bitter night.

In the morning he woke to a cold and spiritless house, empty of Namuunaa's bright and vital presence. The lily flowers had been an intoxicating drug, one that had given him a taste of how it felt to be in her skin and, by the same token, how she might feel inside his. There was something almost magical about it and it had been, he now realized, a gift from her. A gift to make their love-making a more powerful and unforgettable experience. A present for the New Year. That he had the will to resist her, that he would have remained chaste throughout the winter, whether he'd drunk the lily tea or not, he now knew to be false. And on New Year's Eve, his mind undone, he had been no less eager than she.

Forgive me, Lord, for I have sinned, he muttered, but his words rang hollow even to himself.

For the truth was, he had wanted her from the very moment he had seen her. The truth was that he loved her as he had never loved anyone in his life before, with a love so strong it made him tremble at the violence of his feelings.

For three days and nights the storm continued. He paced the house, the wolf's eyes never leaving him. On the fourth day he put on the suit that Namuunaa had made him and his *del*, and left, the wolf at his heels.

It seemed to take a long time between his knocking and the door opening. He stood in the thick of the storm, the wind and the snow raging about him, the sky and the ground grown one, tears that the wind had involuntarily whipped from his eyes frozen against his skin. She stood in the doorway and looked down on him. She seemed to be a little thinner than he remembered, her high cheekbones more prominent. Her dark green eyes glowed in the light like uncut emeralds.

Please, he said, his voice stolen by the roar of the wind, please. Come home.

Now?

Yes, now.

He waited in the doorway, the snow running from him and pooling at his feet. Lena ran over and hugged him round the knees and he lifted her up and held her close, soaking the child in the process.

He led their horses back through the storm, nearly blinded by snowflakes transformed to shards of ice. Once inside the house he turned to her. She was smiling, the smile spilling out of her almost without her knowledge. He was trembling.

I missed you, he said.

I know.

He pulled her to him and rested his cheek against hers and finally, for the first time, he was able to cry.

After the child had gone to bed, he said slowly, hesitantly, You know, you make me feel whole.

He wasn't sure this was what he had meant to say, but it was a start. Her hand closed tightly round his and she half turned and traced the curve of his lips with her finger.

We make each other feel whole, she said.

She moved her hand to caress the side of his face, his jaw, and kissed him softly, tiny kisses along the edge of his lips. He remained as impassive as stone, gripping her other hand, before his resistance broke.

This time her body felt real to him, not fragments from a dream, or a surreal hallucination, but there was a certain clumsiness, an awkwardness on his part as if it were the first time for him now that he was bereft of the herb that made him feel how she felt. They were not in tune and it was as if he were splashing about helplessly on the shore of some great ocean, waiting for a current or the right swimming stroke to sweep him effortlessly out to sea. He felt they were lacking some vital ingredient; she was only partly engaged, the building explosion of sensation that had made her unfurl like a flower, a morning glory greeting the sun, was missing. He stopped.

What is it? she asked.

You, he said. I've lost you, he whispered.

She smiled, wide-eyed, twisted her body, took his hand and showed him what to do; he felt her breath hot against his throat, her pulse quicken, limbs grow taut. He was hanging in deep green water, waves breaking against him, the clean span of the shore attainable in a few slow strokes.

Why, she said afterwards, as he held her trembling gently in his arms, why does your God deny you this?

He stiffened and felt his throat constrict. He had always been told that loving a woman was a distraction, preventing a full and devoted love of God, but now he wondered whether not-loving, the dedication of one's internal resources to the denial of one's feelings, was not, in fact, more all-consuming.

My love, he whispered, and leaned to kiss her shoulder, her breast-bone, tracing the dark line that ran across her belly with his lips.

You know, she said, her voice soft in the dark, you once asked me why I was following you. What Uugan really told me was that my destiny lay with a foreign man. A man not of this country nor of our race who worshipped a God we do not know. And as soon as I saw you, I knew you were the one. You stood there looking at me, so fine, so proud, so pale, with your handsome face and your black hair and deep blue eyes and I felt inexplicably drawn to you. Almost against my will. The spirits said that I would fall in love with you and that you would break my heart. Joseph, don't do it. I love you with all my soul. Please. Don't break my heart.

Do you remember the goose we ate? he asked Lena, while they saddled the horses. The child nodded.

Well, your mother hunted them with the eagle by a lake. Shall we ride down there today?

Lena nodded eagerly and scrambled up the horse as if she were mountaineering. Joseph had given her the roan.

The glare from the snow was blinding. It was an odd sensation, being outside in considerable cold while the sun's heat burned their faces. They picked their way slowly down the mountainside: responsible for a young child, Joseph did not want to encourage any headlong gallops. But when she caught sight of the lake she urged the horse to head for it at full speed and Joseph followed alongside as Lena bounced about in her saddle like an unprofessional jockey, singing and shouting. Vast flocks of waders took flight and the air around them was filled with beating wings. A couple of small downy feathers floated on to Joseph's saddle. Lena stood up in her stirrups and screamed, waving her cap at the birds as they honked loudly in their panic. They slowed to a walk and Joseph gave one of the white feathers to Lena who tucked it in her hair with an impish grin. Joseph leaned over and rearranged her skull cap on her unruly mass of hair. It was blue and red and Namuunaa had embroidered it with flowers in black and gold thread.

Can I go skating?

Skating? The word was unfamiliar to him.

On the ice, said Lena impatiently, not understanding his difficulty.

He assumed that she was going to slide around on the ice since she was hardly likely to possess a pair of ice skates.

Let me go first.

A scattering of crisp crumbs of snow covered the frozen lake. He stood gingerly on the edge. The ice, white with streams of frozen bubbles, was thick and opaque. He moved further out and bounced a little, suddenly skidded and nearly fell. Lena giggled and clapped her hands from the shore. He skated in an ungainly manner towards her.

It appears to be thick but don't go out too far.

He held her hands and guided her on to the edge of the lake, then spun her around as if they were waltzing partners. She laughed happily and let go, spinning away by herself. If this were London, or even Bristol, he imagined there would be fine ladies in long, velvet dresses, their hands in muffs, elegantly skating on thin, metal blades with white lace-up boots; men in striped satin waistcoats and full-length evening coats; street urchins and children like the kind of child he had once been slipping under the barriers and tearing about wantonly; old men with soot-blackened faces selling hot chestnuts and baked potatoes. He checked Lena, who was making a neat figure of eight round two of the bog-oak black trees. He returned to the shore to fetch his gun. He skittered somewhat ineptly from the ice on to the shore, unhooked his gun from the saddle and turned back towards the lake.

Lena was gone. He stood still for a couple of seconds in disbelief, thinking that perhaps he was mistaking one of the twisted tree trunks for her. But nothing moved. He half ran, half slipped across the ice to where he'd last seen her. There were smooth glassy tracks where she'd been skating round the two tree stumps and then one leading off at an angle towards the centre of the lake. He followed the marks she'd made as she'd slid across the ice. In the distance something twinkled in the bright heat of the sun. He stumbled and skidded as fast as he could towards it. It was her hat. He could feel the ice thinning beneath him, creaking ominously, protesting at his weight.

His throat was dry and he felt sick to the pit of his stomach. Faint lines like an optical illusion were threading through the ice. He could see it now, the dark heart from which they had their source, a jagged hole a few yards ahead of him. He suppressed his urge to run straight at it, but edged gingerly forwards. The ruins of a tree stuck out of the ice and he wrapped his arm around its trunk as he prepared to stretch himself out full-length on the ice. Something coloured caught his eye. He gave it no more than a passing glance but as he slid on his belly towards the hole, the after-image of this thing hit him with the full realization of what it was. He leapt to his feet and the ice creaked and cracked about him. He looked down.

It was Lena, floating beneath him, her hair spread in the dark water like an ice maiden. He hit the ice with the butt of his gun. Chips of ice flew away from the indentation, and fracture marks spread outwards in a geometric ripple, but he had done little more than create a small indentation. He swung the gun again but still made little impact. He shrugged off his *del* and slid towards the hole in the ice. A whole plate of ice split and cracked beneath him, tipping him into the freezing water. He struggled blindly for a few seconds, attempting to orient himself, his body collapsing into shock at the cold. He swam under the ice towards the tree. Lena's dress had become tangled on a dead branch. He tried to work it free but it was caught fast and he was running out of air. He braced his feet against the trunk and leaned back until the material ripped. Holding her beneath his arm, he swam towards the hole in the ice and held her aloft.

As he tried to push her back on to the ice, the sheet broke and tilted and her dead and watery weight came down upon him, pushing him under once more. He kicked hard to get back to the surface and leaned against another part of the ice. He tried a second time and the same thing happened. He was starting to panic. He attempted to push her out a third time, in the direction of the oak, and this time the ice held. He pushed her as far away from himself as he could and then he struggled to get out. His hands stuck to the frozen ice and he was shaking with the cold so much his muscles hardly worked at all. Eventually he managed to get his face and shoulders out and could reach the oak with one hand to lever himself on to the ice. He wrapped Lena in his *del* and staggered towards the shore.

At the side of the lake he dropped to the ground. Her face was pale, her lips tinged blue and her eyelids were mauve. Her tiny hands, the fingers white and wrinkled, made him want to weep. The sun seemed heartlessly bright; above his head flocks of gulls spun and screamed.

He started to pray: Our Father, who art in heaven, hallowed be Thy name, Thy Kingdom come, Thy will be done . . .

How long this continued for he could not say, but as he was on the point of burying his head in the snow and howling at the sky, he realized that she was breathing. He tore her dress open and placed his hand upon her heart. He felt its shallow beat. He started to cry with relief, choking on his own tears as he ran with her over to his horse. Placing her across his knee, he rode back up the mountainside. Lena drifted in and out of consciousness throughout the journey. He himself was chilled to the bone and racked with shivers that convulsed his entire body but the whole way to the house he thanked God over and over again, a litany that was as much part of retaining his own sanity as asserting his gratitude.

What he felt on that ride back as he urged the horses to gallop faster through the thick snow was an almost grim realignment of his priorities, the values that he had held so dear throughout his life. In those few minutes from when he'd seen her face pressed against the thickened ice as if floating in some macabre fish tank he had realized that there was nothing he would not have given to make her live again: his entire plant collection, a whole valley of lily bulbs dug out by hand, his faith, his soul, his heart.

Namuunaa looked down at Lena and back at him.

What have you done with my child? she screamed.

He pushed past her and placed Lena by the fire.

She's alive but not conscious. Don't let her warm up too quickly, he said.

Don't tell me how to look after my own child.

Her voice had an edge of hysteria to it. Joseph brought over blankets and clothes and helped her wrap Lena in as many layers as possible. He carried her over to her cot. Beads of moisture had sprung on her brow; there was a greenish tinge to her skin. He poured out hot water and gave the bowl and a rag to Namuunaa to wipe the child's face with, then heated some milk for her. He went back out to catch the horses and tie them up. His hands were so cold they were like claws, hooked, frozen and useless. Back inside he built up the fire and put on more water to boil before he changed out of his clothes, which had partly frozen into stiff sheets.

Lena came round a little and they were able to get her to drink a small amount.

What happened? asked Namuunaa, now grown quiet, as they knelt looking at the child.

He told her, I should never have left her for one moment. I should have held on to her. It was stupid to let her skate on the ice at all.

We skate there sometimes. She went with the twins this year. She knows she's supposed to stay by the edge.

I didn't think that it would be so thin so near the shore. I never thought she would . . .

It's all right. It was not your fault.

Will she . . . ?

I hope so. She'll have a severe cold, maybe a fever. If we can get her through that . . .

Shall I get Uugan?

Yes. Go now.

The horses are very tired, I made them gallop back up the mountain, and my horse is limping quite badly.

Take them to Boshigt when you've brought Uugan over. He'll look after them. Joseph?

He paused at the door, struggling to put on her *del*.

Are you all right?

He nodded, and then came back and kissed her.

Namuunaa, he whispered, I love you. I love you.

It was with a mixture of joyful anticipation and dread that Joseph watched the snow begin to thaw and saw the first signs of spring as rosettes of green appeared on the larches. Mendo and Tsem arrived at the start of March and spoke of favourable weather in the south; uncommonly little snow in the valleys, crocuses already blooming on the mountain slopes, an unseasonably warm spring in Suanhwa.

He embraced his two friends, overjoyed to see them again, an ache burning in his heart.

Delger and Amgalan have said you can stay with them for a few days. Let's have some tea here and then we'll ride over.

Namuunaa and Lena were already standing on the door-step grinning at them. Within minutes of their arrival, it seemed, Batbaatar and Boshigt had come over to see what all the commotion was about. Their journey was uneventful this time – no robbers or robber barons – and they did not stay long enough in any of the monasteries to become terrified by mad monks.

Tsem slapped his thigh at the memory of it and recounted the story to Boshigt and Batbaatar.

Without Joseph looking under every crevice for a flower or taking pot shots at passing birds, we travelled a lot faster, Tsem said. We're thinking of leaving him behind on the way back.

Joseph smiled thinly, Namuunaa not at all. Her whole expression was brittle.

It's good to see you again, my friend, said Joseph quietly to Mendo.

The monk looked at him with his dark, almost melancholy eyes and smiled.

I am happy to see you looking so well. How's your leg?

It hurts when it's about to snow or if there is a frost. I feel like an old man. But apart from that, it's good. It healed well. I haven't shot too many birds since then.

Too many?

Well, the odd one or two as I was accompanying Namuunaa when she was hunting. How did you spend the winter?

At Suanhwa with the Lazarists. Meditating and recuperating. Thinking of you. I suppose you want to know about your plants? I spoke to Delaware and he arranged everything as you had requested. I asked him to pass a message on to Patrick to warn him of your delay, and I have some letters for you.

He pulled four from the folds of his habit. Joseph inspected the handwriting and the postmark. Two were from Patrick, one was from Jeremy, and the fourth, which also had a Bristol postmark, was probably from the Royal Botanical Gardens. He put them in his jacket pocket to read later. There was something not quite right. He could not put his finger on it. It might be because Mendo was tired and would never show it, it might simply be an awkwardness at meeting after several months apart, an awkwardness it had taken them some little time to overcome initially, but he had a feeling it was deeper than that. He could see it in Mendo's eyes but they were so unfathomable he was unable to read their true expression.

Look what I've got, said Tsem loudly, producing a large bottle of fine brandy. We saved it for this occasion.

Lena, run and fetch some bowls, said Namuunaa. She had started to build up the fire and put on a pot of water to boil. Joseph, seeing this, went to the food store to bring in some yak meat for the stew she was about to make.

Lena, go and tell Uugan that Mendo and Tsem are here, he said, taking the bowls from her and passing round the brandy. He had automatically taken on the role of man of the house. Mendo watched with his inscrutable expression, bowing his head when he received the brandy. Tsem patted him on the shoulder, and started to roll a cigarette.

I should be using those bits of paper up there. He nodded to the flower paintings that covered one wall.

Don't even consider thieving scraps from those ones.

Tsem chuckled. We have something else for you too.

He rummaged about in his *del* and passed Joseph a brown paper package tied with bamboo leaf. Joseph held it to his face and took a long deep sniff.

Thank you, he said.

What is it? I want to smell too.

He passed it to Lena who smelled it and screwed up her face.

Yuk!

It's coffee. You might like it when you're older.

Lena, Joseph asked you to go and tell Grandma to come over.

I'm getting ready, she lied.

Joseph helped her put on her coat and boots.

All right, you're ready now. Don't be long, it's getting dark.

It was a late night, fuelled by brandy and yak's milk vodka, the stew too little and too slow in coming, for the whole village turned up. Joseph had a job to persuade Delger and Amgalan to leave; Mendo was bound to be tired and in need of his bed, though Tsem looked, as he usually did on such occasions, as if he could roll over and sleep anywhere.

Namuunaa held him tightly, fiercely, all through the night. He slept badly, the unaccustomed brandy disagreeing with his system. As he stared up at the ceiling, he felt Namuunaa stir next to him. He stroked her shoulder.

Are you happy? she asked quietly.

He traced the outline of her cheekbone, brushed the hair from her face. For a person who prided himself on rationality and accuracy, it would be possible to describe many permutations of his emotional state. But he told her the truth he knew she would want to hear.

No, he said.

She leaned on her elbow and looked down at him.

That's not entirely true, she said.

The following afternoon Mendo appeared. He looked slightly awkward.

Come in, come in. Namuunaa held the door open for him but he hovered outside.

I was wondering if you wished to take a walk with me, he said to Joseph. Take some fresh air.

Getting fresh air seemed to be an alien term in Mongolia given the sufficiency of it.

I should be glad to, he answered. I'm feeling a little fragile this morning.

Mendo grinned sheepishly. I think the brandy was not as good as we thought.

Nonsense, my friend, I drank too much of it, that's all.

He smiled at Namuunaa as he left.

I'll take you to a waterfall in the woods where I pray sometimes, Joseph said. You would find it conducive to meditation – were it not so cold, he added.

In some parts of Tibet the monks practise *tummo*, the art of heating the body through concentrated meditation even in the bitterest winter. I've seen monks in training sitting naked in the snow wrapped in sheets soaked in cold water. They dry the sheets with the heat from their bodies and they're replaced with wet sheets, over and over again for eight to twelve hours.

They walked in silence for some while and then Joseph asked, Is everything all right?

Mendo stopped and turned to him. Will you be travelling back with us?

Of course, Joseph said, deliberately turning away and walking on. After a moment he heard Mendo's footsteps crunching through the snow towards him. The monk caught up with him.

Why do you ask? he said, staring straight ahead.

Joseph, surely we know each other well enough.

Well enough for what? asked Joseph coldly.

Mendo sighed. I am Mongolian, he said. We hate confrontation.

Spit it out, my friend, whatever it is you must say, say it.

Joseph, you are my brother. You have become as dear to me as my own kin. So I say this to you as a friend. You must realize how cruel this will be?

How cruel what will be? He turned to look at Mendo.

Mendo looked away, composed himself and turned back, presenting an expression that to anyone else would have seemed like a blank mask but Joseph could see the hidden signs of anxiety.

Don't make me spell it out, he said with dignity.

If you are referring to Namuunaa . . .

Who else would I be speaking of? And the child. Can you not see what it will do to them?

You left me with her.

You are responsible for your own karma.

Joseph stared off into the mountains in the distance, fuming quietly, defensively. They walked on in silence, the sound of the waterfall growing louder. When they reached the stream, they both stood side by side, mesmerized, watching the water, newly freed from the ice.

Forgive me, said Joseph with difficulty. You saved my life and here I am behaving like a spoiled child with you. You know me better than maybe I even know my own self. So you will understand how hard this is for me to say. I know that there is nothing I can say that could excuse my behaviour. I have fallen in love with a woman, a beautiful woman, and her child. I have created a false family that I will tear apart. I have broken my own vows of chastity. In front of my own God, I have sinned.

Mendo suddenly turned and hugged him.

You could stay.

And you know why I can't. You are a stronger man than me, Mendo. Munke . . .

Yes, said Mendo sadly. I have loved Munke my whole life. Long before my brother. And though I loved him greatly, he never recognized her true worth. When he died, I wondered whether I should stop being a lama.

And you decided not to. You have kept your faith and your morals intact.

Joseph, I make that decision every day. Every single day I make my vows anew. Who knows how long I will hold out, how long my faith will sustain me? She struggles, Joseph, I see her struggling to raise Boldt by herself. Surely it would be an act of charity, of goodness, to marry her and help her raise my brother's child? This is the thought that torments me, night after night. I envy you, my brother. You have loved and been loved even if the leaving of that love will break your heart.

He turned abruptly away and strode up the hill towards the cabins. Joseph remained, watching the waterfall, and tried to pray. But he could find no words with which to speak to his God and the desolation he felt swelled and grew, spreading within him like a canker hollowing out the marrow of his bones.

When he reached the cabin it was after dark. He opened the door and hesitated at the threshold. Lena wasn't there. There was a fire crackling in the hearth and the room was filled with candles. It smelled of beeswax and pine and musk. Namuunaa uncoiled from where she had been sitting in front of the flickering flames. She was wearing the dark blood-red coat he had first seen her in and was naked beneath it. The candlelight glimmered in her hair, casting auburn sparks amid its blackness, and the fire threw shadows of light and dark on the curve of her breast, the plane of her stomach. He shut the door and leaned against it.

It's one night. Our last night, she said, walking softly towards him.

He swallowed. She was so beautiful it hurt him to look at her. He knew that as soon as she reached him, he would be undone. He would not have the willpower to turn away from her. She was halfway between him and the fire. This was his only chance to leave if he was going to. He felt as if he had been pierced through with iron nails that tore his lungs as he tried to breathe. She stopped in front of him. She did not touch him. Tall and lithe, she was almost level with him and when she looked at him it was as if she were seeing into his soul.

Such pain, Joseph, there is so much pain in your eyes, she whispered.

He slid his hands around her waist. Her skin was smooth and she felt sleekly muscled, as a dolphin might. He ran his hands up her back and round her ribcage. He bent and kissed her in a line down her neck into the curve of her shoulder and felt her tremble beneath his lips. He cupped his hands over her breasts, felt the heavy, soft weight of them, as her nipples hardened, grazing his palms. She stroked his jaw, his cheekbones and then pulled him towards her, kissing him deeply. Their tongues met and he felt himself dissolve, like wax melting in the heat. She stepped back slightly and removed his clothes, one by one, and then led him to the thick fur rug in front of the fire.

She moaned softly as he entered her; in the firelight her eyes widened and glowed and he could see into their depths as if into the green shallows of the sea where waves whisper over rocks and bones. And, like the tide, he felt surges of ecstasy and utter sadness wash over him.

Afterwards, she lay in his arms and he stroked her all over as if attempting to memorize her body in its entirety, to imprint her on his palms for the rest of his life. He hugged her tightly to him, wishing he could incorporate her into his own flesh.

Flesh of my flesh, blood of my blood . . .

There was a price to be paid for such a pleasure. A price for cheating God and taking his heart's desire. And he was already starting to pay.

As if she could sense his thoughts, she said quietly, You were the one. I knew as soon as I looked into your blue eyes. I knew that one day I would love you. And you would love me too. But the spirits were right. Tomorrow you will leave. Tomorrow you will break my heart.

PART III

The three of them lined up at the edge and peered over.

Dear Lord, what do we do now?

Fly?

Flying indeed seems to be our only option, Joseph answered Tsem.

The crevasse was relatively narrow but deep, the sides sheer cliff, and at the bottom was a raging black torrent of meltwater from the mountains. There had been a bridge; the remnants remained. The crevasse stretched as far as the eye could see in either direction.

Could the horses swim it? asked Mendo.

They should be swept away surely.

Tsem nodded. We'd need to tie them together.

How?

Loop rope through the bridles; stretch the rope across the river. But they couldn't carry the baggage. It would be too much for them – they'd drown; and even if they didn't, the bags would get wet.

How will we get them down?

There must be a way, said Tsem. A path chipped into the cliff.

So we can get the horses across, possibly. What about us? asked Joseph.

We will make a rope bridge, said Mendo, who had been studying the crevasse silently. One rope to stand on, one rope to hold on to. The top rope will be a pulley system so that we can winch the bags across.

Our thickest rope is thin.

It is all we have.

We can loop it round the trees on either side, but how are we going to get it across?

We'll just have to wait until we see someone, throw the rope to them, said Tsem.

We could be here for days.

He nodded.

What about the wolf? asked Joseph suddenly.

Mendo shook his head. She will drown. The current is too strong for her.

There was silence for a few moments, then Joseph said, I am going to have to carry her. Across the rope. It's the only way.

Mendo shook his head again. She will be too scared. The drop – look at it.

I am looking at it, said Joseph grimly.

Tsem suddenly grinned. We'll tie a scarf round her eyes.

It's not such a bad idea, said Mendo and the two of them turned to look at Joseph who shut his eyes in horror at the thought of walking across a piece of rope above a gorge carrying a blind, half-grown wolf in his arms.

When they'd left, Namuunaa had given him Wolf as a gift. At first he had not wanted to accept; Wolf, after all, was useful to her and, in any case, what would he do with a predator from the Mongolian steppes? He could not take her to Bristol with him. But then he saw Mendo shaking his head at him so he thanked Namuunaa and called Wolf to his side.

I'll look after her, said Mendo once they were on the road. You can collect her when you come back.

We'll have no trouble with robbers, that's for sure, said Tsem.

Joseph said nothing.

Now as they waited for a traveller to appear on the other side of the crevasse, the time seemed endless. He sat with his arm around Wolf. Tsem wandered up and down the bank until he found a track in the cliff that the horses, unencumbered by people and luggage, could get down. Mendo checked and rechecked the ropes round the bags and kept their own thin coils of rope ready.

Perhaps one of us could swim across, said Joseph.

Who?

Well, I'm a strong swimmer.

The water is freezing.

I know.

Tsem shook his head. We're not going to carry your wolf for you; you can't go.

They were right to wait; despite the vastness of Mongolia, there was always someone about somewhere and after a couple of hours, a horseman appeared in the distance. Tsem took out his blue silk scarf and waved it and Mendo blew into a conch shell he had hidden on his person.

The herder, in true Mongolian fashion, had to debate all the options with them until he arrived at the same conclusions they had already come to hours earlier. But he caught their ropes, tied one to the base of the tree, looped the second one higher up the tree and threw it back to Tsem who knotted it together with its own end. They winched the bags over one by one to the herder who unhooked them from the rope.

Let's get the horses over next, said Tsem. He threaded his yak hide lasso through the horses' bridles and tied a stone round one end. He led the horses down the steep cliff path and fastened the other end of the hide to a tree growing out of a crevice in the rock. He threw the stone across to the herder who had scrambled down the opposite bank and he hitched the hide to a piece of stone jutting out from the cliff. Now Tsem climbed up the cliff face slightly above the horses and almost kicked them into the water. The minute the horses were in the river, Joseph could see just how strong and malevolent a force it was. They struggled furiously, their eyes rolling, Tsem and the herder shouting encouragement at them. Just at the point where they were about to be swept away, they managed to get a purchase on the river bottom and scramble out dripping and shaking.

But the last horse was in trouble right from the start. It didn't manage to get into a swimming stroke sufficiently early and as a result was swept quickly downstream. The herder was half hanging from the cliff edge trying to untie the previous horse's bridle and release it from the yak hide, for the rope was pulling the horse back down the cliff towards the river. The horse itself was not being co-operative, shaking its head, showing its teeth, whinnying in fear. The herder gave a last desperate yank and the whole bridle broke off, the horse's neck snapped back and it made a mad and desperate bid to clamber up the cliff towards the others. The horse in the river was not so lucky. The hide was stretched to breaking point between the tree on one side and the rock on the other but it was the horse's bridle that snapped first. It was swept away within seconds. They watched it in horrified silence. Tsem undid the hide and the herder on the far side pulled it in and coiled it up ready for him.

The only thing that remained was to cross the crevasse themselves. Joseph sat Wolf down in front of him and stroked her all over, generally making a fuss of her. He tied Tsem's scarf around her eyes, then tied his own scarf round his *del* lower and tighter than normal to make a larger pouch. With Tsem's help, they lifted her in. She growled and showed her white incisors at this unwelcome manhandling. Once she was in the pouch, Mendo tied another rope loosely round both Joseph and the wolf to hold her in. Joseph held her to him with his left arm, with his right he held the rope. Crossing the tight rope was one of the most frightening experiences he'd ever encountered.

Do not look down, do not look down, they yelled at him.

He inched his way across, feeling with each foot for the rope, praying it was secured tightly enough, praying he would not lose his balance, praying the wolf would not suddenly move. His weight was all out of kilter and he struggled to remain upright and not tilt to one side, for he knew that if he did, all would be lost. He kept his eyes firmly fixed on the herder who, for all Joseph cared, could have been shouting in Siberian. At the far side he grasped his hand and the herder helped him on to the cliff edge. When he untied the rope from around his middle, Wolf stuck her head out and growled ferociously at the man but seemed unwilling to leave the pouch. Joseph had to turn her out and she cowered by his ankles.

Are you going to cross? Tsem asked the herder when he and Mendo had arrived safely.

The herder uttered something, which Joseph didn't fully understand, but took to be both rude and negative. He burst into laughter and he and Tsem hugged each other. They caught the horses who had no spirit to run from them and, as the occasion demanded, took tea together. The herder, whose name was Chinbaatar, invited them back to his *ger*.

That night Joseph lay looking at the stars through the sky hole in Chinbaatar's *ger* and thought of falling from the rope, clutching the wolf to his chest, falling through black water, falling down the side of the mountain in an inexorable torrent of melted snow.

After a few more days they reached the flat plains of the steppes and, in the distance, could see the Temple of the Larks, the sun glancing across the glazed green roof. Mendo and Tsem picked up the pace and Tsem started to whistle. Since there was no festival taking place this time, Joseph imagined that Mendo was looking forward to staying with the monks for a couple of days. They would be kindred spirits for him and it would be a welcome break to sleep indoors, even in one of the brothers' spartan cells. But he himself could summon no feeling about it either way: he felt utterly wretched; his whole being ached for Namuunaa and Lena. He could not rid his mind of the image of Namuunaa on the day he left, standing on the mountain top, watching him until she was but a speck in the distance; knowing it was the last time he should ever see her pale and beautiful face, grave with grief at his leaving. Knowing that what he had lost could not be measured nor calibrated, but its magnitude would haunt him for the rest of his days.

As they neared the temple, Mendo suddenly slowed his horse from a jerky trot to a walk and Tsem stopped whistling. Joseph had been staring down at his horse's mane and not paying attention to his surroundings and it was only after a few minutes that he noticed and looked up. When he did, he had an uncomfortable sensation that all was not well but he couldn't quite comprehend why. It was the absence of sound that struck him first. He could hear no birdsong. A thin wind sliced across the tips of the grass, bending it into pale shapes like the parting of a woman's hair. There were no voices from the temple and, now that he had thought about it, no monks either: those brief flashes of orange robe, disappearing past the white walls; the high-altitude tinkle of their prayer bells was missing too. As they drew nearer it became apparent that something was terribly wrong. Joseph felt his skin slowly chill and corrugate into goose-flesh. The terracotta monkeys, dragons, fish and horses that had once marched across the gables now lay shattered on the ground in front of the temple along with green shards of slate from the smashed roof tiles. The gold prayer wheels and the flags were missing. The wolf started to snarl and pace and when the three of them urged their horses through the bent and twisted gates into the inner courtyard she put her ears flat to her skull and her tail between her legs and refused to follow them. The statue of

Maidari had been hacked to pieces, the head cleaved in two; one ear lay flat on the stone floor. Mendo jumped from his horse and picked up a piece of rock. It was part of a lotus petal, a smooth, shell-pink curve. The ornate onyx tiles with gold filigree had been prised away, leaving only dark blood-red stains against the white walls.

Who could have done this? asked Joseph, his voice sounding loud in the unnaturally quiet, echoing chamber, only the sound of the wind keening round the corners.

I'm going inside, said Mendo. Will you wait here with the horses?

Tsem can look after them. I'm coming with you.

He slid from his horse and handed the reins to Tsem. When he turned back, Mendo had already disappeared inside the building. Joseph hurried to catch up with him, wondering if this was wise. Could whoever had done this still be here? He prayed that the monks had escaped in time. He paused in the doorway, hesitant to step into the darkness until his eyes began to adjust. He could hear Mendo striding down the corridor, his footsteps echoing and crunching through the broken artefacts that littered the ground. Joseph hastened after him, just as Mendo, his *del* flaring out behind him, turned a corner and disappeared into the blackness.

It looked as if a small army had looted the temple: the gold leaf and statues had been shorn from the walls and the intricately carved screens were strewn across the corridor, the exposed wood raw against their polished outer surfaces. Joseph remembered going to meet the Yolros lama, incense drifting, sweet and smoky, in gunmetal-grey clouds through this passageway. Joseph hurried after the sound of Mendo's footsteps down the opposite side of the quadrant. Mendo was pushing open broken doors and peering into empty, desecrated rooms, disappearing in and out of the half-light. He caught up with him and put his hand on his shoulder. Mendo covered it briefly with his own.

I think you should go back and wait with Tsem. I do not have a good feeling about this.

I'll stay with you, said Joseph.

Mendo started to speed up, pushing doors open, kicking apart screens with an agitation Joseph had never seen in him before. And it was at that point that the smell hit Joseph. It grew in strength until it felt like a physical object, a cloying stench that crept down the back of his throat making him retch. Mendo looked up at the winding stairway to the upper levels but turned away and instead stepped through the remains of the doorway into what had once been the great hall. The smell was overpowering. Joseph held his scarf over his mouth as he climbed over and through the ruined wooden panels, snagging his *del* and feeling a splinter slice into his skin. The room was suddenly eerily still. Mendo stood silently in the centre, surrounded by lances of light falling through the shutters where they had been pierced by a legion of swords. In front of him was a pile of bodies, almost heaped to the ceiling. Those who were whole were twisted, bent the way the human body cannot bend. There were arms and legs and severed heads. The tide of blood had spread in a slick as black as oil and dried like a glaze of varnish across the floor. Criss-crossing one another were trails of footprints and smears where someone had slipped in the blood, where someone had been dragged through it. By Joseph's feet lay a hand: so perfect he could have stretched out and shaken it, imagined its dry warmth; so terrible in its immolation it was like a nightmarish insect that might rise and scuttle into a crevice. Joseph doubled over and vomited. He continued to throw up even after he had rid himself of all the bile in his stomach and his stomach had tightened into a clenched fist. He felt Mendo seize him by the shoulders and pull him upright.

Come, brother, he said, and putting his arm around him helped him back through the broken door.

They took the nearest exit into the courtyard, Joseph practically falling into the daylight. He staggered upright and took a huge juddering breath. It felt as if the universe were out of kilter: the thin wind still dragged skeins of cloud across the perfect cerulean blue of the sky; the soft pad of his palm throbbed around the buried splinter of wood. Tsem gripped his other arm and poured water across his face, wiping away cold sweat and involuntary tears, and he drank from the goatskin bottle, feeling the acrid sting of the bile at the back of his throat and in his nostrils.

Are you all right, my friend? said Joseph as he handed the water to Mendo.

Mendo drank and said nothing but when he looked at Joseph it was as if part of his soul had been extinguished.

You think it was the White Warlord? asked Tsem.

Mendo nodded. We should go. Find someone to speak to. Find where his army is.

Tsem sucked his teeth and spat and shook his head. He helped Joseph back on his horse as if he were an invalid and led him like a child out of the courtyard and into the wide, open steppe.

The following day there was a rainstorm that gradually became colder and more vicious until the water turned to ice. Through the blinding rain of grit and hail they saw, with astonishment, a girl rounding up sheep. She was riding a white horse flecked strawberry-brown, single-mindedly wheeling and calling around her flock, a thin black and white mongrel streaking between her horse and the herd. Her *del* was made of pink Chinese silk, torn in many places, and she wore a tangerine orange scarf around her face and a black and red hat that covered her ears and rose to a peak like a minaret. Tsem shouted until she saw them and galloped over, melded to her horse. As she drew near Joseph saw that she had silver hoops in her ears and a headdress of coral. She was probably only sixteen or seventeen and she stared frankly at them with dark, slanting eyes. The shepherdess gestured to the east and said something briefly to Tsem, then cantered back to the sheep. Joseph followed Mendo and Tsem in the direction she had pointed. In the distance was a *ger* and a well, but the longer they journeyed towards it, the further away the dwelling appeared to be.

After what seemed an interminable length of time, they reached the *ger*. Joseph fumbled over his horse's reins but Tsem took them from him and tied up the animal with the other horses and the wolf. He was so cold he shook violently, his body jerking in uncontrollable spasms. Mendo and Tsem bundled him between them next to the hearth in the centre of the *ger*. The owners stared at the three of them and in particular at Joseph with the open and friendly curiosity he had grown accustomed to. It was warm, hot with stale air and the thick steam from his party and the owners' damp *dels*. The woman of the household served them the rancid milk tea; he forced it down, glad of its warming and restorative properties. There were twin girls with light brown hair tied in ribbons, about six years old, a toddler crawling around the floor with almost no clothes, a thin thirteen-year-old girl whose trouser cuffs and sleeves failed to cover her bony ankles and wrists, the woman's mother, in a jade *del*, who was wearing a silver ring with a giant moss-green stone, and the father of the girls, a lean man whose face was corrugated with lines and who leaned hunched into the fire. A little later the shepherdess strode in and hung her hat by the door.

Where are your boys? asked Tsem.

Even he sounded despondent and weary, as if he was only asking for form's sake.

The man replied that he had none. He said that the oldest was as strong as a boy, but that she would need to be married soon, and then he would have no one to help him.

The twin girls turned away and buried their giggling heads in one of the beds when Joseph stared at them, and the baby crawled over to him and dribbled on his knee. The woman served them bowls of mutton stew, which were rich and full of meat. It was still mutton, still greasy, still vegetable-free, but at least it was not the watery concoction most families could only afford to give their guests. The couple seemed very nervous, constantly glancing at each other out of the corners of their eyes.

Joseph asked the woman if he could borrow one of her pans. He put in a little water from a bucket by the door and set it on the hearth to boil. Braving the wind, which tore at him like a demented creature, he searched through his bags until he found what he wanted. The wolf whined and strained at her leash, her coat dark with rain. The whole family watched him with interest; even the shepherdess peered through her coral headdress at him. He added a twist of coffee, grown in Africa, shipped to Bristol where it had been roasted and ground, and which had sailed halfway round the world again. It was the last of his coffee and the smell made him long for home. He used a square of muslin to strain the coffee into a jar and then poured everyone a measure, Turkish cup size. He added a few drops of brandy to the men's cups, including his own. The twin girls sniffed the coffee and ran away laughing; the thirteen-year-old sipped a little, made a terrible face and handed her bowl back to her mother. In the silence they could hear the wind moaning, and the trellis of wooden struts that held up the *ger* creaked and swayed like the mast of a tall ship.

We came past the Temple of the Larks, said Mendo eventually.

The man blew on his coffee and shook his head as if the situation was so terrible no words could describe it.

Was it the White Warlord's men?

He nodded.

And where are they now?

We don't know. They left a week ago. They travel from lamasery to lamasery. The army has grown.

Joseph poured more coffee and felt his pulse begin to race at the unaccustomed stimulation.

Do they leave the people alone?

So far. They stole some of our sheep but they did not touch the girl. They mean to rid us of the monks. They say they are parasites on the system, that the taxes are unfair and too high. You are not safe, said the man, glancing at the three of them and then back at Mendo.

We will leave you, said Mendo. Thank you for your hospitality.

No, please, said the woman. Stay until the morning at least.

The man said nothing, only continued to sit with his head bowed over his empty coffee bowl.

You cannot let them go, said the woman turning to her husband. Look outside, it's still hailing.

He said nothing and Mendo, Joseph and Tsem rose to their feet.

Thank you, you've been most kind to us, said Joseph.

The three of them turned and pushed their way through the flaps of the *ger* outside into the night. Chips of ice flew into their faces.

At least our bellies are full, said Tsem. Come on, he added, slapping their shoulders, get on your horses, keep warm.

We cannot even see the stars, said Mendo glumly. How will we navigate?

We won't, said Tsem, whistling through his teeth. We'll just ride and then camp. We'll see where we are in the morning.

They followed Tsem's voice as he sang, his song a thin, steely strand stretching into that bitter night. In the early hours of the morning they came across an outcrop of rock and hobbled the horses together and sheltered against the stone, wrapping the canvas of their tent around them. Mendo sat silent and pale in between Joseph and Tsem, bowed down under the weight of bodies. And when Joseph, shaking with a cold that had seeped into his very bones, closed his eyes, he saw maggots writhing in the flesh of men. The wolf, curled up beside him, licked his hand.

They had reached the treeline. Joseph took his bowl of tea and wandered under the edge of the canopy. Tsem had decided the next morning that they should head up towards the trees – it would give them cover if they did need to hide. It would be a much longer way to Pekin but Tsem was hopeful that at some point they would be able to drop back down to their original route.

Beneath the trees the needle-carpeted earth was soft and springy, the cool air smelled of the crisp freshness of pine and a gentle breeze stirred the branches. Waxy, whey-white orchids grew at the base of some of the trees; small creatures stirred and rustled. Deeper into the forest the trees' limbs were festooned with thick drifts of lichen the sober olive-grey of a magpie's egg.

Joseph thought that in former times on these solitary wanderings of his he would have considered evolution and Darwin. He had once fantasized that Darwin would write another book. He had imagined Darwin citing Father Joseph Jacob and his collection of herbarium specimens from Outer Mongolia; his impressive display of fossils and geological artefacts, his extensive knowledge of the flora and fauna of the steppes and mountains. He remembered composing letters in his mind:

> *Dear Mr Darwin,*
>
> *It has come to my attention that you might be interested in a discovery I made while travelling in Outer . . .*

> *Dear Mr Charles Darwin,*
>
> *It was with great pleasure that I read your book, The Origin of Species. May I congratulate you on your lucidity, profundity, and, above all, bravery? I am, myself, well acquainted with natural selection in the field. I have travelled quite widely, and wished to share with you . . .*

Now it seemed empty vanity to him. Joseph liked minerals, animals, botanical specimens, yet these evolutionary talismans no longer contained the power to move him and he seemed to have lost the better part of himself. He was like a few notes scattered in a strong wind, the backbone of melody long since blown out to sea.

What stretched in front of him on his return to England was months if not years of cataloguing plants and animals. He had no doubt he would be able to write a decent monologue on the flora and fauna of Outer Mongolia. And then, of course, there were the lilies. The bulbs would, he was sure, secure his fame in botanical circles. But this fame that he had once so craved now seemed to him to be hollow: the reality was that he would spend his days by Patrick's side, growing old alongside the old man, the two of them stooped and weary, until his foster father's death. For the rest of his life he would know how utterly and flagrantly he had sinned. He had been sent a test, as if Namuunaa were his fate and he had given in to his destiny, succumbed to temptation the first time it had been presented to him. The God who had spoken to him every day was now silent.

As he walked the enormity of his deed grew and swelled in his mind. On their last night together, after they had made love, Namuunaa had asked him if he wanted to try the lily again and in truth, though he knew every inch of her body, he had longed for that singular feeling of being inside her skin, a chemical closeness no amount of love nor intimacy could simulate. She had grated one of his precious bulbs and made him eat the bitter shreds with honey.

You are altogether beautiful, my love; there is no flaw in you . . .

And in the early hours of the morning, as they made love a second and last time, he had felt that strange conflation of the senses: the heat of the fire rose from his flesh like pyramidal forms of swirling onyx: lazily drifting smoke imprisoned in darkening glass. The smell of pine resin lay like maple syrup on his tongue; Namuunaa's perfume; pollen inflated a thousand thousand times to lie like miscreant jewellery in the palms of his hands.

You have ravished my heart, my sister, my bride, you have ravished my heart with one glance of your eyes . . .

He was wholly at ease in his own body, yet he felt as if he had breasts, as if every inch of his skin had become sensualized, an entire erotic organ that he felt his own hands upon her as he smoothed his palms, his fingertips, over her body, traced her outline, coloured her in, made her whole; trembled as he stroked her nipples, his own touch softening in response.

Who is this that looks forth like the dawn, fair as the moon, bright as the sun, terrible as an army with banners?

He felt himself responding to the memory, heat creeping up his throat. He was glad of the damp chill.

My beloved has gone to gather lilies. I am my beloved's and my beloved is mine; she pastures her flock among the lilies . . .

He felt as if his mind were running on twin train tracks, his love of God and his faith on the one side, and, parallel, his love and desire for Namuunaa. Neither track had deviated and so although he felt as if his mind were being slowly wrenched in two, it was an equal tearing, an equal spoiling which as yet required him to make no choices, only to feel guilt and love and shame in equal measures. For to cease to love her would be to cut his living, beating heart from his body.

He poured the dregs of his tea away. He watched a tree-creeper-like bird glide round the trunk of a pine, skirting the resinous gouts that welled from cracks in the bark. The scent was liquid rock, mint, tar: the essence of the forest. He thought he should start heading back. He turned round in the direction he'd come. The wind had dropped and there was a dead silence. He could no longer hear birds singing. The forest was eerily still. He stopped for a moment. Even the small movements in the undergrowth had ceased. He looked around. The forest was identical whichever way he looked – firm straight trunks of pines, other species that grew low and whose branches grated against one another, cushioned by the dense lichen. The dark leaves, crowded so closely together at the tips of the trees, blocked out what little light there was.

Joseph suddenly realized that he had no idea what direction he had walked in – he had merely wandered aimlessly, randomly, absorbed in his sinful thoughts; he had no concept of how far he had walked and it was impossible to judge the time of day in that green twilight. He picked a direction he felt was most appropriate and set off walking. His strides did not take him far. The wood hemmed him in, the undergrowth became denser, thornier, a tangled web of limbs encrusted with algae. He struggled through for a short while and then turned about ninety degrees, climbing out of the densest part of the thicket. It was certainly much easier walking, and he had encountered no resistance when he had first made his way into the wood but was this the right way? He could easily walk for hours through this monotonous forest and not reach the end of it. And what if that happened? How would he find his way back?

He wondered whether Tsem might be happily or not so happily rolling a cigarette, smoking and whistling, busying himself with the horses and making more tea. Mendo's reaction would be a little more complex: he would have that inner serenity and equanimity that had come from years of meditation and Buddhist teaching, but vying with it would be his concern for Joseph and his impatience, which he would on the one hand try to suppress and, on the other, justify because it was getting late and they would need to find a suitable camp for the night. Joseph half smiled to himself and then peered worriedly through the trees in an attempt to see if he could make out the end of the forest. He could not. A branch snapped suddenly and he jumped. He was bathed in cold sweat and was beginning to be seriously concerned. This could be completely the wrong direction; for all he knew his companions might be directly behind him. The trees seemed to be growing much closer together here and he was forced to weave between them with alarming regularity; he had to duck under low branches and snap his head back to avoid being poked in the eye by the sharp, spindly twigs that stuck straight out from the main trunk.

He paused to get his breath and squinted up at the sky. It was still light outside the wood; inside it appeared to be dusk already. But if he was not mistaken, there was a patch of light ahead of him. He made for the light, half crouching now and still clutching his wretched bowl. When he had almost reached it, he straightened up and looked at it in disappointment. It was a clearing in the wood – a tree had fallen down and its roots were exposed like excavated bones. The first stars were just visible and the sky was turning deep violet. As he watched from the heart of the wood, small bats flitted in front of him, dark visions caught in the corners of his eyes.

He turned, his shoulders slumped, the sweat pooling uncomfortably in the hollow of his back, and walked diagonally away from the clearing. There was, he thought, no point in panicking until he had walked at least as far as he had just walked but in the opposite direction. Even so, his heart beat uneasily and not merely from the exertion of twisting himself through the trees. He could barely see in front of him, lichen brushed against his face, branches scratched him, twigs clawed at him. He longed to stretch out his arms and stand tall. An owl, disturbed by his blundering passage, called, long and low, and there was an answering stirring in the woods from small frightened birds.

He stopped and, cupping his hands to his mouth, shouted at the top of his voice: Mendo. He called twice more. He shouted Tsem's name. And when he stood and listened, he heard nothing: the wood absorbed even the echoes of his cries. He called out once more. This time within two heartbeats there was an answer: the thin, far-off howl of a wolf. He felt the hairs at the back of his neck rise and sweat bead across his brow. He could not tell if it was his own wolf or a wild one. He began to half run through the forest, tearing through the mass of spiked twigs, swerving blindly from tree to tree. Joseph was unaware how long he ran for, his breath laboured, his hands and face bleeding from shallow scratches, but suddenly he was at the edge of the wood, as if the trees had spat him out, ejected him from their number. He wiped his hands in the thick grass and rubbed the dew across his face. The area looked vaguely familiar but it was now twilight and he wasn't sure quite where he was, which side of the wood he had come out on. He walked slowly uphill trying to catch his breath.

There was something up ahead of him, a dark shape lying in the grass. He hastened towards it and when he reached it, he picked it up and stared at it in horror. It was the sash from his *del* – he must have dropped it earlier. The awful truth dawned on him. Mendo and Tsem had given up on him and left him here in this wilderness. He tied it round his waist. Over to his right, beyond the forests, came the drawn-out howl of wolves, one after another, crying their hunger into the night. He wondered how long he could survive out here. It was conceivable he could make his way back to the *ger* on foot the following day, but it would take him maybe two days to reach it and he would have no food – he might find wild onions, the odd mushroom, but he would have to eat them raw. He had something to eat them out of, though much good that would do him, he thought bitterly.

What he was now concerned about was lasting the night. It could still become very cold and the wolves in these parts were by no means averse to preying on horses, cattle, even people. His racing mind, running through these practicalities, was skittering round the core issue: what had happened to Mendo and Tsem? Perhaps they had found another *ger* and were sheltering there. He was on the point of slumping into the grass and lying miserably where he fell when he realized how thirsty he was. Jesus had survived forty days in the desert; he could survive the night if he found some water. He continued walking up the mountain, trying not to pay too much attention to the intermittent howling but straining to hear the gentle sounds of running water. Suddenly he was overcome with a great weariness; his legs felt so heavy he could barely move them and he shivered, the sweat chilling him, despite his thick *del*.

He walked with his head bowed, seeing only the dark clumps of grass and the glimmer of white flowers before he crushed them beneath his feet, striving to pick out the sound of the smallest stream. When finally he did look up, he saw a faint light ahead of him. It could only be from a campfire. Tonight at least he should not die of cold or perish with hunger. He hastened towards it.

Nokhoigoo! he called as he neared it, Hold the dogs!

But when he reached the fire he saw there was no *ger*, only a ramshackle, makeshift tent. He stood stupefied and stared. It was their own tent in front of a few embers: all that was left of the fire. Nothing else remained. There was no sign of

Mendo, Tsem, Wolf or the horses. All their possessions had been ransacked. His herbarium was smashed, the pieces scattered over the grass in front of the tent. Sheets of paper to press flowers blew around the campsite. The wooden poles of the tent had been kicked in so that it had collapsed. He lifted the canvas and peered inside. In the dull glow from the remnants of the fire he could see almost nothing – but it looked as if whoever had robbed them had left nothing of substance. He gathered up a few pieces of paper and collected damp twigs and handfuls of pine needles from the edges of the wood to get the fire going and he propped up the tent as best he could.

He drank cold water from the stream and sat in front of the fire until it died. Then he crawled under the canvas and lay on the damp ground. He tried not to think of what might have befallen Mendo and Tsem. How he might survive without them. How he could travel across Mongolia to Pekin. He had a knife, his gun, a bowl and a small coil of rope that he'd been using as Wolf's leash. In the early hours of the morning he woke with a start: they'd taken the lilies too.

He drifted in and out of consciousness throughout the night so that when morning came he had the sensation of never having been asleep but of having floated through the night stretched stiff in a grass-green and chill coffin. He rose and drank at the stream, splashing water across his face. He rolled up the canvas and tied it with the rope across his back. He set a course directly away from the trees, across the steppes where in the early morning the shapes of far-off hills and formations of stone were grey as oysters. It was strange to be on foot; the muscles of his thighs still felt the imprint of the horse. And he felt exposed in that vast wilderness without his comrades or the wolf. As he walked he prayed, his footsteps falling in time with the words until they were threaded through the fabric of his being and he lost their meaning.

It seemed to him that he had mislaid the better part of himself – the woman he loved and the men who meant most to him – and that what had once seemed so important no longer held its charm, as if rocks gathered in excitement riven through with gold had been discovered to sparkle with pyrite. Perhaps it was that he had been too proud, too arrogant, too ambitious, too self-absorbed and this was the price he must pay for the realization that these were the character traits of a hollow, worthless man. Mendo would have said that we cling to the self but that the self has no meaning other than what we ascribe to it. Joseph had always believed Mendo to be wrong, such a firm hold had he once had on who he was and what he considered to be true. Now, in this bleak land, where he seemed the only living, breathing thing, he felt his understanding seep from him.

Just before dusk he set a couple of snares outside a marmot warren and sat and waited until the light turned bronze and the creatures emerged. He caught one, its fur back-lit and golden as it choked in the noose, and cooked it over a fire, eating every bit of charred, half-bloody flesh, even the organs the Mongols believed made the animal part man. He rolled himself in the canvas and lay looking out at the sky ablaze with a million pieces of cold and desolate stone. For the first time he understood the true meaning of loneliness.

*

He walked for three days in the general direction Tsem had indicated Pekin lay. He did not see another human soul. He dug tubers from the ground and ate their crisp, white flesh raw, grit grinding into his teeth. On the third day when he felt his vision go blue at the edges from hunger, he saw a horseman riding towards him. He was a long way away and never seemed to grow closer. Joseph unrolled his canvas and held it out to flap in the wind. There was barely a breeze and it sagged limply. He heaved it into the air and cracked its damp length downwards over and over again. The black dot of the horseman galloped towards him, inching closer. Joseph hoped he had food with him. He thought of steak, the juices easing from it, of potatoes mashed in butter until silky, of green spears of asparagus oily with hollandaise, thick wedges of salmon, lemon dripping between the pale pink flakes, and, unaccountably, of jelly that he had once eaten as a child, the orange morsels shivering before melting in an explosion of tangerine on his tongue. As the rider drew nearer, he wrapped up the canvas again, tied it with the rope and hooked it over his shoulders. He wondered why the rider was travelling towards him at such a furious pace. He had long ago dismissed any hope that the man could be one of his friends, but in the end it was the horse he recognized. He started to run and when Tsem drew near, he threw himself from his horse and ran towards Joseph, his arms outstretched. The two men collided in an embrace.

My friend, I've been looking for you. I never expected to find you. Tsem's nut-brown face was creased with an uncomplicated joy.

What happened? asked Joseph, finally releasing him.

Tsem's expression changed.

Are you hungry? he asked in quite another tone.

Joseph nodded.

They sat down, the horse pulling at the grass next to them. Tsem pulled some strips of dried meat from an inner pocket of his *del*. It was very far from what Joseph had been hoping for but he took a couple and started to chew desperately at them.

They took everything, said Tsem, everything we had. He put his head in his hands.

Mendo? asked Joseph, swallowing the dry clot of meat with difficulty.

We need to go back, said Tsem, wiping his eyes. He's still there.

Where?

Come on, said Tsem, heaving himself slowly to his feet. We don't have much time. I left him. I thought I could get help. I hoped to find you. And you have the gun, he added.

He helped Joseph up and on to his horse and he held the bridle and walked alongside. As they walked, he said that while Joseph had been in the wood, the White Warlord's men had galloped into the camp. They had taken what they wanted and smashed the rest. They had tied Tsem's and Mendo's hands by their wrists and bound them to their horses and taken them to their camp. It was two days' ride away and Mendo and Tsem had to watch while they cooked and ate their food in front of them but gave them almost nothing to eat.

And Mendo is still in the camp?

Yes, but it will take us two days to get there at this rate, said Tsem glumly. We galloped most of the way there and I left as fast as I could.

How did you get away?

They were less interested in me. It was Mendo they wanted. They hit him and punched him at every opportunity. They were careless with me – my rope was not bound as tightly, and I gradually worked it loose but kept it tied as if it were tight. In the night I crawled across the ground to my horse and worked it free from the other horses and then rode away, he said, as if it had been a simple matter.

But didn't they have men watching? Were there no guards?

Yes, said Tsem, but they were drunk and it was late. A couple of them chased me but they gave up. It was Mendo they wanted, he repeated.

How many were in the camp? asked Joseph, finishing the last of the biltong.

Tsem shrugged. Hard to say. Maybe thirty, forty men. Lots of horses. A few other prisoners. It was like a small army camp. Most of the men were out on raids or training. There were a handful in the camp during the day. I was only there for a day, he added apologetically.

Do you have a plan? asked Joseph, his stomach suddenly clenching and churning with fear and the unaccustomed meat.

Tsem continued to walk, staring at his boots and said nothing.

It seemed to Joseph to be a hopeless situation and yet there was nothing he could do other than head towards certain death in order to mount what would undoubtedly be a futile attempt to save his friend. If this had happened on the way here, he would have known he should ultimately be victorious because God was on his side. Now he no longer held such sureties.

They continued to journey until they reached the bank of a small stream and followed its course until it was too dark even to see by the light of the stars reflected from the flickering surface of black water. They rolled under the damp canvas together, fully clothed, sharing each other's small warmth.

Joseph awoke to the smell of mildewed canvas. Their makeshift tent had fallen over his face in the night. He stared through its green glow and pushed it aside. His ribs were so bruised from the hard ground that it hurt to breathe and as he crawled to his feet, his lower body sparked in pain as the blood rushed to his extremities. He walked along the bank of the stream like a crooked old man until he could feel his feet once more. Tsem had lit a small fire from dried dung and was heating a bowl of *tsamba*, shredding pieces of dried meat into it. Joseph washed his face and joined him, as ever admiring Tsem's practical abilities: not only had he escaped with a horse, he'd also managed to steal some food and a small pan. They scooped the barley mush into their mouths with their fingers and continued on their journey. Tsem would not hear of Joseph walking but insisted he ride the horse again. Joseph, still hungry, half dozed in the saddle and longed for a cup of hot, black coffee.

He felt weak, like a man of milk; it took him all his strength not to think about Namuunaa and now Mendo and what might have happened to him. It was, it seemed to him, the central problem, the eternal question: why does evil exist in the world? How could God let it exist? Even in his narrow life he had seen things he would not wish another human being to witness, much less experience. No matter where one was in the world, one did not have to look far or hard to see man's inhumanity to man. Why does an all-powerful God allow this to happen? He remembered that Mendo had once said that the fundamental difference between Buddhism and Christianity is that Buddhists believe evil is a mistake, a skewed way of looking at the world; an odd way of behaving. He had said that our nature is to be perfect; this perfection is hidden within us like an olive stone within an olive, we have but to seek it out. Whereas Christians believe that sin is inherent in our very make-up.

The wicked go astray from the womb, they err from their birth, speaking lies, they have venom like the venom of a serpent . . .

Mendo had said that Christians cannot have it both ways: he said that you cannot have an all-powerful God who is good, because how can God be good if He is responsible for evil? And if He is not responsible for evil, He is not all-powerful, in which case, He is not God. He said that evil is an incorrect perception of reality. Imagine mistaking a rope for a snake: the snake never existed, it was a rope the whole time. It is only our belief on the matter that has changed. There is no such thing as good or bad according to the Buddhists. There are only actions and thoughts that lead to suffering or happiness. We ourselves are responsible for the evil that befalls us. We inherit the past and create the future.

Joseph had listened carefully and conceded that Mendo did indeed have a point. He himself had always struggled with the idea of original sin.

He had said to Mendo, I believe we are responsible for evil, and for producing evil through our own actions.

He liked the idea of goodness welling up within a person, golden and precious as olive oil. As they rode out across the steppe on that grey and silent day, where hardly a bird called or the wind stirred, Joseph remembered that their conversation had taken place at night, huddled round the fire, the wolf crouched at his heels, her hackles rising and falling, a snow-storm raging about them.

There is no reality. It is all illusion, Mendo had said, holding up his hands like a conjurer, snow burning to nothing before it touched his palms, his face half hidden in his cowl, his eyes ablaze in the glowing embers.

We can never truly see the world, for we see it through the veil of our own senses; we have no way of knowing if and how the world exists independently of us. What is the true nature of a rock? A bird? A red petal? A white lily? A flaming branch? We cannot know, because these properties – the heat, the redness, the whiteness, the strength – they lie in our perception of objects.

He had held his hands up to the fire to warm them and then said, In the Buddhist scriptures there is a story of two blind men who wanted to know what colour was. They stopped two travellers and asked them to explain this secret that had been denied them. One man took up a handful of snow, and he said, White is the colour of snow, and he let the snow fall on to the blind man's palm.

Ah, said the blind man, then white feels like this, it feels like this . . .

Mendo held out a palmful of snow to Joseph, the flakes melting as he spoke. The other traveller said, No, white is the colour of swans. There is one flying over our heads right now. And the blind man tilted his head to one side and he heard the swan's wing beats and he thought, Ah, that is what white is, a rhythmic hiss in the wind.

So you see, Joseph, we each have our own reality which cannot be denied, but it cannot be reality. The world cannot be determined by itself.

The wind howled around them and Mendo sat with his head bowed, snow gathering on his shoulders so that he seemed like a warlock petrified in the darkness.

Eventually he looked up and he said, I tell you this, Joseph, not through some idle whim to explain myself to you, but because I want you to take it to heart. My teacher once said to me, It is not appearances that will bind you, it is your attachment to appearances.

What do you mean? whispered Joseph, his hand buried in the wolf's thick fur.

There is a Zen poem, said Mendo, which translates something like this: To her lover a beautiful woman is a delight, to an ascetic, a distraction, to a wolf, a good meal.

It had not worked: he was too Western for Mendo's philosophy to take root and to Joseph what was important about stones and birds, petals and lilies was their appearance, their inherent property – how a petal held the story of all petals, the bones of birds spoke of sauropod ancestors; it was these things that showed the stamp of evolution and the essential nature of God. He could, on an intellectual level, believe a wolf might view a beautiful woman as meat but she was still a beautiful woman nonetheless.

Your belly is a heap of wheat, encircled with lilies . . .

The more he tried not to think of her, the more she consumed his mind.

My God, he whispered to himself. Why have you forsaken me? *I am poured out like water, and all my bones are out of joint; my heart is like wax; it is melted within my breast . . .*

He rubbed the water that unaccountably had seeped from his eyes and slid from the horse.

Wolf? he asked Tsem.

They tried to catch her. And then they tried to kill her. She ran away towards the mountains. It's for the best, Joseph, said Tsem, patting his shoulder. If they'd trapped her they would only have kept her chained up and muzzled. And she's a wild creature.

It seemed somehow like the final blow.

Tsem dug up ground squirrel burrows with his bare hands until they bled. He found a few tubers the squirrels had forgotten to eat over winter. It was barely a handful and they were shrivelled and dried. They ate them with roasted squirrel but the following day Tsem said they should not light a fire as they were nearing the White Warlord's army camp and, in any case, there was no food left. Tsem took them the long way round, in a snaking route past a rocky hill and through a narrow valley into a small wood where they spent the night in fitful wakefulness.

Joseph, his back against a pine tree, the bark digging into his skin, looked up at the sky through the maze of branches, stars caught in a gap-toothed net. Less than two miles away were the Warlord's soldiers. Joseph imagined them crouched round a fire tearing lamb off the bone with their teeth, Mendo tied up in the shadows, firelight curling across one cheek. Rooks stirred in the trees and the cracking of twigs made Joseph jump. He hugged his pistol to his belly. It was slick and heavy in his hand: he'd greased it with fat from the squirrel's carcass but he was afraid that in the last few days he had not taken as much care of it as he should. He wondered how many men were on lookout duty, prowling round the camp – perhaps through this very wood – curved swords balanced in their palms. In the early hours of the morning Tsem fell asleep against him, snoring heavily. Joseph watched the rooks stir and caw before leaving their untidy nests to circle above the trees, scraps of black, like particles of soot, dancing against the lightening sky.

He carefully extricated himself from Tsem and started to climb, hauling himself up using the jagged teeth of limestone rocks. He felt light as air, as thistledown, high on hunger. When he felt the wind against his face he crouched down almost flat to the pine needle-strewn ground and crawled slowly to the edge of the wood. The rest of the hill, treeless and bare, the grass shorn to the stone beneath, stretched up above him. Directly in front of him was a sheer drop down to the flat steppe below. He shielded his eyes from the rising sun and looked across to where he thought the camp might be. He could see nothing. The light lay in a thin, nacreous wash over the land. There were dark marks that could be the remains of fires: one breathed a few wisps of smoke. The Warlord's men had gone. They were too late. He bowed his head, resting his forehead against stone. The cold burned into his skull. Eventually he looked up, hoping to fathom which way the men might have gone. In the distance, on a small undulation in the landscape, something fluttered. He strained his eyes in the grey dawn. It was some way away from the remnants of the fires and it looked as if it was orange. His heart began to beat faster.

The quickest way down was straight over the lip of the gorge. He steeled himself for a moment and then turned and lowered himself over the edge. He scrabbled to gain a purchase on the rock face, digging his toes into crevices, twisting his hands through knots of grass and round the roots of saplings as he made his perilous way down. At one point his feet slipped and he hung momentarily from his hands, the rock biting into his skin; his arms felt as if they had been jerked from their sockets. A few feet from the ground, he pushed himself out and dropped, hitting the earth hard, his heart hammering. He turned and began to run in the direction of the dead fires. His breath burned and rasped in his throat and he felt as if he no longer had mastery over his legs. He slowed to a jog when he realized that, hungry as he was, he could not keep up the pace. As he neared where the camp had been he could smell the dead fires, the tang of wood smoke heavy on the air, and he passed the detritus of men: heaps of bones, fragments of rope, charred paper that he recognized as his own and which had once held the frail lives of flowers, pressed between the sheaves.

As he drew closer he saw that what he had seen was a stake of wood standing upright atop a small rise. Whoever was tied to it was clad in an orange robe that fluttered gently in the breeze, the sun shining through the fabric so it glowed as if it were a fallen kite. Above, vultures circled, drifting on the thermals. Joseph began to sprint. He ran as if his very life depended upon it, gasping for air as though he might drown. The man's hands were tied behind his back and they appeared to him in his weakened state not to be hands at all but something alien and other. When he reached the bottom of the knoll and looked up he saw why: every joint had been severed so that only stumps below the knuckles remained. The man's head was bowed and shaven, the tendons standing out at the back of his naked neck. Joseph saw, as he had hoped and prayed that he would not, the scars of letters carved into his skull. There was a terrible stench and Joseph thought he had come too late.

He cried, Mendo, and ran towards his friend.

As he reached him he saw that the monk had been disembowelled and his guts had spewed from the dark cavity of his abdomen down the front of his robe: the orange that denoted his status as a lama was dark and stiff with drying blood. Blood had run down his neck and pooled across his collar bone from the place where his ears had been.

Mendo, he whispered, reaching out to him.

He cupped his face between his hands and with a shock realized he was still warm. He was still alive.

Shaking with the effort, Mendo slowly raised his head. The lower part of his face was caked with blood, flaking like rust. When he tried to open his mouth, fresh blood bubbled out and he coughed and choked. Joseph realized that they had cut out his tongue. For what seemed like a long time Joseph cradled Mendo's face between his palms as the monk struggled to speak. Eventually Joseph stepped back and drew out his pistol. Mendo's eyes were black with pain; unreadable. He half nodded when he saw the gun and shut his mouth, swallowing with difficulty the thick blood that had pooled in his throat.

Joseph's eyes filled with tears. The monk and the sky behind him were now a blur: orange, gold, red and blue. With shaking hands he rested the barrel against Mendo's forehead and drew his finger back on the trigger. He felt the gun's mechanism slowly lock into place. He had only one bullet left but there was no chance that he would miss.

Lord, my God, he whispered, as he squeezed the trigger, bracing himself for the impact of the pistol as it ricocheted, for the explosion of sound and the implosion of blood and brains across his own face.

He closed his eyes. Nothing happened. The pistol had jammed. He was shaking almost uncontrollably now as he took it away from Mendo and examined it. When he looked up, the imprint of the muzzle still branded Mendo's forehead. Mendo's eyes were closed, his head slumped as if his last hope had been extinguished. As if he knew Joseph was looking at him, he raised his head agonizingly slowly once more and opened his eyes. It felt as if Mendo were staring deep into his soul. Joseph flung the pistol to the ground and took out his knife. He pulled the robe apart and laid his hand flat against Mendo's chest. He stood for a long moment, his head bowed, his forehead touching Mendo's, feeling his heart beating against his palm. He placed the tip of his knife against Mendo's skin in the exact point where his hand had lain and he looked into Mendo's eyes as with both hands on the handle of the knife he drove it through bone and flesh into his brother's heart. The monk's entire body stiffened and writhed against the rope that bound him to the wooden stake and Joseph cried out as if in Mendo's place, as if racked with his pain. Mendo opened his eyes wide and Joseph, blood gushing over his hands, thought that at the last, there was one clear moment of serenity, before every spark of life was extinguished. Joseph crumpled to the ground and lay in the grass slick with blood and wept as he had never wept before.

With what felt like his last ounce of strength he screamed at the sky.

Dear God, is this my punishment for what I have done?

When he finally got up, avoiding looking at the limp body hanging next to him, Tsem was sitting a few yards away crying, his shoulders heaving and shuddering. He wiped his hands and gripped the knife, pulling it with difficulty from his friend's body. He cleaned the blade and the handle in the grass and then he cut the ropes that bound Mendo to the wooden stake. He lowered him to the ground and gathered up his intestines in his hands, sliding them as well as he was able on top of and within the body. Then he slid the robe from the monk and wrapped it tightly around his whole body. In this orange, blood-stained shroud, he carried Mendo to the horse and laid him across the saddle. Only once he had done this did his body give way and he doubled over and retched and retched. Tsem rubbed his eyes on his sleeve and fetched the rope. It was dyed with blood in a random pattern. He helped Joseph to his feet and they tied Mendo's body to the horse.

We should take him to Munke, said Joseph quietly.

Tsem nodded. We should rest today and travel at night.

He stepped round the horse and embraced Joseph. Then he picked up the horse's reins and the two of them started to walk, the horse between them.

They went back to the small wood where they'd spent the night. He and Tsem laid Mendo's body on the ground under a large pine to give the horse a rest and then he went to wash in the stream. The dark flakes of blood on his hands turned to skeins of red that unfurled in long tendrils in the icy water. The blood had settled into the lines across the base of his wrists where the skin was white and fragile and the veins glowed blue. He rubbed them with his thumbs to clean them and then cut a hazel switch and peeled back the bark to reveal the fraying pith with which he cleaned his teeth.

While Tsem made tiny snares using fine roots from the pine trees as cord, he slept, leaden and dreamless, the sleep of the dead.

When Munke saw them approaching, she started to run towards them but then she stopped and stood waiting for them, her hands clasped. They had travelled for three weeks and lived off the kindness of strangers. They had bought two horses – fortunately Joseph had had a small amount of money secreted in a pocket in his *del* – and now they rode with Mendo's body between them, the wind tugging at the orange robe. By the time they reached Munke, her beautiful pale green eyes were full of tears. Tsem jumped from his horse and hugged her. She turned to Joseph. When he held her he could feel her trembling beneath his hands. He suddenly thought of Namuunaa and how her naked back had felt, the ridge of muscle either side of her spine.

I've been afraid this would happen, she said as she walked up to Mendo's body.

As she put out her hand to touch him, Tsem grasped her wrist and shook his head.

It's better if you don't look, said Joseph quietly. He died three weeks ago. We need to bury him quickly.

She nodded. You need some food first, she said. You both look as if you haven't eaten for a long time.

They followed her into the *ger*. Tsem stocked up the fire and she hung a pot of mutton stew above it. The fat was congealed in a thick, white layer across the top.

Boldt is out with the sheep, she said as she stirred the meat.

The smell made Joseph ravenous. He could hardly bear waiting for the food to warm up. When she served him a bowl of the stew, he ate it so fast he barely chewed any of it. She silently served him another bowlful.

Tell me what happened, she said eventually, when he and Tsem had finished eating.

I'll start preparing the body, said Tsem, getting up.

Munke silently handed him a length of white silk. Joseph waited until Tsem had left the *ger*. He didn't know where to start, what to say.

Instead he told her about Mendo coming back for him. About the lamasery where Mendo had found him wandering the corridors. He told her about praying alongside Mendo as he meditated. How Mendo had saved his life and said that they were brothers. And then finally how Mendo was captured and how he had found him. He tried to spare her the

297

details. As he spoke, she put her hand in his and held him tightly. He found that his body was racked with dry sobs, as he if were some desiccated creature that could not afford water for tears. He could not remember having talked as much since he'd come to Mongolia and now his throat was sore.

Munke rose and made him some yak butter tea.

As she handed him the tea he said, No wonder Mendo loved you.

Her face crumpled and for the first time she cried. He held her until she had stopped and then passed her the tea. He went outside to find Tsem. The blood had drained from his face and he was smoking, leaning against a cart he'd hitched to one of the horses. He'd burned the orange robe – charred fragments drifted across the grass. Instead he had wrapped Mendo in the silk.

The burial ground is in that direction, said Tsem, pointing east.

He stubbed out his cigarette and started to walk, leading the horse.

Normally, he said, a lama would carry out the ceremony, but it's too dangerous to ask anyone. Any who might still be alive. You're the nearest thing we've got, he added.

Joseph nodded. He walked on the other side of the horse and took its reins. As he prayed out loud, Tsem sang and their voices mingled in the still, clear air. Munke and Boldt caught up with them but rode several paces behind the horse and cart and did not speak.

They have to walk behind us, said Tsem, seeing Joseph looking at them. It's the tradition.

Joseph lost track of time, but when they finally reached the burial ground it was late evening and the sun was setting; light lay like honey across the steppes. It was a rounded hillock littered with stones and bones. Fragments of fabric had snagged on the rocks and fluttered in the faint breeze. The two of them carried Mendo's body into the centre of the mound and placed him on the ground, resting on wide, flat pebbles. Joseph looked up to see Boldt and Munke standing at the edge of the circle of stones. She was holding his hand and he was watching them with wide, black eyes. Above them, circling in the last thermals of the day, were the outlines of lammergeyers. The great, dark shapes were vultures that thrived by smashing bone against stone to release the marrow within.

They both looked down at the body of their dearest friend. Joseph wondered what to do. It felt inappropriate now to say a prayer for a Buddhist. And hypocritical when he himself was like a hollow man, bereft of God. He stood and thought instead of Mendo, his quiet goodness, the light in his eyes blinding him. Tsem crouched down and muttered a few words, then reached across and put his arm round Joseph's shoulder. He led him back to the horses.

Munke was weeping, her long hair blowing in the wind. She clutched Boldt's hand in both of hers. Joseph hugged her briefly and rested his hand on top of the small boy's dark, warm head.

You ride, Tsem said, taking out his tobacco, I'll sit in the cart.

I want to go in the cart too, said Boldt suddenly.

Tsem grinned and put his arm round him as he jumped in.

Joseph took Boldt's horse instead and led the cart horse. He looked back out over the darkening steppe. The body of his friend, wrapped in the white silk, glowed in the dusk. No flowers, he thought, no bibles, grave or grave stone, no crosses or ashes. No words, no ceremony, no tears. Just a body left for the animals. It was, he thought, what Mendo would have wanted.

As if on cue he saw a dog-like creature trotting towards them. A fox, perhaps, or a sable. He watched, almost in spite of himself. But the creature did not turn towards the ring of rocks. Instead it continued to lope towards them. It was bigger than he had initially thought and a stab of fear ran through him. There were wolves here and fearless ones too, attacking the sheep.

Joseph's horse started to whinny and half reared in fright, its ears flat to its head. He wheeled it round, and he took out his knife. The wolf had picked up speed and was running flat out towards them. Just before it reached him, it skittered to a halt and half barked at him, crouching down beneath his heel in a fawning position. Joseph jumped from the horse and the wolf leapt up and licked his face, whining and wagging her tail. It was Wolf, his own wolf.

Tsem, he shouted. Look who has found us!

Tsem ran over and took the reins of the rearing, plunging horse from him and handed them to Munke before he came back to stroke Wolf.

She's Namuunaa's wolf, said Joseph to Boldt, who was crouched in the back of the cart. She gave her to me when we left, but she went missing when the Warlord's men attacked us.

300

He felt her ribs and then each leg and her stomach. Although she was thin, she seemed to be in good shape. He retrieved his horse from Munke and took the reins of the horse pulling the cart. All the horses cantered nervously back to the *ger*, with Wolf loping along near by. And in spite of his grief and tiredness, Joseph smiled to see the animal racing alongside them, her tongue hanging out, almost as if Namuunaa herself were still with him.

There's a message for you, said Munke the next morning as they ate *tsamba* for breakfast.

Mendo had told Joseph about the Mongolian *orto* system of messengers on horseback. Munke looked through a small wooden box she kept by her bed but, when she drew out the handwritten note, she said it was for Tsem. It had been written by a scribe but was from his wife. Munke read it out loud.

Tsem whooped and slapped his thigh. He jumped up grinning and hugged Joseph and Munke.

I have a son, he shouted. A son!

Congratulations, said Joseph, hugging him back. When was he born?

Tsem looked back at the note again. He scrunched up his forehead.

I think it must have been three or four months ago. He looked up. This calls for a celebration.

I have a bottle of *airag*, said Munke, smiling at him.

They clinked their shot glasses together. Tsem drained his at once and poured himself another measure.

You should go and see her, said Joseph.

Tsem shook his head. Another couple of days won't make any more difference. Munke might need our help. But yes, then we'll go. Thank you, my friend, he said, patting Joseph on the knee. He drained the second glass and looked as if he might cry. You must come back with me – see my new son – and then I'll take you to Pekin.

Joseph was silent. When he looked up he saw Munke watching him as if trying to divine his thoughts. To his surprise Tsem sealed the bottle instead of drinking the rest of it.

Come on, young man, he said to Boldt, let's take a look at those sheep of yours.

A couple were lame and one had been attacked by a wolf and was badly in need of stitches. Munke followed the two of them, leaving Joseph sitting alone in the dim and smoky *ger*.

Joseph had spotted a small sheaf of paper and a pen and ink in Munke's wooden box. He took them out and dipped the pen in the navy ink. He thought he should set his thoughts in order. What he should do. How to organize his return journey home. At least, thankfully, many of his specimens had already made it to Bristol. He hesitated, his pen poised and a drop of ink landed on the paper. But instead this is what he wrote:

We are like two wild birds destined to blow where the wilderness of the wind takes us. Your spirit is as untrammelled as an eagle's, as loyal, as courageous. It is the secret of our souls: what we have, we have for ever.

Fragments from the Song of Solomon rose unbidden in his mind: that part of the Bible that he'd always felt to be forbidden now flowed from his pen as if the words had somehow been etched indelibly on his mind.

As a lily among brambles, so is my love among maidens . . .

Set me as a seal upon your heart, as a seal upon your arm; for
love is strong as death . . .

Upon my bed at night I sought her whom my soul loves; I
sought her, but found her not; I called her, but she gave no
answer. I will rise now, I will seek her whom my soul loves . . .

And more in his own words where he attempted to describe his pain and confusion though he doubted that she would understand. Where he tried to say that though he loved her and though she was a constant in his mind, he had been and always would be a priest and that this carried with it inconvertible duties. This was why, he wrote, he had left her. Now he suddenly stopped and looked at what he had written and wondered whether it made sense any longer. Whether he was still a priest in anything more than name.

He tied up the bundle with a piece of string and laid it to one side. Munke would know how to summon a *bukhia*, one of the young men who would ride day and night from one outpost to another across that vast and limitless landscape, carrying mail in the traditional *orto* system. He imagined one man's untrammelled gallop beneath a galaxy of stars and Namuunaa, how she would feel receiving these strange love letters from a man who could no longer be her lover.

We cannot take the route we took before. It would be a considerable risk.

There is no other way.

Yes, there is.

No.

We can cross the Gobi and then cut north into the mountains.

It can't be done, said Tsem. No man comes out alive.

Jesus wandered in the desert for forty days and nights. I can cross the Gobi.

Well, this man Jesus was a damn fool. You can't expect to be as lucky. There is virtually no water and no food. No people. No shelter. The sun will burn you. You'll freeze at night. The robber barons have a fort out there, almost a city some say.

They won't expect me to travel in that direction.

The souls of men lie trapped in the sand and howl at night. They rise up and plague the living.

God will protect me.

Tsem sighed. Ah, my friend, I think you will surely die.

Joseph looked at him questioningly and Tsem looked away shiftily.

I don't expect you to accompany me.

Relief spread across Tsem's face. My family, my baby son . . .

I understand. I wouldn't want to place you in any more danger.

Well, if I can't persuade you not to go, then you must buy camels. The horses will be useless.

As Tsem mounted his horse he looked back at the priest and half smiled. Now if it was a woman you were searching for . . .

Tsem took Joseph's pistol, now useless to him without bullets, his pocket watch and two of the horses to exchange for the camels and food and a shotgun. Joseph waited for him outside a grey and windswept village, which was barely more than tumbledown huts clinging to a barren, rocky slope.

They'd spent several days with Munke, resting and eating and helping her. Joseph had given her his letters for Namuunaa but he suspected that she had read them before she passed them on to a messenger because when he told her and Tsem that he must return to the mountains she had looked calmly and placidly at him as if she had known that he would be drawn back against his better judgement. But Joseph then said that he must return because he needed the lilies and he saw a delicate line appear in the middle of her smooth, clear forehead.

The lilies were what would make his name, he had said. The lilies were the one flower in his entire collection that would be universally loved. He described how he would write scientific papers about them; how ladies would cut their long stems and arrange them in vases, their incomparable scent would spread through the country's parlours; how they would grace bridal bouquets, spilling their golden pollen from white, waxen petals; how they would grow in conservatories among cold stone and dank green ferns. He tried to sound passionate but he was aware that he merely sounded tired as he paraphrased his old arguments. He concluded by saying that the Warlord's men had stolen his bulbs from him and he meant to travel to the mountains to dig up more.

Munke was now actively frowning at him but she said nothing. Tsem looked at him in astonishment to begin with and as Joseph continued to speak he slowly rolled a cigarette.

I have lost my God, said Joseph carefully, trying to explain to himself as much as to them, and I have lost the woman I love. What is left is this trip. I need to salvage my journey and satisfy those who paid for me to come here. And to do that I must have the lilies.

She's still there. She'll still be waiting for you, said Tsem.

I can't have both. I can't have her and be a priest.

For several minutes no one said anything. Tsem put his hand on Joseph's shoulder. His touch was light and as he spoke he breathed out a cloud of tobacco.

He said, We'll leave tomorrow. We'll see my family and then we'll talk about your trip.

Joseph eventually fell asleep, resting against the small bag of clothes and provisions Munke had given him, the wolf in his arms, and dreamt of a man dressed in black who hacked his fingers off with a blunt blade orange with rust. It was several days later. They had visited Tsem's family and now the two of them had reached the last town before the Gobi Desert. The wolf stirred and growled and he woke instantly, shivering with cold and fear and exhaustion. Coming towards him swaying like tall ships were two camels led by Tsem who rode in front of them on his horse, as if they were galleons and he was a small but stout tug.

The camels had bones through their noses and one of them, considerably smaller than the other, was already laden, with barley flour, Joseph presumed. Both of them had sagging humps and did not seem to be in good condition. Tsem grinned proudly when he saw Joseph watching. Tsem's emotions seemed to sweep through him like clouds; he was almost cheerful as he ordered the camels to kneel and inspected Joseph's luggage. Joseph felt like lying down in the sand and howling at God. His grief at Mendo's burial had turned into a raging, seething anger. How could He let him die? And a living death as torturous as that? He stood on the other side of the camel from Tsem and together they pulled the ropes tightly round his luggage to secure the little he was to take with him. The camel rumbled in protest.

Tsem handed him a pot of fried rice and egg and a bladder of water. The rice was still faintly warm and Joseph ate greedily. Wolf was watching his every movement. He scooped half out and she licked it from the palm of his hand. It was midday and still cold though the sun burned a sickle shape into the back of his neck.

My friend, you must leave now. Keep going through the night and rest tomorrow during the day. You should travel north-west to avoid the towns and then turn west into the Gobi.

Joseph nodded dumbly and the two of them embraced. Tsem had tears in his eyes.

I will pray for you, he said gravely.

Say one for yourself too, said Tsem, releasing him.

He helped him on to the camel and yelled at it and tugged its nose until the vast beast lumbered to its feet, bellowing in ire. The second followed suit, given a little encouragement by Tsem. He stood next to his horse and watched as Joseph hauled the camels round to face north-west and urged them into a ragged, ambling walk, the sun bright above Joseph's head, blinding him as he faced towards the Black Desert.

Towards evening he passed Genghis Khan's anvil, a towering pinnacle of rock that shimmered into lucidity in the twilight, twin shadows of sun and moon lengthening, falling sharp and angular. It was marked on his rudimentary map and he'd read of it as a child. The grey, dusty plains had given way to steppe – a faint covering of grass skimmed the stone and, in the softening light of the setting sun, the land glowed gold. In spite of his heavy heart, he felt almost at peace in his familiarity with this alien landscape. From the great height of his camel he rode on into the night.

He woke the following evening as the cold began to seep into his bones in a sea of horsetail grasses that swept towards him in waves and hissed and lashed at imaginary shores without shells. He built a fire and cooked his miserly gruel.

The only explanation for it, as far as he could see, was that evil was inherent in the world. God had created it, or allowed it to spawn, and while man had free will, there would always be a choice; one man's love had not been enough to staunch the evil in men's hearts. He saw now that it was arrogant to have presumed that Mendo had died because of something he, Joseph, had done. He had sinned and he would suffer but he had not caused Mendo's death. No, God had allowed Mendo to live in agony, a slow shedding of life, drop by drop, of his own blood because that was a choice made long ago when the world was but a barren rock spinning through space.

He remembered the words that Jesus had spoken with a cold heart: *Do not think that I have come to bring peace to earth; I have not come to bring peace but a sword.*

He loved God, more than a lover, more than words could say. Could he adjust to a God who was not indifferent, but watched, as an observer watched, a cruel charade of the world He had created?

Dear Lord, he prayed, let me love you with this new knowledge yet as I loved before.

Three days later Joseph reached the edge of the desert and decided that it was safe enough for him to travel during the day, for few would pass this way. Wolf, though still gaunt, had caught hares at night, and brought them back to him. They'd shared the meat and she was looking a little less starved. The dawn was petrifyingly cold, the sun as sharp as knife blades springing open over the horizon, and the world, sliced apart in the morning light, was unlike anything he had witnessed before. Giant blood-red rocky crags dwarfed him, black and pearl teeth erupted from the sand in serried rows; there were few trees and those that existed were twisted, stunted with peeling bark and wounds amber with resin. The sand was cold as ice beneath his feet.

When Jeremy had accused him of paganism, he was wrong, thought Joseph. What he felt was closer to pantheism – he saw a spirit in grains of sand, some clear as glass, others stippled as trout; in the crabbed liquorice trees, the vultures that hovered overhead hoping vainly – but it was one spirit that moved him, the one spirit that dwelt in needle-thin leaves and the horns of beetles alike, the word of God like a living, breathing fire. He felt it now, the feeling that had been present to him almost as long as he lived and which he thought he might have lost, for his faith, like a shed snake's skin, had remained intact but lifeless. And he felt too, as he cajoled the camels into motion, that though he had never walked this way, every step connected him to Namuunaa: every bird, every rock, every early lizard basking in the baking heat, spoke to him of her. He swayed across the desert: a collection of notes once scattered silently on the wind gaining in strength, tone, timbre: as he travelled towards her, the potential of a melody was beginning to form.

He passed waves of sand like those on the beach, only these ones were higher than a man's head; he saw a lake in the distance and a shining purple mountain and urged the camels towards it only to find the mountain a mirage and the lake a cracked bed of salt. On his seventh day in the desert, the wind whipped the sand into a terrible storm, dust devils skittered at his feet and veils of sand swept the blackened sky. In the distance tornadoes 300 feet high spun like dervishes over the salt and sand plain. This was the Ordos, the Bad Lands, where none dared cross, where legends told of legions of slaughtered men who lay buried beneath the sand and rose howling and furious when they heard the tread of a free man; the Ordos where the little water that existed was foul with salt and sulphur, the sun's heat could flay a man and there was no shelter. He crouched with his camels and the wolf in the midst of the desert and prayed to God to let the storm pass them by without harm.

He drank brandy in an attempt to quench his thirst and visions swept through him like water through wine: of his father shipwrecked, drowning at sea, screaming lungfuls of black and salted water; of Mendo, unable to see, hear, speak or smell, his throat clotted with blood, silent red tears weeping from his finger joints; of Patrick, his skin so frail he could see his heart beating bluely in his chest, his pulse slower than the hall clock, and Namuunaa, her green eyes draining of life as the tide leaves the shore.

The day after the storm dawned bright as if new-minted, the sky soft blue. He was coated with sand like lice. He and the animals struggled on and he came across many strange things that were unquestionably old: a woman's comb, an amulet, part of a sword. The sand had uncovered them and he thought that he was the first living being to have seen them since their owners had perished.

Near a crag that had been split, its base exposed like a woman's arched throat, he saw something glinting. Thinking it was yet another artefact, he gave it no more than a cursory glance. It had a dull gleam, a spark extinguished in all but the harshest sunlight. He bent and dusted the sand from its surface. It was a set of tiny teeth. He used his knife to try to free it from the rock that had shattered and was already loose about it. It took him two days. It was, he discovered, part of a fossil, only the jaw bone and a small section of the skull. The bone was hollow as a bird's yet shaped like a lizard's with a long, beak-like protuberance, the lustre of the enamel on its minute teeth intact. He held its frail weight in the palm of his hand and weighed its worth. It was, he thought, incomparable. Two years before he had left England, a similar fossil had been uncovered in Germany, part avian, part reptile, remnants of fossil feathers clinging to its wings, four hooked claws curling from the wing tips, a lizard-like tail. It was old, old as the dinosaurs. Darwin had predicted that such a creature might be found, an intermediary between earth and sky.

What he had discovered was a small section of that very same creature that once must have flown above these valleys long before the desert became a desert. It was, he thought, another link in evolution's bright chain that binds us, from the first creatures that crawled out of the primordial swamp, to him, as he stood in the sand in a barren wasteland, a fragment of rock in his hand that had once been a conscious being. It was this branching chain that had given rise to beetles, bower birds, bilberries and bleeding heart flowers, that had led to apes and finally to us; as creatures gradually became more complex, raw emotions and instincts evolved and finessed, this chain of being gave birth to man and his finer passions, twinned with the darker side of his heart where true evil walks hand in hand with love.

He walked on, still holding his fossil as if he could not bear to let it go and in the distance he thought he saw another mirage, a shape conjured from sand to bewitch him. It was a giant fortress, its ruined walls crumbling like burned sugar, watch towers leaning drunkenly, the entrance wide open, the wood long since gone. He hobbled the camels and, beckoning Wolf, he entered the fort. It had occurred to him that this might be the home of the White Warlord but if that had been the case, he was sure he would have been ambushed long before. It was a reminder that he should take better care.

Inside there was a network of streets and tumbledown houses in rigid geometrical lines, small courtyards and squares as if for the buying and selling of wares, the windows dark as caves, sand piled in drifts against the lintels. At the opposite end of the fort was a temple and, to his surprise, a blue silk scarf was tied to one of its pillars. Next to it was a *ger*.

A man stepped out of the tent and watched him with a look of horror as he and the wolf walked down the cobbled street of the dead, desert citadel. He supposed in retrospect it looked as if he had appeared from nowhere, a dead soldier swept from the sand, hollow life breathed into him by the storm.

Please, he said as he neared the man, do you have any water?

With a look of pure fear, the man ran back inside the *ger*. A moment later his wife came out followed by her husband.

Would you please be so kind as to let me have some water? he whispered.

Do you know, she said, turning to her husband, it almost sounds as if he's speaking Mongolian.

He emitted a wheezing sort of splutter which would have been a laugh if his tongue had not been so swollen.

I am speaking Mongolian.

There! You see! she said triumphantly.

Joseph mimed drinking and she immediately turned back into the *ger* and brought out a skin of water. He drank half and poured the rest down the wolf's throat.

Thank you, I cannot thank you enough. My camels are outside the fort; is there anywhere for them to drink?

He is speaking Mongolian, said the man.

Yes, said Joseph, smiling.

Come, I'll show you. He stretched out his hand and touched him, as if to reassure himself that Joseph was indeed flesh and blood.

They walked through the west gate and in a dried-up river bed were tamarisk trees and short green reeds. There was a trough for the man's goats and camels, which were scattered widely across the desert in front of them.

I'll help you bring them round. Where did you leave them? he asked Joseph, giving him another strange and sidelong glance.

At the east gate.

By the time they'd returned to the *ger*, the woman had made tea with goat's milk, which she handed him when he entered. He sat and drank and then looked about him. They were both small and thin, their skin lined and dark from the sun, their cheeks round, their noses and chins sharp. She was wearing a navy blue silk *del* with black flowers and curlicues and a black waistcoat; their clothes were torn and shabby, drab from wear and use. Unlike the other Mongolians he had met, they sat quietly, as if used to the silence, as if hesitant to believe he were not a chimera, waiting for him to speak.

Eventually he felt fortified enough to say, I have come from a land far, far away. I sailed here across the sea and I have travelled from Pekin. I am heading west into the desert and then north into the mountains.

They nodded at him like two birds with bright eyes and no way of expressing their curiosity verbally.

Tell me, he said. Do you see bands of men passing this way?

They nodded in unison. The woman said, They don't disturb us, we have nothing they can steal.

They steal from travellers, rich travellers, he said. You'll be safe here with us, but the desert is a dangerous place.

Joseph nodded. In more ways than one. But tell me, what is this fort? I thought at first it might belong to the robbers.

No, the White Warlord lives much further west. We've never seen his fort, but we have heard that thousands of men live there.

It's a long story, said the man. Perhaps you might like to rest a while?

Joseph said he believed he would and he thanked them for their kindness. He unpacked his bedding roll and lay down on one of their beds, the wolf curled up beneath him.

When he woke they were both sitting watching him, a veil of steam between them. They served him goat stew and ate in silence. When they had finished eating, the man began to speak. He had a slightly high-pitched reedy voice, a voice that might carry on the desert winds thin as the hum of air round rock.

He said, This is the ancient city of Khara Khoto. Long ago this land was green and fertile with trees and grasslands and grazing animals. The city was ruled by Khara Bator Janjyn, the black hero-chief who practised the *Khara ugge*, the art of black magic. His power was so great that the Chinese became concerned and they sent an army of legions of men to kill him. Khara Bator Janjyn retreated into the fort. He knew he and his men could survive for many weeks because they had plenty of food and in one of the towers is a deep well which connected with the river so they would never be thirsty. When he heard that the Chinese were on their way, he sent out emissaries to warn the surrounding tribes and he was confident that they would come to his aid.

But the Chinese, as the Chinese always are, were cunning and they sent out bands of men to circle Khara Khoto and cut off the tribesmen. Still, there seemed to be no way of starving

315

the men out of their fort, so the Chinese Emperor himself came to bring about the downfall of Khara Bator Janjyn. He threw a magic stone into the river and it changed its course travelling far to the west. The Emperor named it after himself – Etsin gol. You can see where the old river used to be.

Now the men of Khara Koto would surely die and Khara Bator was determined that his men would die with honour. He planned to open the great gates and fight the Chinese. But his daughter persuaded him that he would surely lose his life and that he should speak with the Chinese.

He agreed with her and he said to the Emperor that he would give himself up and that the following morning the Chinese would be allowed to enter through the west gate. During the night the vast army amassed before the gate awaiting the dawn. In the meantime Khara Bator and his men escaped from the east gate. Their horses had all died of thirst and they were obliged to travel on foot; only the chief himself rode an ass, the only beast that had survived. As he travelled he spoke the black words and a great sandstorm sprang up hiding the chief and his men, and the land was transformed into a barren desert. His daughter remained behind to fulfil the chief's promise to the Chinese and open the west gates but before dawn broke she took all the treasure in the city and threw it down the deep well. When the Chinese entered, they were enraged to discover the place was empty save for one beautiful young girl. She would not tell them where the treasure was, nor where her father had escaped to, and so the Chinese chopped her into small pieces. And now this place of grasslands and forest has become bleak and windswept and sterile and the Chinese have no use of it.

And what became of the treasure?

It lies there still.

Have you seen it?

They say that many men have searched for it but as soon as anyone looks into the well, flames hundreds of feet high rise up from the depths of the earth, for the spirit of Khara Bator Janjyn lives on.

But sometimes, said the man's wife, in the early hours of the morning when all is still and the dawn gleams like a pearl on the edge of the horizon, we see the girl standing on the ruins of the tower with her long, black hair blowing about her, staring east after her father. Waiting for death.

Joseph stayed for another day in Khara Khoto letting the camels rest and drink; he took as much water as he could carry from the family's well, and they gave him goat's meat and cheese and dried berries they'd collected from liquorice trees. They said if he made haste he might be safe, for many men had already passed this way from the White Warlord's citadel and there must be few left behind, but he must be sure to head north before he drew near the Warlord's dwelling place as it was bound to be securely guarded with lookouts and watch towers posted for miles around it.

The land became more rocky and he wandered through thin canyons where the wind whispered like a lover or howled like an assassin. The stone was layered as a terrine with fossils: the leaves of trees that had existed when the land was fertile; giant pachyderms; the fearsome teeth and claws of rapacious dinosaurs; and once a piece of cranium and part of the jaw bone of a creature that heralded humanity yet whose skull was distinctly ape-like in origin. Joseph held these bones in his hands and felt a connection between himself and the earth that sang a song of evolution, a lost melody he strained to hear like the last lingering notes of perfume belonging to the one woman he loved.

He looked at small details: the circular pattern interlaid with runic drifts cast by blades of grass spun in the wind; the faint calligraphy traced in the sand by tumbleweeds half airborne; knots and fissures in wood ground to the grain through the scouring of sand. He thought he might read some meaning into these things. He was mainly hungry and always thirsty. Most of the wells he came across were salty and alkaline. The camels were thin and lethargic. Every day it was a struggle to make them stand. The wolf was suffering: she was too hot in her thick coat during the day and she had hardly the energy to hunt. The desert was killing her slowly.

He prayed in a half-dream of robbers and bandits; John the Baptist and Jesus.

I am the voice of one crying out in the wilderness . . .

One does not live by bread alone, but by every word that comes from the mouth of God . . .

He thought of Moses waking in the wilderness of Sin to a sweet frost icing the ground; bathed in quails as night falls.

Bread and meat and the one word . . .

In the beginning was the Word, and the Word was God . . .

And one morning he woke up, his breath pure white and crystalline, and saw that the small camel had died in the night. Its eyes were open and it was staring back to the east from whence they had come. He took its load and added it to that of the larger camel's and he walked, leading the recalcitrant animal towards what he could only surmise was its own death also.

The lake lay ahead of him: a vision in blue bleeding shimmering waves into the horizon. He hoped and prayed that it might be real. But the wolf and the camel were not fooled by mirages: Wolf sloped off at a brisk pace, and even the camel walked a little more quickly. When she came back and nuzzled against his leg, her muzzle was wet and for the first time his spirits lifted. He believed he might at last have arrived at Socho-nor, the one great lake in the Black Gobi.

It stretched before him finally, its edges ringed with minerals sharp and bright as cut glass. Flocks of migrant waders rose in clouds before settling like butterflies over its vitreous surface. The desert was a green oasis of tamarisk trees, willows, thorny jujube, reeds and grasses. He knelt and prayed in the sucking sand, thanking God for preserving him thus far. He could hardly persuade the camel to venture towards the water's edge but eventually it did so, sinking to its knees and drinking as if it would never stop. The water was salty; he drank a little and the rest he boiled, condensing the steam.

He killed two birds in snares; he gave one to the wolf and the other he made into stew with *tsamba* to stretch it further. He ate the rest the following morning and then went in search of the camel, which he could no longer see. On the far shore a man wearing a red headscarf was walking towards him. Joseph called Wolf to his side but the man appeared to be on his own. He half bowed before he reached Joseph. He was very tall and broad-shouldered with a square jaw and dark eyes. One ear was pierced with a silver hoop and he wore a necklace of jet-black stones.

Is it your camel?

Yes.

You shouldn't have spent the night here.

Why?

The man gestured to him to follow. The camel was stretched out in the reeds, blinking in the sun. Its body was black with flies and its belly was swollen.

Joseph tried to pull the camel to its feet, but the man put his hand on his arm.

It has lost too much blood. It'll die today or maybe tomorrow.

He found it hard to believe that flies could do this but the camel certainly seemed to have lost all will to live.

I can't leave it here.

The man shrugged. What else can you do?

I could shoot it. Spare its misery.

If you had a gun and you used it, you might as well give up your life now. I believe that even now there will be men on their way to this place. The White Warlord's fortress is not many miles from here on the banks of Etsin gol.

Joseph looked at him. He was not certain if he could trust this man who had appeared from nowhere and looked so little like a Mongol.

Come, he said, gather your things. We can load them on to my horse.

The animal was tied up behind a clump of tamarisk and Joseph led him back to his makeshift camp, sickened at the thought of the camel and its suffering. They loaded his belongings on to the nomad's horse and led the beast back past the camel. This time the man took out a curved silver knife and slit its throat, to relieve his distress, he realized, not that of the camel.

He told him, as he wiped the blood from his knife across the camel's still heaving flank, that he was a Torgut, a race that had come from the north-west the longest time ago when Khara Khoto was a thriving citadel and that his name was Jur. He said that all the men in his tribe wore a ring through their ear in honour of their forefather. This man had been fishing in Etsin gol and he had caught a small boy who had fallen into the river some miles upstream and had nearly drowned. The fishing hook went through the child's ear and he was hauled out of the water like a big fish. Later the child came to the chief and said that the other children teased him for having a fishing hook in his ear, for they had never been able to remove it. The chief then decreed that every boy should have a hook through his ear so that the child would not be alone in his oddity. To this day all the men wore silver rings in their ears from childhood.

He told him the lake was called Socho-nor, Lake of the Water Cattle, because long ago a race of people lived on its banks who were indolent and evil and the gods were determined to punish them. They caused the lake to become salty and laden with minerals so that the water could no longer be drunk, and they made the lake rise and engulf all their houses and drown every one of them. But the cattle the people had owned had committed no great wrong, so the gods turned them into water beasts and they lived at the bottom of the lake. Sometimes, said Jur, you could hear them lowing at night and the brittle mineral edge of the lake was broken by their hoof prints in the morning.

Jur took him to his *ger*, which was so poor that many of the wooden spokes had broken and there was not even a thick felt covering over the whole construction. Joseph could not imagine how cold it must be at night in winter. Jur appeared to live alone but he said that his people were spread out along the southern shores of Socho-nor. Joseph gave him half of the little food he had left and the rest of his brandy in exchange for the horse. Jur said he wanted the wolf but Joseph said she was not for sale and that even if she were, she would not stay with Jur.

He went on foot, leading the horse, and headed north, hoping that the wind would erase his tracks and the emissaries of the White Warlord would not trouble themselves to pursue an elusive and seemingly poor quarry. Ahead of him were the mountains where Namuunaa's tribe lived. He remembered standing on a long spine of land with her beside him, the eagle on her fist, the wolf scouting ahead of them, and staring down at the shimmering ochre mirage of the Black Gobi; strange to think that he now stood here looking up at those self-same mountains, wondering if she were there, galloping across the peaks, her hair flying out behind her, the hawk circling above her. Waiting for his return.

Two days after he had left Jur he saw them. They were many miles in the distance, on the other side of the lake, which shimmered like the memory of water. The White Warlord's horses threw up a great cloud of dust as they progressed inexorably towards him. He looked around. The desert was slowly beginning to bleed into the edge of the mountains. The vegetation was less sparse and the land was not as bleak. Small shrubs bloomed red and white and lilac. The grass was thicker and interlaced with flowers. He had got out of the habit of it but recently he had picked a few of the species that were new to him. Now he looked at the terrain with a fresh eye. There was nowhere to hide. He still had his shotgun and a knife. The pistol he imagined changing hands on the other side of the Gobi, greasy wads of crumpled notes being tucked into *dels*, followed by a handshake and the obligatory slug of *airag* before the smooth slide of the pistol into some other man's pocket. He felt a queasy sensation as he watched the cloud on the horizon begin to draw a little nearer to the lake. He had no saddle for the horse and the animal was so thin he could feel its ribbed spine pressing into his seat. Its head hung low as it shuffled its cracked hooves through the thorny scrub. There was little hope of a quick getaway. Wolf threw nervous glances over her shoulder as she loped alongside and gave a small whine.

He didn't dare stop for food but pressed on, growing increasingly hungry and slightly faint. The heat and lack of water made his tongue swell and his mouth felt as if gummed together. As night fell, the men lit a fire, which glowed against the skyline. Navigating by the stars, he continued into the night, eking out his flagon of warm water. The horse was barely able to break into a trot. The temperature dropped dramatically and he wrapped his *del* more tightly around himself as his breath crystallized in a cloud above the horse's mane.

As dawn broke he came across a thin stream and he offered a prayer to the God who might or might not have been watching over him. The animals drank ravenously and he knelt alongside them and sucked water directly from the stream too. He lit a small fire and hoped that the smoke would not give him away. He stirred water into barley flour to make *tsamba* and broke an egg into it – a present from Jur – which he had carried like a precious object in a pouch of his *del* for some special occasion. He wondered if this would be how he would die: executed ignominiously by henchmen in the depths of the Black Gobi after eating a wild bird's egg. He tried not to think of Namuunaa. He made a bitter brew of tea and herbs that Munke had said would fortify him and filled up his water bottles. He led the horse onwards towards the mountains, forcing his way through waist-high sprawling shrubs. The ground beneath his feet was uneven, strewn with large, iron-coloured boulders. He could no longer see the horsemen but he knew they could not be far behind.

He imagined himself taking a stand against some rock formation; hiding in a cave; disappearing like a shadow between the trunks of trees in some dense forest. But there was nothing. No shelter. Nowhere to hide. He thought about shooting his lame horse and hiding behind its body but realized that he could not in all conscience do that. The longer he continued, the further away the solid mass of the mountains seemed to be. The lukewarm *tsamba* and the curdled egg hung heavily in his stomach and the after-taste of the herb tea was like some bitter medicine. Slowly the sun started to rise and burn away the shadows and he felt himself begin to grow hotter and more uncomfortable, heat crawling and prickling along his skin like a spreading rash.

By midday they reached him. There were three of them and their horses had once been fine but were now drenched with sweat and the foam at their bits was flecked with blood. They snorted and pawed and flared their nostrils at him. The men only reined them in with difficulty. He knew it was because they could smell Wolf but the men had not seen her. She was somewhere behind him, hiding in the bushes, her hackles raised. He could feel her low growl making the hair on the back of his neck rise; if they had noticed her tracks, they would merely have expected a large but decrepit mongrel in keeping with his mount.

He looked at the men. It was clear they thought he had not been worth the effort of tracking down and at one and the same time his life was meaningless to them. They would slit his throat without a second's thought. One of them had long hair tied back in a ponytail and a scar that curved down his cheek and bisected his mouth as if his lips had been broken and clumsily fitted back together. One had hair that was so thick and blunt at the ends it was as if another man had lifted it off the nape of his neck and sliced through it with one sweep of his blade. His nose had a soft, square shape that indicated he had broken it more than once. The third, who was mounted on a piebald pony, was wearing a hat and one of his eyes was the colour of marble.

The men were so close he could smell their rank odour: smoke, mutton fat and the sweetish stench of unwashed flesh. They had the look of soldiers who had travelled long and hard, for they were coated with a patina of dirt and sand and their eyes were empty. The one in the middle with the long hair suddenly opened his mouth in a smile that bared his teeth. He was missing three on the top row and the bottom glinted with silver. He drew his sword and the other two men did so too.

Do you think he will put up much of a fight? he said to the others.

Look at him, said the one with the broken nose, and spat disgustedly in the sand.

The three of them raised their swords and shouted as they charged towards him. But they were slow and it was almost half-hearted. His own horse pinned back its ears and bunched its hind quarters beneath it as if to flee but Joseph held it reined in tightly and waited for a few more seconds until the men were fifteen feet away, closing to ten. Then he swiftly pulled out his shotgun and fired at the man with the broken nose. His horse reared and neighed and he fell heavily.

Joseph took out his knife. He held it for a moment in his hand, thinking of all those days of target practice with Tsem. Then, though, he'd been standing firmly on the ground and the target had been an immobile stuffed sheep's skin. He moved the handle so he held the knife between his fingers as Tsem had taught him, bent his arm back, aimed the knife at the man with the dead eye, took a deep breath and released his breath and the knife at the same time. The blade made a sound as it flew through the air like the rending of silk. It pierced the man's neck just above his clavicle. Joseph closed his eyes for one moment, silently thanking Tsem. The man dropped his sword and fell forward on to the neck of his horse and his blood pulsed scarlet over the animal's white coat. Joseph's horse bolted and he clung on, attempting to reload his shotgun.

The man with the ponytail gave a great cry and urged his horse faster. Joseph looked over his shoulder and the Warlord's soldier was gaining on him, his horse's nose now level with Joseph's mount's rump. Joseph was desperately fumbling with the buckshot, trying to force it into the gun and remain on his horse, which was weaving in and out of the scrub, stumbling on stones. Just as the soldier reached him and raised his sword, Wolf leapt at the man's horse. The horse reared and plunged, falling to its knees and twisting one of its forelegs, Wolf's jaws locked around its throat. The man was thrown to the ground, the sword spinning from his hand. Joseph grabbed the reins and wheeled his horse around. He snapped the shotgun closed and aimed it at the soldier. He waited until the man sat up and turned around and then he pulled the trigger. The ammunition parted into separate pellets as it reached the soldier, hitting his chest and neck and removing most of his face.

The dying horse was trying to trample Wolf. Joseph called her to him and slid from his horse, looping the reins over a bush. Wolf had torn out part of the soldier's horse's throat and it had also broken its leg. Joseph reloaded the gun and pressed the muzzle into the horse's forelock. It was his last bullet. The blast ricocheted through the desert, the kickback burning his shoulder, as the horse fell in front of him.

He walked back through the desert to where the men had first charged him and found the man's hat before he found the body of the man with the one good eye. He pulled his knife from the dead man's throat and wiped the blade with leaves, then picked up the soldier's sword and slid its heavy blade beneath the belt of his *del*. The other two horses had galloped some way off and Joseph debated whether to go after them or not. In the end he decided to leave them and hope that Jur, at least, would find them and benefit from them. He took what food the men had on them and then he stroked Wolf's bloody muzzle and led his horse onwards, towards the mountains.

He had been in the desert for thirty days, and he travelled towards the mountains for another five. As he climbed the mountains he wandered for three days amid trees picked out with plum and apple blossom, the alien eyes of giant rhubarb buds, clumps of orange lilies, spring daisies and sky-blue irises. He could not find the place where he had first met the tribe and when he did, they were not there. He felt like sitting down and weeping: they were nomads, how could he hope to find them? He journeyed further into the mountains to the valley where the lilies grew. They were lush with thick stems and foliage but no buds as yet. He camped at the edge of the forest in a stand of silver birch. He had no luck hunting that night and he had no food left of his own.

At dawn, hungry and exhausted, he crawled through the dewy leaves and pulled up a hundred bulbs, prising them out of the soil with his knife, severing their stems until the bitter juice stained his palms green. He sat at the lip of the valley, the birches whispering in front of him, the smell of plant sap and earth and another mustier, feral scent, rising from his hessian sack full of lily bulbs, and he felt as lonely as if his loneliness had a physical presence. Wolf licked his face and he hardly noticed. Then she wheeled around and stood staring in the direction of the forest, her hair on end, her tail erect. She trotted off and left him sitting beneath the sighing trees. When she returned it was with Delger.

The old man crouched down and held out his hands to him.

She said you would return, he said.

Joseph said nothing.

He stood up, his joints creaking.

She said she wanted lily bulbs. She thought they might be the one thing that would help her, and here, you already have them.

Where is she? Joseph turned to look at him properly for the first time.

In the cabin up in the mountains.

Why?

She is ill, Joseph. Come on, let's go.

He helped Joseph on to his own horse and led Joseph's though he was at least twice the young priest's age.

I'm surprised to see you, said Delger. Many of the monks have been slaughtered. The lamaseries are almost empty. He shook his head. It's a sad and evil time we are living in.

I came across the Gobi.

Delger turned to look at him. It was a long, slow stare, and then he said, That explains it.

Is she bad? asked Joseph when they were almost at Namuunaa's house.

Yes, said Delger, and then said nothing more.

*

She was pale as milk and her cheekbones stood out sharply. Her green eyes were too large in her face and there was a haunted look to them. He took her in his arms and she was light and fragile; he could feel her shoulder blades, her collar bones, her ribs.

Ah, my love, she whispered, I knew you would come back.

He buried his head in her thick black hair and wept, all the tears over all the weeks he had not shed.

When he sat up he saw Delger, Amgalan, Uugan and Lena sitting by the hearth silently watching him. He held out his arms and Lena looked at him awkwardly, almost blankly, twisting her skirt with one hand, her other in her mouth, then she came to him and held out her arms so that he could hug her. She had grown taller and leaner, her hair longer, and her eyes, grey and shaped like Namuunaa's, seemed to contain a knowledge beyond her years. Uugan greeted him quietly. She took a couple of the lily bulbs and boiled them in milk with honey.

Joseph helped Namuunaa sit up and held the bowl so that she could drink.

Will you try a little? she asked.

He shook his head. You should drink it all.

She was so young. He remembered her as strong, powerful, full of life and vitality. It tore his heart to see her like this.

Tell me, he said, what has happened since I saw you last. How have you been?

Oh, she said, as if it were a great effort, I have missed you.

I missed you too, he said. I have thought of nothing else.

She smiled. I am pleased you are back.

Uugan touched him gently on the shoulder. Let her rest, she said, she is very tired.

330

She smoothed the blankets and furs around Namuunaa and replaced the screen around her bed. He followed her back to the hearth and Lena crept into his lap. Uugan handed him a bowl of tea.

She always said you would return but I didn't believe it, said Uugan. I thought we should never see you again. Have you come to stay?

He stroked the child's hair and in a low voice said, No.

You have come for the lilies, she said matter-of-factly.

He nodded.

She wrinkled her small button nose and looked at him sidelong. Yes, I can see that is what you told your people. And yourself.

He drank his tea, the child's familiar weight on his lap.

Is she bad?

Don't tell her what you have told me, she said.

I cannot lie.

It would kill her. She is alive for the hope of you.

What ails her?

Uugan sighed. She went to sell the furs. She came back with a fever.

Can't you cure her?

I am trying.

You helped me.

Sometimes I wonder if we were right to do so. Lena has been so very confused and sad. She's lost two fathers.

Give the man a chance, said Delger, he's only just arrived. He crossed the Gobi to see her. Let him alone.

He crossed the Gobi for the lilies, Uugan gently corrected him.

Yes, yes, so he says, said Delger. Come on, let's go.

He and Amgalan took their leave, promising to return the following day.

Batbaatar is looking after the animals, said Uugan, but I am afraid that the eagle has been neglected of late.

I'll take him out tomorrow, he said.

The eagle had lost some of his condition, his feathers were dull and there was a malevolent glare in his eye. It took some time to fasten the hood over his head. They were all some-what the worse for wear, himself, the bird and the wolf. He took Namuunaa's horse which had grown fat for lack of exercise and carried the eagle on his fist, the wolf loping easily alongside. As they cantered through the mountains, he felt as if her spirit were with him.

He flew Bird twice, tempting him back with a small piece of meat, and then he released him once more into the wide blue sky. For several minutes the bird hovered, suspended in the air, before dropping his wings and hurtling like a stone towards the earth. Even before the bird reached the ground, Wolf was racing over to him. Joseph galloped back with the hare the eagle had caught and fed both the bird and the wolf. He was flushed and out of breath, still weak from lack of food and exhaustion but exhilarated.

He hurried in to tell Namuunaa. She smiled.

You might make a good eagle hunter one day, you're a half-wild creature yourself, she teased. But of course, she added with only the hint of a smile, my teaching days are over.

Nonsense. When you are well you can teach me properly.

That won't happen. How could it?

It could, my love, of course it could. Perhaps we could find an eagle for me too. We could hide out in the mountains, camp near an eagle's nest and wait until the youngster is big enough to catch, and then we should tame him and bring him back home.

He hardly knew what he said, he was babbling to try to ease her suffering, but even as he talked of the eagle it seemed to him at that moment that he could imagine nothing better than to spend summer with Namuunaa, high as an eagle's eyrie, Outer Mongolia spread below them, waiting for the fledgling to grow into a proud and savage beast. They would take a little of that country's wild spirit with them when they left the mountains.

You think that will happen? she whispered and there were tears in her eyes.

Yes, my love, he replied, and kissed her gently.

I think she is getting better, he said. She talked for quite a long time today and she took a little of that stew you made.

Uugan was sewing. She did not look up.

I think you have incredible powers of self-deception. She isn't getting better; she's just pleased that you are here. She's doing things no one as ill as she is should be able to do. Her body will make her pay for it later.

Have you no hope? he cried, before he remembered to keep his voice down. You can't give up like this.

Uugan put down her sewing and looked over at him, a tiny wizened woman with a moss-green stone at her throat and shrewd grey eyes.

I will never give up, she said, but I'm being realistic. You forget, Joseph, that I am losing a daughter. You are not even losing a wife.

A week after he arrived there was a glorious sunset. He ran into the house to tell Namuunaa. She was on her own – Uugan kept Lena with her most of the time now. Namuunaa was staring at the ceiling and the sight of her lying so still as if she no longer had the energy to challenge her fate made his heart shrink.

Let me take you outside to see the sky. It's beautiful. I can carry you, he said, gathering up quilts and blankets all in a rush to try to mask his pain.

She smiled at him as if she were indulging him and he helped her sit up and wrapped a *del* around her. He carried her outside. She had once been so strong and vigorous and now she weighed so little. He built up a nest of blankets for her in front of the cabin. He cocooned her in the blankets until she told him to stop for fear he would suffocate her.

The sky was apricot, lilac, fuchsia, lavender. The light filled her green eyes and made them glow so it was as if they had become the colour of water, emptied of pigment. They watched as the sun sank and the sky deepened and darkened to plum. He held her hand and felt her frail pulse beat against his wrist and it reminded him of the time as a child he'd caught and held a baby bird in the cage of his fingers. The first star shone opposite them and he bit hard on his lip; a minor pain to remove the larger. This was the kind of evening he could have shared, side by side with this beautiful woman, until they both grew old, if he had not behaved as he had, if he had not been the kind of man he was. He felt the loss of all the years that might have been, the life he could have lived, the love he would have received, as if he were being hollowed out from the inside.

You know what I should like? she said, suddenly turning to him.

Anything, he said.

I should like you to wash my hair.

He hesitated momentarily, cast back to that evening last winter when she had knelt before him and the hot water had streamed across her naked skin. The memory had the power to unravel him.

Of course, my love.

He unwrapped some of the blankets and she started to shiver. He carried her back inside and put her in bed, placing extra blankets to support her so that she could sit upright. He stoked the fire with fresh pine logs and then went outside to haul water. He sat in front of the fire, watching the flames licking against the cast-iron pot, waiting for the water to heat. He couldn't bear to sit in the stillness and watch Namuunaa's face in the firelight, now thin and drawn and pallid.

When the water was warm he poured it into a wooden pail and then lifted Namuunaa and placed her gently by the hearth. She unrolled her nightdress past her shoulders and leaned forward, sweeping her hair in one fluid movement from the nape of her neck over her head so that it hung above the basin. He scooped water in a small wooden bowl and poured it over her hair. The tendons in the back of her neck rose. Her wet hair flowed into the pail like a jet-black stream of oil. He poured a little soapwort into the palm of his hands and massaged it into her scalp, then ran the suds through her hair. He could see the bones in her chest standing out and the bones in her shoulders pushing through the skin as if her whole body had suddenly become sharp and the skin translucent. He scooped up more water and slowly washed away the soap, the bubbles bursting and dying against the surface of the water. Then he took her hair in his hands as if it were a rope and twisted it, wringing the water from it. He lifted the rope of hair from her face and wrapped it in a cloth, gently towelling her hair dry.

Thank you, she said, and he could hardly bear to look at her.

He pulled her close and felt her fragile and trembling against his chest.

She moved away from him slightly and reached for her brush, but he took it and gently started to work it through her hair, removing the knots and smoothing through the tangles.

You'll make sure Lena is all right, she said, so quietly he could hardly hear her.

He lifted up her hair in one hand and kissed the back of her neck. Her skin was still damp.

There's no need. You'll be well again soon.

We both know . . . she started to say but he tilted her head towards him and kissed her on the lips.

At first she seemed to resist him and then her lips parted and melted against his. He wound her wet hair round one fist as he cradled her against himself. He could feel the fire hot against his cheek. He felt as if the heat were travelling through him, burning him from the inside out. He picked her up and carried her slowly back to her bed.

*

In the morning he woke to find that she was already awake. As he moved and stretched, she turned imperceptibly towards him.

I read your letters, she said, her voice faint as a whisper. They made me cry.

Why, my darling?

They were so beautiful and so impossible. I wanted so much for them to be true.

They were true, I meant everything I wrote.

You have two loves in your heart, and your love of God is the stronger. Your God is greedy. He won't share you with me.

Why? he said suddenly, voicing his thoughts. I wonder why that should be? Surely God is not capable of jealousy.

I believe, she said, and her voice was so quiet he had to rest his head on the pillow to hear her, that you do not believe in mortal love. Somehow you cannot believe in its constancy and its fidelity; you long for the spiritual because that is the only love you think is true and lasting. And yet I have tried, she said, opening her eyes and looking straight into his, I have tried to show you how strong my love for you is. I would have crossed the world to be with you in a land so strange to me I cannot begin to imagine it; in a land of ships and boats when I have never even seen the sea. I would have made you a home here had you wished to stay; I gave you my wolf and I would have tamed an eagle for you. I have waited to see you again when none believed that you should ever return; I would have waited for ever. Joseph, there is no solidity on this earth; there is nothing that will last. Even the very rocks can be worn away to dust. But, Joseph, you should have trusted your heart, for I would have loved you as long as I lived with a love that was both real and true.

He woke one morning, the child in his arms. The night before, Lena had insisted on staying and around midnight she had woken and crept into his bed and curled up next to him. It was the beginning of July and he could hear the larks singing outside. Fresh light, the colour of newly planed wood, filtered through cracks between the logs and fell from one open window across Namuunaa's bed. He could smell the rich, high notes of pine, meadowsweet, as thick as clotted cream, the thin, fine fragrance of sun-warmed buttercups. It was very still.

He disentangled himself from the child and knelt by Namuunaa. She was lying on her back with her black hair spread out across the pillow and her eyes closed. She looked peaceful, serene, like a saint cast in marble. He held her hand. There was only a faint warmth in her palm. He kept expecting her to open her great, green eyes and turn to him with her wide smile, generously accepting him for who he was in all his inconstancy and ambiguity, her eyes sparkling with life like the wild, free spirit she had been.

He wrapped her body in a white sheet and carried her on horseback to the top of the mountain. The whole of the village rode with him followed by Wolf.

The men had laid out rocks on the mountain top, large chunks of milk-grey granite. He placed her upon them. In the traditional Mongolian way she would be left for the wild creatures. They built a small *ovoo* next to her and tied a blue silk scarf to a stave of pine at the top. Delger played the *morin khuur*, a string of sweet sad notes that trickled like a stream and galloped like a horse over the limitless steppes. Uugan invoked the words of the spirits of the air and earth and they walked clockwise round the *ovoo* as she chanted.

They returned to Namuunaa's log cabin and began what Joseph supposed was the equivalent of a wake with music and food and plenty to drink. He slipped out, taking half the lilies with him. He carried the eagle on his fist and returned to the top of the mountain. Joseph planted the bulbs around her, scattering them in small clusters. The earth was hard and brittle. He thought of his journey since he had left her, across the steppe and then back across the Gobi Desert; he thought of all the days he had spent in a dream-like state transfixed for love of her and unable to eat or sleep without thinking of her, all those days where he barely existed, for every waking thought was a thought he believed he should not have had.

His eyes blurred with tears so that he could hardly see what he was doing and had to plant the bulbs by touch alone. He looked up at her profile, haloed by the setting sun. A scrap of the sheet that wrapped her was caught by the wind and blew gently, flashing rays of light at him as it obscured and revealed the sinking sun. He had no way to calibrate the enormity of his loss. She was the only woman he had ever loved, the only one he would ever love, and life without her living presence was unimaginable. As he knelt in front of Namuunaa, he seemed to hear words on the wind, the feral voice of the Yolros lama who had said to him, *You will journey far beyond the boundaries of your imagination.*

You will meet and seize your heart's desire. It will be the death of your soul.

Joseph tried to pray for her soul and his but no words would come. He felt as if a crevasse were opening inside his very heart, a vastness so great he could feel no limit to the emptiness that expanded within him. He wound his rosary around her hand, leaving traces of earth across her cold fingers. She still wore the Celtic cross he had given her for Christmas.

He undid the eagle's jesses and slid the hood from his head. The eagle blinked slowly and looked at him with a harsh and golden stare. He perched on Joseph's fist for a couple of minutes and spread his wings as if testing their span, then he took off with long, slow wing beats and Joseph watched him fly along the stone spine of the hill and into the blue distance where sky and mountain merged.

He could hardly speak. He said goodbye to each of the villagers in turn almost silently. Lastly he said goodbye to Uugan. She was so tiny she barely reached the middle of his chest.

Will you keep Wolf for me? he asked. I can't take her to England and she'll be happier in the mountains.

The old woman nodded. Maybe she will return to her own kind. She's a wild animal at heart.

That would be for the best, he said, but I fear that she'll remain neither one thing nor the other, neither fully tame nor fully wild.

Remember, she said, avoid the lamaseries on your way back. The nomads will shelter you and conceal you.

He nodded. I intend to visit Munke, Mendo's sister-in-law. I wish to give her the suit Namuunaa made me for Boldt, her son.

Yes, she said, Mendo would have approved.

He mounted Namuunaa's white horse and rode slowly away leading one of Uugan's horses which she had given him for a pack animal.

Joseph, she called when he was a couple of hundred yards away.

He turned and waved.

She called his name more urgently.

What is it? he shouted.

The lilies, Delger shouted back. You forgot the lilies.

I'll get them, said Lena, and she wheeled her horse around and cantered back to her grandmother.

He halted his horse and watched as Delger and Amgalan between them tied his sack of precious bulbs behind Lena's saddle. She hugged her grandmother and the two old men one more time, and then galloped towards him, her mane of curly blonde hair flying behind her. Her cheeks were still flushed from crying but she smiled gravely at him as she approached.

What are you waiting for? she said, as she galloped past.

Acknowledgements

*M*any thanks go to my agent, Patrick Walsh, and to Rob Dinsdale who read numerous drafts of *The Naked Name of Love*. Both made insightful comments for which I'm very grateful. I would also like to thank Kate Parkin for her thoughtful and skilful editing, as well as to the rest of the team at John Murray for their support of the book.

Joseph's character and his journey was principally inspired by and informed by two men: Pierre Teilhard de Chardin and Père Armand David. Teilhard de Chardin was a French Jesuit, paleontologist, biologist, and geologist, who struggled to integrate his religious beliefs with his knowledge of biology and, in particular, evolutionary theory. He travelled to China several times, as well as visiting Mongolia, to carry out geological excavations. He discovered Peking Man, a relative of Pithecanthropus. David was a French Lazarist Missionary, a zoologist and a botanist. He discovered and brought back the handkerchief tree, *Davidia involucrata*, a clematis, *Clematis armandi*, and Père David's deer, as well as numerous other animals and plants that grace our gardens today. His diary of his travels through China and Mongolia at the end of the nineteenth century was invaluable to my research.